THE CAPTAIN'S TOLL-GATE

FRANK R. STOCKTON

With a Memorial Sketch by Mrs. Stockton

1ˢᵗ WORLD
LIBRARY
Literary Society

The Captain's Toll-Gate

Frank R. Stockton

© 1st World Library, 2007
PO Box 2211
Fairfield, IA 52556
www.1stworldlibrary.com
First Edition

LCCN: 2007901787

Softcover ISBN: 978-1-4218-4255-4
Hardcover ISBN: 978-1-4218-4157-1
eBook ISBN: 978-1-4218-4353-7

Purchase *"The Captain's Toll-Gate"*
as a traditional bound book at:
www.1stWorldLibrary.com/purchase.asp?ISBN=978-1-4218-4255-4

1st World Library is a literary, educational organization
dedicated to:

- Creating a free internet library of downloadable ebooks

- Hosting writing competitions and offering book
publishing scholarships.

1ˢᵗ World Library Literary Society

Giving Back to the World

"If you want to work on the core problem, it's early school literacy."

- James Barksdale, former CEO of Netscape

"No skill is more crucial to the future of a child, or to a democratic and prosperous society, than literacy."

- Los Angeles Times

Literacy... means far more than learning how to read and write... The aim is to transmit... knowledge and promote social participation."

- UNESCO

"Literacy is not a luxury, it is a right and a responsibility. If our world is to meet the challenges of the twenty-first century we must harness the energy and creativity of all our citizens."

- President Bill Clinton

"Parents should be encouraged to read to their children, and teachers should be equipped with all available techniques for teaching literacy, so the varying needs and capacities of individual kids can be taken into account."

- Hugh Mackay

CONTENTS

A MEMORIAL SKETCH

As this—The Captain's Toll-Gate—is the last of the works of
Frank R. Stockton that will be given to the public, it is fitting
that it be accompanied by some account of the man whose
bright spirit illumined them all. It is proper, also, that
something be said of the stories themselves; of the
circumstances in which they were written, the influences that
determined their direction, and the history of their evolution.
It seems appropriate that this should be done by the one who
knew him best; the one who lived with him through a long
and beautiful life; the one who walked hand in hand with him
along the whole of a wonderful road of ever-changing scenes:
now through forests peopled with fairies and dryads, griffins
and wizards; now skirting the edges of an ocean with its
strange monsters and remarkable shipwrecks; now on the
beaten track of European tourists, sharing their novel
adventures and amused by their mistakes; now resting in lovely
gardens imbued with human interest; now helping the young
to make happy homes for themselves; now sympathizing with
the old as they look longingly toward a heavenly home; and,
oftenest, perhaps, watching girls and young men as they were
trying to work out the problems of their lives. All this, and
much more, crowded the busy years until the Angel of Death
stood in the path; and the journey was ended.

In regard to the present story—The Captain's Toll-Gate—
although it is now after his death first published, it was all
written and completed by Mr. Stockton himself. No other
hand has been allowed to add to, or to take from it. Mr.

Stockton had so strong a feeling upon the literary ethics involved in such matters that he once refused to complete a book which a popular and brilliant author, whose style was thought to resemble his own, had left unfinished. Mr. Stockton regarded the proposed act in the light of a sacrilege. The book, he said, should be published as the author left it. Knowing this fact, readers of the present volume may feel assured that no one has been permitted to tamper with it. Although the last book by Mr. Stockton to be published, it is not the last that he wrote. He had completed The Captain's Toll-Gate, and was considering its publication, when he was asked to write another novel dealing with the buccaneers. He had already produced a book entitled Buccaneers and Pirates of our Coasts. The idea of writing a novel while the incidents were fresh in his mind pleased him, and he put aside The Captain's Toll-Gate, as the other book—Kate Bonnet—was wanted soon, and he did not wish the two works to conflict in publication. Steve Bonnet, the crazy-headed pirate, was a historical character, and performed the acts attributed to him. But the charming Kate, and her lover, and Ben Greenaway were inventions.

Francis Richard Stockton, born in Philadelphia in 1834, was, on his father's side, of purely English ancestry; on his mother's side, there was a mixture of English, French, and Irish. When he began to write stories these three nationalities were combined in them: the peculiar kind of inventiveness of the French; the point of view, and the humor that we find in the old English humorists; and the capacity of the Irish for comical situations.

Soon after arriving in this country the eldest son of the first American Stockton settled in Princeton, N.J., and founded that branch of the family; while the father, with the other sons, settled in Burlington County, in the same State, and founded the Burlington branch of the family, from which Frank R. Stockton was descended. On the female side he was descended from the Gardiners, also of New Jersey. His was a family with literary proclivities. His father was widely known for his religious writings, mostly of a polemical character, which had a powerful influence in the denomination to which he belonged. His half-brother (much older than Frank) was a preacher of great eloquence, famous a generation ago as a pulpit orator.

When Frank and his brother John, two years younger, came to the age to begin life for themselves, they both showed such decided artistic genius that it was thought best to start them in that direction, and to have them taught engraving; an art then held in high esteem. Frank chose wood, and John steel engraving. Both did good work, but their hearts were not in it, and, as soon as opportunity offered, they abandoned engraving. John went into journalism; became editorially connected with prominent newspapers; and had won a foremost place in his chosen profession; when he was cut off by death at a comparatively early age.

Frank chose literature. He had, while in the engraving business, written a number of fairy tales, some of which had been published in juvenile magazines; also a few short stories, and quite an ambitious long story, which was published in a prominent magazine. He was then sufficiently well known as a writer to obtain without difficulty a place on the staff of Hearth and Home, a weekly New York paper, owned by Orange Judd, and conducted by Edward Eggleston. Mrs. Mary Mapes Dodge had charge of the juvenile department, and Frank went on the paper as her assistant. Not long after Scribner's Monthly was started by Charles Scribner (the elder), in conjunction with Roswell Smith, and J.G. Holland. Later Mr. Smith and his associates formed The Century Company; and with this company Mr. Stockton was connected for many years: first on the Century Magazine, which succeeded Scribner's Monthly, and afterward on St. Nicholas, as assistant to Mrs. Mary Mapes Dodge, and, still later, when he decided to give up editorial work, as a constant contributor. After a few years he resigned his position in the company with which he had been so pleasantly associated in order to devote himself exclusively to his own work. By this time he had written and published enough to feel justified in taking, what seemed to his friends, a bold, and even rash, step, because so few writers then lived solely by the pen. He was never very strong physically; he felt himself unable to do his editorial work, and at the same time write out the fancies and stories with which his mind was full. This venture proved to be the wisest thing for him; and from that time his life was, in great part, in his books; and he gave to the world the novels and stories which bear his name.

I have mentioned his fairy stories. Having been a great lover of fairy lore when a child, he naturally fell into this form of story writing as soon as he was old enough to put a story together. He invented a goodly number; and among them the Ting-a-Ling stories, which were read aloud in a boys' literary circle, and meeting their hearty approval, were subsequently published in The Riverside Magazine, a handsome and popular juvenile of that period; and, much later, were issued by Hurd & Houghton in a very pretty volume. In regard to these, he wrote long afterward as follows:

"I was very young when I determined to write some fairy tales because my mind was full of them. I set to work, and in course of time produced several which were printed. These were constructed according to my own ideas. I caused the fanciful creatures who inhabited the world of fairy-land to act, as far as possible for them to do so, as if they were inhabitants of the real world. I did not dispense with monsters and enchanters, or talking beasts and birds, but I obliged these creatures to infuse into their extraordinary actions a certain leaven of common sense."

It was about this time, while very young, that he and his brother became ambitious to write stories, poems, and essays for the world at large. They sent their effusions to various periodicals, with the result common to ambitious youths: all were returned. They decided at last that editors did not know a good thing when they saw it, and hit upon a brilliant scheme to prove their own judgment. One of them selected an extract from Paradise Regained (as being not so well known as Paradise Lost), and sent it to an editor, with the boy's own name appended, expecting to have it returned with some of the usual disparaging remarks, which they would greatly enjoy. But they were disappointed. The editor printed it in his paper, thereby proving that he did know a good thing if he did not know his Milton. Mr. Stockton was fond of telling this story, and it may have given rise to a report, extensively circulated, that he tried to gain admittance to periodicals for many years before he succeeded. This is not true. Some rebuffs he had, of course—some with things which afterward proved great successes—but not as great a number as falls to the lot of most beginners.

The Ting-a-Ling tales proved so popular that Mr. Stockton followed them at intervals with long and short stories for the young which appeared in various juvenile publications, and were afterward published in book form—Roundabout Rambles. Tales out of School, A Jolly Fellowship, Personally Conducted, The Story of Viteau, The Floating Prince, and others. Some years later, after he had begun to write for older readers, he wrote a series of stories for St. Nicholas, ostensibly for children, but really intended for adults. Children liked the stories, but the deeper meaning underlying them all was beyond the grasp of a child's mind. These stories Mr. Stockton took very great pleasure in writing, and always regarded them as some of his best work, and was gratified when his critics wrote of them in that way. They have become famous, and have been translated into several languages, notably Old Pipes and the Dryad, The Bee Man of Orne, and The Griffin and the Minor Canon. This last story was suggested by Chester Cathedral, and he wrote it in that venerable city. The several tales were finally collected into a volume under the title: The Bee Man of Orne and Other Stories, which is included in the complete edition of his novels and stories. During the whole of his literary career Mr. Stockton was an occasional contributor of short stories and essays to The Youth's Companion.

Mr. Stockton considered his career as an editor of great advantage to him as an author. In an autobiographical paper he writes: "Long-continued reading of manuscripts submitted for publication which are almost good enough to use, and yet not quite up to the standard of the magazine, can not but be of great service to any one who proposes a literary career. Bad work shows us what we ought to avoid, but most of us know, or think we know, what that is. Fine literary work we get outside the editorial room. But the great mass of literary material which is almost good enough to print is seen only by the editorial reader, and its lesson is lost upon him in a great degree unless he is, or intends to be, a literary worker."

The first house in which we set up our own household goods stood in Nutley, N.J. We had with us an elderly *attache* of the Stockton family as maid-of-all-work; and to relieve her of some of her duties I went into New York, and procured from an orphans' home a girl whom Mr. Stockton described as "a middle-sized orphan." She was about fourteen years old, and proved to be a very peculiar individual, with strong characteristics which so appealed to Mr. Stockton's sense of humor that he liked to talk with her and draw out her opinions of things in general, and especially of the books she had read. Her spare time was devoted to reading books, mostly of the blood-curdling variety; and she read them to herself aloud in the kitchen in a very disjointed fashion, which was at first amusing, and then irritating. We never knew her real name, nor did the people at the orphanage. She had three or four very romantic ones she had borrowed from novels while she was with us, for she was very sentimental.

Mr. Stockton bestowed upon her the name of Pomona, which is now a household word in myriads of homes. This extraordinary girl, and some household experiences, induced Mr. Stockton to write a paper for Scribner's Monthly which he called Rudder Grange. This one paper was all he intended to write, but it attracted immediate attention, was extensively noticed, and much talked about. The editor of the magazine received so many letters asking for another paper that Mr. Stockton wrote the second one; and as there was still a clamor for more, he, after a little time, wrote others of the series. Some time later they were collected in a book. For those interested in

Pomona I will add, that while the girl was an actual personage, with all the characteristics given to her by her chronicler, the woman Pomona was a development in Mr. Stockton's mind of the girl as he imagined she would become, for the original passed out of our lives while still a girl.

Rudder Grange was Mr. Stockton's first book for adult readers, and a good deal of comment has been made upon the fact that he had reached middle life when it was published. His biographers and critics assume that he was utterly unknown at that time, and that he suddenly jumped into favor, and they naturally draw the inference that he had until then vainly attempted to get before the public. This is all a misapprehension of the facts. It will be seen from what I have previously stated, that at this time he was already well known as a juvenile writer, and not only had no difficulty in getting his articles printed, but editors and publishers were asking him for stories. He had made but few slight attempts to obtain a larger audience. That he confined himself for so long a time to juvenile literature can be easily accounted for. For one thing, it grew out of his regular work of constantly catering for the young, and thinking of them. Then, again, editorial work makes urgent demands upon time and strength, and until freed from it he had not the leisure or inclination to fashion stories for more exacting and critical readers. Perhaps, too, he was slow in recognizing his possibilities. Certain it is that the public were not slow to recognize him. He did, however, experience difficulties in getting the collected papers of Rudder Grange published in book form. I will quote his own account, which is interesting as showing how slow he was to appreciate the fact that the public would gladly accept the writings of a humorist:

"The discovery that humorous compositions could be used in journals other than those termed comic marked a new era in my work. Periodicals especially devoted to wit and humor were very scarce in those days, and as this sort of writing came naturally to me, it was difficult, until the advent of Puck, to find a medium of publication for writings of this nature. I contributed a good deal to this paper, but it was only partly satisfactory, for articles which make up a comic paper must be terse and short, and I wanted to write humorous tales which should be as long as ordinary magazine stories. I had good reason for my opinion of the gravity of the situation, for the editor of a prominent magazine declined a humorous story (afterward very popular) which I had sent him, on the ground that the traditions of magazines forbade the publication of stories strictly humorous. Therefore, when I found an editor at last who actually *wished* me to write humorous stories, I was truly rejoiced. My first venture in this line was Rudder Grange. And, after all, I had difficulty in getting the series published in book form. Two publishers would have nothing to do with them, assuring me that although the papers were well enough for a magazine, a thing of ephemeral nature, the book-reading public would not care for them. The third publisher to whom I applied issued the work, and found the venture satisfactory."

The book-reading public cared so much for this book that it would not remain satisfied with it alone. Again and again it demanded of the author more about Pomona, Euphemia, and Jonas. Hence The Rudder Grangers Abroad and Pomona's Travels.

The most famous of Mr. Stockton's stories, The Lady or the Tiger?, was written to be read before a literary society of which he was a member. It caused such an interesting discussion in the society that he published it in the Century Magazine. It had no especial announcement there, nor was it heralded in any way, but it took the public by storm, and surprised both the editor and the author. All the world must love a puzzle, for in an amazingly short time the little story had made the circuit of the world. Debating societies everywhere seized upon it as a topic; it was translated into nearly all languages; society people discussed it at their dinners; plainer people argued it at their firesides; numerous letters were sent to nearly every periodical in the country; and public readers were expounding it to their audiences. It interested heathen and Christian alike; for an English friend told Mr. Stockton that in India he had heard a group of Hindoo men gravely debating the problem. Of course, a mass of letters came pouring in upon the author.

A singular thing about this story has been the revival of interest in it that has occurred from time to time. Although written many years ago, it seems still to excite the interest of a younger generation; for, after an interval of silence on the subject of greater or less duration, suddenly, without apparent cause, numerous letters in relation to it will appear on the author's table, and "solutions" will be printed in the newspapers. This ebb and flow has continued up to the present time. Mr. Stockton made no attempt to answer the question he had raised.

We both spent much time in the South at different periods. The dramatic and unconsciously humorous side of the negroes pleased his fancy. He walked and talked with them, saw them in their homes, at their "meetin's," and in the fields. He has drawn with an affectionate hand the genial, companionable Southern negro as he is—or rather as he was—for this type is rapidly passing away. Soon there will be no more of these "old-time darkies." They would be by the world forgot had they not been embalmed in literature by Mr. Stockton, and the best Southern writers.

There is one other notable characteristic that should be referred to in writing of Mr. Stockton's stories—the machines and appliances he invented as parts of them. They are very numerous and ingenious. No matter how extraordinary might be the work in hand, the machine to accomplish the end was made on strictly scientific principles, to accomplish that exact piece of work. It would seem that if he had not been an inventor of plots he might have been an inventor of instru-ments. This idea is sustained by the fact that he had been a wood-engraver only a short time when he invented and patented a double graver which cuts two parallel lines at the same time. It is somewhat strange that more than one of these extraordinary machines has since been exploited by scientists and explorers, without the least suspicion on their part that the enterprising romancer had thought of them first. Notable among these may be named the idea of going to the north pole under the ice, the one that the center of the earth is an immense crystal (Great Stone of Sardis), and the attempt to manufacture a gun similar to the Peace Compeller in The Great War Syndicate.

In all of Mr. Stockton's novels there were characters taken from real persons who perhaps would not recognize themselves in the peculiar circumstances in which he placed them. In the crowd of purely imaginative beings one could easily recognize certain types modified and altered. In The Casting away of Mrs. Leeks and Mrs. Aleshine he introduced two delightful old ladies whom he knew, and who were never surprised at anything that might happen. Whatever emergency arose, they took it as a matter of course, and prepared to meet it. Mr. Stockton amused himself at their expense by writing this story. He was not at first interested in the Dusantes, and had no intention of ever saying anything further about them. When there was a demand for knowledge of the Dusantes Mr. Stockton did not heed it. He was opposed to writing sequels. But when an author of distinction, whose work and friendship he highly valued, wrote to him that if he did not write something about the Dusantes, and what they said when they found the board money in the ginger jar, he would do it himself, Mr. Stockton set himself to writing The Dusantes.

I have been asked to give some account of the places in which Mr. Stockton's stories and novels were written, and their environments. Some of the Southern stories were written in Virginia, and, now and then, a short story elsewhere, as suggested by the locality, but the most of his work was done under his own roof-tree. He loved his home; it had to be a country home, and always had to have a garden. In the care of a garden and in driving, he found his two greatest sources of recreation.

I have mentioned Nutley, which lies in New Jersey, near New York. His dwelling there was a pretty little cottage, where he had a garden, some chickens, and a cow. This was his home in his editorial days, and here Rudder Grange was written. It was a rented place. The next home we owned. It stood at a greater distance from New York, at the place called Convent, half-way between Madison and Morristown, in New Jersey. Here we lived a number of years after Mr. Stockton gave up editorial work; and here the greater number of his tales were written. It was a much larger place than we had at Nutley, with more chickens, two cows, and a much larger garden.

Mr. Stockton dictated his stories to a stenographer. His favorite spot for this in summer was a grove of large fir-trees near the house. Here, in the warm weather, he would lie in a hammock. His secretary would be near, with her writing materials, and a book of her choosing. The book was for her own reading while Mr. Stockton was "thinking." It annoyed him to know he was being "waited for." He would think out pages of incidents, and scenes, and even whole conversations, before he began to dictate. After all had been arranged in his mind he dictated rapidly; but there often were long pauses, when the secretary could do a good deal of reading. In cold weather he had the secretary and an easy chair in the study—a room he had built according to his own fancy. A fire of blazing logs added a glow to his fancies.

I may state here that we always spent a part of every winter in New York. A certain amount of city life was greatly enjoyed. Mr. Stockton thus secured much intellectual pleasure. He liked his clubs, and was fond of society, where he met men noted in various walks of life.[1]

[Footnote 1: Edward Gary, the secretary of the Century Club, in the obituary notice of Mr. Stockton written by him for the club's annual report, says of Mr. Stockton as a member: "It was but a dozen years ago that Frank R. Stockton entered the fellowship of the Century, in which he soon became exceedingly at home, winning friends here, as he won them all over the land and in other lands, by the charm of his keen and kindly mind shining in all that he wrote and said. He had an extraordinary capacity for work and a rare talent for diversion, and the Century was honored by his well-earned fame, and fortunate in its share in his ever fresh and varying companionship."]

I am now nearing the close of a life which had had its trials and disappointments, its struggles with weak health and with unsatisfying labor. But these mostly came in the earlier years, and were met with courage, an ever fresh-springing hope, and a buoyant spirit that would not be intimidated. On the whole, as one looks back through the long vista, much more of good than of evil fell to his lot. His life had been full of interesting experiences, and one of, perhaps, unusual happiness. At the last there came to pass the fulfilment of a dream in which he had long indulged. He became the possessor of a beautiful estate containing what he most desired, and with surroundings and associations dear to his heart.

He had enjoyed The Holt, his New Jersey home, and was much interested in improving it. His neighbors and friends there were valued companions. But in his heart there had always been a longing for a home, not suburban—a place in the *real* country, and with more land. Finally, the time came when he felt that he could gratify this longing. He liked the Virginia climate, and decided to look for a place somewhere in that State, not far from the city of Washington. After a rather prolonged search, we one day lighted upon Claymont, in the Shenandoah Valley. It won our hearts, and ended our search. It had absolutely everything that Mr. Stockton coveted. He bought it at once, and we moved into it as speedily as possible.

Claymont is a handsome colonial residence, "with all modern improvements"—an unusual combination. It lies near the historic old town of Charles Town, in West Virginia, near Harpers Ferry. Claymont is itself an historic place. The land was first owned by "the Father of his Country." This great personage designed the house, with its main building, two cottages (or lodges), and courtyards, for his nephew Bushrod, to whom he had given the land. Through the wooded park runs the old road, now grass grown, over which Braddock marched to his celebrated "defeat," guided by the youthful George Washington, who had surveyed the whole region for Lord Fairfax. During the civil war the place twice escaped destruction because it had once been the property of Washington.

But it was not for its historical associations, but for the place itself, that Mr. Stockton purchased it. From the main road to the house there is a drive of three-quarters of a mile through a park of great forest-trees and picturesque groups of rocks. On the opposite side of the house extends a wide, open lawn; and here, and from the piazzas, a noble view of the valley and the Blue Ridge Mountains is obtained. Besides the park and other grounds, there is a farm at Claymont of considerable size. Mr. Stockton, however, never cared for farming, except in so far as it enabled him to have horses and stock. But his soul delighted in the big, old terraced garden of his West Virginia home. Compared with other gardens he had had, the new one was like paradise to the common world. At Claymont several short stories were written. John Gayther's Garden was prepared for publication here by connecting stories previously published into a series, told in a garden, and suggested by the one at Claymont. John Gayther, however, was an invention. Kate Bonnet and The Captain's Toll-Gate were both written at Claymont.

Mr. Stockton was permitted to enjoy this beautiful place only three years. They were years of such rare pleasure, however, that we can rejoice that he had so much joy crowded into so short a space of his life, and that he had it at its close. Truly life was never sweeter to him than at its end, and the world was never brighter to him than when he shut his eyes upon it. He was returning from a winter in New York to his beloved Claymont, in good health, and full of plans for the summer and for his garden, when he was taken suddenly ill in Washington, and died three days later, on April 20, 1902, a few weeks after Kate Bonnet was published in book form.

Mr. Stockton passed away at a ripe age—sixty-eight years. And yet his death was a surprise to us all. He had never been in better health, apparently; his brain was as active as ever; life was dear to him; he seemed much younger than he was. He had no wish to give up his work; no thought of old age; no mental decay. His last novels, his last short stories, showed no falling-off. They were the equals of those written in younger years. Nor had he lost the public interest. He was always sure of an audience, and his work commanded a higher price at the last than ever before. His was truly a passing away. He gently glided from the homes he had loved to prepare here to one already prepared for him in heaven, unconscious that he was entering one more beautiful than even he had ever imagined.

Mr. Stockton was the most lovable of men. He shed happiness all around him, not from conscious effort but out of his own bountiful and loving nature. His tender heart sympathized with the sad and unfortunate, but he never allowed sadness to be near, if it were possible to prevent it. He hated mourning and gloom. They seemed to paralyze him mentally until his bright spirit had again asserted itself, and he had recovered his balance. He usually looked either upon the best, or the humorous side of life. Pie won the love of every one who knew him—even that of readers who did not know him personally, as many letters testify. To his friends his loss is irreparable, for never again will they find his equal in such charming qualities of head and heart.

This is not the place for a critical estimate of the work of Frank R. Stockton.[2] His stories are, in great part, a reflex of himself. The bright outlook on life; the courageous spirit; the helpfulness; the sense of the comic rather than the tragic; the love of domestic life; the sweetness of pure affection; live in his books as they lived in himself. He had not the heart to make his stories end unhappily. He knew that there is much of the tragic in human lives, but he chose to ignore it as far as possible, and to walk in the pleasant ways which are numerous in this tangled world. There is much philosophy underlying a good deal that he wrote, but it has to be looked for; it is not insistent, and is never morbid. He could not write an impure word, or express an impure thought, for he belonged to the "pure in heart," who, we are assured, "shall see God."

[Footnote 2: I may, however, properly quote from the sketch prepared by Mr. Gary for the Century Club: "He brought to his later work the discipline of long and rather tedious labor, with the capital amassed by acute observation, on which his original imagination wrought the sparkling miracles that we know. He has been called the representative American humorist. He was that in the sense that the characters he created had much of the audacity of the American spirit, the thirst for adventures in untried fields of thought and action, the subconscious seriousness in the most incongruous situations, the feeling of being at home no matter what happens. But how amazingly he mingled a broad philosophy with his fun, a philosophy not less wise and comprehending than his fun was compelling! If his humor was American, it was also cosmopolitan, and had its laughing way not merely with our British kinsmen, but with alien peoples across the usually impenetrable barrier of translation. The fortune of his jesting lay not in his ears, but in the hearts of his hearers. It was at once appealing and revealing. It flashed its playful light into the nooks and corners of our own being, and wove close bonds with those at whom we laughed. There was no bitterness in it. He was neither satirist nor preacher, nor of set purpose a teacher, though it must be a dull reader that does not gather from his books the lesson of the value of a gentle heart and a clear, level outlook upon our perplexing world."]

MARIAN E. STOCKTON.

CLAYMONT, *May 15, 1903.*

CHAPTER I

OLIVE

A long, wide, and smoothly macadamized road stretched itself from the considerable town of Glenford onward and northward toward a gap in the distant mountains. It did not run through a level country, but rose and fell as if it had been a line of seaweed upon the long swells of the ocean. Upon elevated points upon this road, farm lands and forests could be seen extending in every direction. But there was nothing in the landscape which impressed itself more obtrusively upon the attention of the traveler than the road itself. White in the bright sunlight and gray under the shadows of the clouds, it was the one thing to be seen which seemed to have a decided purpose. Northward or southward, toward the gap in the long line of mountains or toward the wood-encircled town in the valley, it was always going somewhere.

About two miles from the town, and at the top of the first long hill which was climbed by the road, a tall white pole projected upward against the sky, sometimes perpendicularly, and sometimes inclined at a slight angle. This was a turnpike gate or bar, and gave notice to all in vehicles or on horses that the use of this well-kept road was not free to the traveling public. At the approach of persons not known, or too well known, the bar would slowly descend across the road, as if it were a musket held horizontally while a sentinel demanded the password.

Upon the side of the road opposite to the great post on which the toll-gate moved, was a little house with a covered doorway, from which toll could be collected without exposing the collector to sun or rain. This tollhouse was not a plain white-washed shed, such as is often seen upon turnpike roads, but a neat edifice, containing a comfortable room. On one side of it was a small porch, well shaded by vines, furnished with a settle and two armchairs, while over all a large maple stretched its protecting branches. Back of the tollhouse was a neatly fenced garden, well filled with old-fashioned flowers; and, still farther on, a good-sized house, from which a box-bordered path led through the garden to the tollhouse.

It was a remark that had been made frequently, both by strangers and residents in that part of the country, that if it had not been for the obvious disadvantages of a toll-gate, this house and garden, with its grounds and fields, would be a good enough home for anybody. When he happened to hear this remark Captain John Asher, who kept the toll-gate, was wont to say that it was a good enough home for him, even with the toll-gate, and its obvious disadvantages.

It was on a morning in early summer, when the garden had grown to be so red and white and yellow in its flowers, and so green in its leaves and stalks, that the box which edged the path was beginning to be unnoticed, that a girl sat in a small arbor standing on a slight elevation at one side of the garden, and from which a view could be had both up and down the road. She was rather a slim girl, though tall enough; her hair was dark, her eyes were blue, and she sat on the back of a rustic bench with her feet resting upon the seat; this position she had taken that she might the better view the road.

With both her hands this girl held a small telescope which she was endeavoring to fix upon a black spot a mile or more away upon the road. It was difficult for her to hold the telescope steadily enough to keep the object-glass upon the black spot, and she had a great deal of trouble in the matter of focusing, pulling out and pushing in the smaller cylinder in a manner which showed that she was not accustomed to the use of this optical instrument.

"Field-glasses are ever so much better," she said to herself; "you can screw them to any point you want. But now I've got it. It is very near that cross-road. Good! it did not turn there; it is coming along the pike, and there will be toll to pay. One horse, seven cents."

She put down the telescope as if to rest her arm and eye. Presently, however, she raised the glass again. "Now, let us see," she said, "Uncle John? Jane? or me?" After directing the glass to a point in the air about two hundred feet above the approaching vehicle, and then to another point half a mile to the right of it, she was fortunate enough to catch sight of it again. "I don't know that queer-looking horse," she said. "It must be some stranger, and Jane will do. No, a little boy is driving. Strangers coming along this road would not be driven by little boys. I expect I shall have to call Uncle John." Then she put down the glass and rubbed her eye, after which, with unassisted vision, she gazed along the road. "I can see a great deal better without that old thing," she continued. "There's a woman in that carriage. I'll go myself." With this she jumped down from the rustic seat, and with the telescope under her arm, she skipped through the garden to the little tollhouse.

The name of this girl was Olive Asher. Captain John Asher, who took the toll, was her uncle, and she had now been living with him for about six weeks. Olive was what is known in certain social circles as a navy girl. About twenty years before she had come to her uncle's she had been born in Genoa, her father at the time being a lieutenant on an American war-vessel lying in the harbor of Villa Franca. Her first schooldays were passed in the south of France, and she spent some subsequent years in a German school in Dresden. Here she was supposed to have finished her education but when her father's ship was stationed on our Pacific coast and Olive and her mother went to San Francisco they associated a great deal with army people, and here the girl learned so much more of real life and her own country people that the few years she spent in the far West seemed like a post-graduate course, as important to her true education as any of the years she had spent in schools.

After the death of her mother, when Olive was about eighteen, the girl had lived with relatives, East and West, hoping for the day when her father's three years' cruise would terminate, and she could go and make a home for him in some pleasant spot on shore. Now, in the course of these family visits she had come to stay with her father's brother, John Asher, who kept the toll-gate on the Glenford pike.

Captain John Asher was an older man than his brother, the naval officer, but he was in the prime of life, and able to hold the command of a ship if he had cared to do it. But having been in the merchant service for a long time, and having made some money, he had determined to leave the sea and to settle on shore; and, finding this commodious house by the toll-gate, he settled there. There were some people who said that he had taken the position of toll-gate keeper because of the house, and there were others who believed that he had bought the house on account of the toll-gate. But no matter what people thought or said, the good captain was very well satisfied with his home and his official position. He liked to meet with people, and he preferred that they should come to him rather than that he should go to them. He was interested in most things that were going on in his neighborhood, and therefore he liked to talk to the people who were going by. Sometimes a good talking acquaintance or an interesting traveler would tie his horse under the shade of the maple-tree and sit a while with the captain on the little porch. Certain it was, it was the most hospitable toll-gate in that part of the country.

There was a road which branched off from the turnpike, about a mile from the town, and which, after some windings, entered the pike again beyond the toll-gate, and although this road was not always in very good condition, it had seen a good deal of travel, which, in time, gave it the name of the shunpike. But since Captain Asher had lived at the toll-gate it was remarked that the shunpike was not used as much as in former times.

There were penurious people who had once preferred to go a long way round and save money whose economical dispositions now gave way before the combined attractions of a better road, and a chat with Captain Asher.

It had been predicted by some of her relatives that Olive would not be content with her life in her uncle's somewhat peculiar household. He was a bachelor, and seldom entertained company, and his ordinary family consisted of an elderly housekeeper and another servant. But Olive was not in the least dissatisfied. From her infancy up, she had lived so much among people that she had grown tired of them; and her good-natured uncle, with his sea stories, the garden, the old-fashioned house, the fields and the woods beyond, the little stream, which came hurrying down from the mountains, where she could fish or wade as the fancy pleased her, gave her a taste of some of the joys of girlhood which she had not known when she was really a girl.

Another thing that greatly interested her was the toll-gate. If she had been allowed to do so, she would have spent the greater part of her time taking money, making change, and talking to travelers. But this her uncle would not permit. He did not object to her doing some occasional toll-gate work, and he did not wonder that she liked it, remembering how interesting it often was to himself, but he would not let her take toll indiscriminately.

So they made a regular arrangement about it. When the captain was at his meals, or shaving, or otherwise occupied, old Jane attended to the toll-gate. At ordinary times, and when any of his special friends were seen approaching, the captain collected toll himself, but when women happened to be traveling on the road, then it was arranged that Olive should go to the gate.

Two or three times it had happened that some young men of the town, hearing their sisters talk of the pretty girl who had taken their toll, had thought it might be a pleasant thing to drive out on the pike, but their money had always been taken by the captain, or else by the wooden-faced Jane, and nothing had come of their little adventures.

The garden hedge which ran alongside the road was very high.

CHAPTER II

MARIA PORT

Olive stood impatiently at the door of the little tollhouse. In one hand she held three copper cents, because she felt almost sure that the person approaching would give her a dime or two five-cent pieces.

"I never knew horses to travel so slowly as they do on this pike!" she said to herself. "How they used to gallop on those beautiful roads in France!"

In due course of time the vehicle approached near enough to the toll-gate for Olive to take an observation of its occupant. This was a middle-aged woman, dressed in black, holding a black fan. She wore a black bonnet with a little bit of red in it. Her face was small and pale, its texture and color suggesting a boiled apple dumpling. She had small eyes of which it can be said that they were of a different color from her face, and were therefore noticeable. Her lips were not prominent, and were closely pressed together as if some one had begun to cut a dumpling, but had stopped after making one incision.

This somewhat somber person leaned forward in the seat behind her young driver, and steadily stared at Olive. When the horse had passed the toll-bar the boy stopped it so that his passenger and Olive were face to face and very near each other.

"Seven cents, please," said Olive.

Frank R. Stockton

The cleft in the dumpling enlarged itself, and the woman spoke. "Bless my soul," she said, "are you Captain Asher's niece?"

"I am," said Olive in surprise.

"Well, well," said the other, "that just beats me! When I heard he had his niece with him I thought she was a plain girl, with short frocks and her hair plaited down her back."

Olive did not like this woman. It is wonderful how quickly likes and dislikes may be generated.

"But you see I am not," she replied. "Seven cents, please."

"Don't you suppose I know what the toll is?" said the woman in the carriage. "I'm sure I've traveled over this road often enough to know that. But what I'm thinkin' about is the difference between what I thought the captain's niece was and what she really is."

"It does not make any difference what the difference is," said Olive, speaking quickly and with perhaps a little sharpness in her voice, "all I want is for you to pay me the toll."

"I'm not goin' to pay any toll," said the other.

Olive's face flushed. "Little boy," she exclaimed, "back that horse!" As the youngster obeyed her peremptory request Olive gave a quick jerk to a rope and brought down the toll-gate bar so that it stretched itself across the road, barely missing in its downward sweep the nose of the unoffending horse. "Now," said Olive, "if you are ready to pay your toll you can go through this gate, and if you are not, you can turn round and go back where you came from."

"I'm not goin' to pay any toll," said the other, "and I don't want to go through the gate. I came to see Captain Asher.— Johnny, turn your horse a little and let me get out. Then you can stop in the shade of this tree and wait until I'm ready to go back.—I suppose the captain's in," she said to Olive, "but if he isn't, I can wait."

"Oh, he's at home," said Olive, "and, of course, if I had known you were coming to see him, I would not have asked you for your toll. This way, please," and she stepped toward a gate in the garden hedge.

"When I've been here before," said the visitor, "I always went through the tollhouse. But I suppose things is different now."

"This is the entrance for visitors," said Olive, holding open the gate.

Captain Asher had heard the voices, and had come out to his front door. He shook hands with the newcomer, and then turned to Olive, who was following her.

"This is my niece, my brother Alfred's daughter," he said, "and Olive, let me introduce you to Miss Maria Port."

"She introduced herself to me," said Miss Port, "and tried to get seven cents out of me by letting down the bar so that it nearly broke my horse's nose. But we'll get to know each other better. She's very different from what I thought she was."

"Most people are," said Captain Asher, as he offered a chair to Miss Port in his parlor, and sat down opposite to her. Olive, who did not care to hear herself discussed, quietly passed out of the room.

"Captain," said Miss Port, leaning forward, "how old is she, anyway?"

"About twenty," was the answer.

"And how long is she going to stay?"

"All summer, I hope," said Captain John.

"Well, she won't do it, I can tell you that," remarked Miss Port. "She'll get tired enough of this place before the summer's out."

"We shall see about that," said the captain, "but she is not tired yet."

"And her mother's dead, and she's wearin' no mournin'."

"Why should she?" said the captain. "It would be a shame for a young girl like her to be wearing black for two years."

"She's delicate, ain't she?"

"I have not seen any signs of it."

"What did her mother die of?"

"I never heard," said the captain; "perhaps it was the bubonic plague."

Miss Port pushed back her chair and drew her skirts about her.

"Horrible!" she exclaimed. "And you let that child come here!"

The captain smiled. "Perhaps it wasn't that," he said. "It might have been an avalanche, and that is not catching."

Miss Port looked at him seriously. "It's a great pity she's so handsome," she said.

"I don't think so; I am glad of it," replied the captain.

Miss Port heaved a sigh. "What that girl is goin' to need," she said, "is a female guardeen."

"Would you like to take the place?" asked the captain with

a grin.

At that instant it might have been supposed that a certain dumpling which has been mentioned was made of very red apples and that its covering of dough was somewhat thin in certain places. Miss Port's eyes were bent for an instant upon the floor.

"That is a thing," she said, "which would need a great deal of consideration."

A sudden thrill ran through the captain which was not unlike a moment in his past career when a gentle shudder had run through his ship as its keel grazed an unsuspected sand-bar, and he had not known whether it was going to stick fast or not; but he quickly got himself into deep water again.

"Oh, she is all right," said he briskly; "she has been used to taking care of herself almost ever since she was born. And by the way, Miss Port, did you know that Mr. Easterfield is at his home?"

Miss Port was not pleased with the sudden change in the conversation, and she remembered, too, that in other days it had been the captain's habit to call her Maria.

"I did not know he had a home," she answered. "I thought it was her'n. But since you've mentioned it, I might as well say that it was about him I came to see you. I heard that he came to town yesterday, and that her carriage met him at the station, and drove him out to her house. I hoped he had stopped a minute as he drove through your toll-gate, and that you might have had a word with him, or at least a good look at him. Mercy me!" she suddenly ejaculated, as a look of genuine disappointment spread over her face; "I forgot. The coachman would have paid the toll as he went to town, and there was no need of stoppin' as they went back. I might have saved myself this trip."

The captain laughed. "It stands to reason that it might have been that way," he said, "but it wasn't. He stopped, and I talked to him for about five minutes."

The face of Miss Port now grew radiant, and she pulled her chair nearer to Captain Asher. "Tell me," said she, "is he really anybody?"

"He is a good deal of a body," answered the captain. "I should say he is pretty nearly six feet high, and of considerable bigness."

"Well!" exclaimed Miss Port, "I'd thought he was a little dried-up sort of a mummy man that you might hang up on a nail and be sure you'd find him when you got back. Did he talk?"

"Oh, yes," said the captain, "he talked a good deal."

"And what did he tell you?"

"He did not tell me anything, but he asked a lot of questions."

"What about?" said Miss Port quickly.

"Everything. Fishing, gunning, crops, weather, people."

"Well, well!" she exclaimed. "And don't you suppose his wife could have told him all that, and she's been livin' here—this is the second summer. Did he say how long he's goin' to stay?"

"No."

"And you didn't ask him?"

"I told you he asked the questions," replied the captain.

"Well, I wish I'd been here," Miss Port remarked fervently. "I'd got something out of him."

"No doubt of that," thought the captain, but he did not say so.

"If he expects to pass himself off as just a common man," continued Miss Port, "that's goin' to spend the rest of his summer here with his family, he can't do it. He's first got to explain why he never came near that young woman and her two babies for the whole of last summer, and, so far as I've heard, he was never mentioned by her. I think, Captain Asher, that for the sake of the neighborhood, if you don't care about such things yourself, you might have made use of this opportunity. As far as I know, you're the only person in or about Glenford that's spoke to him."

The captain smiled. "Sometimes, I suppose," said he, "I don't say enough, and sometimes I say too much, but—"

"Then I wish he'd struck you more on an average," interrupted Miss Port. "But there's no use talkin' any more about it. I hired a horse and a carriage and a boy to come out here this mornin' to ask you about that man. And what's come of it? You haven't got a single thing to tell anybody except that he's big."

The captain changed the subject again. "How is your father?" he asked.

"Pop's just the same as he always is," was the answer. "And now, as I don't want to lose the whole of the seventy-five cents I've got to pay, suppose you call in that niece of yours, and let me have a talk with her. Perhaps I can get something interesting out of her."

The captain left the room, but he did not move with alacrity. He found Olive with a book in a hammock at the back of the house. When he told her his errand she sat up with a sudden bounce, her feet upon the ground.

"Uncle," she said, "isn't that woman a horrid person?"

Frank R. Stockton

The captain was a merry-minded man, and he laughed. "It is pretty hard for me to answer that question," said he; "suppose you go in and find out for yourself."

Olive hesitated; she was a girl who had a very high opinion of herself and a very low opinion of such a person as this Miss Port seemed to be. Why should she go in and talk to her? Still undecided, she left the hammock and made a few steps toward the house. Then, with a sudden exclamation, she stopped and dropped her book.

"Buggy coming," she exclaimed, "and that thing is running to take the toll!" With these words she started away with the speed of a colt.

An approaching buggy was on the road; Miss Maria Port, walking rapidly, had nearly reached the back door of the tollhouse when Olive swept by her so closely that the wind of her fluttering garments almost blew away the breath of the elder woman.

"Seven cents!" cried Olive, standing in the covered doorway, but she might have saved herself the trouble of repeating this formula, for the man in the buggy was not near enough to hear her.

When Olive saw it was a man, she turned, and perceiving her uncle approaching the tollhouse, she hurried by him up the garden path, looking neither to the right nor to the left.

"A pretty girl that is of yours!" exclaimed Miss Port. "She might just as well have slapped me in the face!"

"But what were you going to do in here?" asked Captain Asher. "You know that's against the rules."

"The rules be bothered," replied the irate Maria. "I thought it was Mr. Smiley. He's been away from his parish for a week, and there are a good many things I want to ask him."

"Well, it is the Roman Catholic priest from Marlinsville," said Captain Asher, "and he wouldn't tell you anything if you asked him."

The captain had a cheerful little chat with the priest, who was one of his most valued road friends; and when he returned to his garden he found Miss Port walking up and down the main path in a state of agitation.

"I should think," said she, "that the company would have something to say about your takin' up your time talkin' to people on the road. I've heard that sometimes they get out, and spend hours talkin' and smokin' with you. I guess that's against the rules."

"It is all right between the company and me," replied the captain. "You know I am a stockholder in a small way."

"You are!" exclaimed Miss Port. "Well, I've got somethin' by comin' here, anyway." Stowing away this bit of information in regard to the captain's resources in her mind for future consideration, she continued: "I don't think much of that niece of your'n. Has she never lived anywhere where the people had good manners?"

Olive, who had gone to her room in order to be out of the way of this queer visitor, now sat by an upper window, and it was impossible that she should fail to hear this remark, made by Miss Port in her most querulous tones. Olive immediately left the window, and sat down on the other side of the room.

"Good manners!" she ejaculated, and fell to thinking. Her present situation had suddenly presented itself to her in a very different light from that in which she had previously regarded it. She was living in a very plain house in a very plain way, with a very plain uncle who kept a tollhouse; but she liked him; and, until this moment, she had liked the life. But now she asked herself if it were possible for her longer to endure it if she were to be condemned to intercourse with people like that

Frank R. Stockton

thing down in the garden. If her uncle's other friends in Glenford were of that grade she could not stay here. She smiled in spite of her irritation as she thought of the woman's words—"Anywhere where the people had good manners."

Good manners, indeed! She remembered the titled young officers in Germany with whom she had talked and danced when she was but seventeen years old, and who used to send her flowers. She remembered the people of rank in the army and navy and in the state who used to invite her mother and herself to their houses. She remembered the royal prince who had wished to be presented to her, and whose acquaintance she had declined because she did not like what she had heard of him. She remembered the good friends of her father in Europe and America, ladies and gentlemen of the army and navy. She remembered the society in which she had mingled when living with her Boston aunt during the past winter. Then she thought of Miss Port's question. Good manners, indeed!

"Well," said the perturbed Maria, after having been informed by the captain that his niece was accustomed to move in the best circles, "I don't want to go into the house again, for if I was to meet her, I'm sure I couldn't keep my temper. But I'll say this to you, Captain Asher, that I pity the woman that's her guardeen. And now, if you'll help my boy turn round so he won't upset the carriage, I'll be goin'. But before I go I'll just say this, that if you'd been in the habit of takin' advantage of the chances that come to you, I believe that you'd be a good deal better off than you are now, even if you do own shares in the turnpike company."

It was not difficult for the captain to recognize some of the chances to which she alluded; one of them she herself had offered him several times.

"Oh, I am very well off as I am," he answered, "but perhaps some day I may have something to tell you of the Easterfields and about their doings up on the mountain."

"About her doin's, you might as well say," retorted Miss Port. "No matter what you tell me, I don't believe a word about his ever doin' anything." With this she walked to the little phaeton, into which the captain helped her.

"Uncle John," said Olive, a few minutes later, "are there many people like that in Glenford?"

"My dear child," said the captain, "the people in Glenford, the most of them, I mean, are just as nice people as you would want to meet. They are ladies and gentlemen, and they are mighty good company. They don't often come out here, to be sure, but I know most of them, and I ought to be ashamed of myself that I have not made you acquainted with them before this. As to Maria Port, there is only one of her in Glenford, and, so far as I know, there isn't another just like her in the whole world. Now I come to think of it," he continued, "I wonder why some of the young people have not come out to call on you. But if that Maria Port has been going around telling them that you are a little girl in short frocks it is not so surprising."

"Oh, don't bother yourself, Uncle John, about calls and society," said Olive. "If you can only manage that that woman takes the shunpike whenever she drives this way, I shall be perfectly satisfied with everything just as it is."

CHAPTER III

MRS. EASTERFIELD

On the side of the mountain, a few miles to the west of the gap to which the turnpike stretched itself, there was a large estate and a large house which had once belonged to the Sudley family. For a hundred years or more the Sudleys had been important people in this part of the country, but it had been at least two decades since any of them had lived on this estate. Some of them had gone to cities and towns, and others had married, or in some other fashion had melted away so that their old home knew them no more.

Although it was situated on the borders of the Southern country, the house, which was known as Broadstone, from the fact that a great flat rock on the level of the surrounding turf extended itself for many feet at the front of the principal entrance, was not constructed after ordinary Southern fashions. Some of the early Sudleys were of English blood and proclivities, and so it was partly like an English house; some of them had taken Continental ideas into the family, and there was a certain solidity about the walls; while here and there the narrowness of the windows suggested southern Europe. Some parts of the great stone walls had been stuccoed, and some had been whitewashed. Here and there vines climbed up the walls and stretched themselves under the eaves. As the house stood on a wide bluff, there was a lawn from which one could see over the tree tops the winding river sparkling far below. There were gardens and fields on the open slopes, and beyond these the forests rose to the top of the mountains.

The ceilings of the house were high, and the halls and rooms were wide and airy; the trees on the edge of the woods seemed always to be rustling in a wind from one direction or another, and a lady; Mrs. Easterfield; who several years before had been traveling in that part of the country; declared that Broadstone was the most delightful place for a summer residence that she had ever seen, either in this country or across the ocean. So, with the consent and money of her husband, she had bought the estate the summer before the time of our story, and had gone there to live.

Mr. Easterfield was what is known as a railroad man, and held high office in many companies and organizations. When his wife first went to Broadstone he was obliged to spend the summer in Europe, and had agreed with her that the estate on the mountains would be the best place for her and the two little girls while he was away. This state of affairs had occasioned a good deal of talk, especially in Glenford, a town with which the Easterfields had but little to do, and which therefore had theorized much in order to explain to its own satisfaction the conduct of a comparatively young married woman who was evidently rich enough to spend her summers at any of the most fashionable watering-places, but who chose to go with her young family to that old barracks of a house, and who had a husband who never came near her or his children, and who, so far as the Glenford people knew, she never mentioned.

Mrs. Margaret Easterfield was a very fine woman, both to look at and to talk to, but she did not believe that her duty to her fellow-beings demanded that she should devote her first summer months at her new place to the gratification of the eyes and ears of her friends and acquaintances, so she had gone to Broadstone with her family—all females—with servants enough, and for the whole of the summer they had all been very happy.

But this summer things were going to be a little different at Broadstone, for Mrs. Easterfield had arranged for some house parties. Her husband was very kind and considerate about her plans, and promised her that he would make one of the good company at Broadstone whenever it was possible for him to do so.

So now it happened that he had come to see his wife and children and the house in which they lived; and, having had some business at a railroad center in the South, he had come through Glenford, which was unusual, as the intercourse between Broadstone and the great world was generally maintained through the gap in the mountains.

With his wife by his side and a little girl on each shoulder, Mr. Tom Easterfield walked through the grounds and the gardens and out on the lawn, and looked down over the tops of the trees upon the river which sparkled far below, and he said to his wife that if she would let him do it he would send a landscape-gardener, with a great company of Italians, and they would make the place a perfect paradise in about five days.

"It could be ruined a great deal quicker by an army of locusts," she said, "and so, if you do not mind, I think I will wait for the locusts."

It was not time yet for any of the members of the house parties to make their appearance, and it was the general desire of his family that Mr. Easterfield should remain until some of the visitors arrived, but he could not gratify them. Three days after his arrival he was obliged to be in Atlanta; and so, soon after breakfast one fine morning, the Easterfield carriage drove over the turnpike to the Glenford station, Mr. and Mrs. Easterfield on the back seat, and the two little girls sitting opposite, their feet sticking out straight in front of them.

When they stopped at the toll-gate Captain Asher came down to collect the toll—ten cents for two horses and a carriage. Olive was sitting in the little arbor, reading. She had noticed the approaching equipage and saw that there was a lady in it, but for some reason or other she was not so anxious as she had been to collect toll from ladies. If she could have arranged the matter to suit herself she would have taken toll from the male travelers, and her Uncle John might attend to the women; she did not believe that men would have such absurd ideas about people or ask ridiculous questions.

There was no conversation at the gate on this occasion, for the carriage was a little late, but as it rolled on Mrs. Margaret said to Mr. Tom:

"It seems to me as though I have just had a glimpse of Dresden. What do you suppose could have suggested that city to me?"

Mr. Tom could not imagine, unless it was the dust. She laughed, and said that he had dust and ballast and railroads on the brain; and when the oldest little girl asked what that meant, Mrs. Margaret told her that the next time her father came home she would make him sit down on the floor and then she would draw on that great bald spot of his head, which they had so often noticed, a map of the railroad lines in which he was concerned, and then his daughters would understand why he was always thinking of railroad-tracks and that sort of thing with the inside of his head, which, as she had told them, was that part of a person with which he did his thinking.

"Don't they sell some sort of annual or monthly tickets for this turnpike?" asked Mr. Tom. "If they do, you would save your-self the trouble of stopping to pay toll and make change."

"I so seldom use this road," she said, "that it would not be worth while. One does not stop on returning, you know."

But notwithstanding this speech, when Mrs. Easterfield returned from the Glenford station, one little girl sitting beside her and the other one opposite, both of them with their feet sticking out, she ordered her coachman to stop when he reached the toll-gate.

Olive was still sitting in the arbor, reading. The captain was not visible, and the wooden-faced Jane, noticing that the travelers were a lady and two little girls, did not consider that she had any right to interfere with Miss Olive's prerogatives; so that young lady felt obliged to go to the toll-gate to see what was wanted.

"You know you do not have to pay going back," she said.

"I know that," answered Mrs. Easterfield, "but I want to ask about tickets or monthly payments of toll, or whatever your arrangements are for that sort of thing."

"I really do not know," said Olive, "but I will go and ask about it."

"But stop one minute," exclaimed Mrs. Easterfield, leaning over the side of the carriage. "Is it your father who keeps this toll-gate?"

For some reason or other which she could not have explained to herself, Olive felt that it was incumbent upon her to assert herself, and she answered: "Oh, no, indeed. My father is Lieutenant-Commander Alfred Asher, of the cruiser Hopatcong."

Without another word Mrs. Easterfield pushed open the door of the carriage and stepped to the ground, exclaiming: "As I passed this morning I knew there was something about this place that brought back to my mind old times and old friends, and now I see what it was; it was you. I caught but one glimpse of you and I did not know you. But it was enough. I knew your father very well when I was a girl, and later I was with him and your mother in Dresden. You were a girl of twelve or thirteen, going to school, and I never saw much of you. But it is either your father or your mother that I saw in your face as you sat in that arbor, and I knew the face, although I did not know who owned it. I am Mrs. Easterfield, but that will not help you to know me, for I was not married when I knew your father."

Olive's eyes sparkled as she took the two hands extended to her. "I don't remember you at all," she said, "but if you are the friend of my father and mother—"

"Then I am to be your friend, isn't it?" interrupted Mrs. Easterfield.

"I hope so," answered Olive.

"Now, then," said Mrs. Easterfield, "I want you to tell me how in the world you come to be here."

There were two stools in the tollhouse, and Olive, having invited her visitor to seat herself on the better one, took the other, and told Mrs. Easterfield how she happened to be there.

"And that handsome elderly man who took the toll this morning is your uncle?"

"Yes, my father's only brother," said Olive.

"A good deal older," said Mrs. Easterfield.

"Oh, yes, but I do not know how much."

"And you call him captain. Was he also in the navy?"

"No," said Olive, "he was in the merchant service, and has retired. It seems queer that he should be keeping a toll-gate, but my father has often told me that Uncle John does not care for appearances, and likes to do things that please him. He likes to keep the tollhouse because it brings him in touch with the world."

"Very sensible in him," said Mrs. Easterfield. "I think I would

Frank R. Stockton

like to keep a toll-gate myself."

Captain Asher had seen the carriage stop, and knew that Mrs. Easterfield was talking to Olive, but he did not think himself called upon to intrude upon them. But now it was necessary for him to go to the tollhouse. Two men in a buggy with a broken spring and a coffee bag laid over the loins of an imperfectly set-up horse had been waiting for nearly a minute behind Mrs. Easterfield's carriage, desiring to pay their toll and pass through. So the captain went out of the garden-gate, collected the toll from the two men, and directed them to go round the carriage and pass on in peace, which they did.

Then Mrs. Easterfield rose from her stool, and approached the tollhouse door, and, as a matter of course, the captain was obliged to step forward and meet her. Olive introduced him to the lady, who shook hands with him very cordially.

"I have found the daughter of an old friend," said she, and then they all went into the tollhouse again, where the two ladies reseated themselves, and after some explanatory remarks Mrs. Easterfield said:

"Now, Captain Asher, I must not stay here blocking up your toll-gate all the morning, but I want to ask of you a very great favor. I want you to let your niece come and make me a visit. I want a good visit—at least ten days. You must remember that her father and I, and her mother, too, were very good friends. Now there are so many things I want to talk over with Miss Olive, and I am sure you will let me have her just for ten short days. There are no guests at Broadstone yet, and I want her. You do not know how much I want her."

Captain Asher stood up tall and strong, his broad shoulders resting against the frame of the open doorway. It was a positive delight to him to stand thus and look at such a beautiful woman. So far as he could see, there was nothing about her with which to find fault. If she had been a ship he would have said that her lines were perfect, spars and rigging just as he would have them. In addition to her other perfections, she was large enough. The captain considered himself an excellent judge of female beauty, and he had noticed that a great many fine women were too small. With Olive's personal appearance he was perfectly satisfied, although she was slight, but she was young, and would probably expand. If he had had a daughter he would have liked her to resemble Mrs. Easterfield, but that feeling did not militate in the least against Olive. In his mind it was not necessary for a niece to be quite as large as a daughter ought to be.

"But what does Olive say about it?" he asked.

"I have not been asked yet," replied Olive, "but it seems to me that I—"

"Would like to do it," interrupted Mrs. Easterfield. "Now, isn't that so, dear Olive?"

The girl looked at the captain. "It depends upon what you say about it, Uncle John."

The captain slightly knitted his brows. "If it were for one night, or perhaps a couple of days," he said, "it would be different. But what am I to do without Olive for nearly two weeks? I am just beginning to learn what a poor place my house would be without her."

At this minute a man upon a rapidly trotting pony stopped at the toll-gate.

"Excuse me one minute," continued the captain, "here is a person who can not wait," and stepping outside he said good morning to a bright-looking young fellow riding a sturdy pony and wearing on his cap a metal plate engraved "United States Rural Delivery."

The carrier brought but one letter to the tollhouse, and that was for Captain Asher himself. As the man rode away the captain thought he might as well open his letter before he went back. This would give the ladies a chance to talk further over the matter. He read the letter, which was not long, put it in his pocket, and then entered the tollhouse. There was now no doubt or sign of disturbance on his features.

"I have considered your invitation, madam," said he, "and as I see Olive wants to visit you, I shall not interfere."

"Of course she does," cried Mrs. Easterfield, springing to her feet, "and I thank you ever and ever so much, Captain Asher. And now, my dear," said she to Olive, "I am going to send the carriage for you to-morrow morning." And with this she put her arm around the girl and kissed her. Then, having warmly shaken hands with the captain, she departed.

"Do you know, Uncle John," said Olive, "I believe if you were twenty years older she would have kissed you."

With a grim smile the captain considered; would he have been willing to accept those additional years under the circumstances? He could not immediately make up his mind, and contented himself with the reflection that Olive did not think him old enough for the indiscriminate caresses of young people.

CHAPTER IV

THE SON OF AN OLD SHIPMATE

When Olive came down to breakfast the next morning she half repented that she had consented to go away and leave her uncle for so long a time. But when she made known her state of mind the captain laughed at her.

"My child," said he, "I want you to go. Of course, I did not take to the notion at first, but I did not consider then what you will have to tell when you come home. The people of Glenford will be your everlasting debtors. It might be a good thing to invite Maria Port out here. You could give her the best time she ever had in her life, telling her about the Broadstone people."

"Maria Port, indeed!" said Olive. "But we won't talk of her. And you really are willing I should go?"

"I speak the truth when I say I want you to go," replied the captain.

Whereupon Olive assured him that he was truly a good uncle.

After the Easterfield carriage had rolled away with Olive alone on the back seat, waving her handkerchief, the captain requested Jane to take entire charge of the toll-gate for a time; and, having retired to his own room, he took from his pocket the letter he had received the day before.

"I must write an answer to this," he said, "before the postman comes."

The letter was from one of the captain's old shipmates, Captain Richard Lancaster, the best friend he had had when he was in the merchant service. Captain Lancaster had often been asked by his old friend to visit him at the toll-gate, but, being married and rheumatic, he had never accepted the invitation. But now he wrote that his son, Dick, had planned a holiday trip which would take him through Glenford, and that, if it suited Captain Asher, the father would accept for the son the long-standing invitation. Captain Lancaster wrote that as he could not go himself to his old friend Asher, the next best thing would be for his son to go, and when the young man returned he could tell his father all about Captain Asher. There would be something in that like old times. Besides, he wanted his former shipmate to know his son Dick, who was, in his eyes, a very fine young fellow.

"There never was such a lucky thing in the world," said Captain Asher to himself, when he had finished rereading the letter. "Of course, I want to have Dick Lancaster's son here, but I could not have had him if Olive had been here. But now it is all right. The young fellow can stay here a few days, and he will be gone before she gets back. If I like him I can ask him to come again; but that's my business. Handsome women, like that Mrs. Easterfield, always bring good luck. I have noticed that many and many a time."

Then he set himself to work to write a letter to invite young Richard Lancaster to spend a few days with him.

For the rest of that day, and the greater part of the next, Captain Asher gave a great deal of thinking time to the consideration of the young man who was about to visit him, and of whom, personally, he knew very little. He was aware that Captain Lancaster had a son and no other children, and he was quite sure that this son must now be a grown-up young man. He remembered very well that Captain Lancaster was a fine young fellow when he first knew him, and he did not doubt at all that the son resembled the father. He did not believe that young Dick was a sailor, because he and old Dick had often said to each other that if they married their sons should not go to sea. Of course he was in some business; and Captain Lancaster ought to be well able to give him a good start in life; just as able as he himself was to give Olive a good start in housekeeping when the time came.

"Now, what in the name of common sense," ejaculated Captain Asher, "did I think of that for? What has he to do with Olive, or Olive with him?" And then he said to himself, thinking of the young man in the bosom of his family and without reference to anybody outside of it: "Yes, his father must be pretty well off. He did a good deal more trading than ever I did. But after all, I don't believe he invested his money any better than I did mine, and it is just as like as not if we were to show our hands, that Olive would get as much as Dick's son. There it is again. I can't keep my mind off the thing." And as he spoke he knocked the ashes out of his pipe, and began to stride up and down the garden walk; and as he did so he began to reproach himself.

What right had he to think of his niece in that way? It was not doing the fair thing by her father, and perhaps by her, for that matter. For all he knew she might be engaged to somebody out West or down East, or in some other part of the world where she had lived. But this idea made very little impression on him. Knowing Olive as he did, he did not believe that she was engaged to anybody anywhere; he did not want to think that she was the kind of girl who would conceal her engagement from him, or who could do it, for that matter. But, everything considered, he was very glad Olive had gone to Broadstone, for, whatever the young fellow might happen to be, he wanted to know all about him before Olive met him.

Captain Asher firmly believed that there was nothing of the matchmaker in his disposition, but notwithstanding this estimate of himself, he went on thinking of Olive and the son of his old shipmate, both separately and together. He had never said to anybody, nor intimated to anybody, that he was going to give any of his moderate fortune to his niece. In fact, before this visit to him he had not thought much about it, nor did it enter his mind that Olive's Boston aunt, her mother's sister, had favored this visit of the girl to her toll-gate uncle, hoping that he might think about it.

In consequence of these cogitations, and in spite of the fact that he despised matchmaking, Captain Asher was greatly interested in the coming advent of his shipmate's son.

When the same phaeton, the same horse, and the same boy that had brought Maria Port to the tollhouse, conveyed there a young man with two valises, one rather large, Captain Asher did not hurry from the house to meet his visitor. He had seen him coming, and had preferred to stand in his doorway and take a preliminary observation of him. Having taken this, Captain Asher was obliged to confess to himself that he was disappointed.

The first cause of his disappointment was the fact that the young man wore a colored shirt and no vest, and a yellow leather belt. Now, Captain Asher for the greater part of his active life had worn colored shirts, sometimes very dark ones, with no vests, but he had not supposed that a young man coming to a house where there was a young lady accustomed to the best society would present himself in such attire. The captain instantly remembered that his visitor could not know that there was a young lady at the house, but this did not satisfy him. Such attire was not respectful, even to him. The leather belt especially offended him. The captain was not aware of the *neglige* summer fashions for men which then prevailed.

The next thing that disappointed him was that young Lancaster, seen across the garden, did not appear to be the strapping young fellow he had expected to see. He was moderately tall, and moderately broad, and handled his valise with apparent ease, but he did not look as though he were his father's son. Dick Lancaster had married the daughter of a captain when he was only a second mate, and that piece of good fortune had been generally attributed to his good looks.

But these observations and reflections occupied a very short time, and Captain Asher walked quickly to meet his visitor. As he stepped out of the garden-gate he was disappointed again. The young man's trousers were turned up above his shoes. The weather was not wet, there was no mud, and if Dick Lancaster's son had not bought a pair of ready-made trousers that were too long for him, why should he turn them up in that ridiculous way?

In spite of these first impressions, the captain gave his old friend's son a hearty welcome, and took him into the house. After dinner he subjected the young man to a crucial test; he asked him if he smoked. If the visitor had answered in the negative he would have dropped still further in the captain's estimation. It was not that the captain had any theories in regard to the sanitary advantages or disadvantages of tobacco; he simply remembered that nearly all the rascals with whom he had been acquainted had been eager to declare that they never used tobacco in any form, and that nearly all the good fellows he had known enjoyed their pipes. In fact, he could not see how good fellowship could be maintained without good talk and good tobacco, so he waited with an anxious interest for his guest's answer.

"Oh, yes," said he, "I am fond of a smoke, especially in company," and so, having risen several inches in the good opinion of his host, he followed him to the little arbor in the garden.

"Now, then," said Captain Asher, when his pipe was alight, "you have told me a great deal about your father, now tell me something about yourself. I do not even know what your business is."

"I am Assistant Professor of Theoretical Mathematics in

Sutton College," answered the young man.

Captain Asher put down his pipe and gazed at his visitor across the arbor. This answer was so different from anything he had expected that for the moment he could not express his astonishment, and was obliged to content himself with asking where Sutton College was.

"It is what they call a fresh-water college," replied the young man, "and I do not wonder that you do not know where it is. It is near our town. I graduated there and received my present appointment about three years ago. I was then twenty-seven."

"Your father was good at mathematics," said Captain Asher. "He was a great hand at calculations, but he went in for practise, as I did, and not for theories. I suppose there are other professors who teach regular working mathematics."

"Oh, yes," replied the young man, with a smile, "there is the Professor of Applied Mathematics, but of course the thorough student wants to understand the theories on which his practise is to be based."

"I do not see why he should," replied the other. "If a good ship is launched for me, I don't care anything about the stocks she slides off of."

"Perhaps not," said Lancaster, "but somebody has to think about them."

In the afternoon Captain Asher showed his visitor his little farm, and took him out fishing. During these recreations he refrained, as far as possible, from asking questions, for he did not wish the young man to suppose that for any reason he had been sent there to undergo an examination. But in the evening he could not help talking about the college, not in reference to the work and life of the students, a subject that did not interest him, but in regard to the work and the prospects of the faculty.

"What does your president teach?" he asked. "I believe all presidents have charge of some branch or other."

"Oh, yes," said Lancaster, "our president is Professor of Mental and Moral Philosophy."

"I thought it would be something of the kind," said the captain to himself. "Even the head Professor of Mathematical Theories would never get to the top of the heap. He is not useful enough for that."

After he had gone to bed that night Captain Asher found himself laughing about the events of the day. He could not help it when he remembered how his mind had been almost constantly occupied with a consideration of his old shipmate's son with reference to his brother's daughter. And when he remembered that neither of these two young people had ever seen or heard of the other, it is not surprising that he laughed a little.

"It's none of my business, anyway," thought the captain, "and I might as well stop bothering my head about it. I suppose I might as well tell him about Olive, for it is nothing I need keep secret. But first I'll see how long he is going to stay. It's none of his business, anyway, whether I have a niece staying with me or not."

Frank R. Stockton

CHAPTER V

OLIVE PAYS TOLL

It is needless to say that Olive was charmed with Broadstone; with its mistress; with the two little girls; with the woods; the river; the mountains; and even the sky; which seemed different from that same sky when viewed from the tollhouse. She was charmed also with the rest of the household, which was different from anything of that kind that she had known, being composed entirely, with the exception of some servants, of women and little girls. Olive, accustomed all her life to men, men, men, grew rapturous over this Amazonian paradise.

"Don't be too enthusiastic," said Mrs. Easterfield; "for a while you may like fresh butter without salt, but the longing for the condiment will be sure to come."

There was Mrs. Blynn, the widow of a clergyman, with dark-brown eyes and white hair, who was always in a good humor, who acted as the general manager of the household, and also as particular friend to any one in the house who needed her services in that way. Then there was Miss Raleigh, who was supposed to be Mrs. Easterfield's secretary. She was a slender spinster of forty or more, with sad eyes and very fine teeth. She had dyspeptic proclivities, and never differed with anybody except in regard to her own diet. She seldom wrote for Mrs. Easterfield, for that lady did not like her handwriting, and she did not understand the use of the typewriter; nor did she read to the lady of the house, for Mrs. Easterfield could not endure to have anybody read to her. But in all the other duties of a secretary she made herself very useful. She saw that the books, which every morning were found lying about the house, were put in their proper places on the shelves, and, if necessary, she dusted them; if she saw a book turned upside down she immediately set it up properly. She was also expected to exert a certain supervision over the books the little girls were allowed to look at. She was an excellent listener and an appropriate smiler; Mrs. Easterfield frequently said that she never knew Miss Raleigh to smile in the wrong place. She took a regular walk every day, eight times up and down the whole length of the lawn.

Mrs. Easterfield gave herself almost entirely to the entertainment of her guest. They roamed over the grounds, they found the finest points of view, at which Olive was expert, being a fine climber, and they tramped for long distances along the edge of the woods, where together they killed a snake. Mrs. Easterfield also allowed Olive the great privilege of helping her work in her garden of nature. This was a wide bed which was almost entirely shaded by two large trees. The peculiarity about this bed was that its mistress carefully pulled up all the flowering plants and cultivated the weeds.

"You see," said she to Olive, "I planted here a lot of flower-seeds which I thought would thrive in the shade, but they did not, and after a while I found that they were all spindling and puny-looking, while the weeds were growing as if they were out in the open sunshine, so I have determined to acknowledge the principle of the survival of the fittest, and whenever anything that looks like a flower shows itself I jerk it out. I also thin out all but the best weeds. I hoe and rake the others, and water them if necessary. Look at that splendid Jamestown weed—here they call it jimson weed—did you ever see anything finer than that with its great white blossoms and dark-green leaves? I expect it to be twice as large before the summer is over. And all these others. See how graceful they are, and what delicate flowers some of them have!"

Frank R. Stockton

"I wonder," said Olive, "if I should have had the strength of mind to pull up my flowers and leave my weeds."

"The more you think about it," said Mrs. Easterfield, "the more you like weeds. They have such fine physiques, and they don't ask anybody to do anything for them. They are independent, like self-made men, and come up of themselves. They laugh at disadvantages, and even bricks and flagstones will not keep them down."

"But, after all," said Olive, "give me the flowers that can not take care of themselves." And she turned toward a bed of carnations, bright under the morning sun.

"Do you suppose, little girl," said Mrs. Easterfield, following her, "that I do not like flowers because I do like weeds? Everything in its place; weeds are for the shady spots, but I keep my flowers out of such places. This flower, for instance," touching Olive on the cheek. "And now let us go into the house and see what pleasant thing we can find to do there."

In the afternoon the two ladies went out rowing on the river, and Mrs. Easterfield was astonished at Olive's proficiency with the oar. She had thought herself a good oarswoman, but she was nothing to Olive. She good-naturedly acknowledged her inferiority, however. How could she expect to compete with a navy girl? she said.

"Are you fond of swimming?" asked Olive, as she looked down into the bright, clear water.

"Oh, very," said Mrs. Easterfield. "But I am not allowed to swim in this river. It is considered dangerous."

Olive looked up in surprise. It seemed odd that there should be anything that this bright, free woman was not allowed to do, or that there should be anybody who would not allow it.

Then followed some rainy days, and the first clear day Mrs.

Easterfield told Olive that she would take her a drive in the afternoon.

"I shall drive you myself with my own horses," she said, "but you need not be afraid, for I can drive a great deal better than I can row. We must lose no time in seizing all the advantages of this Amazonian life, for to-morrow some of our guests will arrive, the Foxes and Mr. Claude Locker."

"Who are the Foxes?" asked Olive.

"They are the pleasantest visitors that any one could have," was the answer. "They always like everything. They never complain of being cold, nor talk about the weather being hot. They are interested in all games, and they like all possible kinds of food that one can give them to eat. They are always ready to go to bed when they think they ought to, and sit up just as long as they are wanted. Of course, they have their own ideas about things, but they don't dispute. They take care of themselves all the morning, and are ready for anything you want to do in the afternoon or evening. They have two children at home, but they never talk about them unless they are particularly asked to do so. They know a great many people, and you can tell by the way they speak of them that they won't talk scandal about you. In fact, they are model guests, and they ought to open a school to teach the art of visiting."

"And what about Mr. Claude Locker?"

Mrs. Easterfield laughed. "Oh, he is different," she said; "he is so different from the Poxes that words would not describe it. But you won't be long in becoming acquainted with him."

The road over which the two ladies drove that afternoon was a beautiful one, sometimes running close to the river under great sycamores, then making a turn into the woods and among the rocks. At last they came to a cross-road, which led away from the river, and here Mrs. Easterfield stopped her horses.

"Now, Olive," said she, for she was now very familiar with her guest, "I will leave the return route to you. Shall we go back by the river road—and the scenery will be very different when going in the other direction—or shall we drive over to Glenford, and go home by the turnpike? That is a little farther, but the road is a great deal better?"

"Oh, let us go that way," cried Olive. "We will go through Uncle John's toll-gate, and you must let me pay the toll. It will be such fun to pay toll to Uncle John, or old Jane."

"Very well," said Mrs. Easterfield, "we will go that way."

When the horses had passed through Glenford and had turned their heads homeward, they clattered along at a fine rate over the smooth turnpike, and Olive was in as high spirits as they were.

"Whoever comes out to take toll," said she, "I intend to be treated as an ordinary traveler and nothing else. I have often taken toll, but I never paid it in my life. And they must take it—no gratis traveling for me. But I hope you won't mind stopping long enough for me to say a few words after I have transacted the regular business."

"Oh, no," said Mrs. Easterfield, "you can chat as much as you like. We have plenty of time."

Olive held in her hand a quarter of a dollar; she was determined they should make change for her, and that everything should be done properly.

Dick Lancaster sat in the garden arbor, reading. He was becoming a little tired of this visit to his father's old friend. He liked Captain Asher and appreciated his hospitality, but there was nothing very interesting for him to do in this place, and he had thought that it might be a very good thing if the several days for which he had been invited should terminate on the morrow. There were some very attractive plans ahead of him, and he felt that he had now done his full duty by his father and his father's old friend.

Captain Asher was engaged with some matters about his little farm, and Lancaster had asked as a favor that he might be allowed to tend the toll-gate during his absence. It would be something to do, and, moreover, something out of the way.

When he perceived the approach of Mrs. Easterfield's carriage Lancaster walked down to the tollhouse, and stopped for a minute to glance over the rates of toll which were pasted up inside the door as well as out.

The carriage stopped, and when a young man stepped out from the tollhouse Olive gave a sudden start, and the words with which she had intended to greet her uncle or old Jane instantly melted away.

"Don't push me out of the carriage," said Mrs. Easterfield, good-naturedly, and she, too, looked at the young man.

"For two horses and a vehicle," said Dick Lancaster, "ten cents, if you please."

Olive made no answer, but handed him the quarter with which he retired to make change. Mrs. Easterfield opened her mouth to speak, but Olive put her finger on her lips and shook her head; the situation astonished her, but she did not wish to ask that stranger to explain it.

Lancaster came out and dropped fifteen cents into Olive's hand. He could not help regarding with interest the occupants of the carriage, and Mrs. Easterfield looked hard at him. Suddenly Olive turned in her seat; she looked at the house, she looked at the garden, she looked at the little piazza by the side of the tollhouse. Yes, it was really the same place. For an instant she thought she might have been mistaken, but there was her window with the Virginia creeper under the sill where she had trained it herself. Then she made a motion to her companion, who immediately drove on.

"What does this mean?" exclaimed Mrs. Easterfield. "Who is that young man? Why didn't you give me a chance to ask after the captain, even if you did not care to do so?"

"I never saw him before!" cried Olive. "I never heard of him. I don't understand anything about it. The whole thing shocked me, and I wanted to get on."

"I don't think it a very serious matter," said Mrs. Easterfield. "Some passer-by might have relieved your uncle for a time."

"Not at all, not at all," replied Olive. "Uncle John would never give the toll-gate into the charge of a passer-by, especially as old Jane was there. I know she was there, for the basement door was open, and she never goes away and leaves it so. That man is somebody who is staying there. I saw an open book on the arbor bench. Nobody reads in that arbor but me."

"And that young man apparently," said Mrs. Easterfield. "I agree with you that it is surprising."

For some minutes Olive did not speak. "I am afraid," she said, presently, "that my uncle is not acting quite frankly with me. I noticed how willing he was that I should go to your house."

"Perhaps he expected this person and wanted to get you out of the way," laughed Mrs. Easterfield.

"Well, my dear, I do not believe your uncle is such a schemer. He does not look like it. Take my word for it, it will all be as simple as a-b-c when it is explained to you."

But Olive could not readily take this view of the case, and the drive home was not nearly so pleasant as it would have been if her uncle or old Jane had taken her quarter and given her fifteen cents in change.

That night, soon after the family at Broadstone had retired to their rooms, Olive knocked at the door of Mrs. Easterfield's chamber.

"Do you know," she exclaimed, when she had been told to enter, "that a horrible idea has come into my head? Uncle John may have been taken sick, and that man looked just like a doctor. Old Jane was busy with uncle, and as the doctor had to wait, he took the toll. Oh, I wish we had asked! It was cruel in me not to!"

"Now, that is all nonsense," said Mrs. Easterfield. "If anything serious is the matter with your uncle he most surely would have let you know, and, besides, both the doctors in Glenford are elderly men. I do not believe there is the slightest reason for your anxiety. But to make you feel perfectly satisfied, I will send a man to Glenford early in the morning. I want to send there anyway."

"But I would not like my uncle to think that I was trying to find out anything he did not care to tell me," said Olive.

"Oh, don't trouble yourself about that," answered Mrs. Easterfield. "I will instruct the man. He need not ask any questions at the toll-gate. But when he gets to Glenford he can find out everything about that young man without asking any questions. He is a very discreet person. And I am also a discreet person," she added, "and you shall have no connection with my messenger's errand."

After breakfast the next morning Mrs. Easterfield took Olive aside. "My man has returned," she said; "he tells me that Captain Asher took the toll, and was smoking his pipe in perfect health. He also saw the young man, and his natural curiosity prompted him to ask about him in the town. He heard that he is the son of one of the captain's old shipmates who is making him a visit. Now I hope this satisfies you."

"Satisfies me!" exclaimed Olive. "I should have been a great deal better satisfied if I had heard he was sick, provided it was nothing dangerous. I think my uncle is treating me shamefully. It is not that I care a snap about his visitor, one way or another, but it is his want of confidence in me that hurts me. Could he have supposed I should have wanted to stay with him if I had known a young man was coming?"

"Well, my dear," said Mrs. Easterfield, "I can not send anybody to find out what he supposed. But I am as certain as I can be certain of anything that there is nothing at all in this bugbear you have conjured up. No doubt the young man dropped in quite accidentally, and it was his bad luck that prevented him from dropping in before you left."

Olive shook her head. "My uncle knew all about it. His manner showed it. He has treated me very badly."

CHAPTER VI

MR. CLAUDE LOCKER

The Foxes arrived at Broadstone at the exact hour of the morning at which they had been expected. They always did this; even trains which were sometimes delayed when other visitors came were always on time when they carried the Foxes. They were both perfectly well and happy, as they always were.

As rapidly as it was possible for human beings to do so they absorbed the extraordinary advantages of the house and it surroundings, and they said the right things in such a common-sense fashion that their hostess was proud that she owned such a place, and happy that she had invited them to see it.

In their hearts they liked everything about the place except Olive, and they wondered how they were going to get along with such a glum young person, but they did not talk about her to Mrs. Easterfield; there was too much else.

Mr. Claude Locker was expected on the train by which the Foxes had come, but he did not arrive; and this made it necessary to send again for him in the afternoon.

Mrs. Easterfield tried very hard to cheer up Olive, and to make her entertain the Foxes in her usual lively way, but this was of no use; the young person was not in a good humor, and retired for an afternoon nap. But as this was an indulgence she very

Frank R. Stockton

seldom allowed herself, it was not likely that she napped.

Mr. Fox spoke to Mrs. Fox about her. "A queer girl," he said; "what do you suppose is the matter with her?"

"The symptoms are those of green apples," replied Mrs. Fox, "and probably she will be better to-morrow."

The carriage came back without Mr. Locker. But just as the soup-plates were being removed from the dinner-table he arrived in a hired vehicle, and appeared at the dining-room door with his hat in one hand, and a package in the other. He begged Mrs. Easterfield not to rise.

"I will slip up to my room," said he, "if you have one for me, and when I come down I will greet you and be introduced."

With this he turned and left the room, but was back in a moment. "It was a woman," he said, "who was at the bottom of it. It is always a woman, you know, and I am sure you will excuse me now that you know this. And you must let me begin wherever you may be in the dinner."

"I have heard of Mr. Locker," said Mr. Fox, "but I never met him before. He must be very odd."

"He admits that himself," said Mrs. Easterfield, "but he asserts that he spends a great deal of his time getting even with people."

In a reasonable time Mr. Locker appeared and congratulated himself upon having struck the roast.

"As a matter of fact," he said, "we will now all begin dinner together. What has gone before was nothing but overture. If I can help it I never get in until the beginning of the play."

He bowed parenthetically as Mrs. Easterfield introduced him to the company; and, as she looked at him, Olive forgot for a moment her uncle and his visitor.

"Don't send for soup, I beg of you," said Mr. Locker, as he took his seat. "I regard it as a rare privilege to begin with the inside cut of beef."

Mr. Locker was not allowed to do all the talking; his hostess would not permit that; but under the circumstances he was allowed to explain his lateness.

"You know I have been spending a week with the Bartons," he said, "and last night I came over from their house to the station in a carriage. There is a connecting train, but I should have had to take it very early in the evening, so I saved time by hiring a carriage."

"Saved time?" exclaimed Mrs. Easterfield.

"I saved all the time from dinner until the Bartons went to bed, which would have been lost if I had taken the train. Besides, I like to travel in carriages. One is never too late for a carriage; it is always bound to wait for you."

In the recesses of his mind Mr. Fox now said to himself, "This is a fool." And Mrs. Fox, in the recesses of her mind, remarked, "I am quite sure that Mr. Fox will look upon this young man as a fool."

"I spent what was left of the night at a tavern near the station," continued Mr. Locker, "where I would have had to stay all night if I had not taken the carriage. And I should have been in plenty of time for the morning train if I had not taken a walk before breakfast. Apparently that is a part of the world where it takes a good deal longer to go back to a place than it does to get away from it."

"But where did the woman come in?" asked Mrs. Easterfield.

"Oh, she came in with some tea and sandwiches in the middle of the afternoon," said Mr. Locker. "I was waiting in the parlor of the tavern. She was fairly young, and as I ate she stood and talked. She talked about Horace Walpole." At this even Olive smiled. "It was odd, wasn't it?" continued Mr. Locker, glancing from one to the other. "But that is what she did. She had been reading about him in an old book. She asked me if I knew anything about him, and I told her a great deal. It was so very interesting to tell her, and she was so interested, that when the train arrived I was too much occupied to think that it might start again immediately, but it did that very thing, and so I was left. However, the Walpole young woman told me there was a freight-train along in about an hour, and so we continued our conversation. When this train came I asked the engineer how many cigars he would take to let me ride in the cab. He said half a dozen, but as I only had five, I promised to send him the other by mail. However, as I smoked two of his five, I suppose I ought to send him three."

"This young man," said Mr. Fox to himself, "is trying to appear more of a fool than he really is."

"I have no doubt," said Mrs. Fox to herself, "that Mr. Fox is of the opinion that this young man is making an effort to appear foolish."

That evening was a dull one. Mrs. Easterfield did her best, Claude Locker did his best, and Mr. and Mrs. Fox did their best to make things lively, but their success was poor. Miss Raleigh, the secretary, sat ready to give an approving smile to any liveliness which might arise, and Mrs. Blynn, with the dark eyes and soft white hair, sat sewing and waiting; never before had it been necessary for her to wait for liveliness in Mrs. Easterfield's house. A mild rain somewhat assisted the dullness, for everybody was obliged to stay indoors.

Early the next morning Olive Asher went down-stairs, and stood in the open doorway looking out upon the landscape, glowing in the sunshine and brighter and more odorous from the recent rain. Some time during the night this young woman had made up her mind to give no further thought to her uncle who kept the toll-gate. There was no earthly reason why he, or anything he wanted to do, or did not want to do, or did, should trouble and annoy her. A few months before she had scarcely known him, not having seen him since she was a girl; and, in fact, he was no more to her now than he was before she went to his house. If he chose to offer her any explanation of his strange conduct, that would be very well; if he did not choose, that would also be very well. The whole affair was of no consequence; she would drop it entirely from her mind.

Olive's bounding spirits now rose very high, and when Claude Locker came in with his shoes soaked from a tramp in the wet grass she greeted him in such a way that he could scarcely believe she was the grumpy girl of the day before. As they went into breakfast Mrs. Fox remarked to her husband in a low voice that Miss Asher seemed to have recovered entirely from her indisposition.

In the course of the morning Mr. Locker found an opportunity to speak in private with Mrs. Easterfield. "I am in great trouble," he said; "I want to marry Miss Asher."

"You show unusual promptness," said Mrs. Easterfield.

"Not at all," replied Locker. "This sort of thing is not unusual with me. My mind is a highly sensitive plate, and receives impressions almost instantaneously. If it were a large mind these impressions might be placed side by side, and each one would perhaps become indelible. But it is small, and each impression claps itself down on the one before. This last one, however, is the strongest of them all, and obliterates everything that went before."

"It strikes me," said Mrs. Easterfield, "that if you were to pay more attention to your poems and less to young ladies it would be better."

"Hardly," said Mr. Locker; "for it would be worse for

the poems."

The general appearance of Mr. Locker gave no reason to suppose that he would be warranted in assuming a favorable issue from any of the impressions to which his mind was so susceptible. He was small, rather awkwardly set up, his head was large, and the features of his face seemed to have no relation to each other. His nose was somewhat stubby, and had nothing to do with his mouth or eyes. One of his eyebrows was drawn down as if in days gone by he had been in the habit of wearing a single glass. The other brow was raised over a clear and wide-open light-blue eye. His mouth was large, and attended strictly to its own business. It transmitted his odd ideas to other people, but it never laughed at them. His chin was round and prominent, suggesting that it might have been borrowed from somebody else. His cheeks were a little heavy, and gave no assistance in the expression of his ideas.

His profession was that of a poet. He called himself a practical poet, because he made a regular business of it, turning his poetic inspirations into salable verse with the facility and success, as he himself expressed it, of a man who makes boxes out of wood. Moreover, he sold these poems as readily as any carpenter sold his boxes. Like himself, Claude Locker's poems were always short, always in request, and sometimes not easy to understand.

The poem he wrote that night was a word-picture of the rising moon entangled in a sheaf of corn upon a hilltop, with a long-eared rabbit sitting near by as if astonished at the conflagration.

"A very interesting girl, that Miss Asher," said Mr. Fox to his wife that evening. "I do not know when I have laughed so much."

"I thought you were finding her interesting," said Mrs. Fox. "To me it was like watching a game of roulette at Monte Carlo. It was intensely interesting, but I could not imagine it as having anything to do with me."

"No, my dear," said Mr. Fox, "it could have nothing to do with you."

After Mrs. Easterfield retired she sat for a long time, thinking of Olive. That young person and Mr. Locker had been boating that afternoon, and Olive had had the oars. Mr. Locker had told with great effect how she had pulled to get out of the smooth water, and how she had dashed over the rapids and between the rocks in such a way as to make his heart stand still.

"I should like to go rowing with her every day," he had remarked confidentially. "Each time I started I should make a new will."

"Why a new one?" Mrs. Easterfield had asked.

"Each time I should take something more from my relatives to give to her," had been the answer.

As she sat and thought, Mrs. Easterfield began to be a little frightened. She was a brave woman, but it is the truly brave who know when they should be frightened, and she felt her responsibility, not on account of the niece of the toll-gate keeper, but on account of the daughter of Lieutenant Asher, whom she had once known so well. The thing which frightened her was the possibility that before anybody would be likely to think of such a thing Olive might marry Claude Locker. He was always ready to do anything he wanted to do at any time; and for all Mrs. Easterfield knew, the girl might be of the same sort.

But Mrs. Easterfield rose to the occasion. She looked upon Olive as a wild young colt who had broken out of her paddock, but she remembered that she herself had a record for speed. "If there is to be any running I shall get ahead of her," she said to herself, "and I will turn her back. I think I can trust

Frank R. Stockton

myself for that."

Olive slept the sound sleep of the young, but for all that she had a dream. She dreamed of a kind, good, thoughtful, and even affectionate, middle-aged man; a man who looked as though he might have been her father, and whom she was beginning to look upon as a father, notwithstanding the fact that she had a real father dressed in a uniform and on a far-away ship. She dreamed ever so many things about this newer, although elder, father, and her dream made her very happy.

But in the morning when she woke her dream had entirely passed from her mind, and she felt just as much like a colt as when she had gone to bed.

CHAPTER VII

THE CAPTAIN AND HIS GUEST GO FISHING AND COME HOME HAPPY

When Dick Lancaster told Captain Asher he had taken toll from two ladies in a phaeton he was quite eloquent in his description of said ladies. He declared with an impressiveness which the captain had not noticed in him before that he did not know when he had seen such handsome ladies. The younger one, who paid the toll, was absolutely charming. She seemed a little bit startled, but he supposed that was because she saw a strange face at the toll-gate. Dick wanted very much to know who these ladies were. He had not supposed that he would find such stylish people, and such a handsome turnout in this part of the country.

"Oh, ho," said Captain Asher, "do you suppose we are all farmers and toll-gate keepers? If you do, you are very much mistaken, although I must admit that the stylish people, as you call them, are scattered about very thinly. I expect that carriage was from Broadstone over on the mountain. Was the team dapple gray, pony built?"

"Yes," said Lancaster.

"Then it was Mrs. Easterfield driving some of her company. I have seen her with that team. And by George," he exclaimed, "I bet my head the other one was Olive! Of course it was. And she paid toll! Well, well, if that isn't a good one! Olive paying toll! I wish I had been here to take it! That truly would have been a lark!"

Dick Lancaster did not echo this wish of his host. He was very glad, indeed, that the captain had not been at the toll-gate when the ladies passed through. Captain Asher was still laughing.

"Olive must have been amazed," he said. "It was queer enough for her to go through my gate and pay toll, but to pay it to an Assistant Professor of Theoretical Mathematics was a good deal queerer. I can't imagine what she thought about it."

"She did not know I am that!" exclaimed Dick Lancaster. "There is nothing of the professor in my outward appearance—at least, I hope not."

"No, I don't think there is," replied the captain. "But she must have been amazed, all the same. I wish I had been here, or old Jane, anyway. But, of course, when a stranger showed himself she would not have said anything."

"But who is Olive?" asked Lancaster.

"She's my niece," said the captain. "I don't think I have mentioned her to you. She is on a visit to me, but just now she is staying at Broadstone. I suppose she will be there about a week longer."

"It's odd he has not mentioned her to me," thought Lancaster, and then, as the captain went to ask old Jane if she had seen Olive pass, the young man retired to the arbor with a book which he did not read.

His desire to inform his host that it would be necessary to take leave of him on the morrow had very much abated. It would be very pleasant, he thought, to be a visitor in a family of which that girl was a member. But if she were not to return for a week, how could he expect to stay with the captain so long?

There would be no possible excuse for such a thing. Then he thought it would be very pleasant to be in a country of which that young woman was one of the inhabitants. Anyway, he hoped the captain would invite him to make a longer stay. The great blue eyes with which the young lady had regarded him as she paid the toll would not fade out of his mind.

"She must have wondered who it was that took the toll," said old Jane. "And there wasn't no need of it, anyway. I could have took it as I always have took it when you was not here, and before either of them came."

"Either of them" struck the captain's ear strangely. Here was this old woman coupling these two young people in her mind!

The next morning Captain Asher sat on his little piazza, smoking his pipe and thinking about Olive driving through the gate and paying toll to a stranger. But he now considered the incident from a different point of view. Of course, Olive had been surprised when she had seen the young man, but she might also have wondered how he happened to be there and she not know of it. If he were staying long enough to be entrusted with toll-taking it might—in fact, the captain thought it probably would—appear very strange to her that she should not know of it. So now he asked himself if it would not be a good thing if he were to write her a little note in which he should mention Mr. Lancaster and his visit. In fact, he thought the best thing he could do would be to write her a playful sort of a note, and tell her that she should feel honored by having her toll taken up by a college professor. But he did not immediately write the note. The more he thought about it, the more he wished he had been at the toll-gate when Mrs. Easterfield's phaeton passed by.

Captain Asher did not write his note at all. He did not know what to say; he did not want to make too much of the incident, for it was really a trifling matter, only worthy of being mentioned in case he had something more important to write about. But he had nothing more important; there was no

Frank R. Stockton

reason why he should write to Olive during her short stay with Mrs. Easterfield. Besides, she would soon be back, and then he could talk to her; that would be much better. Now, two strong desires began to possess him; one was for Olive to come home; and the other for Dick Lancaster to go away. There had been moments when he had had a shadowy notion of bringing the two together, but this idea had vanished. His mind was now occupied very much with thoughts of his beautiful niece and very little with the young man in the colored shirt and turned-up trousers who was staying with him.

Dick Lancaster, in his arbor, was also thinking a great deal about Olive, and very little about that stalwart sailor, her uncle. If he had merely seen the young woman, and had never heard anything about her, her face would have impressed him, but the knowledge that she was an inmate of the house in which he was staying could not fail to affect him very much. He was puzzling his mind about the girl who had given him a quarter of a dollar, and to whom he had handed fifteen cents in change. He wondered how such a girl happened to be living at such a place. He wondered if there were any possibility of his staying there, or in the neighborhood, until she should come back; he wondered if there were any way by which he could see her again. He might have wondered a good many other things if Captain Asher had not approached the arbor. The captain having been aroused from his mental contemplation of Olive by a man in a wagon, had glanced over at the arbor and had suddenly been struck with the conviction that that young man looked bored, and that, as his host, he was not doing the right thing by him.

"Dick," said the captain, "let's go fishing. It's not late yet, and I'll put my mare to the buggy, and we can drive to the river. We will take something to eat with us, and make a day of it."

Lancaster hesitated a moment; he had been thinking that the time had come when he should say something about his departure, but this invitation settled the matter for that day; and in half an hour the two had started away, leaving the toll-gate in charge of old Jane, who was a veteran in the business, having lived at the toll-gate years before the captain.

As they drove along the smooth turnpike Lancaster remembered with great interest that this road led to the gap in the mountains; that the captain had told him Broadstone was not very far from the gap; and that the river was not very far from Broadstone; and his face glowed with interest in the expedition.

But when, after a few miles, they turned into a plain country road which, as the captain informed him, led in a southeasterly direction, to a point on the river where black bass were to be caught and where a boat could be hired, the corners of Dick Lancaster's mouth began to droop. Of necessity that road must reach the river miles to the south of Broadstone.

It was a very good day for fishing, and the captain was pleased to see that the son of his old shipmate was a very fair angler. Toward the close of the afternoon, with the conviction that they had had a good time and that their little expedition had been a success, the two fishermen set out for home with a basket of bass: some of them quite a respectable size; stowed away under the seat of the buggy. When they reached the turnpike the old mare, knowing well in which direction her supper lay, turned briskly to the left, and set out upon a good trot. But this did not last very long. To her great surprise she was suddenly pulled up short; a carriage with two horses which had been approaching had also stopped.

On the back seat of this carriage sat Mrs. Easterfield; on one side of her was a little girl, and on the other side was another little girl, each with her feet stuck out straight in front of her.

"Oh, Captain Asher," exclaimed the lady, with a most enchanting smile, "I am so glad to meet you. I was obliged to go to Glenford to take one of my little girls to the dentist, and I inquired for you each time I passed your gate."

The captain was very glad he had been so fortunate as to meet her, and as her eyes were now fixed upon his companion, he felt it incumbent upon him to introduce Mr. Richard Lancaster, the son of an old shipmate.

"But not a sailor, I imagine," said Mrs. Easterfield.

"Oh, no," said the captain, "Mr. Lancaster is Assistant Professor of Theoretical Mathematics in Sutton College."

Dick could not imagine why the captain said all this, and he flushed a little.

"Sutton College?" said Mrs. Easterfield. "Then, of course, you know Professor Brent."

"Oh, yes," said Lancaster. "He is our president."

"I never met him," said she, "but he was a classmate of my husband, and I have often heard him speak of him. And now for my errand, Captain Asher. Isn't it about time you should be wanting to see your niece?"

The captain's heart sank. Did she intend to send Olive home?

"I always want to see her," he said, but without enthusiasm.

"But don't you think it would be nice," said the lady, "if you were to come to lunch with us to-morrow? It was to ask you this that I inquired for you at the toll-gate."

Now, this was another thing altogether, and the captain's earnest acceptance would have been more coherent if it had not been for the impatience of his mare.

"And I want you to bring your friend with you," continued Mrs. Easterfield. "The invitation is for you both, of course."

Dick's face said that this would be heavenly, but his mouth

was more prudent.

"It will be strictly informal," continued Mrs. Easterfield. "Only myself and family, three guests, and Olive. We shall sit down at one. Good-by."

Mrs. Easterfield was entirely truthful when she said she was glad to meet the captain. Her anxiety about Olive and Claude Locker was somewhat on the increase. She was very well aware that the most dangerous thing for one young woman is one young man; and in thinking over this truism she had been impressed with the conviction that it was not well for Mr. Claude Locker to be the one man at Broadstone. Then, in thinking of possible young men, her mind naturally turned to the young man who was visiting Olive's uncle. She did not know anything about him, but he was a young man, and if he proved to be worth something, he could be asked to come again. So it was really to Dick Lancaster, and not to Captain Asher, that the luncheon invitation had been given.

The appointment with the Glenford dentist had made it necessary for her to leave home that afternoon. To be sure, she had sent the Foxes with Olive and Claude Locker upon the drive through the gap, and, under ordinary circumstances, and with ordinary people, there would have been no reason for her to trouble herself about them, but neither the circumstances nor the people were ordinary, and she now felt anxious to get home and find out what Claude Locker and Olive had done with Mrs. and Mr. Fox.

CHAPTER VIII

CAPTAIN ASHER IS NOT IN A GOOD HUMOR

The next morning was very bright for Captain Asher; he was going to see Olive, and he did not know before how much he wished to see her.

When Dick Lancaster came from the house to take his seat in the buggy the sight of the handsome suit of dark-blue serge, white shirt and collar, and patent-leather shoes, with the trousers hanging properly above them, placed Dick very much higher in the captain's estimation than the young man with the colored shirt and rolled-up trousers could ever have reached. The captain, too, was well dressed for the occasion, and Mrs. Easterfield had no reason whatever to be ashamed of these two gentlemen when she introduced them to her other visitors.

She liked Professor Lancaster. Having lately had a good deal of Claude Locker, she was prepared to like a quiet and thoroughly self-possessed young man.

Olive was the latest of the little company to appear, and when she came down she caused a genuine, though gentle sensation. She was most exquisitely dressed, not too much for a luncheon, and not enough for a dinner. This navy girl had not studied for nothing the art of dressing in different parts of the world. Her uncle regarded her with open-eyed astonishment.

"Is this my brother's daughter?" he asked himself. "The little girl who poured my coffee in the morning and went out to take toll?"

Olive greeted her uncle with absolute propriety, and made the acquaintance of Mr. Lancaster with a formal courtesy to which no objection could be made. Apparently she forgot the existence of Mr. Locker, and for the greater part of the meal she conversed with Mr. Fox about certain foreign places with which they were both familiar.

The luncheon was not a success; there was a certain stiffness about it which even Mrs. Easterfield could not get rid of; and when the gentlemen went out to smoke on the piazza Olive disappeared, sending a message to Mrs. Easterfield that she had a bad headache and would like to be excused. Her excuse was a perfectly honest one, for she was apt to have a headache when she was angry; and she was angry now.

The reason for her indignation was the fact that her uncle's visitor was an extremely presentable young man. Had it been otherwise, Olive would have given the captain a good scolding, and would then have taken her revenge by making fun of him and his shipmate's son. But now she felt insulted that her uncle should conceal from her the fact that he had an entirely proper young gentleman for a visitor. Could he think she would want to stay at his house to be with that young man? Was she a girl from whom the existence of such a person was to be kept secret? She was very angry, indeed, and her headache was genuine.

Captain Asher was also angry. He had intended to take Olive aside and tell her all about Dick Lancaster, and how he had refrained from saying anything about him until he found out what sort of a young man he was. If, then, she saw fit to scold him, he was perfectly willing to submit, and to shake hands all around. But now he would have no chance to speak to her; she had not treated him properly, even if she had a headache. He admitted to himself that she was young and probably sensitive, but it was also true that he was sensitive, although old. Therefore, he was angry.

Mrs. Easterfield was disturbed; she saw there was something wrong between Olive and her uncle, and she did not like it. She had invited Lancaster with an object, and she did not wish that other people's grievances should interfere with said object. Olive was grumpy up-stairs and Claude Locker was in the doleful dumps under a tree, and if these two should grump and dump together, it might be very bad; consequently, Mrs. Easterfield was more anxious than ever that there should be at least two young men at Broadstone.

For this reason she asked Lancaster if he were fond of rowing; and when he said he was, she invited him to join them in a boat party the next day to help her and Olive pull the big family boat. Mr. Fox did not like rowing, and Mr. Locker did not know how.

On the drive home Captain Asher and Lancaster did not talk much. Even the young man's invitation to the rowing party did not excite much interest in the captain. These two men were both thinking of the same girl; one pleasantly, and the other very unpleasantly. Dick was charmed with her, although he had had very little opportunity of becoming acquainted with her, but he hoped for better luck the next day.

The captain did not know what to make of her. He felt sure that she was at fault, and that he was at fault, and he could not see how things could be made straight between them. Only one thing seemed plain to him, and this was that, with things as they were at present, she was not likely to come back to his house; and this would not be necessary; he knew very well that there were other places she could visit; and that early in the fall her father would be home.

Dick Lancaster walked to Broadstone the next morning because Captain Asher was obliged to go to Glenford on business, but the young man did not in the least mind a six-mile walk on a fine morning.

All the way to Glenford the captain thought of Olive; some-times he wished she had never come to him. Even now, with Lancaster to talk to, he missed her grievously, and if she should not come back, the case would be a great deal worse than if she had never come at all. But one thing was certain: If she returned as the young lady with whom he had lunched at Broadstone, he did not want her. He felt that he had been in the wrong, that she had been in the wrong; and it seemed as if things in this world were gradually going wrong. He was not in a good humor.

When he stopped his mare in front of a store, Maria Port stepped up to him and said: "How do you do, captain? What have you done with your young man?"

The captain got down from his buggy, hitched his mare to a post, and then shook hands with Miss Port.

"Dick Lancaster has gone boating to-day with the Broadstone people," he said.

"What!" exclaimed Miss Port. "Gone there again already? Why it was only yesterday you took dinner with them."

"Lunch," corrected the captain.

"Well, you may call it what you please," said Maria, "but I call it dinner. And them two's together without you, that you tried so hard to keep apart!"

"I did not try anything of the kind," said the captain a little sharply; "it just happened so."

"Happened so!" exclaimed Miss Port. "Well, I must say, Captain Asher, that you've a regular genius for makin' things happen. The minute she goes, he conies. I wish I could make things happen that way."

Frank R. Stockton

The captain took no notice of this remark, and moved toward the door of the store.

"Look here, captain," continued Miss Port, "can't you come and take dinner with us? You haven't seen Pop for ever so long. It won't be lunch, though, but an honest dinner."

The captain accepted the invitation; for old Mr. Port was one of his ancient friends; and then he entered the store. Miss Port was on the point of following him; she had something to say about Olive; but she stopped.

"I'll keep that till dinner-time," she said to herself.

Old Mr. Port had always been a very pleasant man to visit, and he had not changed now, although he was nearly eighty years old. He had been a successful merchant in the days when Captain Asher commanded a ship, and there was good reason to believe that a large measure of his success was due to his constant desire to make himself agreeable to the people with whom he came in business contact. He was just as agreeable to his friends, of whom Captain Asher was one of the oldest.

The people of Glenford often puzzled themselves as to what sort of a woman Maria's mother could have been. None of them had ever seen her, for she had died years before old Mr. Port had come into that healthful region to reside; but all agreed that her parents must have been a strangely assorted pair, unless, indeed, as some of the wiser suggested, she got her disposition from a grandparent.

"That navy niece of yours must be a wild girl," said Miss Port to the captain as she carved the beef.

"Wild!" exclaimed the captain. "I never saw anything wild about her."

"Perhaps not," said his hostess, "but there's others that have. It was only three days ago that she took that young man, that goggle-eyed one, out on the river in a boat, and did her best to upset him. Whether she stood up and made the boat rock while he clung to the side, or whether she bumped the boat against rocks and sand-bars, laughin' the louder the more he was frightened, I wasn't told. But she did skeer him awful. I know that."

"You seem to know a good deal about what is going on at Broadstone," remarked the captain, somewhat sarcastically.

"Indeed I do," said she; "a good deal more than they think. They've got such fine stomachs that they can't eat the beef they get at the gap, and Mr. Morris goes there three times a week, all the way from Glenford, to take them Chicago beef. The rest of the time they mostly eat chickens, I'm told."

"And so your butcher takes meat and brings back news," said the captain. "The next time he passes the toll-gate I will tell him to leave the news with me, and I will see that it is properly distributed." And with this, he began to talk with Mr. Port.

"Oh, you needn't be so snappish about her," insisted Maria. "If you are in that temper often, I don't wonder the young woman wanted to go away."

The captain made no answer, but his glance at the speaker was not altogether a pleasant one. Old Mr. Port did not hear very well; but his eyesight was good, and he perceived from the captain's expression that his daughter had been saying something sharp. This he never allowed at his table; and, turning to her, he said gently, but firmly:

"Maria, don't you think you'd better go up-stairs and go to bed?"

"He's all the time thinkin' I'm a child," said Miss Maria, with a grin; "but how awfully he's mistook." Then she added: "Has that teacher got money enough to support a wife when he marries her? I don't suppose his salary amounts to much. I'm

Frank R. Stockton

told it's a little bit of a college he teaches at."

"I do not know anything about his salary," said the captain, and again attempted to continue the conversation with the father.

But the daughter was not to be put down. "When is Olive Asher coming back to your house?" she asked.

The captain turned upon her with a frown. "I did not say she was coming back at all," he snapped.

Now old Mr. Port thought it time for him to interfere. To him Maria had always been a young person to be mildly counseled, but to be firmly punished if she did not obey said counsels. It was evident that she was now annoying his old friend; Maria had a great habit of annoying people, but she should not annoy Captain Asher.

"Maria," said Mr. Port, "leave the table instantly, and go to bed."

Miss Port smiled. She had finished her dinner, and she folded her napkin and dusted some crumbs from her lap. She always humored her father when he was really in earnest; he was very old and could not be expected to live much longer, and it was his daughter's earnest desire that she should be in good favor with him when he died. With a straight-cut smile at the captain, she rose and left the two old friends to their talk, and went out on the front piazza. There she saw Mr. Morris, the butcher, on his way home with an empty wagon. She stepped out to the edge of the sidewalk and stopped him.

"Been to Broadstone?" she asked.

"Yes," said the butcher with a sigh, and stopping his horse. Miss Port always wanted to know so much about Broadstone, and he was on his way to his dinner.

"Well," said Miss Port, "what monkey tricks are going on there now? Has anybody been drowned yet? Did you see that young man that's stayin' at the toll-gate?"

"Yes," said the butcher, "I saw him as I was crossing the bridge. He was in the big boat helping to row. Pretty near the whole family was in the boat, I take it."

"That's like them, just like them!" she exclaimed. "The next thing we'll hear will be that they've all gone to the bottom together. I don't suppose one of them can swim. Was the captain's niece standin' up, or sittin' down?"

"They were all sitting down," said the butcher, "and behaving like other people do in a boat." And he prepared to go on.

"Stop one minute," said Miss Port. "Of course you are goin' out there day after to-morrow?"

"No," said Mr. Morris. "I'm going to-morrow. They've ordered some extra things." Then he said, with a sort of conciliatory grin, "I'll get some more news, and have more time to tell it."

"Now, don't be in such a hurry," said Miss Port, advancing to the side of the wagon. "I want very much to go to Broadstone. I've got some business with that Mrs. Blynn that I ought to have attended to long ago. Now, why can't I ride out with you to-morrow? That's a pretty broad seat you've got."

The butcher looked at her in dismay. "Oh, I couldn't do that, Miss Port," he said. "I always have a heavy load, and I can't take passengers, too."

"Now, what's the sense of your talkin' like that?" said Miss Port. "You've got a great big horse, and plenty of room, and would you have me go hire a carriage and a driver to go out there when you can take me just as well as not?"

The butcher thought he would be very willing. He did not care for her society, and, moreover, he knew that both at Broadstone and in the town he would be ridiculed when it should be known that he had been taking Maria Port to drive.

"Oh, I couldn't do it," he replied. "Of course, I'm willing to oblige—"

"Oh, don't worry yourself any more, Mr. Morris," interrupted Miss Port. "I'm not askin' you to take me now, and I won't keep you from your dinner."

The next morning as Mr. Morris, the butcher, was driving past the Port house at rather a rapid rate for a man with a heavy wagon, Miss Maria appeared at her door with her bonnet on. She ran out into the middle of the street, and so stationed herself that Mr. Morris was obliged to stop. Then, without speaking, she clambered up to the seat beside him.

"Now, you see," said she, settling herself on the leather cushion, "I've kept to my part of the bargain, and I don't believe your horse will think this wagon is a bit heavier than it was before I got in. What's the name of the new people that's comin' to Broadstone?"

CHAPTER IX

MISS PORT TAKES A DRIVE WITH THE BUTCHER

As the butcher and Miss Port drove out of town the latter did not talk quite so much as was her wont. She seemed to have something on her mind, and presently she proposed to Mr. Morris that he should take the shunpike for a change.

"That would be a mile and a half out of my way!" he exclaimed. "I can't do it."

"I should think you'd get awfully tired of this same old road," said she.

"The easiest road is the one I like every time," said Mr. Morris, who was also not inclined to talk.

Miss Port did not care to pass the toll-gate that day; she was afraid she might see the captain, and that in some way or other he would interfere with her trip, but fortune favored her, as it nearly always did. Old Jane came to the gate, and as this stolid old woman never asked any questions, Miss Port contented herself with bidding her good morning, and sitting silent during the process of making change.

This self-restraint very much surprised old Jane, who straightway informed the captain that Miss Port was riding with the butcher to Broadstone—she knew it was Broadstone, for he had no other customers that way—and she guessed something must be the matter with her, for she kept her mouth shut, and didn't say nothing to nobody.

As the wagon moved on Miss Port heaved a sigh. Fearful that she might see the captain somewhere, she had not even allowed herself to survey the premises in order to catch a glimpse of the shipmate's son. This was a rare piece of self-denial in Maria, but she could do that sort of thing on occasion.

When the butcher's wagon neared the Broadstone house Miss Port promptly got down, and Mr. Morris went to the kitchen regions by himself. She never allowed herself to enter a house by the back or side door, so now she went to the front, where, disappointed at not seeing any of the family although she had made good use of her eyes, she was obliged to ask a servant to conduct her to Mrs. Blynn. Before she had had time to calculate the cost of the rug in the hall, or to determine whether the walls were calcimined or merely whitewashed, she found herself with that good lady.

Miss Port's business with Mrs. Blynn indicated a peculiar intelligence on the part of the visitor. It was based upon very little; it had not much to do with anything; it amounted to almost nothing; and yet it appeared to contain certain elements of importance which made Mrs. Blynn give it her serious consideration.

After she had talked and peered about as long as she thought was necessary, Maria said she was afraid Mr. Morris would be waiting for her, and quickly took her leave, begging Mrs. Blynn not to trouble herself to accompany her to the door. When she left the house Maria did not seek the butcher's wagon, but started out on a little tour of observation through the grounds. She was quite sure Mr. Morris was waiting for her, but for this she did care a snap of her finger; he would not dare to go and leave her. Presently she perceived a young gentleman approaching her, and she recognized him instantly—it was the goggle-eyed man who had been described to her. Stepping quickly toward Mr. Locker, she asked him if he could tell her where she could find Miss Asher; she had been told she was in the grounds.

The young man goggled his eye a little more than usual. "Do you know her?" said he.

"Oh, yes," replied Maria; "I met her at the house of her uncle, Captain Asher."

"And, knowing her, you want to see her"

Astonished, Miss Port replied, "Of course."

"Very well, then," said he; "beyond that clump of bushes is a seat. She sits thereon. Accept my condolences."

"I will remember every word of that," said Miss Port to herself, "but I haven't time to think of it now. He's just ravin'."

Olive had just had an interview with Mr. Locker which, in her eyes, had been entirely too protracted, and she had sent him away. He had just made her an offer of marriage, but she had refused even to consider it, assuring him that her mind was occupied with other things. She was busy thinking of those other things when she heard footsteps near her.

"How do you do" said Miss Port, extending her hand.

Olive rose, but she put her hands behind her back.

"Oh!" said Miss Port, dropping her hand, but allowing herself no verbal resentment. She had come there for information, and she did not wish to interfere with her own business. "I happened to be here," she said, "and I thought I'd come and tell you how your uncle is. He took dinner with us yesterday, and I was sorry to see he didn't have much appetite. But I suppose he's failin', as most people do when they get to his age. I thought you might have some message you'd like to send him."

Frank R. Stockton

"Thank you," said Olive with more than sufficient coldness, "but I have no message."

"Oh!" said Miss Port. "You're in a fine place here," she continued, looking about her, "very different from the toll-gate; and I expect the Easterfields has everything they want that money can more than pay for." Having delivered this little shot at the reported extravagance of the lady of the manor, she remarked: "I don't wonder you don't want to go back to your uncle, and run out to take the toll. It must have been a very great change to you if you're used to this sort of thing."

"Who said I was not going back?" asked Olive sharply.

"Your uncle," said Miss Port. "He told me at our house. Of course, he didn't go into no particulars, but that isn't to be expected, he's not the kind of man to do that."

Olive stood and looked at this smooth-faced, flat-mouthed spinster. She was pale, she trembled a little, but she spoke no word; she was a girl who did not go into particulars, especially with a person such as this woman standing before her.

Miss Port did not wish to continue the conversation; she generally knew when she had said enough. "Well," she remarked, "as you haven't no message to send to your uncle, I might as well go. But I did think that as I was right on my way, you'd have at least a word for him. Good mornin'." And with this she promptly walked away to join Mr. Morris, cataloguing in her mind as she went the foolish and lazy hammocks and garden chairs, the slow motions of a man who was sweeping leaves from the broad stone, and various other evidences of bad management and probable downfall which met her eyes in every direction.

When Miss Port approached the toll-gate on her return she was very anxious to stop, and hoped that the captain would be at the gate. Fortune favored her again, and there he stood in the doorway of the little tollhouse.

"Oh, captain," she exclaimed, extending herself somewhat over the butcher's knees in order to speak more effectively, "I've been to Broadstone, and I've seen your niece. She's dressed up just like the other fine folks there, and she's stiffer than any of them, I guess. I didn't see Mrs. Easterfield, although I did want to get a chance to tell her what I thought about her plantin' weeds in her garden, and spreadin' new kinds of seeds over this country, which goes to weeds fast enough in the natural way. As to your niece, I must say she didn't show me no extra civility, and when I asked her if she had any message for you, she said she hadn't a word to say."

The captain was not in the least surprised to hear that Olive had not treated Miss Port with extra civility. He remembered his niece treating this prying gossip with positive rudeness, and he had been somewhat amused by it, although he had always believed that young people should be respectful to their elders. He did not care to talk about Olive with Miss Port, but he had to say something, and so he asked if she seemed to be having a good time.

"If settin' behind bushes with young men, and goggle-eyed ones at that, is havin' a good time," replied Miss Port, "I'm sure she's enjoyin' herself." And then, as she caught sight of Lancaster: "I suppose that's the young man who's visitin' you. I hope he makes his scholars study harder than he does. He isn't readin' his book at all; he's just starin' at nothin'. You might be polite enough to bring him out and introduce him, captain," she added in a somewhat milder tone.

The captain did not answer; in fact, he had not heard all that Miss Port had said to him. If Olive had refused to send him a word, even the slightest message, she must be a girl of very stubborn resentments, and he was sorry to hear it. He himself was beginning to get over his resentment at her treatment of him at the Broadstone luncheon, and if she had been of his turn of mind everything might have been smoothed over in a very short time.

"Well?" remarked Maria in an inquiring tone.

"Excuse me," said the captain, "what were you saying?"

Miss Maria settled herself in her seat. "If you and that young man wastin' his time in the garden can't keep your wits from wool-gatherin'," said she, "I hope old Jane has got sense enough to go on with the housekeepin'. I'll call again when you've sent your young man away, and got your young woman back."

Maria said little to the taciturn butcher on their way to Glenford, but she smiled a good deal to herself. For years it had been the desire of her life to go to live in the toll-gate—not with any idea of ousting Captain Asher—oh, no, by no means. Old Mr. Port could not live much longer, and his daughter would not care to reside in the Glenford house by herself. But the toll-gate would exactly suit her; there was life; there was passing to and fro; there was money enough for good living and good clothes without any encroachment on whatever her father might leave her; and, above all, there was the captain, good for twenty years yet, in spite of his want of appetite, which she had mentioned to his niece. This would be a settlement which would suit her in every way, but so long as that niece lived there, there would be no hope of it; even the shipmate's son would be in the way. But she supposed he would soon be off.

CHAPTER X

MRS. EASTERFIELD WRITES A LETTER

When Miss Port had left her, Olive was so much disturbed by what that placid spinster had told her that she totally forgot Claude Locker's proposal of marriage, as well as the other things she had been thinking about. These things had been not at all unpleasant; she had been thinking of her uncle and her return to the toll-gate house. Her visit to Broadstone was drawing to a close, and she was getting very tired of Mr. Locker and Mr. and Mrs. Fox. She found, now her anger had cooled down, that she was actually missing her uncle, and was thinking of him as of some one who belonged to her. Her own father had never seemed to belong to her; for periods of three years he was away on his ship; and, even when he had been on shore duty, she had sometimes been at school; and when she and her parents had been stationed somewhere together, the lieutenant had been a good deal away from home on this or that naval business. When a girl she had taken these absences as a matter of course, but since she had been living with her uncle her ideas on the subject had changed. She wanted now to be at home with him: and as Broadstone was so near the toll-gate she had no doubt that Mrs. Easterfield would some-times want her to come to her when, perhaps, she would have different people staying with her.

This was a very pleasant mental picture, and the more Olive had looked at it, the better she had liked it. As to the reconciliation with her uncle, it troubled her mind but little.

Frank R. Stockton

So often had she been angry with people, and so often had everything been made all right again, that she felt used to the process. Her way was simple enough; when she was tired of her indignation she quietly dropped it; and then, taking it for granted that the other party had done the same, she recommenced her usual friendly intercourse, just as if there had never been a quarrel or misunderstanding. She had never found this method to fail—although, of course, it might easily have failed with one who was not Olive—and she had not the slightest doubt that if she wrote to her uncle that she was coming on a certain day, she would be gladly received by him when she should arrive.

But now? After what that woman had told her, what now? If her uncle had said she was not coming back, there was an end to her mental pictures and her pleasant plans. And what a hard man he must be to say that!

Slowly walking over the grass, Olive went to look for Mrs. Easterfield, and found her in her garden on her knees by a flower-bed digging with a little trowel.

"Mrs. Easterfield," said she, "I am thinking of getting married."

The elder lady sprang to her feet, dropping her trowel, which barely missed her toes. She looked frightened. "What?" she exclaimed. "To whom?"

"Not to anybody in particular," replied Olive. "I am considering the subject in general. Let's go sit on that bench, and talk about it."

A little relieved, Mrs. Easterfield followed her. "I don't know what you mean," she said, when they were seated. "Women don't think of marriage in a general way; they consider it in a particular way."

"Oh, I am different," said Olive; "I am a navy girl, and more like a man. I have to look out for myself. I think it is time I was married, and therefore I am giving the subject attention. Don't you think that is prudent?"

"And you say you have no particular leanings?" the other inquired.

"None whatever," said Olive. "Mr. Locker proposed to me less than an hour ago, but I gave him no answer. He is too precipitate, and he is only one person, anyway."

"You don't want to marry more than one person!" exclaimed Mrs. Easterfield.

"No," said Olive, "but I want more than one to choose from."

Mrs. Easterfield did not understand the girl at all. But this was not to be expected so soon; she must wait a little, and find out more. Notwithstanding her apparent indifference to Claude Locker, there was more danger in that direction than Mrs. Easterfield had supposed. A really persistent lover is often very dangerous, no matter how indifferent a young woman may be.

"Have you been considering the professor?" she asked, with a smile. "I noticed that you were very gracious to him yesterday."

"No, I haven't," said Olive. "But I suppose I might as well. I did try to make him have a good time, but I was still a little provoked and felt that I would like him to go back to my uncle and tell him that he had enjoyed himself. But now I suppose I must consider all the eligibles."

"Why now?" asked Mrs. Easterfield quickly; "why now more than any previous time?"

Olive did not immediately answer, but presently she said: "I am not going back to my uncle. There was a woman here just now—I don't know whether she was sent or not—who

Frank R. Stockton

informed me that he did not expect me to return to his house. When my mother was living we were great companions for each other, but now you see I am left entirely alone. It will be a good while before father comes back, and then I don't know whether he can settle down or not. Besides, I am not very well acquainted with him, but I suppose that would arrange itself in time. So you see all I can do is to visit about until I am married, and therefore the sooner I am married and settled the better."

"Perhaps this is a cold-blooded girl!" said Mrs. Easterfield to herself. "But perhaps it is not!" Then, speaking aloud, she said: "Olive Asher, were you ever in love?"

The girl looked at her with reflective eyes. "Yes," she said. "I was once, but that was the only time."

"Would you mind telling me about it?" asked Mrs. Easterfield.

"Not at all," replied the girl. "I was between thirteen and fourteen, and wore short dresses, and my hair was plaited. My father was on duty at the Philadelphia Navy-Yard, and we lived in that city. There was a young man who used to come to bring messages to father; I think he was a clerk or a draftsman. I do not remember his name, except that his first name was Rupert, and father always called him by that. He was a beautiful man-boy or boy-man, however you choose to put it. His eyes were heavenly blue, his skin was smooth and white, his cheeks were red, and he had the most charming mouth I ever saw. He was just the right height, well shaped, and wore the most becoming clothes. I fell madly in love with him the second time I saw him, and continued so for a long time. I used to think about him and dream about him, and write little poems about him which nobody ever saw. I tried to make a sketch of his face once, but I failed and tore it up."

"What did he do?" asked Mrs. Easterfield.

"Nothing whatever," said Olive. "I never spoke to him, or he to me. I don't believe he ever noticed me. Whenever I could I went into the room where he was talking to father, but I was very quiet and kept in the background, and I do not think his eyes ever fell upon me. But that did not make any difference at all. He was beautiful above all other men in the world, and I loved him. He was my first, my only love, and it almost brings tears in my eyes now to think of him."

"Then you really could love the right person if he were to come along," said Mrs. Easterfield.

"Why do you think I couldn't? Of course I could. But the trouble is he doesn't come, so I must try to arrange the matter with what material I have."

When Mrs. Easterfield left the garden she went rapidly to her room. There was a smile on her lips, and a light in her eye. A novel idea had come to her which amused her, pleased her, and even excited her. She sat down at her writing-table and began a letter to her husband. After an opening paragraph she wrote thus:

"Is not Mr. Hemphill, of the central office of the D. and J., named Rupert? It is my impression that he is. You know he has been to our house several times to dinner when you invited railroad people, and I remember him very well. If his name is Rupert will you find out, without asking him directly, whether or not he was engaged about seven years ago at the navy-yard. I am almost positive I once had a conversation with him about the navy-yard and the moving of one of the great buildings there. If you find that he had a position there, don't ask him any more questions, and drop the subject as quickly as you can. But I then want you to send him here on whatever pretext you please—you can send me any sort of an important message or package—and if I find it desirable, I shall ask him to stay here a few days. These hard-worked secretaries ought to have more vacations. In fact, I have a very interesting scheme in mind, of which I shall say nothing now for fear you may think it necessary to reason about it. By the time you come it will have been worked out, and I will tell you all about it. Now, don't fail to send Mr. Hemphill as promptly as possible, if you find his name is Rupert, and that he has ever been engaged in the navy-yard."

This letter was then sent to the post-office at the gap with an immediate-delivery stamp on it.

When Mrs. Easterfield went down-stairs, her face still glowing with the pleasure given by the writing of her letter, she met Claude Locker, whose face did not glow with pleasure.

"What is the matter with you?" she asked.

"I feel like a man who has been half decapitated," said he. "I do not know whether the execution is to be arrested and my wound healed, or whether it is to go on and my head roll into the dust."

"A horrible idea!" said Mrs. Easterfield. "What do you really mean?"

"I have proposed to Miss Asher and I was treated with indifference, but have not been discarded. Don't you see that I can not live in this condition? I am looking for her."

"It will be a great deal better for you to leave her alone," replied Mrs. Easterfield. "If she has any answer for you she will give it when she is ready. Perhaps she is trying to make up her mind, and you may spoil all by intruding yourself upon her."

"That will not do at all," said Locker, "not at all. The more Miss Asher sees of me in an unengaged condition the less she will like me. I am fully aware of this. I know that my general aspect must be very unpleasant, so if I expect any success whatever, the quicker I get this thing settled the better."

"Even if she refuses you," said Mrs. Easterfield.

"Yes," he answered; "then down comes the axe again, away goes my head, and all is over! Then there is another thing," he said, without giving Mrs. Easterfield a chance to speak. "There is that mathematical person. When will he be here again?"

"I do not know," replied Mrs. Easterfield; "he has merely a general invitation."

"I don't like him," said Locker. "He has been here twice, and that is two times too many. I hate him."

"Why so?"

"Because he is unobjectionable," Locker answered, "and I am very much afraid Miss Asher likes unobjectionable people. Now I am objectionable—I know it—and the longer I remain unengaged the more objectionable I shall become. I wish you would invite nobody but such people as the Foxes."

"Why?"

"Because they are married," replied Locker. "But I must not wait here. Can you tell me where I shall be likely to find her?"

"Yes," said Mrs. Easterfield, "she is with the Foxes, and they are married."

CHAPTER XI

MR. LOCKER IS RELEASED ON BAIL

Nearly the whole of that morning Dick Lancaster sat in the arbor in the tollhouse garden, his book in his hand. Part of the time he was thinking about what he would like to do, and part of the time he was thinking about what he ought to do. He felt sure he had stayed with the captain as long as he had been expected to, but he did not want to go away. On the contrary, he greatly desired to remain within walking distance of Broadstone. He was in love with Olive. When he had seen her at luncheon, cold and reserved, he had been greatly impressed by her, and when he went out boating with her the next day he gave her his heart unreservedly. When people fell in love with Olive they always did it promptly.

As he sat, with Olive standing near the footlights of his mental stage and the drop-curtain hanging between her and all the rest of the world, the captain strolled up to him.

"Dick," said he, "somehow or other my tobacco does not taste as it ought to. Give me a pipeful of yours."

When the captain had filled his pipe from Dick's bag he lighted it and gave a few puffs. "It isn't a bit better than mine," said he, "but I will keep on and smoke it. Dick, let's go and take a walk over the hills. I feel rather stupid to-day. And, by the way, I hope you will be able to stay with me for the rest of your vacation. Have you made plans to go anywhere else?"

"No plans of the slightest importance," answered Lancaster with joyous vivacity. "I shall be delighted to stay."

This prompt acceptance somewhat surprised the captain. He had spoken without premeditation, and without thinking of anything at all except that he did not want everybody to go away and leave him. He had begun to know something of the pleasures of family life; of having some one to sit at the table with him; to whom he could talk; on whom he could look. In fact, although he did not exactly appreciate such a state of things, some one he could love. He was getting really fond of Dick Lancaster.

As for Olive, he did not know what to think of her; sometimes he was sure she was not coming back, and at other times he thought it likely he might get a letter that very day appointing the time for her return. He stood puffing his pipe and thinking about this after Dick had spoken.

"But it does not matter," he said to himself, "which way it happens. If she doesn't come I want him here, and if she does come, he is good enough for anybody, and perhaps she may be pleased." And then he indulged in a little fragment of the dream which had come to him before; he saw two young people in a charming home, not at the toll-gate, and himself living with them. Plenty of money for all moderate needs, and all happy and satisfied. Then with a sigh he knocked the tobacco from his pipe and said to himself: "If I hear she is coming, I will let her know he is still here, and then she must judge for herself."

As they walked together over the hills, Dick Lancaster was very anxious to know something about Olive's return, but he did not like to ask. The captain had been very reticent on the subject of his niece, and Dick was a gentleman. But to his surprise, and very much to his delight, the captain soon began to talk about Olive. He told Dick how his brother had entered the navy when the elder was first mate on a merchant vessel; how Alfred had risen in the service; had married; and how his

Frank R. Stockton

wife and daughter had lived in various parts of the world. Then he spoke of a good many things he had heard about Olive, and other things he had found out since she had lived with him; and as he went on his heart warmed, and Dick Lancaster listened with as warm a heart as that from which the captain spoke.

And thus they walked over the hills, this young man and this elderly man, each in love with the same girl.

During all the walk Dick never asked when Miss Asher was coming back to the tollhouse, nor did Captain Asher make any remarks upon the subject. It was not really of vital importance to Dick, as Broadstone was so near, and it was of such vital importance to the captain that it was impossible for him to speak of it.

The next day the bright-hearted Richard trod buoyantly upon the earth; he did not care to read; he did not want to smoke; and he was not much inclined to conversation; he was simply buoyant, and undecided. The captain looked at him and smiled.

"Why don't you walk over to Broadstone?" he said. "It will do you good. I want you to stay with me, but I don't expect you to be stuck down to this tollhouse all day. I am going about the farm to-day, but I shall expect you to supper."

When he was ready to start Dick Lancaster felt a little perplexed. His ideas of friendly civility impelled him to ask the captain if there was anything he could do for him, if there was any message or missive he could take to his niece, or anything he could bring from her, but he was prudent and refrained; if the captain wished service of this sort he was a man to ask for it.

The first person Dick met at Broadstone was Mrs. Easterfield, cutting roses.

"I am very glad to see you, Professor Lancaster," said she, as she put down her roses and her scissors. "Would you mind, before you enter into the general Broadstone society, sitting down on this bench and talking a little to me?"

Dick could not help smiling. What man in the world, even if he were in love with somebody else, could object to sitting down by such a woman and talking to her?

"What I am going to say," said Mrs. Easterfield, "is impertinent, unwarranted, and of an officious character. You and I know each other very slightly; neither of us has long been acquainted with Captain Asher, you have met his niece but twice, and I have never really known her until what you might call the other day. But in spite of all this, I propose that you and I shall meddle a little in their affairs. I have taken the greatest fancy to Miss Asher, and, if you can do it without any breach of confidence, I would like you to tell me if you know of any misunderstanding between her and her uncle."

"I know of nothing of the kind," said Dick with great interest, "but I admit I thought there might be something wrong somewhere. He knew I was coming here to-day—in fact, he suggested it—but he sent Miss Asher no sort of message."

"Can it be possible he is cherishing any hard feelings against her?" she remarked. "I should not have supposed he was that sort of man."

"He is not that sort of man," said Dick warmly. "He was talking to me about her yesterday, and from what he said, I am sure he thinks she is the finest girl in the world."

"I am glad to hear that," said she, "but it makes the situation more puzzling. Can it be possible that she is treating him badly?"

"Oh, I could not believe that!" exclaimed Dick fervently. "I can not imagine such a thing."

Mrs. Easterfield smiled. He had really known the girl but for one day, for the first meeting did not count; and here he was defending the absolute beauty of her character. But the assumption of the genus young man often overtops the pyramids. She now determined to take him a little more into her confidence.

"Miss Asher has intimated to me that she does not expect to go back to her uncle's house, and this morning she made a reference to the end of her visit here, but I thought you might be able to tell me something about her uncle. If he really does not expect her back I want her to stay here."

"Alas," said Dick, "I can not tell you anything. But of one thing I feel sure, and that is that he would like her to come back."

"Well," said Mrs. Easterfield, "I am not going to let her go away at present, and if Captain Asher should say anything to you on the subject, you are at liberty to tell him that. From what you said the other day, I suppose you will soon be leaving this quiet valley for the haunts of men."

"Oh, no," exclaimed Dick. "He wants me to stay with him as long as I can, and I shall certainly do it."

"Now," said Mrs. Easterfield, rising, "I must go and finish cutting my roses. I think you will find everybody on the tennis grounds."

Mrs. Easterfield had cut in all twenty-three roses when Claude Locker came to her from the house. His face was beaming, and he skipped over the short grass.

"Congratulate me," he said, as he stepped before her.

Mrs. Easterfield dropped her roses and her scissors and turned pale. "What do you mean?" she gasped.

"Oh, don't be frightened," he said. "I have not been acquitted, but the execution has been stopped for the present, and I am out on bail. I really feel as though the wound in my neck had healed."

"What stuff!" said Mrs. Easterfield, her color returning. "Try to speak sensibly."

"Oh, I can do that," said Mr. Locker; "upon occasion I can do that very well. I proposed again to Miss Asher not twenty minutes ago. She gave me no answer, but she made an arrangement with me which I think is going to be very satisfactory; she said she could not have me proposing to her every time I saw her—it would attract attention, and in the end might prove annoying—but she said she would be willing to have me propose to her every day just before luncheon, provided I did not insist upon an answer, and would promise to give no indication whatever at any other time that I entertained any unusual regard for her. I agreed to this, and now we understand each other. I feel very confident and happy. The other person has no regular time for offering himself, and if any effort of mine can avail he shall not find an irregular opportunity."

Mrs. Easterfield laughed. "Come pick up my roses," she said. "I must go in."

"It is like making love," said Locker as he picked up the flowers, "charming, but prickly." At this moment he started. "Who is that?" he exclaimed.

Mrs. Easterfield turned. "Oh, that is Monsieur Emile Du Brant. He is one of the secretaries of the Austrian legation. He is to spend a week with us. Suppose you take my flowers into the house and I will go to meet him."

Claude Locker, his arms folded around a mass of thorny roses, and a pair of scissors dangling from one finger, stood and gazed with savage intensity at the dapper little man—black eyes, waxed mustache, dressed in the height of fashion—who, with one hand outstretched, while the other held his hat, advanced with smiles and bows to meet the lady of the house. Locker had seen him before; he had met him in Washington; and he had received forty dollars for a poem of which this Austrian young person was the subject.

He allowed the lady and her guest to enter the house before him, and then, like a male Flora, he followed, grinding his teeth, and indulging in imprecations.

"He will have to put on some other kind of clothes," he muttered, "and perhaps he may shave and curl his hair. That will give me a chance to see her before lunch. I do not know that she expected me to begin to-day, but I am going to do it. I have a clear field so far, and nobody knows what may happen to-morrow."

As Locker stood in the hallway waiting for some one to come and take his flowers, or to tell him where to put them, he glanced out of the back door. There, to his horror, he saw that Mrs. Easterfield had conducted her guest through the house, and that they were now approaching the tennis ground, where Professor Lancaster and Miss Asher were standing with their rackets in their hands, while Mr. and Mrs. Fox were playing chess under the shade of a tree.

"Field open!" he exclaimed, dropping the roses and the scissors. "Field clear! What a double-dyed ass am I!" And with this he rushed out to the tennis ground; Mrs. Easterfield did not play.

Before Mrs. Easterfield returned to the house she stood for a moment and looked at the tennis players.

"Olive and three young men," she said to herself; "that will do very well."

A little before luncheon Claude Locker became very uneasy,

and even agitated. He hovered around Olive, but found no opportunity to speak to her, for she was always talking to somebody else, mostly to the newcomer. But she was a little late in entering the dining-room, and Locker stepped up to her in the doorway.

"Is this your handkerchief?" he asked.

"No," said she, stopping; "isn't it yours?"

"Yes," he replied, "but I had to have some way of attracting your attention. I love you so much that I can scarcely see the table and the people."

"Thank you," she said, "and that is all for the next twenty-four hours."

Frank R. Stockton

CHAPTER XII

MR. RUPERT HEMPHILL

That afternoon it rained, so that the Broadstone people were obliged to stay indoors. Dick Lancaster found Mr. Fox a very agreeable and well-informed man, and Mrs. Fox was also an excellent conversationalist. Mrs. Easterfield, who, after the confidences of the morning, could not help looking at him as something more than an acquaintance, talked to him a good deal, and tried to make the time pass pleasantly, at which business she was an adept. All this was very pleasant to Dick, but it did not compensate him for the almost entire loss of the society of Olive, who seemed to devote herself to the entertainment of the Austrian secretary. Mrs. Easterfield was very sorry that the young foreigner had come at this time, but he had been invited the winter before; the time had been appointed; and the visit had to be endured.

When the rain had ceased, and Dick was about to take his leave, his hostess declared she would not let him walk back through the mud.

"You shall have a horse," she said, "and that will insure an early visit from you, for, of course, you will not trust the animal to other hands than your own. I would ask you to stay, but that would not be treating the captain kindly."

As Dick was mounting Mr. Du Brant was standing at the front door, a smile on his swarthy countenance. This smile said as plainly as words could have done so that it was very amusing to this foreign young man to see a person with rolled-up trousers and a straw hat mount upon a horse. Claude Locker, whose soul had been chafing all the afternoon under his banishment from the society of the angel of his life, was also at the front door, and saw the contemptuous smile. Instantly a new and powerful emotion swept over his being in the shape of a strong feeling of fellowship for Lancaster. It made his soul boil with indignation to see the sneer which the Austrian directed toward the young man, a thoroughly fine young man, who, by said foreigner's monkeyful impudence, and another's mistaken favor, had been made a brother-in-misfortune of himself, Claude Locker.

"I will make common cause with him against the enemy," thought Locker. "If I should fail to get her I will help him to." And although Dick's brown socks were plainly visible as he cantered away, Mr. Locker looked after him as a gallant and honored brother-in-arms.

That evening Claude Locker fought for himself and his comrade. He persisted in talking French with Mr. Du Brant; and his remarkable management of that language, in which ignorance and a subtle facility in intentional misapprehension were so adroitly blended that it was impossible to tell one from the other, amused Olive, and so provoked the Austrian that at last he turned away and began to talk American politics with Mr. Fox, which so elated the poet that the ladies of the party passed a merry evening.

"Would you like me to take him out rowing to-morrow?" asked Claude apart to his hostess.

"With you at the oars?" she asked.

"Of course," said Locker.

"I am amazed," said she, "that you should suspect me of such cold-blooded cruelty."

"You know you don't want him here," said Claude. "His salary can not be large, and he must spend the greater part of it on clothes—and oil."

"Is it possible," she asked, "that you look upon that young man as a rival?"

"By no means," he replied; "such persons never marry. They only prevent other people from marrying anybody. Therefore it is that I remember what sort of a boatman I am."

"My dear," said Mr. Fox, when he and his wife had retired to their room, "after hearing what that Austrian has to say of the American people, I almost revere Mr. Locker."

"I heard some of his remarks," she said, "and I imagined they would have an effect of that kind upon you."

When the Broadstone surrey came from the train the next morning it brought a gentleman.

"What!" exclaimed Mrs. Fox, when from the other side of the lawn she saw him alight. "Another young man with a valise! It seems to me that this is an overdose!"

"Overdoses," remarked Mr. Fox, "are often less dangerous than just enough poison."

Mrs. Easterfield received this visitor at the door. She had been waiting for him, and did not wish him to meet anybody when she was not present. After offering his respectful salutations, Mr. Hemphill, Mr. Easterfield's secretary in the central office of the D. and J., delivered without delay a package of which he was the bearer, and apologized for his valise, stating that Mr. Easterfield had told him he must spend the night at Broadstone.

"Most assuredly you would do that," said she, and to herself she added, "If I want you longer I will let you know."

Mr. Rupert Hemphill was a very handsome man; his nose was fine; his eyes were dark and expressive; he wore silky side-whiskers, which, however, did not entirely conceal the bloom upon his cheeks; his teeth were very good; he was well shaped; and his clothes fitted him admirably.

As has been said before, Mrs. Easterfield was exceedingly interested; she was even a little agitated, which was not common with her. She had Mr. Hemphill conducted to his room, and then she waited for him to come down; this also was not common with her.

"Mr. Locker," she called from the open door, "do you know where Miss Asher is?"

The poet stopped in his stride across the lawn, and approached the lady. "Oh, she is with the Du Brant," said he. "I have been trying to get in some of my French, but neither of them will rise to the fly. However, I am content; it is now three hours before luncheon, and if she has him to herself for that length of time, I think she will be thoroughly disgusted. Then it will be my time, as per agreement."

Mrs. Easterfield was a little disappointed. She wanted Olive by herself, but she did not want to make a point of sending for her. But fortune favored her.

"There she is," exclaimed Locker; "she is just going into the library. Let me go tell her you want her."

"Not at all," said Mrs. Easterfield. "Don't put yourself into danger of breaking your word by seeing her alone before luncheon. I'll go to her."

Mr. Locker continued his melancholy stroll, and Mrs. Easterfield entered the library. Olive must not be allowed to go away until the moment arrived which had been awaited with so much interest.

"I am looking for a copy of *Tartarin sur les Alps*. I am sure I saw it among these French books," said Olive, on her knees before a low bookcase. "Would you believe it, Mr. Du Brant has never read it, and he seems to think so much of education."

Mrs. Easterfield knew exactly where the book was, but she preferred to allow Olive to occupy herself in looking for it, while she kept her eyes on the hall.

"Wait a moment, Olive," said she; "a visitor has just arrived, and I want to make him acquainted with you."

Olive rose with a book in her hand, and Mrs. Easterfield presented Mr. Hemphill to Miss Asher. As she did so, Mrs. Easterfield kept her eyes steadily fixed upon the young lady's face. With a pleasant smile Olive returned Mr. Hemphill's bow. She was generally glad to make new acquaintances.

"Mr. Hemphill is one of my husband's business associates," said Mrs. Easterfield, still with her eyes on Olive. "He has just come from him."

"Did he send us this fine day by you?" said Olive. "If so, we are greatly obliged to him."

The young man answered that, although he had not brought the day, he was delighted that he had come in company with it.

"What atrocious commonplaces!" thought Mrs. Easterfield. "The girl does not know him from Adam!"

Here was a disappointment; the thrill, the pallor, the involuntary start, were totally absent; and the first act of the little play was a failure. But Mrs. Easterfield hoped for better things when the curtain rose again. She conducted Mr. Hemphill to the Foxes and let Olive go away with her book; and, as soon as she had the opportunity, she read the letter from her husband.

"With this I send you Mr. Hemphill," he wrote. "I don't know what you want to do with him, but you must take good care of him. He is a most valuable secretary, and an estimable young man. As soon as you have done with him please send him back."

"I am glad he is estimable," said Mrs. Easterfield to herself. "That will make the matter more satisfactory to Tom when I explain it to him."

When Dick Lancaster, properly booted and wearing a felt hat, returned the borrowed horse, he was met by Mr. Locker, who had been wandering about the front of the house, and when he had dismounted Dick was somewhat surprised by the hearty handshake he received.

"I am sorry to have to tell you," said the poet, "that there is another one."

"Another what?" asked Dick.

"Another unnecessary victim," replied Locker. And with this he returned to the front of the house.

At last Olive came down the stairs, and she was alone. Locker stepped quickly up to her.

"If I should marry," he said, "would I be expected to entertain that Austrian?"

She stopped, and gave the question her serious consideration. "I should think," she said, "that that would depend a good deal upon whom you should marry."

"How can you talk in that way?" he exclaimed. "As if there were anything to depend upon!"

"Nothing to depend upon," said Olive, slightly raising her eyebrows. "That is bad." And she went into the dining-room.

Frank R. Stockton

The afternoon was an exceptionally fine one, but the party at Broadstone did not take advantage of it; there seemed to be a spirit of unrest pervading the premises, and when the carriage started on a drive along the river only Mr. and Mrs. Fox were in it. Mrs. Easterfield would not leave Olive and Mr. Hemphill, and she did not encourage them to go. Consequently there were three young men who did not wish to go.

"It seems to me," said Mr. Fox, as they rolled away, "that a young woman, such as Miss Asher, has it in her power to interfere very much with the social feeling which should pervade a household like this. If she were to satisfy herself with attracting one person, all the rest of us might be content to make ourselves happy in such fashions as might present themselves."

"The rest of us!" exclaimed Mrs. Fox.

"Yes," replied her husband. "I mean you, and Mrs. Easterfield, and myself, and the rest. That young woman's indeterminate methods of fascination interfere with all of us."

"I don't exactly see how they interfere with me," said Mrs. Fox rather stiffly.

"If the carriage had been filled, as was expected," said her husband, "I might have had the pleasure of driving you in a buggy."

She turned to him with a smile. "Immediately after I spoke," she said, "I imagined you might be thinking of something of that kind."

Mrs. Easterfield was not a woman to wait for things to happen in their own good time. If possible, she liked to hurry them up. In this Olive and Hemphill affair there was really nothing to wait for; if she left them to themselves there would be no happenings. As soon as was possible, she took Olive into her own little room, where she kept her writing-table, and into whose sacred precincts her secretary was not allowed to penetrate.

"Now, then," said she, "what do you think of Mr. Hemphill?"

"I don't think of him at all," said Olive, a little surprised. "Is there anything about him to think of?"

"He sat by you at luncheon," said Mrs. Easterfield.

"I know that," said Olive, "and he was better than an empty chair. I hate sitting by empty chairs."

"Olive," exclaimed Mrs. Easterfield with vivacity, "you ought to remember that young man!"

"Remember him?" the girl ejaculated.

"Certainly," said Mrs. Easterfield. "After what you told me about him, I expected you would recognize him the moment you saw him. But you did not know him; you did not do anything I expected you to do; and I was very much disappointed."

"What are you talking about?" asked Olive.

"I am talking about Mr. Hemphill; Mr. Rupert Hemphill; who, about seven years ago, was engaged in the Philadelphia Navy-Yard, and who came to your house on business with your father. From what you told me of him I conjectured that he might now be my husband's Philadelphia secretary, for his name is Rupert, and I had reason to believe that he was once engaged in the navy-yard. When I found out I was entirely correct in my supposition I had him sent here, and I looked forward with the most joyous anticipations to being present when you first saw him. But it was all a fiasco! I suppose some people might think I was unwarrantably meddling in the affairs of others, but as it was in my power to create a most charming romance, I could not let the opportunity pass."

Frank R. Stockton

Olive did not hear a word of Mrs. Easterfield's latest remarks; her round, full eyes were fixed upon the wall in front of her, but they saw nothing. Her mind had gone back seven years.

"Is it possible," she exclaimed presently, "that that is my Rupert, my beautiful Rupert of the roseate cheeks, the Rupert of my heart, my only love! The Endymion-like youth I watched for every day; on whom I gazed and gazed and worshiped and longed for when he had gone; of whom I dreamed; to whom my soul went out in poetry; whose miniature I would have painted on the finest ivory if I had known how to paint; and whose image thus created I would have worn next my heart to look at every instant I found myself alone, if it had not been that my dresses were all fastened down the back! I am going to him this instant! I must see him again! My Rupert, my only love!" And with this she started to the door.

"Olive," cried Mrs. Easterfield, springing from her chair, "stop, don't you do that! Come back. You must not—"

But the girl had flown down the stairs, and was gone.

CHAPTER XIII

MR. LANCASTER'S BACKERS

Olive found Mr. Hemphill under a tree upon the lawn. He was sitting on a low bench with one little girl upon each knee. He was not a stranger to the children, for they had frequently met him during their winter residences in cities. He was telling them a story when Olive approached. He made an attempt to rise, but the little girls would not let him put them down.

"Don't move, Mr. Hemphill," said Olive; "I am going to sit down myself." And as she spoke she drew forward a low bench. "I am so glad to see you are fond of children, Mr. Hemphill," she continued; "you must have changed very much."

"Changed!" he exclaimed. "I have always been fond of them."

"Excuse me," said Olive, "not always. I remember a child you did not care for, on whom you did not even look, who was absolutely nothing to you, although you were so much to her."

Mr. Hemphill stared. "I do not remember such a child," said he.

"She existed," said Olive. "I was that child." And then she told him how she had seen him come to her father's house.

Mr. Hemphill remembered Lieutenant Asher, he remembered going to his house, but he did not remember seeing there a

Frank R. Stockton

little girl.

"I was not so very little," said Olive; "I was fourteen, and I was just at an age to be greatly attracted by you. I thought you were the most beautiful young man I had ever beheld. I don't mind telling you, because I can not look upon you as a stranger, that I fell deeply in love with you."

As Mr. Hemphill sat and listened to these words his face turned redder than the reddest rose, even his silky whiskers seemed to redden, his fine-cut red lips were parted, but he could not speak. The two little girls had been gazing earnestly at Olive. Now the elder one spoke.

"I am in love," she said.

"And so am I," piped up the younger one.

"She's in love with Martha's little Jim," said the first girl, "but I am in love with Henry. He's eight. Both boys."

"I wouldn't be in love with a girl," said the little one contemptuously.

This interruption was a help to Mr. Hemphill, and his redness paled a little.

"Of course you could not be expected to know anything of my feelings for you," said Olive, "and perhaps it is very well you did not, for business is business, and the feelings of girls should not be allowed to interfere with it. But my heart went out to you all the same. You were my first love."

Now Mr. Hemphill crimsoned again worse than before. He had not yet spoken a word, and there was no word in the English language which he thought would be appropriate for the occasion.

"You may think I am a little cruel to plump this sort of thing upon you," said Olive, "in such a sudden way, but I am not. All this was seven years ago, and a person of my age can surely speak freely of what happened seven years ago. I did not even know you when I met you, but Mrs. Easterfield told me about you, and now I remember everything, and I think it would have been inhuman if I had not told you of the part you used to play in my life. You have a right to know it."

If Mr. Hemphill could have reddened any more he would have done so, but it was not possible. The thought flashed into his mind that it might be well to say something about her having found him very much changed, but in the next instant he saw that that would not do. How could he assume that he had ever been beautiful; how could he force her to say that he was not beautiful now, or that he still remained so?

"I am very glad I have met you," said Olive, "and that I know who you are. And I am glad, too, to tell you that I forgive you for not taking notice of me seven years ago."

"Is that all of your story?" asked the elder little girl.

"Yes," said Olive, laughing, "that is all."

"Well, then, let Mr. Hemphill go on with his," said she.

"Oh, certainly," said Olive, jumping up; "and you must all excuse me for interfering with your story."

Mr. Hemphill sat still, a little girl on each knee. He had not spoken a word since that beautiful girl had told him she had once loved him. And he could not speak now.

"You look as if you had a plaster taken off," said the younger little girl. And, after waiting a moment for an answer, she slipped off his knee; the other followed; and the story was postponed.

When Mrs. Easterfield heard Olive's account of this incident she was utterly astounded. "What sort of a girl are you" she exclaimed. "What are you going to do about it now?"

"Do?" said Olive quietly. "I have done."

Mrs. Easterfield was in a state of great perplexity. She had already asked Mr. Hemphill to stay until Saturday, three days off, and she could not tell him to go away, and the awkwardness of his remaining in the same house with Olive was something not easy to deal with.

During Olive's interview with Mr. Hemphill and the little girls Claude Locker had been sitting alone at a distance, gazing at the group. He was waiting for an opportunity of social converse, for this was not forbidden him even if the time did not immediately precede the luncheon hour. He saw Hemphill's blazing face, and deeply wondered. If it had been the lady who had flushed he would have bounced upon the scene to defend her, but Olive was calm, and it was the conscious guilt of the man that made his face look like a freshly painted tin roof. This was an affair into which he had no right to intrude himself, and so he sat and sighed, and his heart grew heavy. How many ante-luncheon avowals would have to be made before she would take so much interest in him, one way or the other!

Mr. Du Brant also sat at a distance. He was reading, or at least appearing to read; but he was so unaccustomed to holding a book in his hands that he did it very awkwardly, and Miss Raleigh, who was looking at him from the library window, made up her mind that if he dropped it, as she expected him to do, she would get the book and rub the dirt off the corners before it was put back into the bookcase. But when Olive left Mr. Hemphill she went so quickly into the house that the Austrian was unable to join her, and he, therefore, went to his room to prepare for dinner.

Dick Lancaster had also been waiting, although not watching. He had hoped that he might have a chance for a little talk with

Olive. But there was really no good reason to expect it, for he knew that two, and perhaps three, young men had stayed at home that afternoon in the hope that they might have the same opportunity. The odds against him were great.

He began to think that perhaps he was engaged in a foolish piece of business, and was in danger of making himself disagreeably conspicuous. The other young men were guests at Broadstone, but if he came there every day as he had been doing, and as he wanted to do, it might be thought that he was taking advantage of Mrs. Easterfield's kindness. At that moment he heard the rustle of skirts, and, glancing up, saw Mrs. Easterfield, who was looking for him.

Mrs. Easterfield's regard for Lancaster was growing, partly on account of the confidence she had already reposed in him. In her present state of mind she would have been glad to give him still more, for she did not know what to do about Olive and Mr. Hemphill, and there was no one with whom she could talk upon the subject; even if she had known Dick better her loyalty to Olive would have prevented that.

"Have you found out anything about the captain and Olive?" she asked. "Has he spoken of her return?"

"No," replied Dick; "he has not said a word on the subject, but I am very sure he would be overjoyed to have her come back. Every day when the postman arrives I believe he looks for a letter from her, and he shows that he feels it when he finds none. He is good-natured, and pleasant, but he is not as cheerful as when I first came."

"Every day," said Mrs. Easterfield, as they walked together, "I love Olive more and more."

"So do I," thought Dick.

"But every day I understand her less and less," she continued. "She is truly a navy girl, and repose does not seem to be one of

Frank R. Stockton

her characteristics. From what she has told me, I believe she has never lived in domestic peace and quiet until she came to stay with her uncle. It would delight me to see her properly married. I wish you would marry her."

Dick stopped, and so did she, and they stood looking at each other. He did not redden, for he was not of the flushing kind; his face even grew a little hard.

"Do you believe," said he, in a very different tone from his ordinary voice, "that I have the slightest chance?"

"Of course I do," she answered. "I believe you have a very good chance, or I should not have spoken to you. I flatter myself that I have excellent judgment concerning young men, and I am very fond of Olive."

"Mrs. Easterfield," exclaimed Dick, "you know I am in love with her. I suppose that has been easy enough to see, but it has all been very quick work with me; in fact, I have had very little to say to her, and have never said anything that could in the slightest degree indicate how I felt toward her. But I believe I loved her the second day I met her, and I am not sure it did not begin the day before."

"I think that sort of thing is always quick work where Olive is concerned," said Mrs. Easterfield. "I think it likely that many young men have fallen in love with her, and that they have to be very lively if they want a chance to tell her so. But don't be jealous. I know positively that none of them ever had the slightest chance. But now all that is passed. I know she is tired of an unsettled life, and it is likely she may soon be thinking of marrying, and there will be no lack of suitors. She has them now. But I want her to marry you."

"Mrs. Easterfield," exclaimed Dick, "you have known me but a very little while—"

"Don't mention that," she interrupted. "I do quick work as

well as other people. I never before engaged in any match-making business, but if this succeeds, I shall be proud of it to the end of my days. You are in love with Olive, and she is worthy of you. I want you to try to win her, and I will do everything I can to help you. Here is my hand upon it."

As Dick held that hand and looked into that face a courage and a belief in himself came into his heart that had never been there before. By day and by night his soul had been filled with the image of Olive, but up to this moment he had not thought of marrying her. That was something that belonged to the future, not even considered in his state of inchoate adoration. But now that he had been told he had reason to hope, he hoped; and the fact that one beautiful woman told him he might hope to win another beautiful woman was a powerful encouragement. Henceforth he would not be content with simply loving Olive; if it were within his power he would win, he would have her.

"You look like a soldier going forth to conquest," said Mrs. Easterfield with a smile.

"And you," said he impulsively, "you not only look like, but you are an angel."

This was pretty strong for the young professor, but the lady understood him. She was very glad, indeed, that he could express himself impulsively, for without that power he could not win Olive.

As Dick started away from Broadstone on his walk to the toll-gate he heard quick steps behind him and was soon overtaken by Claude Locker.

"Hello," said that young man, "if you are on your way home I am going to walk a while with you. I have not done a thing to-day."

When Dick heard these words his heart sank. He was on his

way home accompanied by Olive—Olive in his heart, Olive in his soul, Olive in his brain, Olive in the sky and all over the earth—how dared a common mortal intrude himself upon the scene?

"There is another thing," said Locker, who was now keeping step with him. "My soul is filled with murderous intent. I thirst for human life, and I need the restraints of companionship."

"Who is it you want to kill?" asked Dick coldly.

"It is an Austrian," replied the other. "I will not say what Austrian, leaving that to your imagination. I don't suppose you ever killed an Austrian. Neither have I, but I should like to do it. It would be a novel and delightful experience."

Dick did not think it necessary that he should be told more; he perfectly understood the state of the case, for it was impossible not to see that this young man was paying marked attention to Olive, while Mr. Du Brant was doing the same thing. But still it seemed well to say something, and he remarked:

"What is the matter with the Austrian?"

"He is in love with Miss Asher," said Locker, "and so am I. I am beginning to believe he is positively dangerous. I did not think so at first, but I do now. He has actually taken to reading. I know that man; I have often seen him in Washington. He was always running after some lady or other, but I never knew him to read before. It is a dangerous symptom. He reads with one eye, while the other sweeps the horizon to catch a glimpse of her. By the way, that would be a splendid idea for a district policeman; if he stood under a lamp-post in citizen's dress reading a book, no criminal would suspect his identity, and he could keep one eye on the printed page, and devote the other to the cause of justice. But to return to our sallow mutton, or black sheep, if you choose. That Austrian ought to be killed!"

Dick smiled sardonically. "He is not your only obstacle," he said.

"I know it," replied Locker. "There's that Chinese laundried fellow, smooth-finished, who came up this morning. He must be an old offender, for I saw her giving it to him hot this morning. I am sure she was telling him exactly what she thought of him, for he turned as red as a pickled beet. So he will have to scratch pretty hard if he expects to get into her good graces again, and I suppose that is what he came here for. But I am not so much afraid of him as I am of that Austrian. If he keeps on the literary lay, and reads books with her, looking up the words in the dictionary, it is dangerous."

"I do not see," said Lancaster, somewhat loftily, "why you speak of these things to me."

"Then I'll tell you," said Locker quickly. "I speak of them to you because you are just as much concerned in them as I am. You are in love with Miss Asher—anybody can see that—and, in fact, I should think you were a pretty poor sort of a fellow if you were not, after having seen and talked with her. Consequently that Austrian is just as dangerous to you as he is to me. And as I have chosen you for my brother-in-arms, it is right that I tell you everything I know."

"Brother-in-arms?" ejaculated Dick.

"That is what it is," said Locker, "and I will tell you how it came about. The Austrian looked upon you with scorn and contempt because you rode a horse wearing rolled-up trousers and low shoes. As you did not see him and could not return the contempt, I did it for you. Having done this, a fellow feeling for you immediately sprang up within me. That is what always happens, you know. After that the feeling became a good deal stronger, and I said to myself that if I found I could not get Miss Asher; and it's seventy-six I don't, for that's generally the state of my luck; I would help you to get her, partly because I like you, and partly because that Austrian

　　　　Frank R. Stockton

must be ousted, no matter what happens or how it is done. So I became your brother-in-arms, and if I find I am out of the race, I am going to back you up just as hard as I can, and here's my hand upon it."

Dick stopped as he had stopped half an hour before, and gazed upon his companion.

"Now don't thank me," continued Locker, "or say anything nice, because if I find I can come in ahead of you I am going to do it. But if we work together, I am sure we need not be afraid of that Austrian, or of that fiery-faced model for a ready-made-clothes shop. It is to be either you or me—first place for me, if possible."

Dick could not help laughing. "You are a jolly sort of a fellow," said he, "and I will be your brother-in-arms. But it is to be first place for me, if possible." And they shook hands upon the bargain.

That evening Mr. Hemphill found Olive alone. "I have been trying to get a chance to speak to you, Miss Asher," said he. "I want to ask you to help me, for I do not know what in the world to do."

Olive looked at him inquiringly.

"Since you spoke to me this afternoon," he went on, "I have been in a state of most miserable embarrassment; I can not for the life of me decide what I ought to say or what I ought to do, or what I ought not to say or what I ought not to do. If I should pass over as something not necessary to take into consideration the—the—most unusual statement you made to me, it might be that you would consider me as a boor, a man incapable of appreciating the—the—highest honors. Then again, if I do say anything to show that I appreciate such honors, you may well consider me presumptuous, conceited, and even insulting. I thought a while ago that I would leave this house before it would be necessary for me to decide how I should act when I met you, but I could not do that. Explanations would be necessary, and I would not be able to make them, and so, in sheer despair, I have come to you. Whatever you say I ought to do I will do. Of myself, I am utterly helpless."

Olive looked at him with serious earnestness. "You are in a queer position," she said, "and I don't wonder you do not know what to do. I did not think of this peculiar consequence which would result from my revelation. As to the revelation itself, there is no use talking about it; it had to be made. It would have been unjust and wicked to allow a man to live in ignorance of the fact that such a thing had happened to him without his knowing it. But I think I can make it all right for you. If you had known when you were very young, in fact, when you were in another age of man, that a young girl in short dresses was in love with you, would you have disdained her affection?"

"I should say not!" exclaimed Rupert Hemphill, his eyes fixed upon the person who had once been that girl in short dresses.

"Well, then," said Olive, "there could have been nothing for her to complain of, no matter what she knew or what she did not know, and there is nothing he could complain of, no matter what he knew or did not know. And as both these persons have passed entirely out of existence, I think you and I need consider them no longer. And we can talk about tennis or bass fishing, or anything we like. And if you are a fisherman you will be glad to hear that there is first-rate bass fishing in the river now, and that we are talking of getting up a regular fishing party. We shall have to go two or three miles below here where the water is deeper and there are not so many rocks."

That night Mr. Hemphill dreamed hard of a girl who had loved him when she was little, and who continued to love him now that she had grown to be wonderfully handsome. He was going out to sail with her in a boat far and far away, where nobody could find them or bring them back.

CHAPTER XIV

A LETTER FOR OLIVE

The next morning, about an hour after breakfast, Mr. Du Brant proposed to Olive. He had received a letter the day before which made it probable that he might be recalled to Washington before the time which had been fixed for the end of his visit at Broadstone, and he consequently did not wish to defer for a moment longer than was necessary this most important business of his life. He told Miss Asher that he had never truly loved before; which was probably correct; and that as she had raised his mind from the common things of earth, upon which it had been accustomed to grovel, she had made a new man of him in an astonishingly short time; which, it is likely, was also true.

He assured her that without any regard to outside circumstances, he could not live without her. If at any other time he had allowed his mind to dwell for a moment upon matrimony, he had thought of family, position, wealth, social station, and all that sort of thing, but now he thought of nothing but her, and he came to offer her his heart. In fact, the man was truly and honestly in love.

Inwardly Olive smiled. "I can not ask him," she said to herself, "to say this again every day before dinner. He hasn't the wit of Claude Locker, and would not be able to vary his remarks; but I can not blast his hopes too suddenly, for, if I do that, he will instantly go away, and it would not be treating Mrs. Easterfield properly if I were to break up her party without her knowledge. But I will talk to her about it. And now for him.—Mr. Du Brant," she said aloud, speaking in English, although he had proposed to her in French, because she thought she could make her own language more impressive, "it is a very serious thing you have said to me, and I don't believe you have had time enough to think about it properly. Now don't interrupt. I know exactly what you would say. You have known me such a little while that even if your mind is made up it can not be properly made up, and therefore, for your own sake, I am going to give you a chance to think it all over. You must not say you don't want to, because I want you to; and when you have thought, and thought, and know yourself better—now don't say you can not know yourself better if you have a thousand years in which to consider it—for though you think that it is true it is not"

"And if I rack my brains and my heart," interrupted Mr. Du Brant, "and find out that I can never change nor feel in any other way toward you than I feel now, may I then—"

"Now, don't say anything about that," said Olive. "What I want to do now is to treat you honorably and fairly, and to give you a chance to withdraw if, after sober consideration, you think it best to do so. I believe that every young man who thinks himself compelled to propose marriage in such hot haste ought to have a chance to reflect quietly and coolly, and to withdraw if he wants to. And that is all, Mr. Du Brant. I must be off this minute, for Mrs. Easterfield is over there waiting for me."

Mr. Du Brant walked thoughtfully away. "I do not understand," he said to himself in French, "why she did not tell me I need not speak to her again about it. The situation is worthy of diplomatic consideration, and I will give it that."

From a distance Claude Locker beheld his Austrian enemy walking alone, and without a book.

"Something has happened," he thought, "and the fellow has changed his tactics. Before, under cover of a French novel, he was a snake in the grass, now he is a snake hopping along on the tip of his tail. Perhaps he thinks this is a better way to keep a lookout upon her. I believe he is more dangerous than he was before, for I don't know whether a snake on tip tail jumps or falls down upon his victims."

One thing Mr. Locker was firmly determined upon. He was going to try to see Olive as soon as it was possible before luncheon, and impress upon her the ardent nature of his feelings toward her; he did not believe he had done this yet. He looked about him. The party, excepting himself and Mr. Du Brant, were on the front lawn; he would join them and satirize the gloomy Austrian. If Olive could be made to laugh at him it would be like preparing a garden-bed with spade and rake before sowing his seeds.

The rural mail-carrier came earlier than usual that day, and he brought Olive but one letter, but as it was from her father, she was entirely satisfied, and retired to a bench to read it.

In about ten minutes after that she walked into Mrs. Easterfield's little room, the open letter in her hand. As Mrs. Easterfield looked up from her writing-table the girl seemed transformed; she was taller, she was straighter, her face had lost its bloom, and her eyes blazed.

"Would you believe it!" she said, grating out the words as she spoke. "My father is going to be married!"

Mrs. Easterfield dropped her pen, and her face lost color. She had always been greatly interested in Lieutenant Asher. "What!" she exclaimed. "He? And to whom?"

"A girl I used to go to school with," said Olive, standing as if she were framed in one solid piece. "Edith Marshall, living in Geneva. She is older than I am, but we were in the same classes. They are to be married in October, and she is to sail for this country about the time his ship comes home. He is to be stationed at Governor's Island, and they are to have a house there. He writes, and writes, and writes, about how lovely it will be for me to have this dear new mother. Me! To call that thing mother! I shall have no mother, but I have lost my father." With this she threw herself upon a lounge, and burst into passionate tears. Mrs. Easterfield rose, and closed the door.

Claude Locker had no opportunity to press his suit before luncheon, for Olive did not come to that meal; she had one of her headaches. Every one seemed to appreciate the incompleteness of the party, and even Mrs. Easterfield looked serious, which was not usual with her. Mr. Hemphill was much cast down, for he had made up his mind to talk to Olive in such a way that she should not fail to see that he had taken to heart her advice, and might be depended upon to deport himself toward her as if he had never heard the words she had addressed to him. He had prepared several topics for conversation, but as he would not waste these upon the general company, he indulged only in such remarks as were necessary to good manners.

Mr. Du Brant talked a good deal in a perfunctory manner, but inwardly he was somewhat elated. "Her emotions must have been excited more than I supposed," he thought. "That is not a bad sign."

Mrs. Fox was a little bit—a very little bit—annoyed because Mr. Fox did not make as many facetious remarks as was his custom. He seemed like one who, in a degree, felt that he lacked an audience; Mrs. Fox could see no good reason for this.

When Mrs. Easterfield went up to Olive's room she found her bathing her eyes in cold water.

"Will you lend me a bicycle" said Olive. "I am sure you have one."

Mrs. Easterfield looked at her in amazement.

"I want to go to my uncle," said Olive. "He is now all I have left in this world. I have been thinking, and thinking about everything, and I want to go to him. Whatever has come between us will vanish as soon as he sees me, I am sure of that. I do not know why he did not want me to come back to him, but he will want me now, and I should like to start immediately without anybody seeing me."

"But a bicycle!" exclaimed Mrs. Easterfield. "You can't go that way. I will send you in the carriage."

"No, no, no," cried Olive; "I want to go quietly. I want to go so that I can leave my wheel at the door and go right in. I have a short walking-skirt, and I can wear that. Please let me have the bicycle."

Mrs. Easterfield made Olive sit down and she talked to her, but there was no changing the girl's determination to go to her uncle, to go alone, and to go immediately.

Frank R. Stockton

CHAPTER XV

OLIVE'S BICYCLE TRIP

Despite Olive's desire to set forth immediately on her bicycle trip, it was past the middle of the afternoon when she left Broadstone. She went out quietly, not by the usual driveway, and was soon upon the turnpike road. As she sped along the cool air upon her face refreshed her; and the knowledge that she was so rapidly approaching the dear old toll-gate, where, even if she did not find her uncle at the house, she could sit with old Jane until he came back, gave her strength and courage.

Up a long hill she went, and down again to the level country. Then there was a slighter rise in the road, and when she reached its summit she saw, less than a mile away, the toll-gate surrounded by its trees, the thick foliage of the fruit-trees in the garden, the little tollhouse and the long bar, standing up high at its customary incline upon the opposite side of the road. Down the little hill she went; and then, steadily and swiftly, onward. Presently she saw that some one was on the piazza by the side of the tollhouse; his back was toward her, he was sitting in his accustomed armchair; she could not be mistaken; it was her uncle.

Now and then, while upon the road, she had thought of what she should say when she first met him, but she had soon dismissed all ideas of preconceived salutations, or explanations. She would be there, and that would be enough. Her father's letter was in her pocket, and that was too much. All she meant to do was to glide up to that piazza, spring up the steps, and present herself to her uncle's astonished gaze before he had any idea that any one was approaching.

She was within twenty feet of the piazza when she saw that her uncle was not alone; there was some one sitting in front of him who had been concealed by his broad shoulders. This person was a woman. She had caught sight of Olive, and stuck her head out on one side to look at her. Upon her dough-like face there was a grin, and in her eye a light of triumph. With one quick glance she seemed to say: "Ah, ha, you find me here, do you? What have you to say to that?"

Olive's heart stood still. That woman, that Maria Port, sitting in close converse with her uncle in that public place where she had never seen any one but men! That horrid woman at such a moment as this! She could not speak to her; she could not speak to her uncle in her presence. She could not stop. With what she had on her mind, and with what she had in her pocket, it would be impossible to say a word before that Maria Port! Without a swerve she sped on, and passed the toll-gate. She only knew one thing; she could not stop.

The wildest suspicions now rushed into her mind. Why should her uncle be thus exposing himself to the public gaze with Maria Port? Why did it give the woman such diabolical pleasure to be seen there with him? With a mind already prepared for such sickening revelations, Olive was convinced that it could mean nothing but that her uncle intended to marry Maria Port. What else could it mean? But no matter what it meant, she could not stop. She could not go back.

On went her bicycle, and presently she gained sufficient command over herself to know that she should not ride into the town. But what else could she do? She could not go back while those two were sitting on the piazza. Suddenly she remembered the shunpike. She had never been on it, but she knew where it left the road, and where it reentered it. So she kept on her course, and in a few minutes had reached the narrow country road. There were ruts here and there, and sometimes there were stony places; there were small hills, mostly rough; and there were few stretches of smooth road; but on went Olive; sometimes trying with much effort to make good time, and always with tears in her eyes, dimming the roadway, the prospect, and everything in the world.

"There now!" exclaimed Maria Port, springing to her feet. "What have you got to say to that? If that isn't brazen I never saw brass!"

"What do you mean?" said the captain, rising in his chair.

"Mean?" said Maria Port, leaning over the railing. "Look there! Do you see that girl getting away as fast as she can work herself? That's your precious niece, Olive Asher, scooting past us with her nose in the air as if we was sticks and stones by the side of the road. What have you got to say to that, Captain John, I'd like to know?"

The captain ran down the path. "You don't mean to say that is Olive!" he cried.

"That's who it is," answered Miss Port. "She looked me square in the face as she dashed by. Not a word for you, not a word for me. Impudence! That doesn't express it!"

The captain paid no attention to her, but ran into the garden. Old Jane was standing near the house door. "Was that Miss Olive?" he cried. "Did you see her?"

"Yes," said old Jane, "it was her. I saw her comin', and I came out to meet her. But she just shot through the toll-gate as if she didn't know there was a toll on bicycles."

The captain stood still in the garden-path. He could not believe that Olive had done this to treat him with contempt. She must have heard some news. There must be something the matter. She was going into town at the top of her speed to send a telegram, intending to stop as she came back. She might have stopped anyway if it had not been for that good-for-nothing Maria Port. She hated Maria, and he hated her himself, at this moment, as she stood by his side, asking him what was the matter with him.

"It's no more than you have to expect," said she. "She's a fine lady, a navy lady, a foreign lady, that's been with the aristocrats! She's got good clothes on that she never wore here, and where I guess she had a pretty stupid time, judgin' from how they carry on at that Easterfield place. Why in the world should she want to stop and speak to such persons as you and me?"

The captain paid no attention to these remarks. "If she doesn't want to send a telegram, I don't see what she is going to town for in such a hurry. I suppose she thought she could get there sooner than a man could go on a horse," he said.

"Telegram!" sneered Miss Port. "It's a great deal easier to send telegrams from the gap."

"Then it is something worse," he thought. Perhaps she might be running away, though what in the world she was running from he could not imagine. Anyway, he must see her; he must find out. When she came back she must not pass again, and if she did not come back he must go after her. He ran to the road and put down the bar, calling to old Jane to come there and keep a sharp lookout. Then he quickly returned to the house.

"What are you going to do" asked Miss Port. "I never saw a man in such a fluster."

"If she does not come back very soon," said he, "I shall go to town after her."

"Then I suppose I might as well be going myself," said she. "And by the way, captain, if you are going to town, why don't

Frank R. Stockton

you take a seat in my carriage? Dear knows me and the boy don't fill it."

But the captain would consider no such invitation. When he met Olive he did not want Maria Port to be along. He did not answer, and went into the house to make some change in his attire. Old Jane would not let Olive pass, and if he met her on the road or in the town he wanted to be well dressed.

Miss Port still stood in the path by the house door. "That's not what I call polite," said she, "but he's awful flustered, and I don't mind."

Far from minding, Maria was pleased; it pleased her to know that his niece's conduct had flustered him. The more that girl flustered him the better it would be, and she smiled with considerable satisfaction. If she could get that girl out of the way she believed she would find but little difficulty in carrying out her scheme to embitter the remainder of the good captain's life. She did not put it in that way to herself; but that was the real character of the scheme.

Suddenly an idea struck her. It was of no use for her to stand and wait, for she knew she would not be able to induce the captain to go with her. It would be a great thing if she could, for to drive into town with him by her side would go far to make the people of Glenford understand what was going to happen. But, if she could not do this, she could do something else. If she started away immediately she might meet that Asher girl coming back, and it would be a very fine thing if she could have an interview with her before she saw her uncle.

She made a quick step toward the house and looked in. The captain was not visible, but old Jane was standing near the back door of the tollhouse. The opportunity was not to be lost.

"Good-by, John," said she in a soft tone, but quite loud enough for the old woman to hear. "I'll go home first, for I've got to see to gettin' supper ready for you. So good-by, John, for a little while." And she kissed her hand to the inside of the house.

Then she hurried out of the gate; got into the little phaeton which was waiting for her under a tree; and drove away. She had come there that afternoon on the pretense of consulting the captain about her father's health, which she said disturbed her, and she had requested the privilege of sitting on the toll-gate piazza because she had always wanted to sit there, and had never been invited. The captain had not invited her then, but as she had boldly marched to the piazza and taken a seat, he had been obliged to follow.

Captain Asher, wearing a good coat and hat, relieved old Jane at her post, and waited and waited for Olive to come back. He did not for a moment think she might return by the shunpike, for that was a rough road, not fit for a bicycle. And if she passed this way once, why should she object to doing it again?

When more than time enough had elapsed for her return from the town, he started forth with a heavy heart to follow her. He told old Jane that if for any reason he should be detained in town until late, he would take supper with Mr. Port, and if, although he did not expect this, he should not come back that night, the Ports would know of his whereabouts. He did not take his horse and buggy because he thought it would be in his way. If he met Olive in the road he could more easily stop and talk to her if he were walking than if he had a horse to take care of.

"I hope you're not runnin' after Miss Olive," said old Jane.

The captain did not wish his old servant to imagine that it was necessary for him to run after his niece, and so he answered rather quickly: "Of course not." Then he set off toward the town. He did not walk very fast, for if he met Olive he would rather have a talk with her on the road than in Glenford.

He walked on and on, not with his eyes on the smooth surface of the pike, but looking out afar, hoping that he might soon see the figure of a girl on a bicycle; and thus it was that he passed the entrance to the shunpike without noticing that a bicycle track turned into it.

Olive struggled on, and the road did not improve. She worked hard with her body, but still harder with her mind. It seemed to her as though everything were endeavoring to crush her, and that it was almost succeeding. If she had been in her own room, seated, or walking the floor, indignation against her uncle would have given her the same unnatural vigor and energy which had possessed her when she read her father's letter; but it is impossible to be angry when one is physically tired and depressed, and this was Olive's condition now. Once she dismounted, sat down on a piece of rock, and cried. The rest was of service to her, but she could not stay there long; the road was too lonely. She must push on. So on she pressed, sometimes walking, and sometimes on her wheel, the pedals apparently growing stiffer at every turn. Slight mishaps she did not mind, but a fear began to grow upon her that she would never be able to reach Broadstone at all. But after a time—a very long time it seemed—the road grew more level and smooth; and then ahead she saw the white surface of the turnpike shining as it passed the end of her road. When she should emerge on that smooth, hard road it could not be long, even if she went slowly, before she reached home. She was still some fifty yards from the pike when she saw a man upon it, walking southward.

As Dick Lancaster passed the end of the road he lifted his head, and looked along it. It was strange that he should do so, for since he had started on his homeward walk he had not raised his eyes from the ground. He had reached Broadstone soon after luncheon, before Olive had left on her wheel, and had passed rather a stupid time, playing tennis with Claude Locker, he had seen but little of Mrs. Easterfield, whose mind was evidently occupied. Once she had seemed about to take him into her confidence, but had suddenly excused herself, and had gone into the house. When the game was finished

Locker advised him to go home.

"She is not likely to be down until dinner time," he had said, "and this evening I'll defend our cause against those other fellows. I have several good things in my mind that I am sure will interest her, and I don't believe there's any use courting a girl unless you interest her."

Lancaster had taken the advice, and had left much earlier than was usual.

CHAPTER XVI

MR. LANCASTER ACCEPTS A MISSION

When Dick Lancaster saw Olive he stopped with a start, and then ran toward her.

"Miss Asher!" he exclaimed. "What are you doing here? What is the matter? You look pale."

When she saw him coming Olive had dismounted, not with the active spring usual with her, but heavily and clumsily. She did not even smile as she spoke to him.

"I am glad to see you, Mr. Lancaster," she said. "I am on my way back to Broadstone, and I would like to send a message to my uncle by you."

"Back from where? And why on this road?" he was about to ask, but he checked himself. He saw that she trembled as she stood.

"Miss Asher," said he, "you must stop and rest. Let me take your wheel and come over to this bank and sit down."

She sat down in the shade and took off her hat; and for a moment she quietly enjoyed the cool breeze upon her head. He did not want to annoy her with questions, but he could not help saying:

"You look very tired."

"I ought to be tired," she answered, "for I have gone over a perfectly dreadful road. Of course, you wonder why I came this way, and the best thing for me to do is to begin at the beginning and to tell you all about it, so that you will know what I have been doing, and then understand what I would like you to do for me."

So she told him all her tale, and, telling it, seemed to relieve her mind while her tired body rested. Dick listened with earnest avidity. He lost not the slightest change in her expression as she spoke. He was shocked when he heard of her father; he was grieved when he imagined how she must have felt when the news came to her; he was angry when he heard of the impertinent glare of Maria Port; and his heart was torn when he knew of this poor girl's disappointment, of her soul-harrowing conjectures, of her wearisome and painful progress along that rough road; of which progress she said but little, although its consequences he could plainly see. All these things showed themselves upon his countenance as he gazed upon her and listened, not only with his ears, but his heart.

"I shall be more than glad," he said, when she had finished, "to carry any message, or to do anything you want me to do. But I must first relieve you of one of your troubles. Your uncle has not the slightest idea of marrying Miss Port. I don't believe he would marry anybody; but, of all women, not that vulgar creature. Let me assure you, Miss Asher, that I have heard him talk about her, and I know he has the most contemptuous opinion of her. I have heard him make fun of her, and I don't believe he would have anything to do with her if it were not for her father, who is one of his oldest friends."

She looked at him incredulously. "And yet they were sitting close together," she said; "so close that at first I did not see her; apparently talking in the most private manner in a very public place. They surely looked very much like an engaged couple as I have noticed them. And old Jane has told me that everybody knows she is trying to trap him; and surely there is good reason to believe that she has succeeded."

Dick shook his head. "Impossible, Miss Asher," he said. "He never would have such a woman. I know him well enough to be absolutely sure of that. Of course, he treats her kindly, and perhaps he is sociable with her. It is his nature to be friendly, and he has known her for a long time. But marry her! Never! I am certain, Miss Asher, he would never do that."

"I wish I could believe it," said she.

"I can easily prove it to you," he said. "I will take your message to your uncle, I will tell him all you want me to tell him, and then I will ask him, frankly and plainly, about Miss Port. I do not in the least object to doing it. I am well enough acquainted with him to know that he is a frank, plain man. I am sure he will be much amused at your supposition, and angry, too, when I tell him of the way that woman looked at you and so prevented you from stopping when you had come expressly to see him. Then I will immediately come to Broadstone to relieve your mind in regard to the Maria Port business, and to bring you whatever message your uncle has to send you."

"No, no," said Olive, "you must not do that. It would be too much to come back to-day. You have relieved my mind some-what about that woman, and I am perfectly willing to wait until to-morrow, when you can tell me exactly how everything is, and let me know when my uncle would like me to come and see him. I think it will be better next time not to take him by surprise. But I would be very, very grateful to you, Mr, Lancaster, if you would come as early in the morning as you can. I can wait very well until then, now that my mind is easier, but I am afraid that when to-morrow begins I shall be very impatient. My troubles are always worse in the morning. But you must not walk. My uncle has a horse and buggy. But perhaps it would be better to let Mrs. Easterfield send for you. I know she will be glad to do it."

Dick assured her that he did not wish to be sent for; that he would borrow the captain's horse, and would be at Broadstone as early as was proper to make a visit.

"Proper!" exclaimed Olive. "In a case like this any time is proper. In Mrs. Easterfield's name I invite you to breakfast. I know she will be glad to have me do it. And now I must go on. You are very, very good, and I am very grateful."

Dick could not say that he was more grateful for being allowed to help her than she could possibly be for being helped, but his face showed it, and if she had looked at him she would have known it.

"Miss Asher," he exclaimed as she rose, "your skirt is covered with dust. You must have fallen."

"I did have one fall," she said, "but I was so worried I did not mind."

"But you can not go back in that plight," he said; "let me dust your skirt." And breaking a little branch from a bush, he proceeded to make her look presentable. "And now," said he, when she had complimented him upon his skill, "I will walk with you to the entrance of the grounds. Perhaps as you are so tired," he said hesitatingly, "I can help you along, so that you will not have to work so hard yourself."

"Oh, no," she answered; "that is not at all necessary. When I am on the turnpike I can go beautifully. I feel ever so much rested and stronger, and it is all due to you. So you see, although you will not go with me, you will help me very much." And she smiled as she spoke. He truly had helped her very much.

Dick was unwilling that she should go on alone, although it was still broad daylight and there was no possible danger, and he was also unwilling because he wanted to go with her, but there was no use saying anything or thinking anything, and so he stood and watched her rolling along until she had passed the top of a little hill, and had departed from his view. Then he ran to the top of the little hill, and watched her until she was entirely out of sight.

The rest of the way to the toll-gate seemed very short to Dick, but he had time enough to make up his mind that he would see the captain at the earliest possible moment; that he would deliver his message and the letter of Lieutenant Asher; that he would immediately bring up the matter of Maria Port and let the captain know the mischief that woman had done. Then, armed with the assurances the captain would give him, he would start for Broadstone after supper, and carry the good news to Olive. It would be a shame to let that dear girl remain in suspense for the whole night, when he, by riding, or even walking an inconsiderable number of miles, could relieve her. He found old Jane in the tollhouse.

"Where is the captain" he asked.

"The captain?" she repeated. "He's in town takin' supper with his sweetheart."

Dick stared at her.

"Perhaps you haven't heard that he's engaged to Maria Port," said the woman; "and I don't wonder you're taken back! But I suppose everybody will soon know it now, and the sooner the better, I say."

"What are you talking about" exclaimed Dick. "You don't mean to tell me that the captain is going to marry Miss Port?"

"Whether he wants to or not, he's gone so far he'll have to. I've knowed for a long time she's been after him, but I didn't think she'd catch him just yet."

"I don't believe it." cried Dick. "It must be a mistake! How do you know it?"

"Know!" said old Jane, who, ordinarily a taciturn woman, was now excited and inclined to volubility. "Don't you suppose I've got eyes and ears? Didn't I see them for ever and ever so long sittin' out on this piazza, where everybody could see 'em, a-spoonin' like a couple of young people? And didn't I see 'em tearin' themselves asunder as if they couldn't bear to be apart for an hour? And didn't I hear her tell him she was goin' home to get an extry good supper for him? And didn't I hear her call him 'dear John,' and kiss her hand to him. And if you don't believe me you can go into the kitchen and ask Mary; she heard the 'dear John' and saw the hand-kissin'. And then didn't he tell me he was goin' to the Ports' to supper, and if he stayed late and anybody asked for him—meaning you, most probable, and I think he might have left somethin' more of a message for you—that he was to be found with the Ports— with Maria most likely, for the old man goes to bed early?"

Dick made no answer; he was standing motionless looking out upon the flowers in the garden.

"And perhaps you haven't heard of Miss Olive comin' past on a bicycle," old Jane remarked. "I saw her comin', and I knew by the look on her face that it made her sick to see that woman sittin' here, and I don't blame her a bit. When he started so early for town I thought he might be intendin' to look for her, and yet be in time for the Ports' supper, but she didn't come back this way at all, and I expect she went home by the shunpike."

"Which she did," said Dick, showing by this remark that he was listening to what the old woman was saying.

"But he cut me mighty short when I asked him," continued old Jane. "I tried to ease his mind, but as I found his mind didn't need no easin', I minded my own business, just as he was mindin' his. And now, sir, you'll have to eat your supper alone this time."

If Dick's supper had consisted of nectar and the brains of

nightingales he would not have noticed it; and, until late in the evening, he sat in the arbor, anxiously waiting for the captain's return. About ten o'clock old Jane, sleepy from having sat up so long, called to him from the door that he might as well come in and let her lock up the house. The captain was not coming home that night. He had stayed with the Ports once before, when the old man was sick.

"I guess he's got a better reason for stayin' tonight," she said. "It'll be a great card for that Maria when the Glenford people knows it, and they'll know it you may be sure, if she has to go and walk the soles of her feet off tellin' them. One thing's mighty sure," she continued. "I'm not goin' to stay here with her in the house. He'll have to get somebody else to help him take toll. But I guess she'll want to do that herself. Nothin' would suit her better than to be sittin' all day in the tollhouse talkin' scandal to everybody that goes by."

CHAPTER XVII

DICK IS NOT A PROMPT BEARER OF NEWS

When the captain reached Glenford, and before he went to the Ports' he went to the telegraph-office, and made inquiries at various other places, but his niece had not been seen in town. He wandered about so long and asked so many questions that it was getting dark when he suddenly thought of the shunpike. He had not thought of it before, for it was an unfit road for bicycles, but now he saw that he had been a fool. That was the only way she could have gone back.

Hurrying to a livery-stable, he hired a horse and buggy and a lantern, and drove to the shunpike. There he plainly saw the track of the bicycle as it had turned into that rough road. Then he drove on, examining every foot of the way, fearful that he might see, lying senseless by the side of the road, the figure of a girl, perhaps unconscious from fatigue, perhaps dead from an accident.

When at last he emerged upon the turnpike he lost the track of the bicycle, but still he went on, all the way to Broadstone; a girl might be lying senseless by the side of the road, even on the pike, which at this time was not much frequented. Thus assuring himself that Olive had reached Broadstone in safety, or at least had not fallen by the way, he turned and drove back to town upon the pike, passing his own toll-gate, where the bar was always up after dark. He had promised to return the horse that night, and, as he had promised, he intended to do it. It was after nine o'clock when, returning from the livery-stable, he reached the Port house, and saw Maria sitting in the open doorway.

She instantly ran out to meet him, asking him somewhat sharply why he had disappointed them. She had kept the supper waiting ever so long. He went in to see her father, who was sitting up for him, and she busied herself in getting him a fresh supper. Nice and hot the supper was, and although his answers to her questions had not been satisfactory, she concealed her resentment, if she had any. When the meal was over both father and daughter assured him that it was too late for him to go home that night, and that he must stay with them. Tired and troubled, Captain Asher accepted the invitation.

As soon as he could get away from the Port residence the next morning Captain Asher went home. He had hoped he would have been able to leave before breakfast, but the solicitous Maria would not listen to this. She prepared him a most tempting breakfast, cooking some of the things with her own hands, and she was so attentive, so anxious to please, so kind in her suggestions, and in every way so desirous to make him happy through the medium of savory food and tender-hearted concern, that she almost made him angry. Never before, he thought, had he seen a woman make such a coddling fool of herself. He knew very well what it meant, and that provoked him still more.

When at last he got away he walked home in a bad humor; he was even annoyed with Olive. Granting that what she had done was natural enough under the circumstances, and that she had not wished to stop when she saw him in company with a woman she did not like, he thought she might have considered him as well as herself. She should have known that it would give him great trouble for her to dash by in that way and neither stop nor come back to explain matters. She must have known that Maria Port was not going to stay always, and she might have waited somewhere until the woman had gone.

If she had had the least idea of how much he wanted to see her she would have contrived some way to come back to him. But no, she went back to Broadstone to please herself, and left him to wander up and down the roads looking for her in the dark.

When the captain met old Jane at the door of the tollhouse her salutation did not smooth his ruffled spirits, for she told him that she and Mr. Lancaster had sat up until nearly the middle of the night waiting for him, and that the poor young man must have felt it, for he had not eaten half a breakfast.

The captain paid but little attention to these remarks and passed in, but before he crossed the garden he met Dick, who informed him that he had something very important to comm- unicate. Important communications that must be delivered without a moment's loss of time are generally unpleasant, and knowing this, the captain knit his brows a little, but told Dick he would be ready for him as soon as he lighted his pipe. He felt he must have something to soothe his ruffled spirits while he listened to the tale of the woes of some one else.

But at the moment he scratched his match to light his pipe his soul was illuminated by a flash of joy; perhaps Dick was going to tell him he was engaged to Olive; perhaps that was what she had come to tell him the day before. He had not expected to hear anything of this kind, at least not so soon, but it had been the wish of his heart—he now knew that without appreciating the fact—it had been the earnest wish of his heart for some time, and he stepped toward the little arbor with the alacrity of happy anticipation.

As soon as they were seated Dick began to speak of Olive, but not in the way the captain had hoped for. He mentioned the great trouble into which she had been plunged, and gave the captain his brother's letter to read. When he had finished it the captain's face darkened, and his frown was heavy.

"An outrageous piece of business," he said, "to treat a daughter in this way; to put a schoolmate over her head in the family! It is shameful! And this is what she was coming to tell me?"

"Yes," said Dick, "that is it."

Now there was another flash of joy in the captain's heart, which cleared up his countenance and made his frown disappear. "She was coming to me," he thought. "I was the one to whom she turned in her trouble." And it seemed to this good captain as if he had suddenly become the father of a grown-up daughter.

"But what message did she send me?" he asked quickly. "Did she say when she was coming again?"

Dick hesitated; Olive had said that she wanted her uncle to say when he wanted to see her, so that there should be no more surprising, but this request had been conditional. Dick knew that she did not want to come if her uncle were going to marry Miss Port; therefore it was that he hesitated.

"Before we go any further," he said, "I think I would better mention a little thing which will make you laugh, but still it did worry Miss Asher, and was one reason why she went back to Broadstone without stopping."

"What is it" asked the captain, putting down his pipe.

Dick did not come out plainly and frankly, as he had told Olive he would do when he mentioned the Maria Port matter. In his own heart he could not help believing now that Olive's suspicions had had good foundations, and old Jane's announcements, combined with the captain's own actions in regard to the Port family, had almost convinced him that this miserable engagement was a fact. But, of course, he would not in any way intimate to the captain that he believed in such nonsense, and therefore, in an offhand manner, he mentioned Olive's absurd anxiety in regard to Miss Port.

When the captain heard Dick's statement he answered it in the most frank and plain manner; he brought his big hand down on his knee and swore as if one of his crew had boldly contradicted him. He did not swear at anybody in particular; there was the roar and the crash of the thunder and the flash of the lightning, but no direct stroke descended upon any one. He was angry that such a repulsive and offensive thing as his marriage to Maria Port should be mentioned, or even thought of, but he was enraged when he heard that his niece had believed him capable of such disgusting insanity. With a jerk he rose to his feet.

"I will not talk about such a thing as this," he said. "If I did I am sure I should say something hard about my niece, and I don't want to do that." With this he strode away, and proceeded to look after the concerns of his little farm.

Old Jane came cautiously to Dick. "Did he tell you when it was going to be, or anything about it?" she asked.

"No," said Dick, "he would not even speak of it."

"I suppose he expects us to mind our own business," said she, "and of course we'll have to do it, but I can tell him one thing—I'm goin' to make it my business to leave this place the day before that woman comes here."

Dejected and thoughtful, Dick sat in the arbor. Here was a state of affairs very different from what he had anticipated. He had not been able to hurry to her the evening before; he had not gone to breakfast as she had invited him; he had not started off early in the forenoon; and now he asked himself when should he go, or, indeed, why should he go at all? She had no anxieties he could relieve. Anything he could tell her would only heap more unhappiness upon her, and the longer he could keep his news from her the better it would be for her.

Olive had not joined the Broadstone party at dinner the night before. She had been too tired, and had gone directly to her room, where, after a time, Mrs. Easterfield joined her; and the two talked late. One who had overheard their conversation might well have supposed that the elder lady was as much interested in Lieutenant Asher's approaching nuptials as was the younger one. When she was leaving Mrs. Easterfield said:

"You have enough on your mind to give it all the trouble it ought to bear, and so I beg of you not to think for a moment of that absurd idea about your uncle's engagement. I never saw the woman, but I have heard of her; she is a professional scandal-monger; and Captain Asher would not think for a moment of marrying her. When Mr. Lancaster comes to-morrow you will hear that she was merely consulting him on business, and that you are to go to the toll-gate to-morrow as soon as you can. But remember, this time I am going to send you in the carriage. No more bicycles."

In spite of this well-intentioned admonition, Olive did not sleep well, and dreamed all night of Miss Port in the shape of a great cat covered with feathers like a chicken, and trying to get a chance to jump at her. Very early she awoke, and looking at her clock, she began to calculate the hours which must pass before Mr. Lancaster could arrive. It was rather strange that of the two troubles which came to her as soon as she opened her eyes, the suspected engagement of her uncle pushed itself in front of the actual engagement of her father; the one was something she *knew* she would have to make up her mind to bear; the other was something she *feared* she would have to make up her mind to bear.

CHAPTER XVIII

WHAT OLIVE DETERMINED TO DO

Olive was very much disappointed at breakfast time, and as soon as she had finished that meal she stationed herself at a point on the grounds which commanded the entrance. People came and talked to her, but she did not encourage conversation, and about eleven o'clock she went to Mrs. Easterfield in her room.

"He is not coming," she said. "He is afraid."

"What is he afraid of?" asked Mrs. Easterfield.

"He is afraid to tell me that the optimistic speculations with which he tried to soothe my mind arose entirely from his own imagination. The whole thing is exactly what I expected, and he hasn't the courage to come and say so. Now, really, don't you think this is the state of the case, and that if he had anything but the worst news to bring me he would have been here long ago?"

Mrs. Easterfield looked very serious. "I would not give up," she said, "until I saw Mr. Lancaster and heard what he has to say."

"That would not suit me," said Olive. "I have waited and waited just as long as I can. It is as likely as not that he has concluded that he can not do anything here which will be of service to any one, and has started off to finish his vacation at some place where people won't bother him with their own affairs. He told me when I first met him that he was on his way North. And now, would you like me to tell you what I have determined to do?"

"I would," said Mrs. Easterfield, but her expression did not indicate that she expected Olive's announcement to give her any pleasure.

"I have been considering it all the morning," said Olive, "and I have determined to marry without delay. The greatest object of my life at present is to write to my father that I am married. I don't wish to tell him anything until I can tell him that. I would also be glad to be able to send the same message to the toll-gate house, but I don't suppose it will make much difference there."

"Do you think," said Mrs. Easterfield, "that my inviting you here made all this trouble?"

"No," said Olive. "It was not the immediate cause, but uncle knows I do not like that woman, and she doesn't like me, and it would not have suited him to have me stay very much longer with him. I thought at first he was glad to have me go on account of Mr. Lancaster, but now I do not believe that had anything to do with it. He did not want me with him, and what that woman came here and told me about his not expecting me back again was, I now believe, a roundabout message from him."

"Now, Olive," said Mrs. Easterfield, "it would be a great deal better for you to stop all this imagining until you hear from Mr. Lancaster, if you don't see him. Perhaps the poor young man has sprained his ankle, or was prevented in some ordinary way from coming. But what is this nonsense about getting married?"

"There is no nonsense about it," said Olive. "I am going to marry, but I have not chosen any one yet."

Mrs. Easterfield uttered an exclamation of horror. "Choose!" she exclaimed. "What have you to do with choosing? I don't think you are much like other girls, but I did think you had enough womanly qualities to make you wait until you are chosen."

"I intend to wait until I am chosen," said Olive, "but I shall choose the person who is to choose me. I have always thought it absurd for a young woman to sit and wait and wait until some one comes and sees fit to propose to her. Even under ordinary circumstances, I think the young woman has not a fair chance to get what she wants. But my case is extraordinary, and I can't afford to wait; and as I don't want to go out into the world to look for a husband, I am going to take one of these young men here."

"Olive," cried Mrs. Easterfield, "you don't mean you are going to marry Mr. Locker?"

"You forget," said Olive, "that I told you I have not made up my mind yet. But although I have not come to a decision, I have a leaning toward one of them. The more I think of it the more I incline in the direction of my old love."

"Mr. Hemphill!" exclaimed Mrs. Easterfield. "Olive, you are crazy, or else you are joking in a very disagreeable manner. There could be no one more unfit for you than he is."

"I am not crazy, and I am not joking," replied the girl, "and I think Rupert would suit me very well. You see, I think a great deal more of Rupert than I do of Mr. Hemphill, although the latter gentleman has excellent points. He is commonplace, and, above everything else, I want a commonplace husband. I want some one to soothe me, and quiet me, and to give me ballast. If there is anything out of the way to be done I want to do it myself. I am sure he is in love with me, for his anxious efforts to make me believe that the frank avowal of my early affection had no effect upon him proves that he was very much affected. I believe that he is truly in love with me."

Frank R. Stockton

Mrs. Easterfield's sharp eyes had seen this, and she had nothing to say.

"I believe," continued Olive, "that a retrospect love will be a better foundation for conjugal happiness than any other sort of affection. One can always look back to it no matter what happens, and be happy in the memory of it. It would be something distinct which could never be interfered with. You can't imagine what an earnest and absorbing love I once had for that man!"

Mrs. Easterfield sprang to her feet. "Olive Asher," she cried, "I can't listen to you if you talk in this way!"

"Well, then," said Olive, "if you object so much to Rupert—you must not forget that it would be Rupert that I would really marry if I became the wife of Mr. Hemphill—do you advise me to take Mr. Locker? And I will tell you this, he is not to be rudely set aside; he has warm-hearted points which I did not suspect at first. I will tell you what he just said to me. As I was coming up-stairs he hurried toward me, and his face showed that he was very anxious to speak to me. So before he could utter a word, I told him that he was too early; that his hour had not yet arrived. Then that good fellow said to me that he had seen I was in trouble, and that he had been informed it had been caused by bad news from my family. He had made no inquiries because he did not wish to intrude upon my private affairs, and all he wished to say now was that while my mind was disturbed and worried he did not intend to present his own affairs to my attention, even though I had fixed regular times for his doing so. But although he wished me to understand that I need not fear his making love to me just at this time, he wanted me to remember that his love was still burning as brightly as ever, and would be again offered me just as soon as he would be warranted in doing so."

"And what did you say to that?" asked Mrs. Easterfield.

"I felt like patting him on the head," Olive answered, "but

instead of doing that I shook his hand just as warmly as I could, and told him I should not forget his consideration and good feeling."

Mrs. Easterfield sighed. "You have joined him fast to your car," she said, "and yet, even if there were no one else, he would be impossible."

"Why so?" asked Olive quickly. "I have always liked him, and now I like him ever so much better. To be sure he is queer; but then he is so much queerer than I am that perhaps in comparison I might take up the part of commonplace partner. Besides, he has money enough to live on. He told me that when he first addressed me. He said he would never ask any woman to live on pickled verse feet, and he has also told me something of his family, which must be a good one."

"Olive," said Mrs. Easterfield, "I don't believe at all in the necessity or the sense in your precipitating plans of marrying. It is all airy talk, anyway. You can't ask a man to step up and marry you in order that you may sit down and write a letter to your father. But if you are thinking of marrying, or rather of preparing to marry at some suitable time, why, in the name of everything that is reasonable, don't you take Mr. Lancaster? He is as far above the other young men you have met here as the mountains are above the plains; he belongs to another class altogether. He is a thoroughly fine young man, and has a most honorable profession with good prospects, and I know he loves you. You need not ask me how I know it—it is always easy for a woman to find out things like that. Now, here is a prospective husband for you whose cause I should advocate. In fact, I should be delighted to see you married to him. He possesses every quality which would make you a good husband."

Olive smiled. "You seem to know a great deal about him," said she, "and I assure you that so far as he himself is concerned, I have no objections to him, except that I think he might have had the courage to come and tell me the truth this morning, whatever it is."

"Perhaps he has not found out the truth yet," quickly suggested Mrs. Easterfield.

Olive fixed her eyes upon her companion and for a few moments reflected, but presently she shook her head.

"No, that can not be," she answered. "He would have let me know he had been obliged to wait. Oh, no, it is all settled, and we can drop that subject. But as for Mr. Lancaster, his connections would make any thought of him impossible. He, and his father, too, are both close friends of my uncle, and he would be a constant communication between me and that woman unless there should be a quarrel, which I don't wish to cause. No, I want to leave everything of that sort as far behind me as it used to be in front of me, and as Professor Lancaster is mixed up with it I could not think of having anything to do with him."

Mrs. Easterfield was silent. She was trying to make up her mind whether this girl were talking sense or nonsense. What she said seemed to be extremely nonsensical, but as she said it, it was difficult to believe that she did not consider it to be entirely rational.

"Well," said Olive, "you have objected to two of my candidates, and I positively decline the one you offer, so we have left only the diplomat. He has proposed, and he has not yet received a definite answer. You have told me yourself that he belongs to an aristocratic family in Austria, and I am sure that would be a grand match. We have talked together a great deal, and he seems to like the things I like. I should see plenty of court life and high society, for he will soon be transferred from this legation, and if I take him I shall go to some foreign capital. He is very sharp and ambitious, and I have no doubt that some day he will be looked upon as a distinguished foreigner. Now, as it is the ambition of many American girls to marry distinguished foreigners, this alliance is certainly worthy of due consideration."

"Stuff!" said Mrs. Easterfield.

Olive was not annoyed, and replied very quietly: "It is not stuff. You must know young women who have married foreigners and who did not do anything like so well as if they had married rising diplomats."

Mrs. Blynn now knocked at the door on urgent household business.

"I shall want to see you again about all this, Olive," said Mrs. Easterfield as they parted.

"Of course," replied the girl, "whenever you want to."

"Mrs. Blynn," said the lady of the house, "before you mention what you have come to talk about, please tell one of the men to put a horse to a buggy and come to the house. I want to send a message by him."

The letter which was speedily on its way to Mr. Richard Lancaster was a very brief one. It simply asked the young gentleman to come to Broadstone, with bad news or good news, or without any news at all. It was absolutely necessary that the writer should see him, and in order that there might be no delay she sent a conveyance for him. Moreover, she added, it would give her great pleasure if Mr. Lancaster would come prepared to spend a couple of days at her house. She felt sure good Captain Asher would spare him for that short time. She believed that at this moment more gentlemen were needed at Broadstone, and, although she did not go on to say that she thought Dick was not having a fair chance at this very important crisis, that is what she expected the young man to understand.

Just before luncheon, at the time when Claude Locker might have been urging his suit had he been less kind-hearted and

Frank R. Stockton

generous, Olive found an opportunity to say a few words to Mrs. Easterfield.

"A capital idea has come into my head," she said. "What do you think of holding a competitive examination among these young men?"

"More stuff, and more nonsense!" ejaculated Mrs. Easterfield. "I never knew any one to trifle with serious subjects as you are trifling with your future."

"I am not trifling," said Olive. "Of course, I don't mean that I should hold an examination, but that you should. You know that parents—foreign parents, I mean—make all sorts of examinations of the qualifications and merits of candidates for the hands of their daughters, and I should be very grateful if you would be at least that much of a mother to me."

"No examination would be needed," said the other quickly; "I should decide upon Mr. Lancaster without the necessity of any questions or deliberations."

"But he is not a candidate," said Olive; "he has been ruled out. However," she added with a little laugh, "nothing can be done just now, for they have not all entered themselves in the competition; Mr. Hemphill has not proposed yet."

At that instant the rest of the family joined them on their way to luncheon.

The meal was scarcely over when Olive disappeared up-stairs, but soon came down attired in a blue sailor suit, which she had not before worn at Broadstone, and although the ladies of that house had been astonished at the number of costumes this navy girl carried in her unostentatious baggage, this was a new surprise to them.

"Mr. Hemphill and I are going boating," said Olive to Mrs. Easterfield.

"Olive!" exclaimed the other.

"What is there astonishing about it?" asked the girl. "I have been out boating with Mr. Locker, and it did not amaze you. You need not be afraid; Mr. Hemphill says he has had a good deal of practise in rowing, and if he does not understand the management of a boat I am sure I do. It is only for an hour, and we shall be ready for anything that the rest of you are going to do this afternoon."

With this, away she went, skipping over the rocks and grass, down to the river's edge, followed by Mr. Hemphill, who could scarcely believe he was in a world of common people and common things, while he, in turn, was followed by the mental anathemas of a poet and a diplomat.

Frank R. Stockton

CHAPTER XIX

THE CAPTAIN AND DICK LANCASTER DESERT THE TOLL-GATE

When Captain Asher, in an angry mood, left his young friend and guest and went out into his barnyard and his fields in order to quiet his soul by the consideration of agricultural subjects, he met with but little success. He looked at his pigs, but he did not notice their plump condition; he glanced at his two cows, cropping the grass in the little meadow, but it did not impress him that they also were in fine condition; nor did he care whether the pasture were good or not. He looked at this; and he looked at that; and then he folded his arms and looked at the distant mountains. Suddenly he turned on his heel, walked straight to the stable, harnessed his mare to the buggy, and, without saying a word to anybody, drove out of the gate, and on to Glenford.

Dick Lancaster, who was in the arbor, looked in amazement after the captain's departing buggy, and old Jane, with tears in her eyes, came out and spoke to him.

"Isn't this dreadful" she said to him. "Supper with that woman and there all night, and back again as soon as he can get off this mornin'!"

"Perhaps he is not going to her house," Dick suggested. "He may have business in town which he forgot yesterday."

"If he'd had it he'd forgot it," replied the old woman. "But he hadn't none. He's gone to Maria Port's, and he may bring her back with him, married tight and fast, for all you or me knows. It would be just like his sailor fashion. When the captain's got anything to do he just does it sharp and quick."

"I don't believe that," said Dick. "If he had had any such intention as that he certainly would have mentioned it to you or to me."

The good woman shook her head. "When an old man marries a girl," she said, "she just leads him wherever she wants him to go, and he gives up everything to her, and when an old man marries a tough and seasoned and smoked old maid like Maria Port, she just drives him wherever she wants him to go, and he hasn't nothin' to say about it. It looks as if she told him to come in this mornin', and he's gone. It may be for a weddin', or it may be for somethin' else, but whatever it is, it'll be her way and not his straight on to the end of the chapter."

Dick had nothing to answer. He was very much afraid that old Jane knew what she was talking about, and his mind was occupied with trying to decide what he, individually, ought to do about it. Old Jane was now obliged to go to the toll-gate to attend to a traveler, but when she came back she took occasion to say a few more words.

"It's hard on me, sir," she said, "at my age to make a change. I've lived at this house, and I've took toll at that gate ever since I was a girl, long before the captain came here, and I've been with him a long time. My people used to own this house, but they all died, and when the place was sold and the captain bought it, he heard about me, and he said I should always have charge of the old toll-gate when he wasn't attendin' to it himself, just the same as when my father was alive and was toll-gate keeper, and I was helpin' him. But I've got to go now, and where I'm goin' to is more'n I know. But I'd rather go to the county poorhouse than stay here, or anywhere else, with Maria Port. She's a regular boa-constrictor, that woman is!

Frank R. Stockton

She's twisted herself around people before this and squeezed the senses out of them; and that's exactly what she's doin' with the captain. If she could come here to live and bring her old father, and get him to sell the house in town and put the money in bank, and then if she could worry her husband and her father both to death, and work things so she'd be a widow with plenty of money and a good house and as much farm land as she wanted, and a toll-gate where she could set all day and take toll and give back lies and false witness as change, she'd be the happiest woman on earth."

It had been long since old Jane had said as much at any one time to any one person, but her mind was stirred. Her life was about to change, and the future was very black to her.

When dinner was ready the captain had not yet returned, and Dick ate his meal by himself. He was now beginning to feel used to this sort of thing. He had scarcely finished, and gone down to the garden-gate to look once more over the road toward Glenford, when the man in the buggy arrived, and he received Mrs. Easterfield's letter.

He lost no moments in making up his mind. He would go to Broadstone, of course, and he did not think it at all necessary to stand on ceremony with the captain. The latter had gone off and left him without making any statement whatever, but he would do better, and he wrote a note explaining the state of affairs. As he was leaving old Jane came to bid him good-by.

"I don't know," said she, "that you will find me here when you come back. The fact of it is I don't know nothin'. But one thing's certain, if she's here I ain't, and if she's too high and mighty to take toll in her honeymoon, the captain'll have to do it himself, or let 'em pass through free."

Mrs. Easterfield was on the lawn when Lancaster arrived, and in answer to the involuntary glance with which Dick's eyes swept the surrounding space, even while he was shaking hands with her, she said: "No, she is not here. She has gone boating, and so you must come and tell me everything, and then we can decide what is best to tell her."

For an instant Dick's soul demurred. If he told Olive anything he would tell her all he knew, and exactly what had happened. But he would not lose faith in this noble woman who was going to help him with Olive if she could. So they sat down, side by side, and he told her everything he knew about Captain Asher and Miss Port.

"It does look very much as if he were going to marry the woman," said Mrs. Easterfield. Then she sat silent and looked upon the ground, a frown upon her face.

Dick was also silent, and his countenance was clouded. "Poor Olive," he thought, "it is hard that this new trouble should come upon her just at this time."

But Mrs. Easterfield said in her heart: "Poor fellow, how little you know what has come upon you! The woman who has turned her uncle from Olive has turned Olive from you."

"Well," said the lady at length, "do you think it is worth while to say anything to her about it? She has already surmised the state of affairs, and, so far as I can see, you have nothing of importance to tell her."

"Perhaps not," said Dick, "but as she sent me on a mission I want to make known to her the result of it so far as there has been any result. It will be very unpleasant, of course—it will be even painful—but I wish to do it all the same."

"That is to say," said Mrs. Easterfield with a smile that was not very cheerful, "you want to be with her, to look at her and to speak to her, no matter how much it may pain her or you to do it."

"That's it," answered Dick.

Mrs. Easterfield sat and reflected. She very much liked this young man, and, considering herself as his friend, were there not some things she ought to tell him? She concluded that there were such things.

"Mr. Lancaster," she said, "have you noticed that there are other young men in love with Miss Asher?"

"I know there is one," said Dick, "for he told me so himself."

"That was Claude Locker?" said she with interest.

"And he promised," continued Dick, "that if he failed he would do all he could to help me. I can not say that this is really for love of me, for his avowed object is to prevent Mr. Du Brant from getting her. We assumed that he was her lover, although I do not know that there is any real ground for it."

"There is very good ground for it," said she, "for he has already proposed to her. What do you think of that?"

"It makes no difference to me," said Dick; "that is, if he has not been accepted. What I want is to find myself warranted in telling Miss Asher how I feel toward her; it does not matter to me how the rest of the world feels."

"Then there is another," said Mrs. Easterfield, "with whom she is now on the river—Mr. Hemphill. He is in love with her; and as he can not stay here very long, I think he will soon propose."

"I can not help it," said Dick; "I love her, and the great object of my life just at present is to tell her so. You said you would help me, and I hope you will not withdraw from that promise."

"No, indeed," said she, "but I do not know her as well as I thought I did. But here she comes now, and without the young man. I hope she has not drowned him!"

Without heeding anything that had just been said to him Dick kept his eyes fixed upon the sparkling girl who now approached them. Every step she made was another link in his chain; Mrs. Easterfield glanced at him and knew this. She pitied him for what he had to tell her now, and more for what he might have to hear from her at another time. But Olive saved Dick from any present ordeal. She stepped up to him and offered him her hand.

"I do not wonder, Mr. Lancaster," she said, "that you did not want to come back and tell me your doleful story, but as I know what it is, we need not say anything about it now, except that I am ever so much obliged to you for all your kindness to me. And now I am going to ask another favor. Won't you let me speak to Mrs. Easterfield a few moments?"

As soon as they were seated, with the door shut, Olive began.

"Well," said she, "he has proposed."

"Mr. Hemphill!" exclaimed Mrs. Easterfield.

"Rupert," Olive answered, "yes, it is truly Rupert who proposed to me."

"I declare," cried Mrs. Easterfield, "you come to me and tell me this as if it were a piece of glad news. Yesterday, and even this morning, you were plunged in grief, and now your eyes shine as if you were positively happy."

"I have told you my aim and object in life," said the girl. "I am trying to do something, and to do it soon, and everything is going on smoothly. And as to being happy, I tell you, Mrs. Easterfield, there is no woman alive who could help being made happy by such a declaration as I have just received. No matter what answer she gave him, she would be bound to be happy."

"Most other women would not have let him make it," said

Mrs. Easterfield a little severely.

"There is something in that," said Olive, "but they would not have the object in life I have. I may be unduly exalted, but you would not wonder at it if you had seen him and heard him. Mrs. Easterfield, that man loves me exactly as I used to love him, and he has told me his love just as I would have told him mine if I could have carried out the wish of my heart. His eyes glowed, his frame shook with the ardor of his passion. Two or three times I had to tell him that if he did not trim boat we should be upset. I never saw anything like his impassioned vehemence. It reminded me of Salvini. I never was loved like that before."

"And what answer did you make to him?" asked Mrs. Easterfield, her voice trembling.

"I did not make him any. It would not have been fair to the others or to myself to do that. I shall not swerve from my purpose, but I shall not be rash."

Mrs. Easterfield rose suddenly and stepped to the open window; she could not sit still a moment longer; she needed air. "Olive," she said, "this is mad and wicked folly in you, and it is impertinent in him, no matter how much you encouraged him. I would like to send him back to his desk this minute. He has no right to come to his employer's house and behave in this manner."

Olive did not get angry. "He is not impertinent," said she. "He knows nothing in this world but that I once loved him, and that now he loves me. Employer and employee are nothing to him. I don't believe he would go if you told him to, even if you could do such a thing, which I don't believe you would, for, of course, you would think of me as well as of him."

"Olive Asher," cried Mrs. Easterfield in a voice which was almost a wail, "do you mean to say that you are to be considered in this matter, that for a moment you think of marrying this man?"

"Yes," said Olive; "I do think of it, and the more I think of it the better I think of it. He is a good man; you have told me that yourself; and I can feel that he is good. I know he loves me. There can be no mistake about his words and his eyes. I feel as I never felt toward any other man, that I might become attached to him. And in my opinion a real attachment is the foundation of love, and you must never forget that I once loved him." The girl now stepped close to Mrs. Easterfield. "I am sorry to see those tears," she said; "I did not come here to make you unhappy."

"But you have made me very unhappy," said the elder lady, "and I do not think I can talk any more about this now."

When Olive had gone Mrs. Easterfield hurried down-stairs in search of Lancaster. She did not care what any one might think of her unconventional eagerness; she wanted to find him, and she soon succeeded. He was sitting in the shade with a book, which, when she approached him, she did not believe he was reading.

"Yes," said she, as he started to his feet in evident concern, "I have been crying, and there is no use in trying to conceal it. Of course, it is about Olive, but I can not confide in you now, and I do not know that I have any right to do so, anyway. But I came here to beg you most earnestly not to propose to Miss Asher, no matter how good an opportunity you may have, no matter how much you want to do so, no matter how much hope may spring up in your heart."

"Do you mean," said Dick, "that I must never speak to her? Am I too late? Is she lost to me?"

"Not at all," said she, "you are not too late, but you may be too early. She is not lost to anybody, but if you should speak to her before I tell you to she will certainly be lost to you."

CHAPTER XX

MR. LOCKER DETERMINES TO RUSH THE ENEMY'S POSITION

The party at Broadstone was not in what might be called a congenial condition. There were among them elements of unrest which prevented that assimilation which is necessary to social enjoyment. Even the ordinarily placid Mr. Fox was dissatisfied. The trouble with him was—although he did not admit it—that he missed the company of Miss Asher. He had found her most agreeable and inspiriting, but now things had changed, and he did not seem to have any opportunity for the lively chats of a few days before. He remarked to his wife that he thought Broadstone was getting very dull, and he should be rather glad when the time came for them to leave. Mrs. Fox was not of his opinion; she enjoyed the state of affairs more than she had done when her husband had been better pleased. There was something going on which she did not understand, and she wanted to find out what it was. It concerned Miss Asher and one of the young men, but which one she could not decide. In any case it troubled Mrs. Easterfield, and that was interesting.

Claude Locker seemed to be a changed man; he no longer made jokes or performed absurdities. He had become wonderfully vigilant, and seemed to be one who continually bided his time. He bided it so much that he was of very little use as a member of the social circle.

Mr. Du Brant was also biding his time, but he did not make the fact evident. He was very vigilant also, but was very quiet, and kept himself in the background. He had seen Olive and Mr. Hemphill go out in the boat, but he determined totally to ignore that interesting occurrence. The moment he had an opportunity he would speak to Olive again, and the existence of other people did not concern him.

Mr. Hemphill was walking by the river; Olive had not allowed him to come to the house with her, for his face was so radiant with the ecstasy of not having been discarded by her that she did not wish him to be seen. From her window Mrs. Easterfield saw this young man on his return from his promenade, and she knew it would not be many minutes before he would reach the house. She also saw the diplomat, who was glaring across the grounds at some one, probably Mr. Locker, who, not unlikely, was glaring back at him. She had come up-stairs to do some writing, but now she put down her pen and called to her secretary.

"Miss Raleigh," said she, "it has been a good while since you have done anything for me."

"Indeed it has," said the other with a sigh.

"But I want you to do something this minute. It is strictly confidential business. I want you to go down on the lawn, or any other place where Miss Asher may be, and make yourself *mal a propos*. I am busy now, but I will relieve you before very long. Can you do that? Do you understand?"

The aspect of the secretary underwent a total change. From a dull, heavy-eyed woman she became an intent, an eager emissary. Her hands trembled with the intensity of her desire to meddle with the affairs of others.

"Of course I understand," she exclaimed, "and I can do it. You mean you don't want any of those young men to get a chance to speak to Miss Asher. Do you include Mr. Lancaster? Or

Frank R. Stockton

shall I only keep off the others?"

"I include all of them," said Mrs. Easterfield. "Don't let any of them have a chance to speak to her until I can come down. And hurry! Here is one coming now."

Hurrying down-stairs, the secretary glanced into the library. There she saw Mrs. Fox in one armchair, and Olive in another, both reading. In the hall were the two little girls, busily engaged in harnessing two small chairs to a large armchair by means of a ball of pink yarn. Outside, about a hundred yards away, she saw Mr. Hemphill irresolutely approaching the house. Miss Raleigh's mind, frequently dormant, was very brisk and lively when she had occasion to waken it. She made a dive toward the children.

"Dear little ones," she cried, "don't you want to come out under the trees and have the good Mr. Hemphill tell you a story? I know he wants to tell you one, and it is about a witch and two pussy-cats and a kangaroo. Come along. He is out there waiting for us." Down dropped the ball of yarn, and with exultant cries each little girl seized an outstretched hand of the secretary, and together they ran over the grass to meet the good Mr. Hemphill.

Of course he was obliged to want to tell them a story; they expected it of him, and they were his employer's children. To be sure he had on mind something very practical and sensible he wished to say to Miss Olive, which had come to him during his solitary walk, and which he did not believe she would object to hearing, although he had said so much to her quite recently. As soon as he should begin to speak she would know that this was something she ought to know. It was about his mother, who had an income of her own, and did not in the least depend upon her son. Miss Olive would certainly agree with him that it was proper for him to tell her this.

But the little girls seized his hands and led him away to a bench, where, having seated him almost forcibly, each climbed upon a knee. The good Mr. Hemphill sent a furtive glare after Miss Raleigh, who, with that smile of gentle gratification which comes to one after having just done a good deed to another, sauntered slowly away.

"Don't come back again," cried out the older of the little girls. "He was put out in the last story, and we want this to be a long one. And remember, Mr, Rupert, it is to be about a witch and two pussy-cats—"

"And a kangaroo," added the other.

At the front door the secretary met Miss Asher, just emerging. "Isn't that a pretty picture" she said, pointing to the group under the trees.

Olive looked at them and smiled. "It is beautiful," she said; "a regular family composition. I wish I had a kodak."

"Oh, that would never do!" exclaimed Miss Raleigh. "He is just as sensitive as he can be, and, of course, it's natural. And the dear little things are so glad to get him to themselves so that they can have one of the long, long stories they like so much. May I ask what that is you are working, Miss Asher?"

"It is going to be what they call a nucleus," said Olive, showing a little piece of fancy work. "You first crochet this, and then its ultimate character depends on what you may put around it. It may be a shawl, or a table cover, or even an apron, if you like crocheted aprons. I learned the stitch last winter. Would you like me to show it to you?"

"I should like it above all things," said the secretary. And together they walked to a rustic bench quite away from the story-telling group. "So far I have done nothing but nucleuses," said Olive, as they sat down. "I put them away when they are finished, and then I suppose some time I shall take up one and make it into something."

"Like those pastry shells," said Miss Raleigh, "which can be laid away and which you can fill up with preserves or jam whenever you want a pie. How many of these have you, Miss Asher?"

"When this is finished there will be four," said Olive.

At some distance, and near the garden, Dick Lancaster, strolling eastward, encountered Claude Locker, strolling westward.

"Hello!" cried Locker. "I am glad to see you. Brought your baggage with you this time, I see. That means you are going to stay, of course."

"A couple of days," replied Dick.

"Well, a man can do a lot in that time, and you may have something to do, but I am not sure. No, sir," continued Locker, "I am not sure. I am on the point of making a demonstration in force. But the enemy is always presenting some new force. By enemy you understand me to mean that which I adore above all else in the world, but which must be attacked, and that right soon if her defenses are to be carried. Step this way a little, and look over there. Do you see that Raleigh woman sitting on a bench with her? Well, now, if I had not had such a beastly generous disposition I might be sitting on that bench this minute. I was deceived by a feint of the opposing forces this morning. I don't mean she deceived me. I did it myself. Although I had the right by treaty to march in upon her, I myself offered to establish a truce in order that she might bury her dead. I did not know who had been killed, but it looked as if there were losses of some kind. But it was a false alarm. The dead must have turned up only missing, and she was as lively as a cricket at luncheon, and went out in a boat with that tailor's model—sixteen dollars and forty-eight cents for the entire suit ready-made; or twenty-three dollars made to order."

Dick smiled a little, but his soul rebelled within him. He

regretted that he had given his promise to Mrs. Easterfield. What he wanted to do that moment was to go over to Captain Asher's niece and ask her to take a walk with him. What other man had a better right to speak to her than he had? But he respected his word; it would be very hard to break a promise made to Mrs. Easterfield; and he stood with his hands in his pockets, and his brows knit.

"Now, I tell you what I am going to do," said Locker. "I am going to wait a little while—a very little while—and then I shall bounce over my earthworks, and rush her position. It is the only way to do it, and I shall be up and at her with cold steel. And now I will tell you what you must do. Just you hold yourself in reserve; and, if I am routed, you charge. You'd better do it if you know what's good for you, for that Austrian's over there pulverizing his teeth and swearing in French because that Raleigh woman doesn't get up and go. Now, I won't keep you any longer, but don't go far away. I can't talk any more, for I've got to have every eye fixed upon the point of attack."

Dick looked at the animated face of his companion, and began to ask himself if the moment had not arrived when even a promise made to Mrs. Easterfield might be disregarded. Should he consent to allow his fate to depend upon the fortunes of Mr. Locker? He scorned the notion. It would be impossible for the girl who had talked so sweetly, so earnestly, so straight from her heart, when he had met her on the shunpike, to marry such a mountebank as this fellow, generous as he might be with that which could never belong to him. As to the diplomat, he did not condescend to bestow a thought upon such a black-pointed little foreigner.

Frank R. Stockton

CHAPTER XXI

MISS RALEIGH ENJOYS A RARE PRIVILEGE

Miss Raleigh was very attentive to the instructions given her by Miss Asher, and while she exhibited the fashion of the new stitch Olive reflected.

"I wonder," she said to herself, "if Mrs. Easterfield has done this. It looks very much like it, and if she did I am truly obliged to her. There is nothing I want so much now as a rest, and I didn't want to stay in the house either. Miss Raleigh," said she, suddenly changing the subject, "were you ever in love?"

The secretary started. "What do you mean by that?" she asked.

"I don't mean anything," said Olive. "I simply wanted to know."

"It is a queer question," said Miss Raleigh, her face changing to another shade of sallowness.

"I know that," said Olive quickly, "but the answers to queer questions are always so much more interesting than those to any others. Don't you think so?"

"Yes, they are," said Miss Raleigh thoughtfully, "but they are generally awfully hard to get. I have tried it myself."

"Then you ought to have a fellow feeling for me," said Olive.

"Well," said the other, looking steadfastly at her companion, "if you will promise to keep it all to yourself forever, I don't mind telling you that I was once in love. Would you like me to tell you who I was in love with?"

"Yes," said Olive, "if you are willing to tell me."

"Oh, I am perfectly willing," said the secretary. "It was Mr. Hemphill."

Olive turned suddenly and looked at her in amazement.

"Yes, it was Mr. Hemphill over there," said the other, speaking very tranquilly, as if the subject were of no importance. "You see, I have been living with the Easterfields for a long time, and in the winter we see a good deal of Mr. Hemphill. He has to come to the house on business, and often takes meals. He is Mr. Easterfield's private and confidential secretary. And, somehow or other, seeing him so often, and sometimes being his partner at cards when two were needed to make up a game, I forgot that I was older than he, and I actually fell in love with him. You see he has a good heart, Miss Asher; anybody could tell that from his way with children; and I have noticed that bachelors are often nicer with children than fathers are."

"And he?" asked Olive.

Miss Raleigh laughed a little laugh. "Oh, I did all the loving," she answered. "He never reciprocated the least little bit, and I often wondered why I adored him as much as I did. He was handsome, and he was good, and he had excellent taste; he was thoroughly trustworthy in his relations to the family, and I believe he would be equally so in all relations of life; but all that did not account for my unconquerable ardor, which was caused by a certain something which you know, Miss Asher, we can't explain."

Frank R. Stockton

Olive tried hard not to allow any emotion to show itself in her face, but she did not altogether succeed. "And you still—" said she.

"No, I don't," interrupted Miss Raleigh. "I love him no longer. There came a time when all my fire froze. I discovered that there was—"

"I say, Miss Asher—" it was the voice of Claude Locker.

Olive looked around at him. "Well?" said she.

"Perhaps you have not noticed," said he, "that the tennis ground is now in the shade, and if you don't mind walking that way—" He said a good deal more which Miss Raleigh did not believe, understanding the young man thoroughly, and which Olive did not hear. Her mind was very busy with what she had just heard, which made a great impression on her. She did not know whether she was affronted, or hurt, or merely startled.

Here was a man who loved her, a man she had loved, and one about whom she had been questioning herself as to the possibility of her loving him again. And here was a woman, a dyspeptic, unwholesome spinster, who had just said she had loved him. If Miss Raleigh had loved this man, how could she, Olive, love him? There was something repugnant about it which she did not attempt to understand. It went beyond reason. She felt it to be an actual relief to look up at Claude Locker, and to listen to what he was saying.

"You mean," said she presently, "that you would like Miss Raleigh and me to come with you and play tennis."

"I did not know Miss Raleigh played," he answered, "but I thought perhaps—"

"Oh, no," said Olive. "I would not think of such a thing. In fact, Miss Raleigh and I are engaged. We are very busy about some important work."

Mr. Locker gazed at the crocheted nucleus with an air of the loftiest disdain. "Of course, of course," said he, "but you really oblige me, Miss Asher, to speak very plainly and frankly and to say that I really do not care about playing tennis, but that I want to speak to you on a most important subject, which, for reasons that I will explain, must be spoken of immediately. So, if Miss Raleigh will be kind enough to postpone the little matter you have on hand—"

Olive smiled and shook her head. "No, indeed, sir," she said; "I would not hurt a lady's feelings in that way, and moreover, I would not allow her to hurt her own feelings. It would hurt your feelings, Miss Raleigh, wouldn't it, to be sent away like a child who is not wanted?"

"Yes," said the secretary, "I think it would."

Mr. Locker listened in amazement. He had not thought the mature maiden had the nerve to say that.

"Then again," said Olive, "this isn't the time for you to talk business with me, and you should not disturb me at this hour."

"Oh," said Locker, bringing down the forefinger of his right hand upon the palm of his left, "that is a point, a very essential point. I voluntarily surrendered the period of discourse which you assigned to me for a reason which I now believe did not exist, and this is only an assertion of the rights vested in me by you."

Miss Raleigh listened very attentively to these remarks, but could not imagine what they meant.

Olive looked at him graciously. "Yes," she said, "you are very generous, but your period for discourse, as you call it, will have to be postponed."

Frank R. Stockton

"But it can't be postponed," he answered. "If I could see you alone I could soon explain that to you. There are certain reasons why I must speak now."

"I can't help it," said Olive. "I am not going to leave Miss Raleigh, and I am sure she does not want to leave me, so if you are obliged to speak you must speak before her."

Mr. Locker gazed from one to the other of the two ladies who sat before him; each of them wore a gentle but determined expression. He addressed the secretary.

"Miss Raleigh," said he, "if you understood the reason for my strong desire to speak in private with Miss Asher, perhaps you would respect it and give me the opportunity I ask for. I am here to make a proposition of marriage to this lady, and it is absolutely necessary that I make it without loss of time. Do you desire me to make it in your presence?"

"I should like it very much," said Miss Raleigh.

Mr. Locker gave her a look of despair, and turned to Olive. "Would you permit that?" he asked.

"If it is absolutely necessary," she said, "I suppose I shall have to permit it."

Mr. Locker had the soul of a lion in his somewhat circum-scribed body, and he was not to be recklessly dared to action.

"Very well, then," said he, "I shall proceed as if we were alone, and I hope, Miss Raleigh, you will at least see fit to consider yourself in a strictly confidential position."

"Indeed I shall," she replied; "not one word shall ever—"

"I hope not," interrupted Claude, "and I will add that if I should ever be accidentally present when a gentleman is about to propose to you, Miss Raleigh, I shall heap coals of fire upon your head by instantaneously withdrawing."

The secretary was about to thank him, but Olive interrupted. "Now, Claude Locker," said she, "what can you possibly have to say to me that you have not said before?"

"A good deal, Miss Asher, a good deal, although I don't wonder you suppose that no man could say more to you of his undying affection than I have already said. But, since I last spoke on the subject, I have been greatly impressed by the fact that I have not said enough about myself; that I have not made you understand me as I really am. I know very well that most people, and I suppose that at some time you have been among them, look upon me as a very frivolous young man, and not one to whom the right sort of a girl should give herself in marriage. But that is a mistake. I am as much to be depended upon as anybody you ever met. My apparently whimsical aspect is merely the outside—my shell, marked off in queer designs with variegated colors—but within that shell I am as domestic, as sober, and as surely to be found where I am expected to be as any turtle. This may seem a queer figure, but it strikes me as a very good one. When I am wanted I am there. You can always depend upon me."

There was not a smile upon the face of either woman as he spoke. They were listening earnestly, and with the deepest interest. Miss Raleigh's eyes sparkled, and Olive seemed to be most seriously considering this new aspect in which Mr. Locker was endeavoring to place himself.

"Perhaps you may think," Claude continued, "that you would not desire turtle-like qualities in a husband, you who are so bright, so bounding, so much like a hare, but I assure you, that is just the companion who would suit you. All day you might skip among the flowers, and in the fields, and wherever you were, you would always know where I was—making a steady bee-line for home; and you would know that I would be there to welcome you when you arrived."

"That is very pretty!" said Miss Raleigh. And then she quickly added: "Excuse me for making a remark."

"Now, Miss Asher," continued Locker, "I have tried, very imperfectly, I know, to make you see me as I really am, and I do hope you can put an end to this suspense which is keeping me in a nervous tingle. I can not sleep at night, and all day I am thinking what you will say when you do decide. You need not be afraid to speak out before Miss Raleigh. She is in with us now, and she can't get out. I would not press you for an answer at this moment, but there are reasons which I can not say anything about without meddling with other people's business. But my business with you is the happiness of my life, and I feel that I can not longer endure having it momentarily jeopardized."

At the conclusion of this speech a faint color actually stole into Miss Raleigh's face, and she clasped her thin hands in the intensity of her approval.

"Mr. Locker," said Olive, speaking very pleasantly, "if you had come to me to-day and had asked me for a decision based upon what you had already said to me, I think I might have settled the matter. But after what you have just told me, I can not answer you now. You give me things to think about, and I must wait."

"Heavens" exclaimed Mr. Locker, clasping his hands. "Am I not yet to know whether I am to rise into paradise, or to sink into the infernal regions?"

Olive smiled. "Don't do either, Mr. Locker," she said. "This earth is a very pleasant place. Stay where you are."

He folded his arms and gazed at her. "It is a pleasant place," said he, "and I am mighty glad I got in my few remarks before you made your decision. I leave my love with you on approbation, and you may be sure I shall come to-morrow before luncheon to hear what you say about it."

"I shall expect you," said Olive. And as she spoke her eyes were full of kind consideration.

"Now, that's genuine," said Miss Raleigh, when Locker had departed. "If he had not felt every word he said he could not have said it before me."

"No doubt you are right," said Olive. "He is very brave. And now you see this new line, which begins an entirely different kind of stitch!"

In the middle distance Mr. Du Brant still strolled backward and forward, pulverizing his teeth and swearing in French. He seldom removed his eyes from Miss Asher, but still she sat on that bench and crocheted, and talked, and talked, and crocheted, with that everlasting Miss Raleigh! He had seen Locker with her, and he had seen him go; and now he hoped that the woman would soon depart. Then it would be his chance.

The young Austrian had become most eager to make Olive his wife. He earnestly loved her; and, beyond that, he had come to see that a marriage with her would be most advantageous to his prospects. This beautiful and brilliant American girl, familiar with foreign life and foreign countries, would give him a position in diplomatic society which would be most desirable. She might not bring him much money; although he believed that all American girls had some money; but she would bring him favor, distinction, and, most likely, advancement. With such a wife he would be a welcome envoy at any court. And, besides, he loved her. But, alas, Miss Raleigh would not go away.

About half an hour after Claude Locker left Olive he encountered Dick Lancaster.

"Well," said he, "I charged. I was not routed, I can't say that I was even repulsed. But I was obliged to withdraw my forces. I shall go into camp, and renew the attack to-morrow. So, my friend, you will have to wait. I wish I could say that there is no use of your waiting, but I am a truthful person and can't do that."

Lancaster was not pleased. "It seems to me," he said, "that you trifle with the most important affairs of life."

"Trifle!" exclaimed Locker. "Would you call it trifling if I fail, and then to save her from a worse fate, were to back you up with all my heart and soul?"

Dick could not help smiling. "By a worse fate," he said, "I suppose you mean—"

"The Austrian," interrupted Locker. "Mrs. Easterfield has told me something about him. He may have a title some day, and he is about as dangerous as they make them. Instead of accusing me of trifling, you ought to go down on your knees and thank me for still standing between him and her."

"That is a duty I would like to perform myself," said Dick.

"Perhaps you may have a chance," sighed Locker, "but I most earnestly hope not. Look over there at that he-nurse. Those children have made him take them walking, and he is just coming back to the house."

CHAPTER XXII

THE CONFLICTING SERENADES

Mrs. Easterfield worked steadily at her letter, feeling confident all the time that her secretary was attending conscientiously to the task which had been assigned to her, and which could not fail to be a most congenial one. One of the greatest joys of Miss Raleigh's life was to interfere in other people's business; and to do it under approval and with the feeling that it was her duty was a rare joy.

The letter was to her husband, and Mrs. Easterfield was writing it because she was greatly troubled, and even frightened. In the indulgence of a good-humored and romantic curiosity to know whether or not a grown-up young woman would return to a sentimental attachment of her girlhood, she had brought her husband's secretary to the house with consequences which were appalling. If this navy girl she had on hand had been a mere flirt, Mrs. Easterfield, an experienced woman of society, might not have been very much troubled, but Olive seemed to her to be much more than a flirt; she would trifle until she made up her mind, but when she should come to a decision Mrs. Easterfield believed she would act fairly and squarely. She wanted to marry; and, in her heart, Mrs. Easterfield commended her; without a mother; now more than ever without a father; her only near relative about to marry a woman who was certainly a most undesirable connection; Olive was surely right in wishing to settle in life. And, if piqued and affronted by her father's intended marriage, she wished immediately to declare her independence, the girl could not be blamed. And, from what she had said of Mr. Hemphill, Mrs. Easterfield could not in her own mind dissent. He was a good young man; he had an excellent position; he fervently loved Olive; she had loved him, and might do it again. What was there to which she could object? Only this: it angered and frightened her to think of Olive Asher throwing herself away upon Rupert Hemphill. So she wrote a very strong letter to her husband, representing to him that the danger was very great and imminent, and that he was needed at Broadstone just as soon as he could get there. Business could be set aside; his wife's happiness was at stake; for if this unfortunate match should be made, it would be her doing, and it would cloud her whole life. Of herself she did not know what to do, and if she had known, she could not have done it. But if he came he would not only know everything, but could do anything. This indicated her general opinion of Mr. Tom Easterfield.

"Now," said she to herself, as she fixed an immediate-delivery stamp upon the letter, "that ought to bring him here before lunch to-morrow."

When Olive saw fit to go to her room Miss Raleigh felt relieved from guard, and went to Mrs. Easterfield to report. She told that lady everything that had happened, even including her own emotions at various points of the interview. The amazed Mrs. Easterfield listened with the greatest interest.

"I knew Claude Locker was capable of almost any wild proceeding," she said, "but I did not think he would do that!"

"There is one thing I forgot," said the secretary, "and that is that I promised Mr. Locker not to mention a word of what happened."

"I am very glad," replied Mrs. Easterfield, "that you remembered that promise after you told me everything, and not before. You have done admirably so far."

"And if I have any other opportunities of interpolating myself, so to speak," said Miss Raleigh, "shall I embrace them?"

Mrs. Easterfield laughed. "I don't want you to be too obviously zealous," she answered. "I think for the present we may relax our efforts to relieve Miss Asher of annoyance." Mrs. Easterfield believed this. She had faith in Olive; and if that young woman had promised to give Claude Locker another hearing the next day she did not believe that the girl would give anybody else a positive answer before that time.

Miss Raleigh went away not altogether satisfied. She did not believe in relaxed vigilance; for one thing, it was not interesting.

Olive was surprised when she found that Mr. Lancaster was to stay to dinner, and afterward when she was informed that he had been invited to spend a few days, she reflected. It looked like some sort of a plan, and what did Mrs. Easterfield mean by it? She knew the lady of the house had a very good opinion of the young professor, and that might explain the invitation at this particular moment, but still it did look like a plan, and as Olive had no sympathy with plans of this sort she determined not to trouble her head about it. And to show her non-concern, she was very gracious to Mr. Lancaster, and received her reward in an extremely interesting conversation.

Still Olive reflected, and was not in her usual lively spirits. Mr. Fox said to Mrs. Fox that it was an abominable shame to allow a crowd of incongruous young men to swarm in upon a country house party, and interfere seriously with the pleasures of intelligent and self-respecting people.

That night, after Mrs. Easterfield had gone to bed, and before she slept, she heard something which instantly excited her attention; it was the sound of a guitar, and it came from the lawn in front of the house. Jumping up, and throwing a dressing-gown about her, she cautiously approached the open window. But the night was dark, and she could see nothing.

Pushing an armchair to one side of the window, she seated herself, and listened. Words now began to mingle with the music, and these words were French. Now she understood everything perfectly. Mr. Du Brant was a musician, and had helped himself to the guitar in the library.

From the position in which she sat Mrs. Easterfield could look upon a second-story window in a projecting wing of the house, and upon this window, which belonged to Olive's room, and which was barely perceptible in the gloom, she now fixed her eyes. The song and the thrumming went on, but no signs of life could be seen in the black square of that open window.

Mrs. Easterfield was not a bad French scholar, and she caught enough of the meaning of the words to understand that they belonged to a very pretty love song in which the flowers looked up to the sky to see if it were blue, because they knew if it were the fair one smiled, and then their tender buds might ope; and, if she smiled, his heart implored that she might smile on him. There was a second verse, much resembling the first, except that the flowers feared that clouds might sweep the sky; and they lamented accordingly.

Now, Mrs. Easterfield imagined that she saw something white in the depths of the darkness of Olive's room, but it did not come to the front, and she was very uncertain about it. Suddenly, however, something happened about which she could not be in the least uncertain. Above Olive's room was a chamber appropriated to the use of bachelor visitors, and from the window of this room now burst upon the night a wild, unearthly chant. It was a song with words but without music, and the voice in which it was shot out into the darkness was harsh, was shrill, was insolently blatant. And thus the clamorous singer sang:

"My angel maid—ahoy!
If aught should you annoy,
By act or sound,

From sky or ground,
I then pray thee
To call on me
My angel maid—ahoy,
My ange—my ange—l maid
Ahoy! Ahoy! Ahoy!"

The music of the guitar now ceased, and no French words
were heard. No ditty of Latin origin, be it ever so melodious
and fervid, could stand against such a wild storm of Anglo-
Saxon vociferation. Every ahoy rang out as if sea captains were
hailing each other in a gale!

"What lungs he has" thought Mrs. Easterfield, as she put her
hand over her mouth so that no one should hear her laugh. At
the open window, at which she still steadily gazed, she now felt
sure she saw something white which moved, but it did not
come to the front.

A wave of half-smothered objurgation now rolled up from
below; it was not to be readily caught, but its tone indicated
rage and disappointment. But the guitar had ceased to sound,
and the French love song was heard no more. A little irrepres-
sible laugh came from somewhere, but who heard it beside
herself Mrs. Easterfield could not know. Then all was still, and
the insects of the night, and the tree frogs, had the stage to
themselves.

Early in the morning Miss Raleigh presented herself before
Mrs. Easterfield to make a report. "There was a serenade last
night," she said, "not far from Miss Asher's window. In fact,
there were two, but one of them came from Mr. Locker's
room, and was simply awful. Mr. Du Brant was the gentleman
who sang from the lawn, and I was very sorry when he felt
himself obliged to stop. I do not think very much of him, but
he certainly has a pleasant voice, and plays well on the guitar. I
think he must have been a good deal cut up by being
interrupted in that dreadful way, for he grumbled and growled,
and did not go into the house for some time. I am sure he

Frank R. Stockton

would have been very glad to fight if any one had come down."

"You mean," said Mrs. Easterfield, "if Mr. Locker had come."

"Well," said the secretary, "if Mr. Hemphill had appeared I have no doubt he would have answered. Mr. Du Brant seemed to me ready to fight anybody."

"How do you know so much about him?" asked Mrs. Easterfield. "And why did you think of Mr. Hemphill?"

"Oh, he was looking out of his window," said Miss Raleigh. "He could not see, but he could hear."

"I ask you again," said Mrs. Easterfield, "how do you know all this?"

"Oh, I had not gone to bed, and, at the first sound of the guitar, I slipped on a waterproof with a hood, and went out. Of course, I wanted to know everything that was happening."

"I had not the least idea you were such an energetic person," remarked Mrs. Easterfield, "and I think you were entirely too rash. But how about Mr. Lancaster? Do you know if he was listening?"

Miss Raleigh stood silent for a moment, then she exclaimed: "There now, it is too bad! I entirely forgot him! I have not the slightest idea whether he was asleep or awake, and it would have been just as easy—"

"Well, you need not regret it," said Mrs. Easterfield. "I think you did quite enough, and if anything of the kind occurs again I positively forbid you to go out of the house."

"There is one thing we've got to look after," said Miss Raleigh, without heeding the last remark, "this may result in bloodshed."

"Nonsense," said Mrs. Easterfield; "nothing of that kind is to be feared from the gentlemen who visit Broadstone."

"Still," said Miss Raleigh, "don't you think it would be well for me to keep an eye on them?"

"Oh, you may keep both eyes on them if you want to," said Mrs. Easterfield. Then she began to talk about something else, but, although she dismissed the matter so lightly, she was very glad at heart that she had sent for her husband. Things were getting themselves into unpleasant complications, and she needed Tom.

There was a certain constraint at the breakfast table. Mr. Fox had heard the serenades, although his consort had slept soundly through the turmoil; and, while carefully avoiding any reference to the incidents of the night, he was anxiously hoping that somebody would say something about them. Mrs. Easterfield saw that Mr. Du Brant was in a bad humor, and she hoped he was angry enough to announce his early departure. But he contented himself with being angry, and said nothing about going away.

Mr. Hemphill was serious, and looked often in the direction of Olive. As for Dick Lancaster, Miss Raleigh, whose eye was fixed upon him whenever it could be spared from the exigencies of her meal, decided that if there should be a fight he would be one of the fighters; his brow was dark and his glance was sharp; in fact, she was of the opinion that he glared. Claude Locker did not come to breakfast until nearly everybody had finished. His dreams had been so pleasant that he had overslept himself.

In the eyes of Mrs. Easterfield Olive's conduct was positively charming. No one could have supposed that during the night she had heard anything louder than the ripple of the river. She talked more to Mr. Du Brant than to any one else, although she managed to draw most of the others into the conversation; and, with the assistance of the hostess, who gave her most

Frank R. Stockton

good-humored help, the talk never flagged, although it did not become of the slightest interest to any one who engaged in it. They were all thinking about the conflict of serenades, and what might happen next.

Shortly after breakfast Miss Raleigh came to Mrs. Easterfield. "Mr. Du Brant is with her," she said quickly, "and they are walking away. Shall I interpolate?"

"No," said the other with a smile, "you can let them alone. Nothing will happen this morning, unless, indeed, he should come to ask for a carriage to take him to the station."

Mrs. Easterfield was busy in her garden when Dick Lancaster came to her. "What a wonderfully determined expression you have!" said she. "You look as if you were going to jump on a street-car without stopping it!"

"You are right," said he, "I am determined, and I came to tell you so. I can't stand this sort of thing any longer. I feel like a child who is told he must eat at the second table, and who can not get his meals until every one else is finished."

"And I suppose," she said, "you feel there will be nothing left for you."

"That is it," he answered, "and I don't want to wait. My soul rebels! I can't stand it!"

"Therefore," she said, "you wish to appear before the meal is ready, and in that case you will get nothing." He looked at her inquiringly. "I mean," said she, "that if you propose to Miss Asher now you will be before your time, and she will decline your proposition without the slightest hesitation."

"I do not quite understand that," said Dick. "Would she decline all others?"

"I am afraid not."

"But why do you except me?" asked Dick. "Surely she is not engaged. I know you would tell me at once if that were so."

"It is not so," said Mrs. Easterfield.

"Then I shall take my chances. With all this serenading and love-making going on around me and around the woman I love with all my heart. I can not stand and wait until I am told my time has come. The intensity and the ardor of my feelings for her give me the right to speak to her. Unless I know that some one else has stepped in before me and taken the place I crave, I have decided to speak to her just as soon as I can. But I thought it was due to you to come first and tell you."

"Mr. Lancaster," said Mrs. Easterfield, speaking very quietly, "if you decide to go to Miss Asher and ask her to marry you, I know you will do it, for I believe you are a man who keeps his word to himself, but I assure you that if you do it you will never marry her. So you really need not bother yourself about going to her; you can simply decide to do it, and that will be quite sufficient; and you can stay here and hold these long-stemmed dahlias for me as I cut them."

A troubled wistfulness showed itself upon the young man's face. "You speak so confidently," he said, "that I almost feel I ought to believe you. Why do you tell me that I am the only one of her suitors who would certainly be rejected if he offered himself?"

Mrs. Easterfield dropped the long-stemmed dahlias she had been holding; and, turning her eyes full upon Lancaster, she said, "Because you are the only one of them toward whom she has no predilections whatever. More than that, you are the only one toward whom she has a positive objection. You are the only one who is an intimate friend of her uncle, and who would be likely, by means of that intimate friendship, to bring her into connection with the woman she hates, as well as with a relative she despises on account of his intended marriage with that woman."

"All that should not count at all," cried Dick. "In such a matter as this I have nothing to do with Captain Asher! I stand for myself and speak for myself. What is his intended wife to me? Or what should she be to her?"

"Of course," said Mrs. Easterfield, "all that would not count at all if Olive Asher loved you. But you see she doesn't. I have had it from her own lips that her uncle's intended marriage is, and must always be, an effectual barrier between you and her."

"What" cried Dick. "Have you spoken to her of me? And in that way?"

"Yes," said Mrs. Easterfield, "I have. I did not intend to tell you, but you have forced me to do it. You see, she is a young woman of extraordinary good sense. She believes she ought to marry, and she is going to try to make the very best marriage that she possibly can. She has suitors who have very strong claims upon her consideration—I am not going to tell you those claims, but I know them. Now, you have no claim—special claim, I mean—but for all this, I believe, as I have told you before, that you are the man she ought to marry, and I have been doing everything I can to make her cease considering them, and to consider you. And this is the way she came to give me her reasons for not considering you at all. Now the state of the case is plain before you."

Dick bowed his head and fixed his eyes upon the dahlias on the ground.

"Don't tread on the poor things," she said, "and don't despair. All you have to do is to let me put a curbed bit on you, and for you to consent to wear it for a little while. See," said she, moving her hands in the air, as if they were engaged upon the bridle of a horse, "I fasten this chain rather closely, and buckle the ends of the reins in the lowest curb. Now, you must have a steady hand and a resolute will until the time comes when the curb is no longer needed."

"And do you believe that time will come?" he asked.

"It will come," she said, "when two things happen; when she has reason to love you, and has no reason to object to you; and, in my opinion, that happy combination may arrive if you act sensibly."

"But—" said Dick.

At this moment a quick step was heard on the garden-path and they both turned. It was Olive.

"Mr. Lancaster," she cried, "I want you; that is, if Mrs. Easterfield can spare you. We are making up a game of tennis. Mr. Du Brant and Mr. Hemphill are there, but I can not find Mr. Locker."

Mrs. Easterfield could spare him, and Dick Lancaster, with the curbed chain pressing him very hard, walked away with Olive Asher.

CHAPTER XXIII

THE CAPTAIN AND MARIA

When the captain drove into Glenford on the day when his mind had been so much disturbed by Dick Lancaster's questions regarding a marriage between him and Maria Port, he stopped at no place of business, he turned not to the right nor to the left, but went directly to the house of his old friend with whom he had spent the night before.

Mr. Simeon Port was sitting on his front porch, reading his newspaper. He looked up, surprised to see the captain again so soon.

"Simeon," said the captain, "I want to see Maria. I have something to say to her."

The old man laid down his newspaper. "Serious?" said he.

"Yes, serious," was the answer, "and I want to see her now."

Mr. Port reflected for a moment. "Captain," said he, "do you believe you have thought about this as much as you ought to?"

"Yes, I have," replied the captain; "I've thought just as much as I ought to. Is she in the house?"

Mr. Port did not answer. "Captain John," said he presently, "Maria isn't young, that's plain enough, considerin' my age;

but she never does seem to me as if she'd growed up. When she was a girl she had ways of her own, and she could make water bile quick, and now she can make it bile just as quick as ever she did, and perhaps quicker. She's not much on mindin' the helm, Captain John, and there're other things about her that wouldn't be attractive to husbands when they come to find them out. And if I was you I'd take my time."

"That's just what I intend to do," said the captain. "This is my time, and I am going to take it."

Miss Port, who was busy in the back part of the house, heard voices, and now came forward. She was wiping her hands upon her apron, and one of them she extended to the captain.

"I am glad to see you—John," she said, speaking in a very gentle voice, and hesitating a little at the last word.

The captain looked at her steadfastly, and then, without taking her hand, he said: "I want to speak to you by yourself. I'll go into the parlor."

She politely stepped back to let him pass her, and then her father turned quickly to her.

"Did you expect to see him back so soon?" he asked.

She smiled and looked down. "Oh, yes," said she, "I was sure he'd come back very soon."

The old man heaved a sigh, and returned to his paper.

Maria followed the captain. "John," said she, speaking in a low voice, "wouldn't you rather come into the dinin'-room? He's a little bit hard of hearin', but if you don't want him to hear anything he'll take in every word of it."

"Maria Port," said the captain, speaking in a strong, upper-deck voice, "what I have to say I'll say here. I don't want the

Frank R. Stockton

people in the street to hear me, but if your father chooses to listen I would rather he did it than not."

She looked at him inquiringly. "Well," she answered, "I suppose he will have to hear it some time or other, and he might as well hear it now as not. He's all I've got in the world, and you know as well as I do that I run to tell him everything that happens to me as soon as it happens. Will you sit down?"

"No," said the captain, "I can speak better standing. Maria Port, I have found out that you have been trying to make people believe that I am engaged to marry you."

The smile did not leave Maria's face. "Well, ain't you?" said she.

A look of blank amazement appeared on the face of the captain, but it was quickly succeeded by the blackness of rage. He was about to swear, but restrained himself.

"Engaged to you?" he shouted, forgetting entirely the people in the street; "I'd rather be engaged to a fin-back shark!"

The smile now left her face. "Oh, thank you very much," she said. "And this is what you meant by your years of devotion! I held out for a long time, knowing the difference in our ages and the habits of sailors, and now—just when I make up my mind to give in, to think of my father and not of myself, and to sacrifice my feelin's so that he might always have one of his old friends near him, now that he's got too feeble to go out by himself, and at his age you know as well as I do he ought to have somebody near him besides me, for who can tell what may happen, or how sudden—you come and tell me you'd rather marry a fish. I suppose you've got somebody else in your mind, but that don't make no difference to me. I've got no fish to offer you, but I have myself that you've wanted so long, and which now you've got."

The angry captain opened his mouth to speak; he was about to ejaculate Woman! but his sense of propriety prevented this. He would not apply such an epithet to any one in the house of a friend. Wretch rose to his lips, but he would not use even that word; and he contented himself with: "You! You know just as well as you know you are standing there that I never had the least idea of marrying you. You know, too, that you have tried to make people think I had, people here in town and people out at my house, where you came over and over again pretending to want to talk about your father's health, when it did not need any more talking about than yours does. You know you have made trouble in my family; that you so disgusted my niece that she would not stop at my house, which had been the same thing as her home; you sickened my friends; and made my very servants ashamed of me; and all this because you want to marry a man who now despises you. I would have despised you long ago if I had seen through your tricks, but I didn't."

There was a smile on Miss Port's face now, but it was not such a smile as that with which she had greeted the captain; it was a diabolical grin, brightened by malice. "You are perfectly right," she said; "everybody knows we are engaged to be married, and what they think about it doesn't matter to me the snap of my finger. The people in town all know it and talk about it, and what's more, they've talked to me about it. That niece of your'n knows it, and that's the reason she won't come near you, and I'm sure I'm not sorry for that. As for that old thing that helps you at the toll-gate, and as for the young man that's spongin' on you, I've no doubt they've got a mighty poor opinion of you. And I've no doubt they're right. But all that matters nothin' to me. You're engaged to be married to me; you know it yourself; and everybody knows it; and what you've got to do is to marry, or pay. You hear what I say, and you know what I'm goin' to stick to."

It may be well for Captain Asher's reputation that he had no opportunity to answer Miss Port's remarks. At that instant Mr. Simeon Port appeared at the door which opened from the parlor on the piazza. He stepped quickly, his actions showing nothing of that decrepitude which his dutiful daughter had feared would prevent him from seeking the society of his friends. He fixed his eyes on his daughter and spoke in a loud, strong voice.

"Maria," said he, "go to bed! I've heard what you've been saying, and I'm ashamed of you. I've been ashamed of you before, but now it's worse than ever. Go to bed, I tell you! And this time, go!"

There was nothing in the world that Maria Port was afraid of except her father, and of him personally she had not the slightest dread. But of his dying without leaving her the whole of his fortune she had an abiding terror, which often kept her awake at night, and which sent a sickening thrill through her whenever a difficulty arose between her and her parent. She was quite sure what he would do if she should offend him sufficiently; he would leave her a small annuity, enough to support her; and the rest of his money would go to several institutions which she had heard him mention in this connection. If she could have married Captain Asher she would have felt a good deal safer; it would have taken much provocation to make her father leave his money out of the family if his old friend had been one of that family.

Now, when she heard her father's voice, and saw his dark eyes glittering at her, she knew she was in great danger, and the well-known chill ran through her. She made no answer; she cared not who was present; she thought of nothing but that those eyes must cease to glitter, and that angry voice must not be heard again. She turned and walked to her room, which was on the same floor, across the hall.

"And mind you go to bed!" shouted her father. "And do it regular. You're not to make believe to go to bed, and then get up and walk about as soon as my back is turned. I'm comin' in presently to see if you've obeyed me."

She answered not, but entered her room, and closed the door

after her.

Mr. Port now turned to the captain. "I never could find out," he said, "where Maria got that mind of her'n. It isn't from my side, for my father and mother was as good people as ever lived, and it wasn't from her mother, for you knew her, and there wasn't anything of the kind about her."

"No," said Captain Asher, "not the least bit of it."

"It must have been from her grandmother Ellis," said the old man. "I never knew her, for she died before I was acquainted with the family, but I expect she died of deviltry. That's the only insight I can get into the reasons for Maria's havin' the mind she's got. But I tell you, Captain John, you've had a blessed escape! I didn't know she was in the habit of goin' out to your house so often. She didn't tell me that."

"Simeon," said the captain, "I think I will go now. I have had enough of Maria. I don't suppose I'll hear from her very soon again."

The old man smiled. "No," said he, "I don't think she'll want to trouble you any more."

Miss Port, whose ear was at the keyhole of her door not twelve feet away, grinned malignantly.

Soon after Captain Asher had gone Mr. Port walked to the door of his daughter's room, gave a little knock, and then opened the door a little.

"You are in bed, are you?" said he. "Well, that's good for you. Turn down that coverlid and let me see if you've got your nightclothes on." She obeyed. "Very well," he continued; "now you stay there until I tell you to get up."

Captain Asher went home, still in a very bad humor. He had ceased to be angry with Maria Port, he was done with her; and

Frank R. Stockton

he let her pass out of his mind. But he was angry with other people, especially with Olive. She had allowed herself to have a most contemptuous opinion of him; she had treated him shamefully; and as he thought of her his indignation increased instead of diminishing. And young Lancaster had believed it! And old Jane! It was enough to make a stone slab angry, and the captain was not a stone slab.

CHAPTER XXIV

MR. TOM ARRIVES AT BROADSTONE

After the conclusion of the game of tennis in which Olive and three of her lovers participated, Claude Locker, returning from a long walk, entered the grounds of Broadstone. He had absented himself from that hospitable domain for purposes of reflection, and also to avoid the company of Mr. Du Brant. Not that he was afraid of the diplomat, but because of the important interview appointed for the latter part of the morning. He very much wished that no unpleasantness of any kind should occur before the time for that interview.

Having found that he had given himself more time than was necessary for his reflections and his walk, he had rested in the shade of a tree and had written two poems. One of these was the serenade which he would have roared out on the night air on a very recent occasion if he had had time to prepare it. It was, in his opinion, far superior to the impromptu verses of which he had been obliged to make use, and it pleased him to think that if things should go well with him after the interview to which he was looking forward, he would read that serenade to its object, and ask her to substitute it in her memory for the inharmonic lines which he had used in order to smother the degenerate melody of a foreign lay. The other poem was intended for use in case his interview should not be successful. But on the way home Mr. Locker experienced an entire change of mind. He came to believe that it would be unwise for him to arrange to use either of those poems on that day. For all he

Frank R. Stockton

knew, Miss Asher might like foreign degenerate lays, and she might be annoyed that he had interfered with one. He remembered that she had told him that if he had insisted on an immediate answer to his proposition it would have been very easy to give it to him. He realized what that meant; and, for all he knew, she might be quite as ready this morning to act with similar promptness. That Du Brant business might have settled her mind, and it would therefore be very well for him to be careful about what he did, and what he asked for.

About half an hour before luncheon, when he neared the house and perceived Miss Asher on the lawn, it seemed to him very much as if she were looking for him. This he did not like, and he hurried toward her.

"Miss Asher," said he, "I wish to propose an amendment."

"To what?" asked Olive. "But first tell me where you have been and what you have been doing? You are covered with dust, and look as hot as if you had been pulling the boat against the rapids. I have not seen you the whole morning."

"I have been walking," said he, "and thinking. It is dreadful hot work to think. That should be done only in winter weather."

"It would be a woeful thing to take a cold on the mind," said Olive.

"That is so!" he replied. "That is exactly what I am afraid of this morning, and that is the reason I want to propose my amendment. I beg most earnestly that you will not make this interview definitive. I am afraid if you do I may get chills in my mind, soul, and heart from which I shall never recover. I have an idea that the weather may not be as favorable as it was yesterday for the unveiling of tender emotions."

"Why so?" asked Olive.

"There are several reasons," returned Mr. Locker. "For one thing, that musical uproar last night. I have not heard anything about that, and I don't know where I stand."

Olive laughed. "It was splendid," said she. "I liked you a great deal better after that than I did before."

"Now tell me," he exclaimed hurriedly, "and please lose no time, for here comes a surrey from the station with a gentleman in it—do you like me enough better to give me a favorable answer, now, right here?"

"No," said Olive. "I do not feel warranted in being so precipitate as that."

"Then please say nothing on the subject," said Locker. "Please let us drop the whole matter for to-day. And may I assume that I am at liberty to take it up again to-morrow at this hour?"

"You may," said Olive. "What gentleman is that, do you suppose?"

"I know him," said Locker, "and, fortunately, he is married. He is Mr. Easterfield."

"Here's papa! Here's papa!" shouted the two little girls as they ran out of the front door.

"And papa," said the oldest one, "we want you to tell us a story just as soon as you have brushed your hair! Mr. Rupert has been telling us stories, but yours are a great deal better."

"Yes," said the other little girl, "he makes all the children too good. They can't be good, you know, and there's no use trying. We told him so, but he doesn't mind."

There was story-telling after luncheon, but the papa did not tell them, and the children were sent away. It was Mrs. Easterfield who told the stories, and Mr. Tom was a most

Frank R. Stockton

interested listener.

"Well," said he, when she had finished, "this seems to be a somewhat tangled state of affairs."

"It certainly is," she replied, "and I tangled them."

"And you expect me to straighten them?" he asked.

"Of course I do," she replied, "and I expect you to begin by sending Mr. Hemphill away. You know I could not do it, but I should think it would be easy for you."

"Would you object if I lighted a cigar?" he asked.

"Of course not," she said. "Did you ever hear me object to anything of the kind?"

"No," said he, "but I never have smoked in this room, and I thought perhaps Miss Raleigh might object when she came in to do your writing."

"My writing!" exclaimed Mrs. Easterfield. "Now don't trifle! This is no time to make fun of me. Olive may be accepting him this minute."

"It seems to me," said Mr. Easterfield, slowly puffing his cigar, "that it would not be such a very bad thing if she did. So far as I have been able to judge, he is my favorite of the claimants. Du Brant and I have met frequently, and if I were a girl I would not want to marry him. Locker is too little for Miss Asher, and, besides, he is too flighty. Your young professor may be good enough, but from my limited conversation with him at the table I could not form much of an opinion as to him one way or another. I have an opinion of Hemphill, and a very good one. He is a first-class young man, a rising one with prospects, and, more than that, I think he is the best-looking of the lot."

"Tom," said Mrs. Easterfield, "do you suppose I sent for you to talk such nonsense as that? Can you imagine that my sense of honor toward Olive's parents would allow me even to consider a marriage between a high-class girl, such as she is—high-class in every way—to a mere commonplace private secretary? I don't care what his attributes and merits are; he is commonplace to the backbone; and he is impossible. If what ought to be a brilliant career ends suddenly in Rupert Hemphill I shall have Olive on my conscience for the rest of my life."

"That settles it," said Mr. Tom Easterfield; "your conscience, my dear, has not been trained to carry loads, and I shall not help to put one on it. Hemphill is a good man, but we must rule him out."

"Yes," said she, "Olive is a great deal more than good. He must be ruled out."

"But I can't send him away this afternoon," Tom continued. "That would put them both on their mettle, and, ten to one, he would considerately announce his engagement before he left."

"No," said she. "Olive is very sharp, and would resent that. But now that you are here I feel safe from any immediate rashness on their part."

"You are right," said Mr. Tom. "My very coming will give them pause. And now I want to see the girl."

"What for?" asked Mrs. Easterfield.

"I want to get acquainted with her. I don't know her yet, and I can't talk to her if I don't know her."

"Are you going to talk to her about Hemphill?"

"Yes, for one thing," he answered.

Frank R. Stockton

"Well," said she, "you will have to be very circumspect. She is both alert, and sensitive."

"Oh, I'll be circumspect enough," he replied. "You may trust me for that."

It was not long after this that Mrs. Easterfield, being engaged in some hospitable duties, sent Olive to show Mr. Tom the garden, and it was rather a slight to that abode of beauty that the tour of the rose-lined paths occupied but a very few minutes, when Mr. Easterfield became tired, and desired to sit down. Having seated themselves on Mrs. Easterfield's favorite bench, Olive looked up at her companion, and asked:

"Well, sir, what is it you brought me here to say to me?"

Mr. Tom laughed, and so did she.

"If it is anything about the gentlemen who are paying their addresses to me, you may as well begin at once, for that will save time, and really an introduction is not necessary."

Mr. Easterfield's admiration for this young lady, which had been steadily growing, was not decreased by this remark. "This girl," said he to himself, "deserves a nimble-witted husband. Hemphill would never do for her. It seems to me," he said aloud, "that we are already well enough acquainted for me to proceed with the remarks which you have correctly assumed I came here to make."

"Yes," said she, "I have always thought that some people are born to become acquainted, and when they meet they instantly perceive the fact, and the thing is accomplished. They can then proceed."

"Very well," said he, "we will proceed."

"I suppose," said Olive, "that Mrs. Easterfield has explained everything, and that you agree with her and with me that it is a sensible thing for a girl in my position to marry, and, having no one to attend wisely to such a matter for me, that I should endeavor to attend to it myself as wisely as I can. Also, that a little bit of pique, caused by the fact that I am to have an old schoolfellow for a stepmother, is excusable."

"And it is this pique which puts you in such a hurry? I did not exactly understand that."

"Yes, it does," said she. "I very much wish to announce my own engagement, if not my marriage, before any arrangements shall be made which may include me. Do you think me wrong in this?"

"No, I don't," said Mr. Easterfield. "If I were a girl in your place I think I would do the same thing myself."

Olive's face expressed her gratitude. "And now," said she, "what do you think of the young men? I feel so well acquainted with you through Mrs. Easterfield that I shall give a great deal of weight to your opinion. But first let me ask you one thing: After what you have heard of me do you think I am a flirt?"

Mr. Tom knitted his brows a little, then he smiled, and then he looked out over the flower-beds without saying anything.

"Don't be afraid to say so if you think so," said she. "You must be perfectly plain and frank with me, or our acquaintanceship will wither away."

Under the influence of this threat he spoke. "Well," said he, "I should not feel warranted in calling you a flirt, but it does seem to me that you have been flirting."

"I think you are wrong, Mr. Easterfield," said Olive, speaking very gravely. "I never saw any one of these young men before I came here except Mr. Hemphill, and he was an entirely different person when I knew him before, and I have given no one of them any special encouragement. If Mr. Locker were not such an impetuous young man, I think the others would have been more deliberate, but as it was easy to see the state of his mind, and as we are all making but a temporary stay here, these other young men saw that they must act quickly, or not at all. This, while it was very amusing, was also a little annoying, and I should greatly have preferred slower and more deliberate movements on the part of these young men. But all my feelings changed when my father's letter came to me. I was glad then that they had proposed already."

"That is certainly honest," said Mr. Tom.

"Of course it is honest," replied Olive. "I am here to speak honestly if I speak at all. Now, don't you see that if under these peculiar circumstances one eligible young man had proposed to me I ought to have considered myself fortunate? Now here are three to choose from. Do you not agree with me that it is my duty to try to choose the best one of them, and not to discourage any until I feel very certain about my choice?"

"That is business-like," said Mr. Easterfield; "but do you love any one of them?"

"No, I don't," answered Olive, "except that there is a feeling in that direction in the case of Mr. Hemphill. I suppose Mrs. Easterfield has told you that when I was a schoolgirl I was deeply in love with him; and now, when I think of those old times, I believe it would not be impossible for those old sentiments to return. So there really is a tie between him and me; even though it be a slight one; which does not exist at all between me and any one of the others."

For a moment neither of them spoke. "That is very bad, young woman," thought Mr. Tom. "A slight tie like that is apt to grow thick and strong suddenly." But he could not discourse about Mr. Hemphill; he knew that would be very dangerous. He would have to be considered, however, and much more seriously than he had supposed.

"Well," said he, "I will tell you this: if I were a young man, unmarried, and on a visit to Broadstone at this time, I should not like to be treated as you are treating the young men who are here. It is all very well for a young woman to look after herself and her own interests, but I should be very sorry to have my fate depend upon the merits of other people. I may not be correct, but I am afraid I should feel I was being flirted with."

"Well, then," said Olive, giving a quick, forward motion on the bench, "you think I ought to settle this matter immediately, and relieve myself at once from the imputation of trifling with earnest affection?"

"Oh, no, no, no!" cried Mrs. Easterfield. "Not at all! Don't do anything rash!"

Olive leaned back on the bench, and laughed heartily. "There is so much excellent advice in this world," she said, "which is not intended to be used. However, it is valuable all the same. And now, sir, what is it you would like me to do? Something plain; intended for every-day use."

Mr. Tom leaned forward, his elbows on his knees. "It does not appear to me," he said, "that you have told me very much I did not know before, for Mrs. Easterfield put the matter very plainly before me."

"And it does not seem to me," said Olive, "that you have given me any definite counsel, and I know that is what you came here to do."

"You are mistaken there," he said. "I came here to find out what sort of a girl you are; my counsels must depend on my discoveries. But there is one thing I want to ask you; you are all the time talking about three young men. Now, there are four of them here."

Frank R. Stockton

"Yes," she answered quickly. "But only three of them have proposed; and, besides, if the other were to do so, he would have to be set aside for what I may call family reasons. I don't want to go into particulars because the subject is very painful to me."

For a moment Mr. Tom did not speak. Then, determined to go through with what he had come to do, which was to make himself acquainted with this girl, he said: "I do not wish to discuss anything that is painful to you, but Mrs. Easterfield and I are very much disturbed for fear that in some way your visit to Broadstone created some misunderstanding or disagreeable feeling between you and your uncle. Now, would you mind telling me whether this is so, or not?"

She looked at him steadily. "There is an unpleasant feeling between me and my uncle, but this visit has nothing to do with it. And I am going to tell you all about it. I hate to feel so much alone in the world that I can't talk to anybody about what makes me unhappy. I might have spoken to Mrs. Easterfield, but she didn't ask me. But you have asked me, and that makes me feel that I am really better acquainted with you than with her."

This remark pleased Mr. Tom, but he did not think it would be necessary to put it into his report to his wife. He had promised to be very circumspect; and circumspection should act in every direction.

"It is very hard for a girl such as I am," she continued, "to be alone in the world, and that is a very good reason for getting married as soon as I can."

"And for being very careful whom you marry," interrupted Mr. Easterfield.

"Of course," said she, "and I am trying very hard to be that. A little while ago I had a father with whom I expected to live and be happy, but that dream is over now. And then I thought I had an uncle who was going to be more of a father to me than my own father had ever been. But that dream is over, too."

"And why?" asked Mr. Easterfield.

"He is going to marry a woman," said Olive, "that is perfectly horrible, and with whom I could not live. And the worst of it all is that he never told me a word about it."

As she said this Olive looked very solemn; and Mr. Tom, not knowing on the instant what would be proper to say, looked solemn also.

"You may think it strange," said she, "that I talk in this way to you, but you came here to find out what sort of girl I am, and I am perfectly willing to help you do it. Besides, in a case like this, I would rather talk to a man than to a woman."

Mr. Tom believed her, but he did not know at this stage of the proceedings what it would be wise to say. He was also fully aware that if he said the wrong thing it would be very bad, indeed.

"Now, you see," said she, "there is another reason why I should marry as soon as possible. In my case most girls would take up some pursuit which would make them independent, but I don't like business. I want to be at the head of a household; and, what is more, I want to have something to do—I mean a great deal to do—with the selection of a husband."

The conversation was taking a direction which frightened Mr. Tom. In the next moment she might be asking advice about the choice of a husband. It was plain enough that love had nothing to do with the matter, and Mr. Tom did not wish to act the part of a practical-minded Cupid. "And now let me ask a favor of you," said he. "Won't you give me time to think over this matter a little?"

"That is exactly what I say to my suitors," said Olive, smiling.

Frank R. Stockton

Mr. Tom smiled also. "But won't you promise me not to do anything definite until I see you again?" he asked earnestly.

"That is not very unlike what some of my suitors say to me," she replied. "But I will promise you that when you see me again I shall still be heart-free."

"There can be no doubt of that," Mr. Tom said to himself as they arose to leave the garden. "And, my young woman, you may deny being a flirt, but you permitted the addresses of two young men before you were upset by your father's letter. But I think I like flirts. At any rate, I can not help liking her, and I believe she has got a heart somewhere, and will find it some day."

When Mr. Tom returned to the house he did not find his wife, for that lady was occupied somewhere in entertaining her guests. Now, although it might have been considered his duty to go and help her in her hospitable work, he very much preferred to attend to the business which she had sent for him to do. And walking to the stables, he was soon mounted on a good horse, and riding away southward on the smooth gray turnpike.

CHAPTER XXV

THE CAPTAIN AND MR. TOM

Captain Asher was standing at the door of the tollhouse when he saw Mr. Easterfield approaching. He recognized him, although he had had but one brief interview with him one day at the toll-gate some time before. Mr. Easterfield was a man absorbed in business, and the first summer Mrs. Easterfield was at Broadstone he was in Europe engaged in large and important affairs, and had not been at the summer home at all. And so far this summer, he had been there but once before, and then for only a couple of days. Now, as the captain saw the gentleman coming toward the toll-gate he had no reason for supposing that he would not go through it. Nevertheless, his mind was disturbed. Any one coming from Broadstone disturbed his mind. He had not quite decided whether or not to ask any questions concerning the late members of his household, when the horseman stopped at the gate, and handed him the toll.

"Good morning, captain," said Mr. Easterfield cheerily, for he had heard much in praise of the toll-gate keeper from his wife.

"Good morning, Mr. Easterfield," said the captain gravely.

"I am glad I do not have to introduce myself," said Mr. Easterfield, "for I am only going through your gate as far as that tree to tie my horse. Then, if convenient to you, I should like to have a little talk with you."

The captain's mind, which had been relieved when Mr. Easterfield paid his toll, now sank again. But he could not say a talk would be inconvenient. "If I had known that you were not going on," he said, "you need not have paid."

"Like most people in this life," said Mr. Easterfield, "I pay for what I have already done, and not for what I am going to do. And now have you leisure, sir, for a short conversation?"

The captain looked very glum. He felt not the slightest desire now to ask questions, and still less desire to be interrogated. However, he was not afraid of anything any one might say to him; and if a certain subject was broached, he had something to say himself.

"Yes," said he; "do you prefer indoors or out of doors?"

"Out of doors, if it suits," replied the visitor, "for I would like to take a smoke."

"I am with you there," said the captain, as he led the way to the little arbor.

Here Mr. Easterfield lighted a cigar, and the captain a pipe.

"Now, sir," said the latter, when the tobacco in his bowl was in a satisfactory glow, "what is it you want to talk about?" He spoke as if he were behind entrenchments, and ready for an attack.

"We have two of your guests with us," answered Mr. Easterfield, "Professor Lancaster, and your niece."

"Oh," said the captain, evidently relieved. "I thought perhaps you had come to ask questions about some reports you may have heard in regard to me."

"Not at all, not at all," said Mr. Easterfield. "I would not think of mentioning your private affairs, about which I have not the slightest right or wish to speak. But as we have apparently appropriated two of your young people, I think, and Mrs. Easterfield agrees with me, that it is but right you should be informed as to their health, and what they are doing."

The captain puffed vigorously. "When is Dick Lancaster coming back" he asked.

"I can't say anything about that," replied Mr. Easterfield, "for I am not master of ceremonies. We would like to keep him as long as we can, but, of course, your claims must be considered."

"I should think so," remarked the captain.

"Professor Lancaster is a remarkably fine young man," said the other, "and as he is a friend of yours, and as I should like him to be a friend of mine, it would give me pleasure to talk to you more about him. But I may as well confess that my real object in coming here is to talk about your niece. Of course, as I said before, it might appear that I have no right to meddle with your family affairs, but in this case I certainly think I am justified; for, as Mrs. Easterfield invited the young lady to leave you and to come to her, and as all that has happened to her has happened at our house, and in consequence of that invitation, I think that you, as her nearest accessible relative, should be told of what has occurred."

The captain made no answer, but gazed steadily into the face of the speaker.

"Therefore," continued Mr. Easterfield, "I will simply state that my wife and I have very good reason to believe that your niece is about to engage herself in marriage; and I will only add that we are very sorry, indeed, that this should have occurred under our roof."

A sudden and curious change came over the face of the captain; a light sparkled in his eye, and a faint flush, as if of pleasure, was visible under his swarthy skin. He leaned toward his companion.

"Is it Dick Lancaster?" he asked quickly.

Mr. Easterfield answered gravely: "I wish it were, but I am very sorry to say it is not."

The light went out of the captain's eye. He leaned back on his bench and the little flush in his cheeks was succeeded by a somber coldness. "Very good," said he; "I don't want to hear anything more about it, and, what is more, it would not be right for you to tell me, even if I did want to know. It is none of my business."

"Now, really, Captain Asher," began Mr. Easterfield.

"No, sir," the captain interrupted. "It is none of my business, and I don't want to hear anything about it. And now, sir, I would like to tell you something. It is something I thought you came here to ask about, and I did not like it, but now I want to tell you of my own free will, in confidence. That is to say, I don't want you to speak of it to anybody in your house. I suppose you have heard something about my intending to marry a woman in town?"

"Yes," said Mr. Easterfield, "I can not deny that I have, but I considered it was entirely your own affair, and I had not—"

"Of course," interrupted the captain, "and I want to tell you— but I don't want my niece to hear it as coming from me—that that whole thing is a most abominable lie! That woman has been trying to make people believe I am going to marry her, and she has made a good many believe it, but I would rather cut my throat than marry her. But I have told her what I think of her in a way she can not mistake. And that ends her! I tell you this, Mr. Easterfield, because I believe you are a good man, and you certainly seem to be a friendly man, and I would like you to know it. I would have liked very much to tell everybody, especially my own flesh and blood, but now I assure you, sir, I am too proud to have her know it through me. Let her go on and marry anybody she pleases, and let her think anything she pleases about me. She has been satisfied with her own opinion of me without giving me a chance to explain to her, or to tell her the truth, and now she can stay satisfied with it until somebody else sets her straight."

"But this is very hard, captain," said Mr. Easterfield; "hard on you, hard on her, and hard on all of us, I may say."

The captain made no answer to these words, and did not appear to hear them. "I tell you, Mr. Easterfield," he said presently, "that I did not know until now how much I cared for that girl. I don't mind saying this to you because you come to me like a friend, and I believe in you. Yes, sir, I did not know how much I cared for her, and it is pretty hard on me to find out how little she cares for me."

"You are wrong there," said Mr. Easterfield. "My wife tells me that Miss Asher has frequently talked to her about you and her life here, and it is certain she has—"

"Oh, that does not make any difference," interrupted the captain. "I am talking about things as they are now. It was all very well as long as things seemed to be going right, but I believe in people who stand by you when things seem to be going wrong, and who keep on standing by you until they know how they are going, and that is exactly what she did not do. Now, there was Dick Lancaster; he came to me and asked me squarely about that affair. To be sure, I cut him off short, for it angered me to think that he, or anybody else, should have such an idea of me, and, besides, it was none of his business. But it should have been her business; she ought to have made it her business; and, even if the thing had stood differently, I would have told her exactly how it did stand; and then she could have said to me what she thought about it, and what she was going to do. But instead of that, she just made up her mind about me, and away went everything. Yes, sir,

Frank R. Stockton

everything. I can't tell you the plans I had made for her and for myself, and, I may say, for Dick Lancaster. If it suited her, I wanted her to marry him, and if it suited her I wanted to go and live with them in his college town, or any other place they might want to go. Again and again, after I knew Dick, have I gone over this thing and planned it out this way, and that way, but always with us three in the middle of everything. Do you see that?" continued the captain after a slight pause, as he drew from his pocket a dainty little pearl paper-cutter. "That belongs to her. She used to sit out here, and cut the leaves of books as she read them. I can see her little hand now as it went sliding along the edges of the pages. When she went away she left it on the bench, and I took it. And I've kept it in my pocket to take out when I sit here, and cut books with it when I have 'em. I haven't many books that ain't cut, but I've sat here and cut 'em till there wasn't any left. And then I cut a lot of old volumes of Coast Survey Reports. It is a foolish thing for an old man to do, but then—but then—well, you see, I did it."

There was a choke in the captain's voice as he leaned over to put the paper-cutter in his pocket and to pick up his pipe, which he had laid on the bench beside him. Mr. Easterfield was touched and surprised. He would not have supposed the captain to be a man of such tender sentiment. And he took him at once to his heart. "It is a shame," his thoughts ran, "for this man to be separated from the niece he so loves. She is a cold-hearted girl, or she does not understand him. It must not be."

Had he been a woman he would have said all this, but, being a man, he found it difficult to break the silence which followed the captain's last words. He did not know what to say, although he had no hesitation in making up his mind what he was going to do about it all. He arose.

"Captain Asher," he said, "I have now told you what I thought you should know, and I must take my departure. I would not presume for a moment to offer you any advice in regard to your family affairs, but there is one thing Mrs. Easterfield and I will interfere with, if we can, for we feel that we have a right to do it, and that is any definite and immediate engagement of your niece. If she should promise herself in marriage at our house we shall feel that we are responsible for it, and that, in fact, we brought it about. Whether the match shall seem desirable to you or not, we do not wish to be answerable for it."

"Oh, I need not be counted in at all," said the captain, who had recovered his composure. "It is her own affair. I suppose it was the news of her father's intended marriage that put her in such a hurry."

"You are right," said Mr. Easterfield.

"Just like her" the captain exclaimed. "And I don't blame her. I'm with her there"

When Mr. Tom reached Broadstone he dismounted at the stable, and walked to the house. Nobody was to be seen on the grounds. It was a warm afternoon when those whose hearts were undisturbed by the turmoils of love were apt to be napping, and those who were in the tumultuous state of mind referred to, preferred to separate themselves from each other and the rest of the world until the cause of their inquietude should consider the heat of the summer day as sufficiently mitigated for her to appear again among her fellow beings.

Mr. Easterfield did not care to meet any of his guests, and hoped to find his wife in her room, that he might report, and consult. But, as he approached the house, he saw at an upper window a female head. It stayed there just long enough for him to see that it was Olive's head; then it disappeared. When he reached the hall door there stood Olive.

Mr. Tom was a little disappointed. He wanted to see his wife immediately, and then to see Olive. But he could not say so.

"Well," said the girl, coming down the steps, "it looks as if we had arranged to meet. But although we didn't, let's take a little walk. I have something I want to say to you."

Mr. Easterfield turned, and walked away from the house. He was a masterful man, and did not like to have his plans interfered with. Therefore he made a dash, and had the first word. "Miss Asher," said he, "I am glad to hear anything you have to say, but first you must really listen to me."

Olive looked at him with surprise. She also was a masterful person, and not accustomed to be treated in this way. But he gave her no chance.

"Miss Asher," said he, "I have come to you to speak for one of your lovers, the truest, best lover you ever had, and I believe, ever will have."

Olive looked at him steadfastly, and her face grew hard. "Mr. Easterfield," she said, "this will not do. I have told you I will not have it. Mrs. Easterfield and you have been very good and kind, and I have told you everything, but you do not seem to remember one thing I have said. I will not have anybody forced upon me; no matter if he happens to be an angel from heaven, or no matter how much better he may be than anybody else on earth. I have my reasons for this determination. They are good reasons, and, above all, they are my reasons. I don't want you to think me rude, but if you persist in forcing that gentleman upon my attention, I shall have to request that the whole subject be dropped between us."

"Who in the name of common sense do you think I am talking about?" exclaimed Mr. Tom. "Do you think I refer to Mr. Lancaster?"

"I do," she said. "You know you would not come to plead the cause of any one of the others."

He looked down at her half doubtfully, wondering a little how she would take what he was going to say. "You are mistaken," he said quietly. "I have nothing whatever to say about Mr. Lancaster. The lover I speak of is your uncle."

Then her face turned red. "Why do you use that expression? Did he send you to say it?"

"Not at all. I came of my own free will. I went to see Captain Asher immediately after I left you. Perhaps you are thinking that I have no right to intrude in your family affairs, but I do not mind your thinking that. I had a long talk with your uncle. I found that the uppermost sentiment of his soul was his love for you. You had come into his life like the break of day. Every little thing you had owned or touched was dear to him because it had been yours, or you had used it. All his plans in life had been remade in reference to you."

They had stopped and were standing facing each other. They could not walk and talk as they were talking.

"Yet, but," she exclaimed, her face pale and her eyes fixed steadfastly upon him, "but what of that—"

"There are no yets and buts," he exclaimed, half angry with her that she hesitated. "I know what you were going to say, but that woman you have heard of is nothing to him. He hates her worse than you hate her. She has imposed upon you; how I know not; but she is an impostor."

At this instant she seized him by the arm. "Mr. Easterfield," she cried, and as she spoke the tears were running down her cheeks, "please let me have a carriage—something covered! I would go on my wheel, for that would be quicker, but I don't want anybody to speak to me or see me! Will you have it brought to the back door, Mr. Easterfield, please? I will run to the house, and be waiting when it comes."

She did not wait for him to answer. He did not ask her where she was going. He knew very well. She ran to the house, and

Frank R. Stockton

he hurried to the stable.

Having given his orders, Mr. Tom went in search of his wife. The moment had arrived when it was absolutely necessary to let her know what was going on.

He found her in her own room. "Where on earth have you been?" she exclaimed. "I have been looking everywhere for you."

In as few words as possible he told her where he had been, and what he had done.

"And where are you going now?" she asked.

"I am going to change my coat," said the good Mr. Tom. "After my ride to the toll-gate and back this jacket is too dusty for me to drive with her."

"Drive with her" exclaimed Mrs. Easterfield. "It will be very well for you to get rid of some of that dust, but when the carriage comes I will drive with Olive to see her uncle."

And thus it happened that Mr. Tom stayed at home with the house party while the close carriage, containing his wife and that dear girl, Olive Asher, rolled swiftly southward over the smooth turnpike road.

CHAPTER XXVI

A STOP AT THE TOLL-GATE

The four lovers at Broadstone walked, and wandered, and waited, after breakfast that morning, but only one of them knew definitely what he was waiting for, and that was Mr. Locker. He was waiting for half-past twelve o'clock, when he would join Miss Asher, if she gave him an opportunity; and he was sure she would give him one, for she was always to be trusted. He intended this interview to be decisive. It would not do for him to wait any longer; yes or no must be her word. She had been walking down by the river with the best clothes on the premises, and he now feared the owner of those clothes more than anybody else. He was a keen-sighted young man, for otherwise how could he have been a poet, and he assured himself that Miss Asher was taking Hemphill seriously.

So Mr. Locker determined to charge the works of the enemy that day before luncheon. When the conflict was over his flag might float high and free or it might lie trampled in the dust, but the battle should be fought, and no quarter would be asked or given.

As for Mr. Hemphill and Mr. Du Brant, they simply wandered, and waited, and bored the rest of the company. They did not care to do anything, for that might embarrass them in case Miss Asher appeared and wished to do something else; they did not want to stay in the house because she might show herself somewhere out of doors; they did not want to stay

Frank R. Stockton

on the grounds because at any moment she might seat herself in the library with a book; above all things, they wanted to keep away from each other; and their indeterminate peregrinations made sick the souls of Mr. and Mrs. Fox.

The diplomat did not know what he was going to do when he saw Miss Asher alone; everything would depend upon surrounding circumstances, for he was quick as well as wary, and could make up his mind on the instant. But good Rupert Hemphill had not even as much decision of purpose as this. He had already spent half an hour with the lady of his love, and he had not been very happy. Delighted that she had permitted him to join her, he had at once begun to speak of the one great object which dominated his existence, but she had earnestly entreated him not to do so.

"It is such a pity," she had said, "for us never to talk of anything but that. There are so many things I like to talk about, especially the things of which I read. I am now reading Charles Lamb—that is, whenever I get a chance—and I don't believe anybody in these days ever does read the works of that dear old man. There is a complete set of his books in the library, and they do not look as if they had ever been opened. Did you ever read his little essays on Popular Fallacies? Some of them are just as true as they can be, although they seem like making fun, especially the one about the angry man being always in the wrong. I am inclined to side with the angry man. I know I am generally right when I am angry."

Mr. Hemphill had not read these little essays, nor had he admitted that he had never read anything else by Mr. Lamb; but he had agreed that it was very common to be both angry and right. Then Olive had talked to him about other books, and his way had become very rough and exceedingly thorny, and he had wished he knew how to bring up the subject of some new figures in the German. But he had not succeeded in doing this. She had been in a bookish mood, and the mood had lasted until she had left him.

Now he began to think that it would be better for him to give up wandering and waiting and go into the library and prepare himself for another talk with Olive, but he did not go; she might see him and suspect his design. He would wait until later. He took some books to his room.

Dick Lancaster wandered and waited, but he was full of a purpose, although it was not exactly definite; he wanted to find Mrs. Easterfield and ask her to release him from his promise. He could not remain much longer at Broadstone, and Olive's morning walk with Hemphill had made him very nervous. She knew that these young men were in love with her, and he had a right to let her know that he was also. It might be imprudent for him to do this, but he could not see why it would not be as imprudent at any other time as now. Moreover, there might come no other time, and he had control of now.

Mrs. Easterfield had not joined her guests because of her anxiety about Olive. Mr. Easterfield did not appear. For a time he was very particularly engaged in the garden. Mr. Fox grew very much irritated.

"I tell you, my dear," said he, "every one who comes here makes this place more stupid and dull. I can't see exactly any reason for it, but these lovers are at the bottom of it. I hate lovers."

"You should be very glad, my dear," replied Mrs. Fox, "that I was not of your opinion in my early life."

But things changed for the better after a time. It is true that Mrs. Easterfield and Olive did not appear, but Mr. Easterfield showed himself, and did it with great advantage. The simple statement that his wife and Miss Asher had gone to make a call caused a feeling of relief to spread over the whole party. Until the callers returned there was no reason why they should not all enjoy themselves, and Mr. Easterfield was there to show them how to do it.

As the Broadstone carriage rolled swiftly on there was not much conversation between its occupants. To the somewhat sensitive mind of Mrs. Easterfield it seemed that Olive was a little disappointed at the change of companions, but this may have been a mere fancy. The girl was so wrapped up in self-concentrated thought that it was not likely that she would have talked much to any one. Suddenly, however, Olive broke out:

"Mr. Easterfield must be a thoroughly good man" she said.

"He is," assented the other.

"And you have always been entirely satisfied with him?"

"Entirely," was the reply, without a smile.

Now Olive turned her face toward her companion and laid her hand upon her arm. "You ought to be a happy woman," she said.

"Now, what is this girl thinking of?" asked Mrs. Easterfield to herself. "Is she imagining that any one of the young fellows who are now besieging her can ever be to her what Tom is to me? Or is she making an ideal of my husband to the disparagement of her own lovers? Whichever way she thinks, she would better give up thinking."

But the somewhat sensitive Mrs. Easterfield need not have troubled herself. The girl had already forgotten the good Mr. Tom, and her mind was intent upon getting to her uncle.

"Will you please ask the man to stop," she said, "before he gets to the gate, and let me out? Then perhaps you will kindly drive on to the tollhouse and wait for me. I will not keep you waiting long."

The carriage stopped, and Olive slipped out, and, before Mrs. Easterfield had any idea of what she was going to do, the girl climbed the rail fence which separated the road from the captain's pasture field. Between this field and the garden was a picket fence, not very high; and, toward a point about midway between the little tollhouse and the dwelling, Olive now ran swiftly. When she had nearly reached the fence she gave a great bound; put one foot on the upper rail to which the pickets were nailed; and then went over. What would have happened if the sharp pales had caught her skirts might well be imagined. But nothing happened.

"That was a fine spring" said Mrs. Easterfield to herself. "She has seen him in the house, and wants to get there before he hears the carriage."

Olive walked quietly through the garden to the house. She knew that her uncle was not at the gate, for from afar she had seen that the little piazza on which he was wont to sit was empty. She went noiselessly into the hall, and looked into the parlor. By a window in the back of the room she saw her uncle writing at a little table. With a rush of air she was at his side before he knew she was in the room. As he turned his head her arms were around his neck, and the pen in his hand made a great splotch of ink upon her white summer dress.

"Now, uncle," she exclaimed, looking into his astonished face, "here I am and here I am going to stay! And if you want to know anything more about it, you will have to wait, for I am not going to make any explanations now. I am too happy to know that I have a dear uncle left to me in this world, and to know that we two are going to live together always to want to talk about whys and wherefores."

"But, Olive" exclaimed the captain.

"There are no buts," she interrupted. "Not a single but, my dear Uncle John! I have come back to stay with you, and that is all there is about it. Mrs. Easterfield is outside in her carriage, and I must go and send her away. But don't you come out, Uncle John; I have some things to say to her, and I will let you know when she is going."

As Olive sped out of the room Captain Asher turned around in his chair and looked after her. Tears were running down his swarthy cheeks. He did not know how or why it had all happened. He only knew that Olive was coming back to live with him!

Meantime old Jane was entertaining Mrs. Easterfield at the toll-gate, where no money was paid, but a great deal of information gained. The old woman had seen Miss Olive run into the house, and she was elated and excited, and consequently voluble. Mrs. Easterfield got the full account of the one-sided courtship of the captain and Miss Port. Even the concluding episode of Maria having been put to bed had somehow reached the ears of old Jane. It is really wonderful how secret things do become known, for not one of the three actors in that scene would have told it on any account. But old Jane knew it, and told it with great glee, to Mrs. Easterfield's intense enjoyment. Then she proceeded to praise Olive for the spirit she had shown under these trying circumstances; and, in this connection, naturally there came into the recital the spirit the old woman herself had shown under these same trying circumstances, and how she had got all ready to leave the minute the nuptial knot was tied and before that Maria Port could reach the toll-gate, although it was like tearing herself apart to leave the spot where she had lived so many years. "But," she concluded, "it is all right now. The captain tells me it's all a lie of her own makin'. She's good at that business, and if lies was salable she'd be rich."

Just as the old woman reached this, what seemed to her unsophisticated mind, impossible business proposition, Olive appeared. Mrs. Easterfield was surprised to see her so soon, and, to tell the truth, a little disappointed. She had been greatly interested and amused by the old woman's rapid tale, which she would not interrupt, but had put aside in her mind several questions to ask, and one of them was in relation to her husband's late visit to the captain. She had had no detailed account from him, and she wondered how much this old body knew about it. She seemed to know pretty much everything.

But Olive's appearance put an end to this absorbing conversation.

"Has you come to stay, dearie?" eagerly asked old Jane, as Olive grasped her hand.

"To be sure I have, Jane! I have come to stay forever!"

"Thank goodness!" exclaimed the old woman. "How the captain will brighten up! But my! I must go and alter the supper!"

"Mrs. Easterfield," said Olive, when the old woman had departed, "you will have to go back without me. I can not leave my uncle, and I am going to stay here right along. You must not think I am ungrateful to you, or unmindful of Mr. Easterfield's great kindness, but this is my place for the present. Some day I know you will be good enough to let me pay you another visit."

"And what am I to do with all those young men?" asked Mrs. Easterfield mischievously. She would have added, "And one of them your future husband?" But she remembered the coachman.

Olive laughed. "They will annoy you less when I am not there. If you will be so good as to ask your maid to pack up my belongings, I will send for my trunk." She glanced at the coachman. "Would you mind taking a little walk with me along the road?"

"I shall be glad to do so," said Mrs. Easterfield, getting out of the carriage.

"Now, my dear Mrs. Easterfield," said Olive when they were some distance from the toll-gate and the house, "I am going to ask you to add to all your kindness one more favor for me."

"That has such an ominous sound," said Mrs. Easterfield, "that

I am not disposed to promise beforehand."

"It is about those three young men you mentioned."

"I mentioned no number, and there are four."

"In what I am going to ask of you one of them can be counted out. He is not in the affair. Only three are in this business. Won't you be so good as to decline them all for me? I know that you can do it better than I can. You have so much tact. And you must have done the thing many a time, and I have not done it once. I am very awkward; I don't know how; and, to confess the truth, I have put myself into a pretty bad fix."

"Upon my word," cried Mrs. Easterfield, "that is a pretty thing for one woman to ask of another!

"I know it is," said Olive, "and I would not ask it of anybody but the truest friend—of no one but you. But you see how difficult it is for me to attend to it. And it must be done. I have given up all idea of marrying, I am going to stay here, and when my father comes with his young lady he will find me settled and fixed, and he and she will have nothing to do with making plans for me. Now, dear Mrs. Easterfield, I know you will do this favor for me, and let me say that I wish you would be particularly gentle and pleasant in speaking to Mr. Locker. I think he is really a very kind and considerate young man. He certainly showed himself that way. I know you can talk so nicely to him that perhaps he will not mind very much. As for Mr. Du Brant, you can tell him plainly that I have carefully considered his proposition—and that is the exact truth—and that I find it will be wise for me not to accept it. He is a man of affairs, and will understand that I have given him a straightforward, practical answer, and he will be satisfied. You must not be sharp with Mr. Hemphill, as I know you will be inclined to be. Please remember that I was once in love with him, and respect my feelings as well as his. Besides, he is good, and he is in earnest, and he deserves fair treatment. I am sorry that I have worried you about him, and I will tell you now that

I have found out he would not do at all. I found it out this morning when I was talking to him about books. His mind is neither broad nor cultivated."

"I could have told you that," said Mrs. Easterfield, "and saved you all the trouble of taking that walk by the river."

"And then there is one more thing," continued Olive; "it is about Professor Lancaster. I am sure you will agree with me that it will not do for him to come back here. I am just going to start housekeeping again. I've got the supper on my mind this minute. You can't imagine how everything has turned topsy-turvy since I left. I suppose he will be wanting to go North, anyway. In fact, he told me so."

Mrs. Easterfield laughed. She did not believe that Mr. Lancaster would want to go North, or West, or East, although South might suit him. But she saw the point of Olive's request; it would be awkward to have him at the tollhouse.

"Oh, I will take care of him," she said, "and he shall continue his vacation trip just as soon as Mr. Easterfield and I choose to give him up."

"You see," said Olive in an explanatory way, "I have not anything in the world to do with him, but I thought he might want to come back to see uncle again. And, really," she added, speaking with a great deal of earnestness, "I don't want to be bothered with any more young men! And now I will call uncle. You know I had to say all these things to you immediately."

Mrs. Easterfield walked quickly back to her carriage, but she did not wait to see Captain Asher. As a hostess it was necessary for her to hurry back home; and as a quick-witted, sensible woman she saw that it would be well to leave these two happy people to themselves. This was not the time for them to talk to her. So, when the captain, unwilling to wait any longer, appeared at the door of the house, these two dear friends had kissed and parted, and the carriage was speeding away.

On her way home Mrs. Easterfield forgot her slight chagrin at what her husband had not done, in her joy at what he had accomplished. He had neglected to take her fully into his confidence, and had acted very much as if he had been a naval commander, who had cut his telegraphic connections in order not to be embarrassed by orders from the home government. But, on the other hand, he had saved her from the terrible shock of hearing Olive declare that she had just engaged herself to Rupert Hemphill. If it had not been for the extraordinary promptness of her good Tom—a style of action he had acquired in the railroad business—it would have been just as likely as not that Olive would have accepted that young man before she had had an opportunity of finding out his want of breadth and cultivation.

CHAPTER XXVII

BY PROXY

About half-past twelve Claude Locker made his appearance in the spacious hall. He looked out of the front door; he looked out of the back door; he peered into the parlor; he glanced up the stairway; and then he peeped into the library. He had not seen the lady of the house since her return, and he was waiting for Olive. This morning his fate was to be positively decided; he would take a position that would allow of no postponement; he would tell her plainly that a statement that she was not prepared to give him an answer that day would be considered by him as a final rejection. She must haul down her flag or he would surrender and present to her his sword.

Claude Locker saw nothing of Miss Asher, but it was not long before the lady of the house came down-stairs.

"Oh, Mr. Locker," she exclaimed, "I am so glad to see you! Come into the library, please."

He hesitated a minute. "I beg your pardon," said he, "but I have an appointment—"

"I know that," said she, "and you may be surprised to hear that it is with me and not with Miss Asher. Come in and I will tell you about it."

Claude Locker actually ran after his hostess into the library,

Frank R. Stockton

both of his eyes wide open.

"And now," said she, "please sit down, and hear what I have to say."

Locker seated himself on the edge of a chair; he did not feel happy; he suspected something was wrong.

"Is she sick?" he asked. "Can't she come down?"

"She is very well," was the reply, "but she is not here. She is with her uncle."

"Then I am due at her uncle's house before one o'clock," said he.

"No," she answered, "you are due here."

He fixed upon her a questioning glance.

"Miss Asher," she continued, "has deputed me to give you her answer. She can not come herself, but she does not forget her agreement with you."

The young man still gazed steadfastly. "If it is to be a favorable decision," said he, "I hope you will be able to excuse any exuberance of demeanor on my part."

Mrs. Easterfield smiled. "In that case," she said, "I do not suppose I should have been sent as an envoy."

His brow darkened, and instinctively he struck one hand with the other. "That is exactly what I expected!" he exclaimed. "The signs all pointed that way. But until this moment, my dear madam, I hoped. Yes, I had presumed to hope that I might kindle in her heart a little nickering flame. I had tried to do this, and I had left but one small match head, which I intended to strike this day. But now I see I had a piece of the wrong end of the match. After this I must be content forever to stay in the cold."

"I am glad you view the matter so philosophically," said Mrs. Easterfield, "and Olive particularly desired me to say—"

"Don't call her Olive, if you please," he interrupted. "It is like speaking to me through the partly open door of paradise, through which I can not enter. Slam it shut, I beg of you, and talk over the top of the wall."

"Miss Asher wants you to know," continued Mrs. Easterfield, "that while she has decided to decline your addresses, she is deeply grateful to you for the considerate way in which you have borne yourself toward her. I know she has a high regard for you, and that she will not forget your kindness."

Mr. Locker put his hands in his pockets. "Do you know," said he, "as this thing had to be done, I prefer to have you do it than to have her do it. Well, it is done now! And so am I!"

"You never did truly expect to get her, did you, Mr. Locker?" asked Mrs. Easterfield.

"Never," he answered; "but I do not flinch at what may be impossibilities. Nobody, myself included, can imagine that I shall rival Keats, and yet I am always trying for it."

"Is it Keats you are aiming at?" she said.

"Yes," he replied; "it does not look like it, does it? But it is."

"And you don't feel disheartened when you fail?" said she.

Mr. Locker took his hands from his pockets, and folded his arms. "Yes, I do," he said; "I feel as thoroughly disheartened as I do now. But I have one comfort; Keats and Miss Asher dropped me; I did not drop them. So there is nothing on my conscience. And now tell me, is she going to take Lancaster? I hope so."

"She could not do that," answered Mrs. Easterfield, "for I know he has not asked her."

"Then he'd better skip around lively and do it," said Mr. Locker, "not only for his own sake, but for mine. If I should be cast aside for the Hemphill clothes I should have no faith in humanity. I would give up verse, and I would give up woman."

"Don't be afraid of anything like that," said Mrs. Easterfield, laughing. "It may be somewhat of a breach of confidence, but I am going to tell you nevertheless; because I think you deserve it; that I am also deputed to decline the addresses of Mr. Hemphill, and Mr. Du Brant."

"Hurrah!" cried Locker. "Mrs. Easterfield, I envy you; and if you don't feel like performing the rest of your mission, you can depute it to me. I don't know anything at this moment that would give me so much joy."

"I would not be so disloyal or so cruel as that," said she. "But I shall not be in a hurry. I shall let them eat their lunch in peace and hope."

"Not much peace," said he. "Her empty chair will put that to flight. I know how it feels to look at her empty chair."

"Then you really love her?" said Mrs. Easterfield, much moved.

"With every fiber," said he.

Mrs. Easterfield found herself much embarrassed at the luncheon table. She had made her husband understand the state of affairs, but had not had time to enter into particulars with him, and she did not find it easy satisfactorily to explain to the company the absence of Miss Asher without calling forth embarrassing questions as to her return, and she wished carefully to avoid telling them that her guest was not coming back for the present. If she made this known then she feared there might be a scene at the table.

Mr. Hemphill turned pale when, that afternoon, his hostess, in an exceedingly clear and plain manner, made known to him his fate. For a few moments he did not speak. Then he said very quietly: "If she had not, of her own accord, told me that she had once loved me, I should never have dared to say anything like that to her."

"I do not think you need any excuse, Mr. Hemphill," said Mrs. Easterfield. "In fact, if you loved her, I do not see how you could help speaking after what she herself said to you."

"That is true," he replied. "And I love her with all my heart!"

"She ought never to have told you of that girlish fancy," said his hostess. "It was putting you in a very embarrassing position, and I am bound to say to you, Mr. Hemphill, that I also am very much to blame. Knowing all this, as I did, I should not have allowed you to meet her."

"Oh, don't say that!" exclaimed Mr. Hemphill. "Don't say that! Not for the world would I give up the memory of hearing her say she once loved me! I don't care how many years ago it was. I am glad you let me come here. I am glad she told me. I shall never forget the happiness I have had in this house. And now, Mrs. Easterfield, let me ask you one thing—"

At this moment Mrs. Easterfield, who was facing the door, saw her husband enter the hall, and by his manner she knew he was looking for her.

"Excuse me," she said to Hemphill, "I will be back in an instant."

And she ran out. "Tom," she cried, "you must go away. I can not see you now. I am very busy declining the addresses of a suitor, and can not be interrupted."

Frank R. Stockton

Mr. Tom looked at her in surprise, although it was not often Mrs. Easterfield could surprise him. He saw that she was very much in earnest.

"Well," said he, "if you are sure you are going to decline him I won't interrupt you. And when you have sealed his fate you will find me in my room. I want particularly to see you."

Mrs. Easterfield went back to the library and Hemphill continued: "You need not answer if you do not think it is right," said he, "but do you believe at any time she thought seriously of me?"

Mrs. Easterfield smiled as she answered: "Now, you see the advantage of an agent in such matters as this. You could not have asked her that question, or if you did she would not answer you. And now I am going to tell you that she did have some serious thought of you. Whatever encouragement she gave you, she treated you fairly. She is a very practical young woman—"

"Excuse me," said Hemphill hurriedly, "but if you please, I would rather you did not tell me anything more. Sometimes it is not well to try to know too much. I can't talk now, Mrs. Easterfield, for I am dreadfully cut up, but at the same time I am wonderfully proud. I don't know that you can understand this."

"Yes, I can," she said; "I understand it perfectly."

"You are very kind," he said. As he was about to leave the room he stopped and turned to Mrs. Easterfield. "Is she going to marry Professor Lancaster?" he asked.

"Really, Mr. Hemphill," she replied, "I can not say anything about that. I do not know any more than you do."

"Well, I hope she may," he said. "It would be a burning shame if she were to accept that Austrian; and as for the other little man, he is too ugly. You must excuse me for speaking of your friends in this way, Mrs. Easterfield, but really I should feel dreadfully if I thought I had been set aside for such a queer customer as he is."

Mrs. Easterfield did not laugh then; but when Hemphill had gone, and she had joined her husband, they had a good time together.

"And so they all recommend Lancaster," said he.

"So far," she answered; "but I have yet to hear what Mr. Du Brant has to say."

"I think you have had enough of this discarding business," said Mr. Tom. "You would better leave Du Brant to me."

"Oh, no," said she; "I promised Olive. And, besides, I think I like it."

"I believe you do," said Mr. Tom. "And now I want to say something important. It is not right that Broadstone should be given up entirely to the affairs of Miss Asher and her lovers. I think, for instance, that our friend Fox looks very much dissatisfied."

"That is because Olive is not here," she replied.

"Not only that," he answered. "He loses her, and does not get anything else in her place. Now, we must make this house lively, as it ought to be. Let Du Brant off for to-day and let us make up a party to go out on the river. We will take two boats, and have some of the men to do the rowing. Postpone dinner so we can have a long afternoon."

Mr. Du Brant did not go on the river excursion. He had some letters to write, and begged to be excused. He had not asked when Miss Asher was expected back, or anything about her return. He did not understand the state of affairs, and was afraid he might receive some misleading information. But if she should come that afternoon or the next day he determined to be on the spot. After that he might not be able to remain at Broadstone, and it would be a glorious opportunity for him if she should come back that afternoon.

It was twilight when the boating party returned. Under the genial influence of Mr. Tom and his wife they had all enjoyed themselves as much as it was possible for them to do so without Olive.

When Claude Locker, a little behind the others, reached the top of the hill he perceived, not far away, Mr. Du Brant strolling. These two had not spoken since the night of the interrupted serenade. Each of them had desired to avoid words or actions which might disturb the peace of this hospitable home, and consequently had very successfully succeeded in avoiding each other. But now Mr. Locker walked straight up to the secretary of legation, holding out his hand.

"Now, Mr. Du Brant," said he, "since we are both in the same boat, let us shake hands and let bygones be bygones."

But the young Austrian did not take the proffered hand. For a moment he looked as though he were about to turn away without taking any notice of Locker, but he had not the strength of mind to do this. He turned and remarked with a scowl:

"What do you mean by same boat? I have nothing to do with you on the water or on the land!"

Mr. Locker shrugged his shoulders. "So you have not been told," said he.

"Told!" exclaimed Du Brant, now very much interested. "Told what?"

"That you will have to find out," said the other. "It is not my business to tell you. But I don't mind saying that as I have been told I thought perhaps you might have been."

"Told what?" exclaimed Mr. Du Brant again, stepping up closer to the other.

"Don't shout so," said Locker; "they will think we are quarreling. Didn't I say I am not the person to tell you anything, and if you did not understand me I will say it again."

For some seconds the Austrian looked steadily at his companion. Then he said, "Have you been refused by Miss Asher?"

"Well," said Locker with a sigh, "as that is my business, I suppose I can talk about it if I want to. Yes, I have."

Again Du Brant was silent for a time. "Did she tell you herself?" he asked.

"No, she did not," was the answer. "She kindly sent me word by Mrs. Easterfield. I suppose your turn has not come yet. I was at the head of the list." And, fearing that if he stayed longer he might say too much, Mr. Locker walked slowly away, whistling disjointedly as he went.

That evening Mrs. Easterfield discovered that she had been deprived of the anticipated pleasure of conveying to Mr. Du Brant the message which Olive had sent him. That gentleman, unusually polite and soft-spoken, found her by herself, and thus accosted her: "You must excuse me, madam, for speaking upon a certain subject without permission from you, but I have reason to believe that you are the bearer of a message to me from Miss Asher."

"How in the world did you find that out?" she asked.

"It was the—Locker," he answered. "I do not think it was his intention to inform me fully; he is not a master of words and expressions; he is a little blundering; but, from what he said, I supposed you were kind enough to be the bearer of such a message."

"Yes," said Mrs. Easterfield; "not being able to be here herself, Miss Asher requested me to say to you that she must decline—"

"Excuse me, madam," he interrupted, "but it is I who decline. I bear toward you, madam, the greatest homage and respect, but what I had the honor to say to Miss Asher I said to her alone, and it is only from her that it is possible for me to receive an answer. Therefore, madam, it is absolutely necessary that I decline to be a party to the interview you so graciously propose. It breaks my heart, my dear madam, even to seem unwilling to listen to anything you might deign to say to me, but in this case I must be firm, I must decline. Can you pardon me, dear madam, for speaking as I have been obliged to speak?"

"Oh, of course," said Mrs. Easterfield. "And really, since you know so much, it is not necessary for me to tell you anything more."

"Ah," said the diplomat, with a little bow and an incredulous expression, as if the lady could have no idea what he might yet know, "I am so much obliged to you! I am so thankful!"

CHAPTER XXVIII

HERE WE GO! LOVERS THREE!

The three discarded lovers of Broadstone—all discarded, although one of them would not admit it—would have departed the next day had not that day been Sunday, when there were no convenient trains. Mr. Du Brant was due in Washington; Mr. Hemphill was needed very much at his desk, especially since Mr. Easterfield had decided to spend a few days with his wife; and Claude Locker wanted to go. When he had finished the thing he happened to be doing it was his habit immediately to begin something else. All was at an end between him and Miss Asher. He acknowledged this, and he did not wish to stay at Broadstone. But, as it could not be helped, they all stayed over Sunday.

Mr. Easterfield planned an early afternoon expedition to a mission church in the mountains; it would be a novel experience, and a delightful trip, and everybody must go.

In the course of the morning Mr. Du Brant strolled in the eastern parts of the grounds, and Mr. Locker strolled over that portion of the lawn which lay to the west. Mr. Du Brant did not meet with any one with whom he cared to talk, but Mr. Locker was fortunate enough to meet Miss Raleigh.

"I am glad to see you," said he; "you are the person above all other persons I wish to talk to."

Frank R. Stockton

"It delights me to hear that," said the lady, her face showing that she spoke the truth.

"Let us go over there and sit down," said he. "Now, then," he continued, "you were present, Miss Raleigh, at a very peculiar moment in my life, a momentous moment, I may say. You enjoyed a privilege—if you consider it such—not vouchsafed to many mortals."

"I did consider it a privilege, you may be sure," exclaimed Miss Raleigh, "and I value it. You do not know how highly I value it!"

"You heard me offer myself, body and soul, to the lady I loved. You were taken into our confidence, you saw me laid upon the table—"

"Oh, dreadful!" cried the lady. "Don't put it that way."

"Well, then," said he, "you saw me postponed for future consideration. You promised you would regard everything you heard as confidential; by so doing you enabled me to speak when otherwise I might not have dared to do so. I am deeply grateful to you; and, as you already know so much about my hopes and my aspirations, I think it right you should know all there is to know."

The conscience of Miss Raleigh stirred itself very vigorously within her, and her voice was much subdued as she said:

"I am sure you are very good."

"Well, then," said Locker, "the proposal you heard me make has been declined. I am discarded; and not directly in a face-to-face interview, but through another by a message. It would have been inconvenient for Miss Asher personally to communicate the intelligence, so as Mrs. Easterfield was coming this way she kindly consented to convey the intelligence."

"I declare," exclaimed Miss Raleigh, "I had not heard of that! Mrs. Easterfield made me her confidant in the early stages of this affair, or I should say, these affairs. But she has not told me that."

"She will doubtless give herself that pleasure later," said Locker.

"No," said she, "she will not think any more about it. I am of no further use. And may I ask if you know anything about the two other gentlemen?"

"Both turned down," said Locker.

"I might have supposed that," answered the lady; "for if Miss Asher would not take you she certainly would not be content with either of them."

"With all my heart I thank you," said Locker warmly. "Such words are welcome to a wounded heart."

For a moment Miss Raleigh was silent, then she remarked, "It is very hard to be discarded."

"You are right there!" exclaimed Locker. "But how do you happen to know anything about it?"

"I have been discarded myself," she answered.

The larger eye of Mr. Locker grew still larger, the other endeavored to emulate its companion's size; and his mouth became a rounded opening. "Discarded?" he cried.

"Yes," said she.

The countenance of the young man was now bright with interest and curiosity. "I don't suppose it would be right to ask you," said he, "even although I have taken you so completely into my confidence—but, never mind. Don't think of it. Of

Frank R. Stockton

course, I would not propose such a question."

"Of course not," said she, "you are too manly for that." And then she was silent again. Naturally she hesitated to reveal the secrets of her heart, and to a gentleman with whom her acquaintance was of such recent date; but she earnestly wanted to repose confidence in another, as well as to receive it, and it was so seldom, so very seldom, that such an opportunity came to her.

"I do not know," she said, "that I ought to, but still—"

"Oh, don't, if you don't want to," said Locker.

"But I think I do want to," she replied. "You are so kind, so good, and you have confided in me. Yes, I was once discarded, not exactly by word of mouth, or even by message, but still discarded."

"A stranger to me, of course," said Locker, his whole form twisting itself into an interrogation-point.

"No," said she, "and as I have begun I will go on. It was Mr. Hemphill."

"What!" he exclaimed. "That—"

"Yes, it was he," said she, speaking slowly, and in a low voice. "He was Mr. Easterfield's secretary and I was Mrs. Easterfield's secretary, and, of course, we were thrown much together. He has very good qualities; I do not hesitate now to say that; and they impressed themselves upon me. In every possible way I endeavored to make things pleasant for him. I do not believe that when he was at work he ever wanted a glass of cold water that he did not find it within reach. I early discovered that he was very fond of cold water."

"A most commendable dissipation," interrupted Locker.

"He had no dissipations," said Miss Raleigh. "His character was unimpeachable. In very many ways I was attracted to him, in very many ways I endeavored to make life pleasant for him; and I am afraid that sometimes I neglected Mrs. Easterfield's interests so that I might do little things for him, such as dusting, keeping his ink-pots full, providing fresh blotting-paper, and many other trifling services which devotion readily suggested."

Locker heaved a sigh of commiseration which she mistook for one of sympathy.

"I will not go into particulars," she continued, "but at last he discovered that—well, I will be plain with you—he discovered that I loved him. Then, sir—it is humiliating to me to say it, but I will not flinch—he discarded me. He did not use words, but his manner was sufficient. Never again did I go near his desk, never did I tender him the slightest service. It was a terrible blow! It was humiliating"

"I should think so," said Locker, "from him"

"But I will say no more," she remarked with a sigh. "I have told you what you have heard that you may understand how thoroughly I sympathize with you, for all is over with me in that direction, as I suppose all is over with you in your direction. And now I must go, for this long conference may be remarked. But before I go, I will say that if ever you—"

"Oh, no, no, no!" interrupted Locker, "it would not do at all! I really have begun to believe that I was cut out for a bachelor."

"What!" said Miss Raleigh, with great severity. "Do you suppose, sir, that I—"

"Not at all, not at all" cried Locker. "Not for one moment do I suppose that you—"

Frank R. Stockton

"If for one moment," said she, "I had imagined you would suppose—"

"But I assure you, Miss Raleigh, I never did suppose that you would imagine I would think—but if you do suppose I thought you imagined I could possibly conceive—"

"But I really did think," said Miss Raleigh, speaking more gently. "But if I was wrong—"

"Nay, think no more about it," Locker interrupted, "and let us be friends again."

He offered her his hand, which she shook warmly, and then departed.

It had been arranged that Lancaster was not to leave Broadstone on the next day. He had expected to do so, but Mr. Easterfield had planned for a day's fishing for himself, Mr. Fox, and the professor, and he would not let the latter off. The ladies had accepted an invitation to luncheon that day; the next day some new visitors were expected; and in order not to interfere with Mr. Easterfield's plans, evidently intended to restore to Broadstone some of the social harmony which had recently been so disturbed, Dick consented to stay, although he really wanted to go. He could not forget that his vacation was passing.

"Very well, then," Mrs. Easterfield remarked to him that Sunday evening, "if you must go on Tuesday, I suppose you must, although I think it would be better for you if I were to keep my eye on you for a little while longer."

"Perhaps so," said Lancaster, "but the time has come when curb-bits, cages, and good advice are not for me. I must burst loose from everything and go my way, right or wrong, whatever it may be."

"I see that," said she; "but if it had not been for the curbed bit and all that, you would be leaving this place a discarded lover, like the rest of them. They depart with their love-affairs finished forever, ended; you go as free to woo, to win, or to lose as you ever were. And you owe this entirely to me, so whatever else you do, don't sneer at my curbs and my cages; to them you owe your liberty."

The professor fully appreciated everything she had done for him, and told her so earnestly and warmly. But she interrupted his grateful expressions.

"It would have been very hard on me," she said, "if Olive had asked me to carry to you the news of your rejection. That is what I did for the others, I suppose you know."

"Oh, yes," said Lancaster; "Locker told me."

"I might have supposed that," said she. "And now I feel bound to tell you also, although it is not a message, that Olive does not expect to see you at her uncle's house. She infers that you are going to continue your vacation journey."

"I have made my plans for my journey," said he, "and I do not think, Mrs. Easterfield, that you will care to have me talk them over with you."

"No, indeed," she replied; "I do not want to hear a word about them, but I am going to give you one piece of advice, whether you like it or not. Don't be in a hurry to ask her to marry you. At this moment she does not want to marry anybody. Her position has entirely changed. She wanted to marry so that her plans might be settled before her father and his new wife arrive; and now she considers that they are settled. So be careful. It is true that the objections she formerly had to you are removed, but before you ask her to marry you, you should seriously ask yourself what reason there is she should do so. She does not know you very well; she is not interested in you; and I am very sure she is not in love with you. Now you know, for I have told you so, that I would be delighted to see you two married. I believe you would suit each other admirably, but although you may agree with me in this opinion, I am quite sure she does not; at least, not yet. Now, this is all I am going to say, except that you have my very best wishes that you may get her."

"I shall never forget that," said he, "but I see I am not to be free from the memory, at least, of the curb and the cage."

After breakfast on Monday the three discarded lovers departed in a dog-cart, Mr. Du Brant in front with the driver, and Claude Locker and Hemphill behind. For some minutes the party was silent. If circumstances had permitted they would have gone separately.

As long as he could see the mansion of Broadstone, Claude Locker spoke no word. When the time had come to go he had not wanted to go. When taking leave of Dick Lancaster he had congratulated that favored young man upon the fact that he had not been rejected, and had assured him that if he had remained at Broadstone he would have done his best to back him up as he had said he would.

Hemphill was not inclined to talk. Of course, Locker did not care to converse with the young diplomat, and consequently he found himself bored, and to relieve his feelings he burst into song. His words were impromptu, and although the verse was not very good, it was very impressive. It began as follows:

"Here we go,
Lovers three,
All steeped deep
In miseree."

At this Mr. Hemphill turned and looked at him, while a deep grunt came from the front seat, but the singer kept on without much attention to meter, and none at all to tune.

"This is so,

Here we go,
Flabbergasted,
Hopes all blasted,
Flags half-masted.
While it lasted,
We poor—"

"Look here," cried Du Brant, turning round suddenly, "I beg you desist that. You are insulting. And what you say is not true, as regards me at least. You can sing for yourself."

"Not true!" cried Locker. "Oh, ho, oh ho! Perhaps you have forgotten yourself, kind sir."

This little speech seemed to make Du Brant very angry, and he fairly shouted at Locker: "No, I haven't forgotten myself, and I have not forgotten you! You have insulted me before, and I should like to make you pay for it! I should like to have satisfaction from you, sir"

"That sounds well," cried Locker. "Do you mean to fight?"

"I want the satisfaction due to a gentleman," answered the young Austrian.

"Good," cried Locker, "that would suit me exactly. It would brighten me up. Let's do it now. I am not going to stop at Washington, and this is the only time I can give you. Driver, can we get to the station in time if we stop a little while?"

The person addressed was a young negro who had become intensely interested in the conversation.

"Oh, yes, sah," he answered. "We'll git dar twenty minutes before de train does, and if you takes half an hour I can whip up. That train's mostly late, anyway."

"All right," cried Locker. "And now, sir, how shall we fight? What have you got to fight with?"

Frank R. Stockton

"This is folly," growled Du Brant. "I have nothing to fight with. I do not fight with fists, like you Americans."

"Haven't you a penknife" coolly asked Locker. "If not, I daresay Mr. Hemphill will lend you one."

Du Brant now fairly trembled with anger. "When I fight," said he, "I fight like a gentleman; with a sword or a pistol."

"I am sorry," said Locker, "but if I remembered to bring my sword and pistol I must have put them in the bottom of my trunk, and that has gone on to the station. Have you two pistols or swords with you? Or do you think you could get sufficient satisfaction out of a couple of piles of stones that we could hurl at each other?"

Du Brant made no English answer to this, but uttered some savage remarks in French.

"Do you understand what all that means?" inquired Locker of Hemphill, who had been quietly listening to what had been going on.

"Yes," said the other, "he is cursing you up hill, and down dale."

"Oh," said Locker, "it sounds to me as if he were calculating his last week's expenses. But when he gets to French cursing, I drop him. I can't fight him that way."

The colored boy now showed that he was very much disappointed. He had expected the pleasure of a fight, and he was afraid he was going to lose it.

"I tell you, sah," he said to Locker, "why don't you try kickshins? Do you know what kick-shins is? You don't know what kick-shins is? Well, kick-shins is this: one fellow stands in front of the other fellow, and one takes hold of the collar of the other fellow, and the other fellow takes hold of his collar, and then they kicks each other's shins, and the one what squeals fust, he's licked, and the other one gits the gal. You've got pretty thin shoes, sah," addressing Du Brant, "and your feet ain't half as big as his'n, but your toes is more p'inted."

"No kick-shins for me," said Locker. "I've got to be economical about my clothes."

Du Brant's rage now became ungovernable. "Do you apologize," he cried, "or I take you by the throat, and I strangle you."

Hemphill, who had been smiling mildly at the kick-shin proposition, now turned himself about. "You will not do that," he said, "and if you don't sit quiet and keep your mouth shut, I'll toss you out of this cart, and make you walk the rest of the way to the station."

As Hemphill looked quite big and strong enough to execute this threat, and as he was too quiet a man to be ignored, Du Brant turned his face to the horse, and said no more.

"I did not know you were such a trump" cried Locker. "Give me your hand. I should hate to be strangled by a foreigner!"

When they took the train Du Brant went by himself into the smoking-car, and Locker and Hemphill had a seat together.

"Do you know," said Locker, "I am beginning to like you, although I must admit that before this morning I can remember no feeling of the sort."

"That is not surprising," said Hemphill. "A man is not generally fond of his rival."

"We will let it go at that," said Locker, "we'll let it go at that! I should not wonder, if we had all stayed at Broadstone; and if the central object of interest had also remained; and, if I had failed, as I have failed, to make the proper impression; and if the professor, whom I promised to back up in case I should find myself out of the combat, should also have failed; I should not wonder if I had backed up you."

CHAPTER XXIX

TWO PIECES OF NEWS

It was nearly two weeks after Mrs. Easterfield drove away from the captain's toll-gate before she went back there again. There were many reasons for thus depriving herself of Olive's society. Mr. Tom had stayed with her for an unusually long time; a house full of visitors, mostly relatives, had succeeded the departed lovers, and Foxes; and, besides, Olive was so very busy and so very happy—as she learned from many little notes—cleaning the house from garret to cellar, and loving her uncle better every day, that it really would have been a misdemeanor to interfere with her ardent pursuits.

But now Olive had written that she wanted to tell her a lot of things which could not go into a letter, and so the Broadstone carriage stopped again at the toll-gate.

Two great things had Olive to tell, and she was really glad that her uncle was not at home so that she might get at once to the telling.

In the first place, old Mr. Port was dead, and Captain Asher was in great trouble about this. Of course, he could not keep away from the deathbed of his old friend, nor could he neglect to do all honor to his memory, but it was a terrible thing for him to have to go into the house where Maria Port lived. After what had happened it was almost too much for his courage, although he was a brave man. But he had conquered his

Frank R. Stockton

feelings, and he was there now. The funeral would be to-morrow.

When Mrs. Easterfield heard all that Olive had to tell her about Maria Port, her heart went out to that brave man who kept the toll-gate.

The next thing that Olive had to tell was that she had heard from her father, who wrote that he would soon arrive in this country; that he would then go West, where he would marry Olive's former schoolmate; and that, on their wedding tour, he would make a little visit at the tollhouse so that Olive might see her new mother.

"Now, isn't this enough," cried Olive, "to make any girl spread her wings and fly to the ends of the earth? But I have no wings; they have all gone away in a dog-cart. But I don't feel about that as I used to feel," she continued, a little hardness coming into her face. "I am settled now just the same as if I were married, and father and Edith Malcolmsen may come just as soon as they please. They shall make no plans for me; I am going to stay here with Uncle John. This house is mine now, and I am seriously thinking of having it painted. I shall stay here just as if I were one of those trees, and my father and my new mother—"

Here tears came into Olive's eyes and Mrs. Easterfield stopped her.

"Olive," said she, "I will give you a piece of advice. When your father and his young wife come here, treat her exactly as if she were your old friend. If you do so I think you will get along very well. This is partly selfish advice, for I greatly desire the opportunity to treat your father hospitably. He was my friend when I was a girl, you remember, and I looked up to him with very great admiration."

And so these two friends sat and talked, and talked, and talked until it was positively shameful, considering that the

Broadstone horses were accustomed to be fed and watered at noon, and that the coachman was very hungry.

When, at last, Mrs. Easterfield drove home, and it must have been three in the afternoon, she left Olive very much comforted, even in regard to the unfortunate obligations which had fallen upon her uncle. For now that her old father had gone, all intercourse with the Port woman would cease.

But in her own mind Mrs. Easterfield was not so very much comforted. It was all well enough to talk about Olive and her uncle and the happiness and safety of the home he had given her, but that sort of thing could not last very long. He was an elderly man and she was a girl. In the natural course of events, she would probably be left alone while she was very young. She would then be alone, for her father's wife could never be a mother to her when he was at sea, and their home would never be a home for her when he was on shore. What Olive wanted, in Mrs. Easterfield's opinion, was a husband. An uncle, such as Captain Asher, was very charming, but he was not enough.

During this pleasant afternoon, when Captain Asher was in town attending to some arrangements for the burial of Mr. Port, Miss Maria was sitting discreetly alone in her darkened chamber. She had a great many things to think about, and if she had allowed her conscience full freedom of action, there would have been much more upon her mind. She might have been troubled by the recollection that since her father's very determined treatment of her when she had endeavored to fix herself upon the affections of Captain Asher, she had so conducted herself toward her venerable parent that she had actually nagged the life out of him; and that had she been the dutiful daughter she ought to have been he might have been living yet. But thoughts of this nature were not common to Maria Port. She had made herself sure that the will was all right, and he was very old. There was a time for all things, and Maria was now about to begin life for herself. To her plans for this new life she now gave almost her sole attention.

Frank R. Stockton

She had one great object in view which overshadowed every-thing else, and this was to marry Captain Asher. This she could have done before, she firmly believed, had it not been for her old father and that horrid girl, the captain's niece. As for the elderly man who kept the toll-gate she did not mind him. If not interfered with, she was sure she could make him marry her, and then the great ambition of her life would be satisfied.

Unpretentious as was her establishment in town, she did not care to spend the money necessary to keep it up, and although she was often an unkind woman, she was not cruel enough to think of inflicting herself as a boarder upon any housewife in the town. No, the toll-gate was the home for her; and if Captain Asher chose to inflict himself upon her for a few years longer, she would try to endure it.

One obstacle to her plans was now gone, and she must devote herself to the work of getting rid of the other one. While Olive Asher remained at the tollhouse there was no chance for her in that quarter.

The funeral was over, and when the bereaved Miss Port took leave of Captain Asher she exhibited a quiet gratitude which was very becoming and suitable. During the short time when he had visited the house every day she had showed him no resentment on account of what had passed between them, and had treated him very much as if he had been one of her father's old friends with whom she was not very well acquainted and to whom she was indebted for various services connected with the sad occasion.

When he took final leave of her he shook her hand, and as he did so he gave her a peculiar grasp which, in his own mind, indicated that he and she had now nothing more to do with each other, and that the acquaintance was adjourned without day. She bade him a simple farewell, and as he left the house she grinned at his broad back. This grin expressed, to herself at least, that the old and rather faulty acquaintance was at an end, and that the new connection which she intended to establish between herself and him would be upon an entirely different basis.

He did not ask her if there was anything more that he could do for her, for he did not desire to mix himself up with her affairs, which he knew she was eminently able to manage for herself, and it was with a deep breath of relief that he got into his buggy and drove home to his toll-gate.

CHAPTER XXX

BY THE SEA

When Lieutenant Asher and his bride arrived at his brother's toll-gate they were surprised as well as delighted by the cordiality of their greeting. Each of them had expected a little stiffness during the first interview, but there was nothing of the kind, although young Mrs. Asher was bound to admit, when she took time to think upon the subject, that Olive treated her exactly as if she had been a dear old schoolmate, and not at all as her father's wife. This made things very pleasant and easy at that time, she thought, although it might have to be corrected a little after a while.

Things were all very pleasant, and there never had been so much talk at the tollhouse since the first stone of its foundation had been laid. The day after the arrival of the newly married couple Mrs. Easterfield called upon them, and invited the whole family to dinner.

"I have never realized how much she must have thought of my parents!" said Olive to herself, as she gazed upon her father and Mrs. Easterfield. "They are so very glad to see each other!"

She did not know that Lieutenant Asher had been to the present Mrs. Easterfield almost as much of a divinity as Mr. Hemphill had been to her girlish fancy; the difference being that the young cadet was well aware of the adoration of this child, not yet in long dresses, and greatly enjoyed and encouraged it. When, a few years later, the child heard of his marriage, she had outgrown the love with the lengthening of the skirts. But she had a tender recollection of it which she cherished.

The dinner the next day was a great success, and after it the lieutenant and Mrs. Easterfield earnestly discussed Olive when they had the opportunity for a *tete-a-tete*. She was so much to each of them, and he was grateful that his daughter had fallen under the influence of this old friend, now a charming woman.

"She is so beautiful," said the lady, "that she ought to be married as soon as possible to the most suitable bachelor in the United States."

"Not so fast! Not so fast" said the lieutenant. "Edith and I are going to housekeeping very soon, and then we shall want Olive."

Mrs. Easterfield smiled, but made no reply.

When the lieutenant and his wife, with Olive, came a few days afterward to make their proper dinner call, he found an occasion to speak to their hostess.

"Do you know," said he, "that this is a strange girl of mine?" She positively refuses to come and live with us. We had counted upon having her, and had made all our arrangements for it. She is as good and nice as she can be, but we can not move her."

"You ought not to try," said Mrs. Easterfield; "it would be a shame for her to go away and leave her uncle. You have one young lady, and you should not ask for both. Olive must marry, and the captain must go and live with her."

"Have you arranged all that?" said he. "I remember you were a great schemer when quite a little girl."

"I am as great as ever," said she. "And I have selected the gentleman."

"Oh, ho!" cried the lieutenant. "And is that all settled? Olive should have told me that."

"She could not do it," said Mrs. Easterfield; "for it is not all settled. There are some obstacles in the way; and the greatest of them is that she does not love him."

The lieutenant laughed. "Then that is settled. I know Olive."

Mrs. Easterfield flushed, and then laughed. "I doubt that knowledge. It is certain you do not know me! The young man loves her with all his heart; there is no objection to him; and I am most earnestly in favor of the match."

"Ah" said the lieutenant, with a bow; "if that is the case, I must get a pencil and paper and calculate what I can give her for her trousseau. I hope the wedding will not come off very soon, for I am decidedly short at present, on account of recent matrimonial expenses. Would you mind telling me his name? Is he naval?"

"Oh, no," said she; "he is pedagogy."

"What!" he cried, his eyes wide open.

Then she laughed and told him all about Dick Lancaster.

"Of course," concluded Mrs. Easterfield, "I can not ask you not to speak to *anybody* about what I have told you, but I do hope you will prevent its getting to Olive's ears. I am afraid it would make a breach between us if she knew that I was trying to make a match for her. And, you see, that is exactly what I am doing."

"And you are right," said the lieutenant; "and what is more, I am with you! You don't know," he added in a softer tone, "how grateful I am to you for your care of Olive now that my dear wife is gone!"

For the moment he totally forgot that his dear wife had merely gone to the edge of the bluff with the captain and Olive to look at the river.

That evening, as they sat together, Lieutenant Asher told his brother all that Mrs. Easterfield had confided to him about Dick Lancaster. The captain was delighted.

"That is what I have wanted," he said, "almost from the beginning, and I want it more than ever now. I am getting to be an old fellow, and I want to see her settled before I sail."

"You know, John," said the lieutenant, "that I find Olive is a little more of a girl of her own mind than she used to be. I don't believe she would rest quietly under the housekeeping of a girl so nearly her own age."

The captain gave some vigorous puffs. "I should think not!" he said to himself. "Olive would have that young woman swabbing the decks before they had been out three days! You are right," said he aloud, "but we must all look out that Olive does not hear anything about this."

It was not until they were continuing their bridal trip that Lieutenant Asher considered the subject of mentioning Dick Lancaster to his wife. Then, after considering it, he concluded not to do it. In the first place, he knew that he was getting to be a little bit elderly, and he did not care about discussing the perfections of the young man who had been selected as a suitable partner for his wife's school friend. This was all very foolish, of course, but people often are very foolish.

Thus it was that Olive Asher never heard of the tripartite alliance between her father, her uncle, and her good friend at Broadstone.

When Captain Asher learned, a few days after his brother had left, that the Broadstone family had gone to the seashore, he sat reflectively and asked himself if he were doing the right thing by Olive. The season was well advanced; it was getting very hot at the toll-gate, and at many other gates in that region; and this navy girl ought to have a breath of fresh air. It is wonderful that he had not thought of it before!

At breakfast the next morning Olive stopped pouring coffee when he told her his plans to go to the sea.

"With you, Uncle John!" she cried. "That would be better than anything in the world! You sail a boat?" she asked inquiringly.

"Sail a boat!" roared the captain. "I have a great mind to kick over this table! My dear, I can sail a boat, keel uppermost, if the water's deep enough! Sail a boat!" he repeated. "I sailed a catboat from Boston to Egg Harbor before your mother was born. By the way, you seem very anxious about boat sailing. Are you afraid of the water?"

She laughed gaily. "I deserve that," she said, "and I accept it. But perhaps I have done something that you never did. I have sailed a felucca."

"Very good," said the captain; "if there's a felucca where we're going you can sail me in one."

They went to a Virginia seaside resort, these two, and left old Jane in charge of the toll-gate.

Early in the day after they arrived they went out to engage a boat. When they found one which suited the captain's critical eye, he said to the owner thereof: "I will take her for the morning, but I don't want anybody to sail me. I will do that myself."

"I don't know about that," said the man; "when my boat goes out—"

He stopped speaking suddenly and looked the captain over and over, up and down. "All right, sir," said he. "And you don't want nobody to manage the sheet?"

"No," interpolated Olive, "I'll manage the sheet."

So they went out on the bounding sea. And as the wind whistled the hat off her head so that she had to fling it into the bottom of the boat, Olive wished that her uncle kept a toll-gate on the sea. Then she could go out with him and stop the little boats and the great steamers, and make them drop seven cents or thirteen cents into her hands as she stood braced in the stern; and she was just beginning to wonder how she could toss up the change to them if they dropped her a quarter, when the captain began to sing Tom Bowline. He was just as gay-hearted as she was.

It was about noon when they returned, for the captain was a very particular man and he had hired the boat only for the morning. Olive had scarcely taken ten steps up the beach before she found herself shaking hands with a young man.

"How on earth!" she exclaimed.

"It was not on earth at all," he said; "I came by water. I wanted to find out if what I had heard of the horrors of a coastwise voyage were true; and I found that it was absolutely correct."

"But here!" she exclaimed. "Why here? You could not have known!"

"Of course not," he answered; "if I had known I am sure I would have felt that I ought not to come. But I didn't know, and so you see I am as innocent as a butterfly. More innocent, in fact, for that little wagwings knows where he ought not to go, and he goes there all the same."

Captain Asher was still at the boat, making some practical suggestions to her owner; who, being not yet forty, had many things to learn about the sails and rigging of a catboat.

"Mr. Locker," said Olive, looking at him very intently, "did you come here to renew any of your previous performances?"

"As a serenader?" said he. "Oh, no! But perhaps you mean as a love-maker?"

"That is it," said Olive.

Mr. Locker took off his hat, and rubbed his head. "No," said he, "I didn't; but I wish I could say I did. But that's impossible. I presume I am right in assuming this impossibility?"

"Entirely," said Olive.

"And, furthermore, I truly didn't know you were here. I think you may rest satisfied that that flame is out, although—By the way, I believe I could make some verses on that subject containing these lines:

"'I do not want the flame,
I better like the coal—'

meaning, of course, that I hope our friendship may continue."

She smiled. "There are no objections to that," she said.

"Perhaps not, perhaps not," he said, clutching his chin with his hand; "but some other lines come into my head. Of course, he didn't want the coal to go out.

"'He blew too hard,
The flame revived.'"

"That will do! That will do!" cried Olive. "I don't want any more of that poem."

"And the result of it all," said he, "is only a burnt match."

"Nothing but a bit of charcoal," added Olive.

At this moment up came the captain. Olive had told him all about Mr. Locker, and he was not glad to see him. Olive noticed this, and she spoke quickly. "Here's Mr. Locker, uncle; he has dropped down quite accidentally at this place."

"Oh" said the captain incredulously.

"You know he used to like me too much. But he knows me better now."

"Charming frankness of friendship!" said Locker.

"And as I like him very much, I am glad he is here," continued Olive.

The young man bowed in gratitude, but Olive's words embarrassed him somewhat, and he did not know exactly what would be suitable for him to say. So he took refuge in a change of subject. "Captain," said he, "can you fish?"

A look of scornful amazement showed itself upon the old mariner's face. "I have tried it," said he.

"And so have I," cried Locker, "but I never had any luck in fishing and—some other things. I am vilely unlucky. I expect that's because I don't know how to fish."

"It is very likely," said Olive, "that your bad luck comes from not knowing where to fish."

The young man took off his hat and held it for a little while, although the sun was very hot.

During the course of that afternoon and evening Captain Asher grew to like Claude Locker. The young man told such gravely comical stories, especially about his experiences in boats and on the water, that the captain was very glad he had

Frank R. Stockton

happened to drop down upon that especial watering-place. He wanted Olive to have some society besides his own, and a discarded lover was better than any other young man they might meet. He knew that Olive was a girl who would not go back on her word.

CHAPTER XXXI

AS GOOD AS A MAN

The next day our three friends went fishing in a catboat belonging to the young seaman of forty, and they took their dinner with them, although Mr. Locker declared that he did not believe that he would want any.

They had a good time on the water, for the captain had made careful inquiries about the best fishing grounds, and the mishaps of Locker were so numerous and so provocative of queer remarks from himself, that the captain and Olive sometimes forgot to pull up their fish, so preengaged were they in laughing. The sky was bright, the water smooth, and even Mr. Locker caught fish, although it might have been thought that he did everything possible to prevent himself doing so.

When their boat ran up the beach late in the afternoon the captain and Olive were still laughing, and Mr. Locker was as sober as a soda-water fountain from which spouts such intermittent sparkle. Dear as was the toll-gate, this was a fine change from that quiet home.

The next morning, upon the sand, Claude Locker approached Olive. "Would you like to decline my addresses for the second time?" he abruptly asked.

"Of course not" she exclaimed.

Frank R. Stockton

"Well, then," said he, extending his hand, "good-by!"

"What are you talking about?" said Olive. "What does this mean?"

"It means," said he, "that I have fallen in love with you again. I think I am rather worse than I was before. If I stay here I shall surely propose. Nothing can stop me—not even the presence of your uncle if it is impossible for me to see you alone—and, if you don't want any of that, it is necessary that I go, and go quickly."

"Of course I don't want it," she said. "But why need you be so foolish? We were getting along so nicely as friends. I expected to have lots of fun here with you and uncle."

"Fun!" groaned Locker. "It might have been fun for you and the captain, but what of the poor torn heart? I know I must go, and now. If I stay here five minutes longer I shall be at your feet, and it will be far better if I take to my own. Good-by!" And, with a warm grasp of her hand, he departed.

Olive looked after him as he walked to the hotel. If he had known how much she regretted to see him go he would have come back, and all his troubles would have begun again.

"Hello!" cried the captain when Locker had entered the house, "I was looking for you. We can run out, and have some fishing this morning. The tide will suit. You did so well yesterday that I think to-day. I can even teach you to take out a hook."

"Take out a hook?" said Locker. "I have a hook within me which no man in this world, and but one woman, can take out. And as this she must not even be asked to do, I go. Farewell!"

"What's the matter with the young man" asked the captain of Olive a little later.

"Oh, he has fallen in love with me again," said Olive, with a sigh, "and, of course, that spoils everything. I wish people could be more sensible."

The captain looked down upon her admiringly. "I don't see any hope for people," he said. And this was the first personal compliment he had ever paid his niece.

When Claude Locker had gone, Olive missed him more than she thought she could miss anybody. Much of the life seemed to have gone out of the place, and the captain's high spirits waned as if he was suffering from the depression which follows a stimulant.

"If that young fellow had been better-looking," said the captain, "if he had more solid sense, and a good business, with both his eyes alike, I might have been more willing to let him go."

"If he had been all that," asked Olive with a smile, "why shouldn't you have been willing to let him stay?"

The captain did not answer. No matter what young Locker might have been, he could never have been Dick Lancaster.

"Uncle," said Olive that afternoon, "where shall we go next?"

"I don't know," said he, "but let's go to-morrow. I don't believe I like so many strangers except when they pay toll."

They traveled about a good deal; and in a general way enjoyed themselves; but they were both old travelers, and mere novelty was not enough for them. Each loved the company of the other, but each would have liked to have Locker along. It grieved Olive to think that she wanted him, or anybody, but she would not even try to deceive herself. The weather grew cooler, and she said to her uncle: "Let us go back to the toll-gate; it must be perfectly beautiful there now, with the mountains putting on their gold and red."

So they started for home, planning for a stop in Washington on their way.

Brightness and people were coming back to Washington. The air was cooler, and city life was stirring. Olive and her uncle stayed several days longer than they had intended; as most people do who visit Washington. On one of these days as they were returning to their hotel from the Smithsonian grounds, where they had been looking at autumn leaves from all quarters of this wide land; many of them unknown to them; they looked with interest from the shaded grounds on one side of the street to the great public building on the other side, which they were then passing, and at the broad steps ascending from the sidewalk to the basement floor.

As they moved on thus slowly they noticed a man standing upon the upper steps of one of these stairs. His back was toward them; and, as their eyes fell upon him he stepped upon the upper sidewalk. He was walking with a cane which seemed to be rather short for him. He stood still for a moment, and appeared to be waiting for some one. Then, suddenly his whole frame thrilled with nervous action; he slightly lowered his head, and, in an instant, he brought his cane to his shoulder, as if it had been a gun. The captain had seen that sort of thing before. It was an air-gun. Without a word he made a dash at the man. He was elderly, but in a case like this he was swift. As he ran he glanced out in the direction in which the gun was aimed. Along the broad, sunlighted avenue a barouche was passing. On the back seat sat two gentlemen, well-dressed, erect. Even in a flash one would notice an air of dignity in their demeanor.

There was not time to strike down the weapon, but before the man had heard steps behind him the captain gave him a tremendous blow between the shoulders which staggered him, and spoiled his aim. Then the captain seized the air-gun. There was a whiz, and a click on the pavement. Then the man turned.

His black eyes flashed out of a swarthy face nearly covered with beard; his soft hat had fallen off when the captain struck him, and his black hair stood up like bristles on a shoe-brush. He was not a large man; he wore a loose woolen jacket; his sleeves were short, and his hands were hairy.

All this Olive saw, for she had been quick to follow her uncle; but the captain, who firmly held the air-gun, saw nothing but the glaring face of a devil.

The man jerked furiously at the gun, but the captain's grasp was too strong. Then the fellow released his hold upon the gun, and, with a savage fury, threw himself upon the older man. The two stood near the top of the steps, and the shock of the attack was so great that both fell, slipping down several of the stone steps.

Olive tried to scream, but in her fright her voice utterly left her. She could not make a sound. As they lay upon the steps, the captain beneath, the man seized his victim by the neck with both hands, pressing his great thumbs deeply into his throat. Apparently he did not notice Olive. All the efforts of his devilish soul were bent upon stifling the voice and the life out of the witness of his attempted crime. Olive sprang down, and stood over the struggling men. Her uncle's eyes stared at her, and seemed bursting from his head. His face was growing dark. Again Olive tried to scream; and, in a frenzy, she seized the man to pull him from the captain. As she did so her hand fell upon something protruding under his woolen jacket. With a quick flash of instinct her sense of feeling recognized this thing. She jerked up the jacket, and there was the stock of a pistol protruding from his hip pocket. In an instant Olive drew it.

A horrid sound issued from the mouth of Captain Asher; he was choking to death. In the same second that she heard it Olive thrust the muzzle of the pistol against the side of the man's head and pulled the trigger.

The man's head fell forward and his hairy hands released their grip, but they still remained at the captain's throat. The latter gave a great gasp, and for an instant he turned his eyes full upon the face of his niece. Then his lids closed.

Now there were footsteps, and, looking up, Olive saw a negro cabman in faded livery and an old silk hat, who stood staring. Before she could speak to him there came another man, a policeman, who, equally amazed, stared at the group below him. Only these two had heard the pistol shots. There were no other people passing on the avenue, and as it was past office hours there was no one in the great public building.

Until they reached the top of the steps the policeman and cabman could see nothing. Now they stood astounded as they stared down upon an elderly man lying on his back on the steps; another man, apparently lifeless, lying on top of him with his hands upon his throat; and a girl standing a little below them with a smoking pistol in her hand.

Before they had time to speak or move Olive called out, "Take that man off my uncle."

In a moment the policeman, followed by the negro, ran down the steps and pulled the black-headed man off the captain, and the limp body slipped down several steps.

The policeman now turned toward Olive. "Take this," she said, handing him the pistol. "I shot him. He was trying to kill my uncle."

The two men raised the captain to a sitting position. He was now breathing, though in gasps, with his eyes opened.

The policeman took the pistol, looked at it, then at Olive, then at the captain, and then down at the body on the steps. He was trying to get an idea of what had happened without asking. If the negro had not been present he might have asked questions, but this was an unusual situation, and he felt his responsibility, and his importance. Olive now stepped toward him, and in obedience to her quick gesture he bent his head, and she whispered something to him. Instantly he was quivering with excitement. He thrust the pistol into his pocket, and turned to the negro. "Run," said he, "and get your cab! Don't say a word to a soul and I will give you five dollars."

The moment the negro had departed Olive said: "Pick up that air-gun. There, on the upper step." Then she went to her uncle and sat down by him.

"Are you hurt?" she said. "Can you speak?"

The captain put his arm around her shoulder, fixing a loving look upon her, and murmured, "You are as good as a man!"

The policeman picked up the air-gun, and gazed upon it as if it had been a telegram in cipher from a detective. Then he tried to conceal it under his coat, but it was too long.

"Let me have it," said Olive; "I will put it behind me."

She had barely concealed it when the cab drove up.

"Now," said the policeman, "you two must go with me. Can you walk, sir?"

"Oh, yes," said the captain in a voice clear, but weak.

Olive rose, holding the air-gun behind her, and the policeman and the cabman helped the captain to the carriage. Olive followed, and the policeman, actuated by some strong instinct, did not look around to see if she were doing so. He had no more idea that she would run away than that the stone steps would move. When he saw that she had taken the air-gun into the carriage with her, he closed the door.

"Did your fall hurt you, uncle?" said Olive, looking anxiously into his face.

"My throat hurts dreadfully," he said, "and I'm stiff. But I'll be stiffer to-morrow."

The policeman picked up the hat of the black-haired man, and going down the steps, he placed it on his head. "Now help me up with this gentleman," he said to the cabman; "we must put him on the box-seat between us. Take him under the arms, and we'll carry him naturally. He must be awfully drunk!"

So they lifted him up the steps, and, after much trouble, got him on the box-seat. Fortunately they were both big men. Then they drove away to police headquarters. The officer was the happiest policeman in Washington. This was the greatest piece of work he had known of during his service; and he was doing it all himself. With the exception of the driver, nobody else was mixed up in it in the least degree. What he was doing was not exactly right; it was not according to custom and regulation. He should have called for assistance, for an ambulance; but he had not, and his guardian angel had kept all foot-passengers from the steps of the public building. He did not know what it all meant, but he was doing it himself, and if that black driver should slip from his seat (of which he occupied a very small portion) and he should break his neck, the policeman would clutch the reins, and be happier than any man in Washington.

There were very many people who looked at the drunken man who was being carried off by the policeman, but the cabman drove swiftly, and gave such people very little opportunity for close observation.

CHAPTER XXXII

THE STOCK-MARKET IS SAFE

There was a great stir at the police station, but Olive and her uncle saw little of it. They were quickly taken to private rooms, where the captain was attended by a police surgeon. He had been bruised and badly treated, but his injuries were not serious.

Olive was put in charge of a matron, who wondered greatly what brought her there. Very soon they were examined separately, and the tale of each of them was almost identical with that of the other; only Olive was able to tell more about the two gentlemen in the barouche, for she had been at her uncle's side, and there was nothing to obstruct her vision.

When the examination was ended the police captain enjoined each of them to say no word to any living soul about what they had testified to him. This was a most important matter, and it was necessary that it be hedged around with the greatest secrecy.

When Olive retired to her plain but comfortable cot she was tired and weak from the reaction of her restrained emotions, but she did not immediately go to sleep for thinking that she had killed a man. And yet for this killing there was not in this girl's mind one atom of regret. She was so grateful that she had been there, and had been enabled to do it. She had seen her uncle almost at his last gasp, and she had saved him from

Frank R. Stockton

making that last gasp. Moreover, she had saved the life of the man who had saved the most important life in the land. She knew the face of the gentleman in the barouche who sat on the side nearest her; she knew what her uncle had done, and she was proud of him; she knew what she had done for him; and she regarded the black-haired man with the hairy hands no more than she would have regarded a wild beast who had suddenly sprung upon them. She thought of him, of course, with horror, but her feelings of thankfulness for her uncle's safety were far too strong. At last her grateful heart closed her eyes, and let her rest.

There were no letters found on the body of the black-haired man which gave any clue to his name; but there were papers which showed that he was from southern France; that he was an anarchist; that he was in this country upon a mission; and that he had been for two weeks in Washington, waiting for an opportunity to fulfil that mission. Which opportunity had at last shown itself in front of him just as Captain John Asher rushed up behind him.

This information was so important that extraordinary methods were pursued. Communications were immediately made with the State Department, and with the higher police authorities; and it was quickly determined that, whatever else might be done, the strictest secrecy must be enforced. The coroner's jury was carefully selected and earnestly admonished; and, early the next morning, when the captain and Olive were required to testify before it, they were made to understand how absolutely necessary it was they should say nothing except to answer the questions which were asked them. The coroner was eminently discreet in regard to his questions; and the verdict was that Olive was acting in her own defense as well as that of her uncle when she shot his assailant.

Among the officials whose positions enabled them to know all these astonishing occurrences it was unanimously agreed that, so far as possible, everybody should be kept in ignorance of the crime which had been attempted, and of the deliverance which had taken place.

Very early the next afternoon the air was filled with the cries of newsboys, and each paper that these boys sold contained a full and detailed account of a remarkable attempt by an unknown foreigner upon the life of Captain John Asher, a visitor in Washington, and the heroic conduct of his niece, Miss Olive Asher, who shot the murderous assailant with his own pistol. There were columns and columns of this story, but strange to say, in not one of the papers was there any allusion to the two gentlemen in the barouche, or to the air-gun.

How this most important feature of the occurrence came to be omitted in all the accounts of it can only be explained by those who thoroughly understand the exigencies of the stock-market, and the probable effect of certain classes of news upon approaching political situations, and who have made themselves familiar with the methods by which the pervasive power of the press is sometimes curtailed.

In the later afternoon editions there were portraits of Olive, and her uncle. Olive was broad-shouldered, with black hair and a determined frown, while the captain was a little man with a long beard. There were no portraits of the anarchist. He passed away from the knowledge of man, and no one knew even his name: his crime had blotted him out; his ambition was blotted out; even the evil of his example was blotted out. There was nothing left of him.

When they were released from detention the captain and Olive quickly left the station—which they did without observation—and entered a carriage which was waiting for them a short distance away. The fact that another carriage with close-drawn curtains had stopped at the station about ten minutes before, and that a thickly veiled lady (the matron) and an elderly man with his collar turned up and his hat drawn down (one of the police officers in plain clothes) had entered the carriage and had been driven rapidly away had drawn off the reporters and the curiosity mongers on the sidewalk and had contributed very much to the undisturbed exit of Captain and Miss Asher.

These two proceeded leisurely to the railroad-station, where they took a train which would carry them to the little town of Glenford. Their affairs at the hotel could be arranged by telegram. There were calls at that hotel during the rest of the day from people who knew Olive or her uncle; calls from people who wanted to know them; calls from people who would be contented even to look at them; calls from autograph hunters who would be content simply to send up their cards; quiet calls from people connected with the Government; and calls from eager persons who could not have told anybody what they wanted. To none of these could the head clerk give any satisfaction. He had not seen his guests since the day before, and he knew naught about them.

When Miss Maria Port heard that that horrid girl, Olive Asher, had shot an anarchist, she stiffened herself to her greatest length, and let her head fall on the back of her chair. She was scarcely able to call to the small girl who endured her service to bring her some water. "Now all is over," she groaned, "for I can never marry a man whose niece's hands are dripping with blood. She will live with him, of course, for he is just the old fool to allow that, and anyway there is no other place for her to go except the almshouse—that is, if they'll take her in." And at the terrified girl, who tremblingly asked if she wanted any more water, she threw her scissors.

The captain and his niece arrived early in the day at Glenford station. The captain engaged a little one-horse vehicle which had frequently brought people to the toll-gate, and informed the driver that there was no baggage. The man, gazing at Olive, but scarcely daring to raise his eyes to her face, proceeded with solemn tread toward his vehicle as if he had been leading the line in a funeral.

As they drove through the town they were obliged to pass the house of Miss Maria Port. The door was shut, and the shutters were closed. She had had a terrible night, and had slept but little, but hearing the sound of wheels upon the street, she had bounced out of bed and had peered through the blinds. When she saw who it was she cursed them both.

"That was the only thing," she snapped, "that could have kept me from gettin' him! So far as I know, that was the only thing!"

When old Jane received the travelers at the toll-gate she warmly welcomed the captain, but she trembled before Olive. If the girl noticed the demeanor of the old woman, she pretended not to do so, and, speaking to her pleasantly, she passed within.

"Will they hang her?" she said to the captain later.

"What do you mean?" he shouted. "Have you gone crazy?"

"The people in the town said they would," replied old Jane, beginning to cry a little.

The captain looked at her steadily. "Did any particular person in the town say that?"

"Yes, sir," she answered; "Miss Maria Port was the first to say it, so I've been told."

"She is the one who ought to be hanged!" said the captain, speaking very warmly. "As for Miss Olive, she ought to have a monument set up for her. I'd do it myself if I had the money."

Old Jane answered not, but in her heart she said: "But she killed a man! It is truly dreadful!"

By nightfall of that day the two hotels of Glenford were crowded, the visitors being generally connected with newspapers. On the next day there was a great deal of travel on the turnpike, and old Jane was kept very busy, the captain having resigned the entire business of toll-taking to her. Everybody stopped, asked questions, and requested to see the captain; and many drove through and came back again, hoping to have better luck next time. But their luck was always bad; old Jane would say nothing; and the captain and Olive were not to be seen. The gate to the little front garden was locked, and there was no passing through the tollhouse. To keep people from getting over the fence a bulldog, which the captain kept at the barn, was turned loose in the yard.

There were men with cameras who got into the field opposite the toll-gate, and who took views from up and down the road, but their work could not be prevented, and Olive and her uncle kept strictly indoors.

It was on the afternoon of the second day of siege that the captain, from an upper window, discovered a camera on three legs standing outside of his grounds at a short distance from the house. A man was taking sight at something at the back of the house. Softly the captain slipped down into the back yard, and looking up he saw Olive sitting at a window, reading.

With five steps the captain went into the house and then reappeared at the back door with a musket in his hand. The man had stepped to his pack at a little distance to get a plate. The captain raised his musket to his shoulder; Olive sprang to her feet at the sound of the report; old Jane in the tollhouse screamed; and the camera flew into splinters.

After this there were no further attempts to take pictures of the inmates of the house at the toll-gate.

After two days of siege the newspaper reporters and the photographers left Glenford. They could not afford to waste any more time. But they carried away with them a great many stories about the captain and his erratic niece, mostly gleaned from a very respectable elderly lady of the town by the name of Port.

CHAPTER XXXIII

DICK LANCASTER DOES NOT WRITE

On the third morning after their arrival at the toll-gate the captain and Olive ventured upon a little walk over the farm. It was very hard upon both of them to be shut up in the house so long. They saw no reporters, nor were there any men with cameras, but the scenery was not pleasant, nor was the air particularly exhilarating. They were not happy; they felt alone, as if they were in a strange place. Some of the captain's friends in the town came to the toll-gate, but there were not many, and Olive saw none of them. The whole situation reminded the girl of the death of her mother.

As soon as it was known that the Ashers were at home there came letters from many quarters. One of these was from Mrs. Easterfield. She would be at Broadstone as soon as she could get her children started from the seashore. She longed to take Olive to her heart, but whether this was in commiseration or commendation was not quite plain to Olive. The letter concluded with this sentence: "There is something behind all this, and when I come you must tell me."

Then there was one from her father in which he bemoaned what had happened. "That such a thing should have come to my daughter!" he wrote. "To my daughter!" There was a great deal more of it, but he said nothing about coming with his young wife to the toll-gate, and Olive's countenance was almost stern when she handed this letter to her uncle.

Frank R. Stockton

Claude Locker wrote:

"How I long, how I rage to write to you, or to go to you! But if I should write, it would be sure to give you pain, and if I should go to you I should also go crazy. Therefore, I will merely state that I love you madly; more now than ever before; and that I shall continue to do so for the rest of my life, no matter what happens to you, or to me, or to anybody.

"Ever turned toward you,

"CLAUDE LOCKER.

"How I wish I had been there with a sledgehammer!"

And then there were the newspapers. Many of these the captain had ordered by the Glenford bookseller, and a number were sent by friends, and some even by strangers. And so they learned what was thought of them over a wide range of country, and this publicity Olive found very hard to bear. It was even worse than the deed she was forced to do, and which gave rise to all this disagreeable publicity. That deed was done in the twinkling of an eye, and was the only thing that could be done; but all this was prolonged torture. Of course, the newspapers were not responsible for this. The transaction was a public one in as public a place as could possibly be selected, and it was clearly their duty to give the public full information in regard to it. They knew what had happened, and how could they possibly know what had not happened? Nor could they guess that this was of more importance than the happening. And so they all viewed the action from the point of view that a young woman had blown out a man's brains on the steps of the Treasury. It was a most unusual, exciting, and tragic incident, and in a measure, incomprehensible; and coming at a time when there was a dearth of news, it was naturally much exploited. Many of the papers recognized the fact that Miss Asher had done this deed to save her uncle's life, and applauded it, and praised her quick-wittedness and courage;

but all this was spoiled for Olive by the tone of commiseration for her in which it was all stated. She did not see why she should be pitied. Rather should she be congratulated that she was, fortunately, on the spot. Other journals did not so readily give in to the opinion that it was an act of self-defense. It might be so; but they expressed strong disapproval of the legal action in this strange affair. A young woman, accompanied by a relative, had killed an unknown man. The action of the authorities in this case had been rapid and unsatisfactory. The person who had fired the fatal shot and her companion had been cleared of guilt upon their own testimony, and the cause of the man who died had no one to defend it. If two persons can kill a man, and then state to the coroner's jury that it was all right, and thereupon repair to their homes without further interference by the law, then had the cause of justice in the capital of the nation reached a very strange pass.

Such were the views of the reputable journals. But there were some which fell into the captain's hands that were well calculated to arouse his ire. Such a sensational occurrence did not often come in their way, and they made the most of it. They scented the idea that the girl had killed an unknown man to save her uncle's life; blamed the authorities severely for not finding out who he was; suggested there must be a secret reason for this; and hinted darkly at a scandal connected with the affair, which, if investigated, would be found to include some well-known names.

"This is outrageous!" cried the captain. "It is too abominable to be borne! Olive, why should we not tell the exact facts of this thing? We did agree—very willingly at the time—to keep the secret. But I am not willing now, and you are being sacrificed to the stock-market. That is the whole truth of it! If these editors knew the truth they would be chanting your praises. If that scoundrel had killed me, he would have killed you, and then he could have run away to go on with his President shooting. I am going to Washington this very day to tell the whole story. You shall not suffer that stocks may not fall and the political situation made alarming at election time.

Frank R. Stockton

That is what it all means, and I won't stand it!"

"You will only make things worse, uncle," said Olive. "Then the whole matter will be stirred up afresh. We will be summoned to investigations, and all sorts of disagreeable things. Every item of our lives will be in the papers, and some will be invented. It is very bad now, but in a little while the public will forget that a countryman and a country girl had a fracas in Washington. But the other thing will never be forgotten. It is very much better to leave it as it is."

The captain, notwithstanding the presence of a lady, cursed the officials, the newspapers, the Government, and the whole country. "I am going to do it!" he cried vehemently. "I don't care what happens!"

But Olive put her arms around him and coaxed him for her sake to let the matter rest. And, finally, the captain, grumblingly, assented.

If Olive had been a girl brought up in a gentle-minded household, knowing nothing of the varied life she had lived when a navy girl; sometimes at this school and sometimes at that; sometimes in her native land, and sometimes in the midst of frontier life; sometimes with parents, and sometimes without them; and, had she been less aware from her own experiences and those of others, that this is a world in which you must stand up very stiffly if you do not want to be pushed down; she might have sunk, at least for a time, under all this publicity and blame. Even the praise had its sting.

But she did not sink. The liveliness and the fun went out of her, and her face grew hard and her manner quiet. But she was not quiet within. She rebelled against the unfairness with which she was treated. No matter what the newspapers knew or did not know, they should have known, and should have remembered, that she had saved her uncle's life. If they had known more they would have been just and kind enough no doubt, but they ought to have been just and kind without knowing more.

Captain Asher would now read no more papers. But Olive read them all.

Letters still came; one of them from Mr. Easterfield. But every time a mail arrived there was a disappointment in the toll-gate household. The captain could scarcely refrain from speaking of his disappointment, for it was a true grief to him that Dick Lancaster had not written a word. Of course, Olive did not say anything upon the subject, for she had no right to expect such a letter, and she was not sure that she wanted one, but it was very strange that a person who surely was, or had been, somewhat interested in her uncle and herself should have been the only one among her recent associates who showed no interest whatever in what had befallen her. Even Mr. and Mrs. Fox had written. She wished they had not written, but, after all, stupidity is sometimes better than total neglect.

"Olive," said the captain one pleasant afternoon, "suppose we take a drive to Broadstone? The family is not there, but it may interest you to see the place where I hope your friends will soon be living again. I can not bear to see you going about so dolefully. I want to brighten you up in some way."

"I'd like it," said Olive promptly. "Let us go to Broadstone."

At that moment they heard talking in the tollhouse; then there were some quick steps in the garden; and, almost immediately, Dick Lancaster was in the house and in the room where the captain and his niece were sitting. He stepped quickly toward them as they rose, and gave Olive his left hand because the captain had seized his right and would not let it go.

"I have been very slow getting here," he said, looking from one to the other. "But I would not write, and I have been unconscionably delayed. I am so proud of you," he said, looking Olive full in the face, but still holding the captain by the hand.

Frank R. Stockton

Olive's hand had been withdrawn, but it was very cheering to her to know that some one was proud of her.

The captain poured out his delight at seeing the young professor—the first near friend he had seen since his adventure, and, in his opinion, the best. Olive said but little, but her countenance brightened wonderfully. She had always liked Mr. Lancaster, and now he showed his good sense and good feeling; for, while it was evidently on his mind, he made no allusion to anything they had done, or that had happened to them. He talked chiefly of himself.

But the captain was not to be repressed, and his tone warmed up a little as he asked if Dick had been reading the newspapers.

At this Olive left the room to make some arrangements for Mr. Lancaster's accommodation.

Seizing this opportunity, Dick Lancaster stopped the captain, who he saw was preparing to go lengthily into the recent affair. "Yes, yes," he said, speaking quickly, "and my blood has run hot as I read those beastly papers. But let me say something to you while I can. I am deeply interested in something else just now. I came here, captain, to propose marriage to your niece. Have I your consent?"

"Consent!" cried the captain. "Why, it is the clearest wish of my heart that you should marry Olive!" And seizing the young man by both arms, he shook him from head to foot. "Consent!" he exclaimed. "I should think so, I should think so! Will she take you, Dick? Is that—"

"I don't know," said Lancaster, "I don't know. I am here to find out. But I hear her coming."

The happy captain thought it full time to go away somewhere. He felt that he could not control his glowing countenance, and that he might say or do something which might be wrong. So he departed with great alacrity, and left the two young people to themselves.

Frank R. Stockton

CHAPTER XXXIV

MISS PORT PUTS IN AN APPEARANCE

The captain clapped on his hat, and walked up the road toward Glenford. He was very much excited and he wanted to sing, but his singing days were over, and he quieted himself somewhat by walking rapidly. There was a buggy coming from town, but it stopped before it reached him and some one in it got out, while the vehicle proceeded slowly onward. The some one waited until the captain came up to her. It was Miss Maria Port.

"How do you do?" she said, holding out her hand. "I was on my way to see you."

The captain put both his hands in his pockets, and his face grew somewhat dark. "Why do you want to see me?" he asked.

She looked at him steadily for a moment, and then answered, speaking very quietly. "I found that Mr. Lancaster had arrived in town, and had gone to your house, and that he was in such a hurry that he walked. So I immediately hired a buggy to come out here. I am very glad I met you."

"But what in the name of common sense," exclaimed the captain, "did you come to see me for? What difference does it make to you whether Mr. Lancaster is here or not? What have you got to do with me and my affairs, anyway?"

She smiled a smile which was very quiet and flat. "Now, don't get angry," she said. "We can talk over things in a friendly way just as well as not, and it will be a great deal better to do it. And I'd rather talk here in the public road than anywhere else; it's more private."

"I don't want a word to say to you," said the captain, preparing to move on. "I have nothing at all to do with you."

"Ah," said Miss Port, with another smile, "but I think you have. You've got to marry me, you know."

Then the captain stopped suddenly. He opened his mouth, but he could find no immediate words.

"Yes, indeed," said Miss Port, now speaking quietly; "and when I saw Mr. Lancaster had come to town, I knew that I must see you at once. Of course, he has come to take away your niece, and that's the best thing to be done, for she wouldn't want to keep on livin' here where so many people have known her. At first I thought that would be a very good thing, for you would be separated from her, and that's what you need and deserve. Young men are young men, and they are often a good deal kinder than they would be if they stopped to think. But a person of mature age is different. He would know what is due to himself and his standing in society. At least, that is what I did think. But it suddenly flashed on me that they might want to get away as quick as they could— which would be proper, dear knows—and it would be just like you to go with them. And so I came right out."

The captain had listened to all this because he very much wanted to know what she had to say, but now he exclaimed: "Do you suppose I shall pay any attention to all the gossip about my affairs?"

"Now, don't go on like that," said Miss Port; "it doesn't do any good, and if you'll only keep quiet, and think pleasantly about it, there will be no trouble at all. You know you've got to marry me; that's settled. Everybody knows about it, and has known about it for years. I didn't press the matter while father was alive because I knew it would worry him. But now I'm going to do it. Not in any anger or bad feelin', but gently, and as firmly as if I was that tree. I don't want to go to any law, but if I have to do it, I'll do it. I've got my proofs and my witnesses, and I'm all right. The people of your own house are witnesses. And there are ever so many more."

"Woman!" cried the captain, "don't you say another word! And don't you ever dare to speak to me again! I'm not going away, and my niece is not going away; and I assure you that I hate and despise you so much that all the law in the world couldn't make me marry you. Although you know as well as I do that all you've been saying has no sense or truth in it."

Miss Port did not get angry. With wonderful self-repression she controlled her feelings. She knew that if she lost that control there would be an end to everything. She grew pale, but she spoke more gently than before. "You know"—she was about to say "John," but she thought she would better not— "that what I say about determination and all that, I simply say because you do not come to meet me half-way, as I would have you do. All I want is to get you to acknowledge my rights, to defend me from ridicule. You know that I am now alone in the world, and have no one to look to but you—to whom I always expected to look when father died—and if you should carry out your cruel words, and should turn from me as if I was a stranger and a nobody, after all these years of visitin' and attention from you, which everybody knows about, and has talked about, I could never expect anybody else—you bein' gone—to step forward—"

At this the face of the captain cleared, and as he gazed upon the unpleasant face and figure of this weather-worn spinster, the idea that any one with matrimonial intentions should "step forward," as she put it, struck him as being so extremely ludicrous that he burst out laughing.

Then leaped into fire every nervelet of Miss Maria Port. "Laugh at me, do you?" cried she. "I'll give you something to laugh at! And if you 're going to stand up for that thing you have in your house, that murderess—"

She said no more. The captain stepped up to her with a smothered curse so that she moved back, frightened. But he did nothing. He was too enraged to speak. She was a woman, and he could not strike her to the ground. Before her sallow venom he was helpless. He was a man and she was a woman, and he could do nothing at all. He was too angry to stay there another second, and, without a word, he left her, walking with great strides toward the town.

Miss Maria Port stood looking after him, panting a little, for her excitement had been great. Then, with a yellow light in her eyes, she hurried toward her vehicle, which had stopped.

As Captain Asher strode into town he asked himself over and over again what should he do? How should he punish this wildcat—this ruthless creature, who spat venom at the one he loved best in the world, and who threatened him with her wicked claws? In his mind he looked from side to side for help; some one must fight his battle for him; he could not fight a woman. He had not reached town when he thought of Mrs. Faulkner, the wife of the Methodist minister. He knew her; she and her husband had been among the friends who had come out to see him; and she was a woman. He would go directly to her, and ask her advice.

The captain was not shown into the parlor of the parsonage, but into the minister's study, that gentleman being away. He heard a great sound of talking as he passed the parlor door, and it was not long before Mrs. Faulkner came in. He hesitated as she greeted him.

"You have company," he said, "but can I see you for a very few minutes? It is important."

"Of course you can," said she, closing the study door. "Our Dorcas Society meets here to-day, but we have not yet come to order. I shall be glad to hear what you have to say."

So they sat down, and he told her what he had to say, and as she listened she grew very angry. When she heard the epithet which had been applied to Olive she sprang to her feet. "The wretch!" she cried.

"Now, you see, Mrs. Faulkner," said the captain, "I can do nothing at all myself, and there is no way to make use of the law; that would be horrible for Olive, and it could not be done; and so I have come to ask help of you. I don't see that any other man could do more than I could do."

Mrs. Faulkner sat silent for a few minutes. "I am so glad you came to me," she said presently. "I have always known Miss Port as a scandal-monger and a mischief-maker, but I never thought of her as a wicked woman. This persecution of you is shameful, but when I think of your niece it is past belief! You are right, Captain Asher; it must be a woman who must take up your cause. In fact," said she after a moment's thought, "it must be women. Yes, sir." And as she spoke her face flushed with enthusiasm. "I am going to take up your cause, and my friends in there, the ladies of the Dorcas Society, will stand by me, I know. I don't know what we shall do, but we are going to stand by you and your niece."

Here was a friend worth having. The captain was very much affected, and was moved with unusual gratitude. He had been used to fighting his own battles in this world, and here was some one coming forward to fight for him.

There came upon him a feeling that it would be a shame to let this true lady take up a combat which she did not wholly understand. He made up his mind in an instant that he would not care what danger might be threatened to other people, or to trade, or to society, he would be true to this lady, to Olive, and to himself. He would tell her the whole story. She should know what Olive had done, and how little his poor girl deserved the shameful treatment she had received.

Mrs. Faulkner listened with pale amazement; she trembled from head to foot as she sat.

"And you must tell no one but your husband," said the captain. "This is a state secret, and he must promise to keep it before you tell."

She promised everything. She would be so proud to tell her husband.

When the captain had gone, Mrs. Faulkner, in a very unusual state of mind, went into the parlor, took the chair, and putting aside all other business, told to the eagerly receptive members the story of Miss Port and Captain Asher. How she had persecuted him, and maligned him, and of the shameful way in which she had spoken of his niece. But not one word did she tell of the story of the two gentlemen in the barouche, and of the air-gun. She was wild to tell everything, but she was a good woman.

"Now, ladies," said Mrs. Faulkner, "in my opinion, the thing for us to do is to go to see Maria Port; tell her what we think of her; and have all this wickedness stopped."

Without debate it was unanimously agreed that the president's plan should be carried out. And within ten minutes the whole Dorcas Society of eleven members started out in double file to visit the house of Maria Port.

CHAPTER XXXV

THE DORCAS ON GUARD

Miss Port had not been home very long and was up in her bedroom, which looked out on the street, when she heard the sound of many feet, and, hurrying to the window, and glancing through the partly open shutters, she saw that a company of women were entering the gate into her front yard. She did not recognize them, because she was not familiar with the tops of their hats; and besides, she was afraid she might be seen if she stopped at the window; so she hurried to the stairway and listened. There were two great knocks at the door—entirely too loud—and when the servant-maid appeared she heard a voice which she recognized as that of Mrs. Faulkner inquiring for her. Instantly she withdrew into her chamber and waited, her countenance all alertness.

When the maid came up to inform her that Mrs. Faulkner and a lot of ladies were down-stairs, and wanted to see her, Miss Port knit her brows, and shut her lips tightly. She could not connect this visit of so many Glenford ladies with anything definite; and yet her conscience told her that their business in some way concerned Captain Asher. He had had time to see them, and now they had come to see her; probably to induce her to relinquish her claims upon him. As this thought came into her mind she grew angry at their impudence, and, seating herself in a rocking-chair, she told the servant to inform the ladies that she had just reached home, and that it was not convenient for her to receive them at present.

Mrs. Faulkner sent back a message that, in that case, they would wait; and all the ladies seated themselves in the Port parlor.

"The impudence!" said Miss Port to herself; "but if they like waitin,' they can wait, I guess they'll get enough of it!"

So Maria Port sat in her room and the ladies sat in the parlor below; and they sat, and they sat, and they sat, and at last it began to grow dark.

"I guess they'll be wantin' their suppers," said Maria, "but they'll go and get them without seein' me. It's no more convenient for me to go down now than when they first came."

There had been, and there was, a great deal of conversation down in the parlor, but it was carried on in such a low tone that, to her great regret, Miss Port could not catch a word of it.

"Now," said Mrs. Pilsbury, "I must go home, for my husband will want his supper and the children must be attended to."

"And so must I," said Mrs. Barney and Mrs. Sloan. They would really like very much to stay and see what would happen next, but they had families.

"Ladies," said Mrs. Faulkner, "of course, we can't all stay here and wait for that woman; but I propose that three of us shall stay and that the rest shall go home. I'll be one to stay. And then, in an hour three of you come back, and let us go and get our suppers. In this way we can keep a committee here all the time. All night, if necessary. When I come back I will bring a candlestick and some candles, for, of course, we don't want to light her lamps. If she should come down while I am away, I'd like some one to run over and tell me. It's such a little way."

At this the ladies arose, and there was a great rustling and chattering, and the face of Miss Maria, in the room above, gleamed with triumph.

Frank R. Stockton

"I knew I'd sit 'em out," said she; "they haven't got the pluck I've got." But when the servant came up and told her that "three of them ladies was a-sittin' in the parlor yet and said they was a-goin' to wait for her," she lost her temper. She sent down word that she didn't intend to see any of them, and she wanted them to go home.

To this Mrs. Faulkner replied that they wished to see her, and that they would stay. And the committee continued to sit.

Now Miss Port began to be seriously concerned. What in the world could these women want? They were very much in earnest; that was certain. Could it be possible that she had said more than she intended to Captain Asher, and that she had given him to understand that she would use any of these women as witnesses if she went to law? However, whatever they meant, she intended to sit them out. So she told her maid to make her some tea and to bring it up with some bread and butter and preserves, and a light. She also ordered her to be careful that the people in the parlor should see her as she went up-stairs. "I guess they'll know I'm in earnest when they see the tea," she said. "I've set out a mess of 'em, and it won't take long to finish up them three!"

She partook of her refreshments, and she reclined in her rocking-chair, and waited for the hungry ones below to depart. "I'll give 'em half an hour," said she to herself.

Before that time had elapsed she heard another stir below, and she exclaimed: "I knew it" and there were steps in the hallway, and some people went out. She sprang to her feet; she was about to run down-stairs and lock and bolt every door; but a sound arrested her. It was the talking of women in the parlor. She stopped, with her mouth wide open, and her eyes staring, and then the servant came up and told her that "them three had gone, and that another three had come back, and they had told her to say that they were goin' to stay in squads all night till she came down to see them."

Miss Port sat down, her elbows on the table, and her chin in her hands. "It must be something serious," she thought. "The ladies of this town are not in the habit of staying out late unless it is to nurse bad cases, or to sit up with corpses." And then the idea struck her that probably there might be something the matter that she had not thought of. She had caused lots of mischief in her day, and it might easily be that she had forgotten some of it. But the more she thought about the matter, the more firmly she resolved not to go down and speak to the women. She would like to send for a constable and have them cleared out of the house, but she knew that none of the three constables in town would dare to use force with such ladies as Mrs. Faulkner and the members of the Dorcas Society.

So she sat and waited, and listened, and grew very nervous, but was more obstinate now than ever, for she was beginning to be very fearful of what those women might have to say to her. She could "talk down one woman, but not a pack of 'em." Thus time passed on, with occasional reports from the servant until the latter fell asleep, and came up-stairs no more. There were sounds of footsteps in the street, and Miss Port put out her light, and went to the front shutters. Three women were coming in. They entered the house, and in a few minutes afterward three women went out. Miss Port stood up in the middle of the floor, and was almost inclined to tear her hair.

"They're goin' to stay all night!" she exclaimed. "I really believe they 're goin' to stay all night!" For a moment she thought of rushing down-stairs and confronting the impertinent visitors, but she stopped; she was afraid. She did not know what they might say to her, and she went to the banisters and listened. They were talking; always in a low voice. It seemed to her that these people could talk forever. Then she began to think of her front door, which was open; but, of course, nobody could come while those creatures were in the parlor. But if she missed anything she'd have them brought up in court if it took every cent she had in the world and constables from some other town. She slipped to the back stairs, and softly called the servant, but there was no answer. She was afraid to go down, for the back door of the parlor commanded all the other rooms on that floor. Now she felt more terribly lonely and more nervous. If she had had a pistol she would have fired it through the floor. Then those women would run away, and she would fasten up the house. But there they sat, chatter, chatter, chatter, till it nearly drove her mad. She wished now she had gone down at first.

After a time, and not a very long time, there were some steps in the street and in the yard, and more women came into the house, but, worse than that, the others stayed. Family duties were over now, and those impudent creatures could be content to stay the rest of the evening.

For a moment the worried woman felt as if she would like to go to bed and cover up her head and so escape these persistent persecutors. But she shook her head. That would never do. She knew that when she awoke in the morning some of those women would still be in the parlor, and, to save her soul, she could not now imagine what it was that kept them there like hounds upon her track.

It was now eleven o'clock. When had the Port house been open so late as that? The people in the town must be talking about it, and there would be more talking the next day. Perhaps it might be in the town paper. The morning would be worse than the night. She could not bear it any longer. There was now nothing to be heard in front but that maddening chatter in the parlor, and up the back stairs came the snores of the servant. She got a traveling-bag from a closet and proceeded to pack it; then she put on her bonnet and shawl and put into her bag all the money she had with her, trembling all the time as if she had been a thief: robbing her own house. She could not go down the back stairs, because, as has been said, she could have been seen from the parlor; but a carpenter had been mending the railing of a little piazza at the back of the house, and she remembered he had left his ladder. Down this ladder, with her bag in her hand, Miss Port silently moved. She looked into the kitchen; she could not see the servant, but she could hear her snoring on a bench. Clapping her hand over the girl's mouth, she whispered into her ear, and without a word the frightened creature sat up and followed Miss Port into the yard.

"Now, then," said Miss Port, whispering as if she were sticking needles into the frightened girl, "I'm goin' away, and don't you ask no questions, for you won't get no answers. You just go to bed, and let them people stay in the parlor all night. They'll be able to take care of the house, I guess, and if they don't I'll make 'em suffer. In the morning you can see Mrs. Faulkner—for she's the ringleader—and tell her that you're goin' home to your mother, and that Miss Port expects her to pull down all the blinds in this house, and shut and bolt the doors. She is to see that the eatables is put away proper or else give to the poor—which will be you, I guess—and then she is to lock all the doors and take the front-door key to Squire Allen, and tell him I'll write to him. And what's more, you can say to the nasty thing that if I find anything wrong in my house, or anything missin', I 'll hold her and her husband responsible for it, and that I'm mighty glad I don't belong to their church."

Then she slipped out of the back gate of the yard, and made her way swiftly to the railroad-station. There was a train for the north which passed Glenford at half-past twelve, and which could be flagged. There was one man at the station, and he was very much surprised to see Miss Port.

"Is anything the matter?" he said.

"Yes," she snapped, "there's some people sick, and I guess there'll be more of 'em a good deal sicker in the morning. I've got to go."

"A case of pizenin'?" asked the man very earnestly.

"Yes," said she, wrapping her shawl around her; "the worse kind of pizenin'!" Then she talked no more.

The servant-girl slept late, and there were a good many ladies in the parlor when she came down. She did not give them a chance to ask her anything, but told her message promptly. It was a message pretty fairly remembered, although it had grown somewhat sharper in the night. When it was finished the girl added: "And I'm to have all the eatables in the house to take home to my mother, and Squire Allen is to pay me four dollars and seventy-five cents, which has been owin' to me for wages for ever so long."

CHAPTER XXXVI

COLD TINDER

Olive and Dick Lancaster sat together in the captain's parlor. She was very quiet—she had been very quiet of late—but he was nervous.

"It is very kind, Mr. Lancaster," said Olive, breaking the silence, "for you to come to see us instead of writing. It is so much pleasanter for friends—"

"Oh, it was not kind," he said, interrupting her. "In fact, it was selfishness. And now I want to tell you quickly, Miss Asher, while I have the chance, the reason of my coming here to-day. It was not to offer you my congratulations or my sympathy, although you must know that I feel for you and your uncle as much in every way as any living being can feel. I came to offer my love. I have loved you almost ever since I knew you as much as any man can love a woman, and whenever I have been with you I could hardly hold myself back from telling you. But I was strong, and I did not speak, for I knew you did not love me."

Olive was listening, looking steadily at him.

"No," she said, "I did not love you."

He paid no attention to this remark, as if it related to something which he knew all about, but went on, "I resolved to speak to you some time, but not until I had some little bit of a reason for supposing you would listen to me; but when I read the account of what you did in Washington, I knew you to be so far above even the girl I had supposed you to be; then my love came down upon me and carried me away. And all that has since appeared in the papers has made me so long to stand by your side that I could not resist this longing, and I felt that no matter what happened, I must come and tell you all."

"And now?" asked Olive.

"There is nothing more," said Dick. "I have told you all there is. I love you so truly that it seems to me as if I had been born, as if I had lived, as if I had grown and had worked, simply that I might be able to come to you and say, I love you. And now that I have told you this, I hope that I have not pained you."

"You have not pained me," said Olive, "but it is right that I should say to you that I do not love you." She said this very quietly and gently, but there was sadness in her tones.

Dick Lancaster sprang up, and stood before her. "Then let me love you" he cried. "Do not deny me that! Do not take the life out of me! the soul out of me! Do not turn me away into utter blackness! Do not say I shall not love you!"

Olive's clear, thoughtful eyes were looking into his. "I believe you love me," she answered slowly. "I believe every word you say. But what I say is also true. I will admit that I have asked myself if I could love you. There was a time when I was in great trouble, when I believed that it might be possible for me to marry some one without loving him, but I never thought that about *you*. You were different. I could not have married you without loving you. I believe you knew that, and so you did not ask me."

His voice was husky when he spoke again.

"But you do not answer me," he said. "You have seen into my

very soul. May I love you?"

She still looked into his glowing eyes, but she did not speak. It was with herself she was communing, not with him.

But there was something in the eyes which looked into his which made his heart leap, and he leaned forward.

"Olive," he whispered, "can you not love me?"

Her lips appeared as if they were about to move, but they did not, and in the next moment they could not. He had her in his arms.

Poor foolish, lovely Olive! She thought she was so strong. She imagined that she knew herself so well. She had seen so much; she had been so far; she had known so many things and people that she had come to look upon herself as the decider of her own destiny. She had come to believe so much in herself and in her cold heart that she was not afraid to listen to the words of a burning heart! *Her* heart could keep so cool!

And now, in a flash, the fire had spread! The coolest hearts are often made of tinder.

Poor foolish, lovely, happy Olive! She scarcely understood what had happened to her. She only knew that she had been born and had lived, and had grown, that he might come to her and say he loved her. What had she been thinking of all this time?

"You are so quick," she said, as she put back some of her disheveled hair.

"Dearest," he whispered, "it seems to me as if I had been so slow, so slow, so very slow!"

It was a long time before Captain Asher returned, and when he entered the parlor he found these two still there. They had been sitting by the window, and when they came forward to meet him Dick's arm was around the waist of Olive. The captain looked at them for a moment, and then he gave a shout, and encircled them both in his great arms.

When they were cool enough to sit down and Olive and Dick had ceased trying to persuade the captain that he was not the happiest of the three, Olive said to him: "I have told Dick everything—about the air-gun and all. Of course, he must know it."

"And I have been looking at you," said Dick, putting his hand upon the captain's shoulder, "as the only hero I have ever met. Not only for what you have done, but for what you have refrained from doing."

"Nonsense!" said the captain. "Olive now—"

"Oh! Olive is Olive!" said Dick. And he did not mind in the least that the captain was present.

* * * * *

It was on the next afternoon that the Broadstone carriage stopped at the toll-gate. Mrs. Easterfield sprang out of it, asking for nobody, for she had spied Olive in the arbor.

"It seems to me," she said, as she burst into tears and took the girl into her arms, "it does seem to me as if I were your own mother!"

"The only one I have," said Olive, "and very dear!"

It was some time after this that Mrs. Easterfield was calm enough to stop the flow of exciting conversation and to say to Olive, taking both her hands tenderly within her own: "My dear, we have been talking a great deal of sentiment, and now I want seriously to speak to you on a matter of business."

"Business!" asked Olive in surprise.

"Yes, it is really business from your point of view; and I have come round to that point of view myself. Olive, I want you to marry!"

"Oh," said Olive, "that is it, is it? That is what you call business?"

"Yes, dear; I am now looking at your future, and at marriage in the very sensible way you regarded those matters when you were staying with me."

"But," said Olive, who could scarcely help laughing, "there was a good reason then for my being so sensible, and that reason no longer exists. I can now afford single-blessedness."

"No, Olive, dear, you can not. Circumstances are all against that consummation. You are not made for that sort of thing. And your uncle is an old man, and even with him you need a young protector. I want you to marry Richard Lancaster. You know my heart has been set on it for some time, and now I urge it. You could never bring forth a single objection to him."

"Except that I did not love him."

"Neither did you love the young men you were considering as eligible. Now, do try to be a sensible girl."

"Mrs. Easterfield, are you laughing at me?" asked Olive.

"Far from it, my dear. I am desperately in earnest. You see, recent events—"

"Dick Lancaster and I are engaged to be married," said Olive demurely, not waiting for the end of that sentence. "And," she added, laughing at Mrs. Easterfield's astonished countenance, "I have not yet considered whether or not it is sensible."

After Mrs. Easterfield had given a half dozen kisses to partly express her pleasure, she said: "And where is he now? I must see him!"

"He went back to his college late last night; it was impossible for him to stay here any longer at present."

As Mrs. Easterfield was going away—she had waited and waited for the captain who had not come—Olive detained her.

"You are so dear," she said, "that I must tell you a great thing." And then she told the story of the two men in the barouche.

Mrs. Easterfield turned pale, and sat down again. She had actually lost her self-possession. She made Olive tell her the story over and over again. "It is too much," she said, "for one day. I am glad the captain is not here, I would not know what to say to him. I may tell Tom?" she said. "I must tell him; he will be silent as a rock."

Olive smiled. "Yes, you may tell Tom," she said.

"I have told Dick, but on no account must Harry ever know anything about it."

Mrs. Easterfield looked at her in amazement. That the girl could joke at such a moment!

When the captain came home Olive told him how she had entrusted the great secret to Mrs. Easterfield and her husband.

"Well," said he, "I intended to tell you, but haven't had a chance yet, that I spoke of the matter to Mrs. Faulkner. So I have told two persons and you have told three, and I suppose that is about the proportion in which men and women keep secrets."

CHAPTER XXXVII

IN WHICH SOME GREAT CHANGES ARE RECORDED

A few days after his return to his college Prof. Richard Lancaster found among his letters one signed "Your backer, Claude Locker."

The letter began:

> "You owe her to me. You should never forget that. If I had done better no one can say what might have been the result. This proposition can not be gainsaid, for as no one ever saw me do better, how should anybody know? I knew I was leaving her to you. She might not have known it, but I did. I did not suppose it would come so soon, but I was sure it would ultimately come to pass. It has come to pass, and I feel triumphant. In the great race in which I had the honor to run, you made a most admirable second. The best second is he who comes in first. In order for a second to take first place it is necessary that the leader in the race, be that leader horse, man, or boat, should experience a change in conditions. I experienced such a change, voluntary or involuntary it is unnecessary to say. You came in first, and I congratulate you as no living being can congratulate you who has not felt for a moment or two that it was barely possible that he might, in some period of existence, occupy the position which you now hold.

> "Do not be surprised if you hear of my early marriage.

Frank R. Stockton

Some woman no better-looking than I am may seek me out. If this should happen, and you know of it, please think of me with gratitude, and remember that I was once

"Your backer,

"CLAUDE LOCKER."

Olive also received a letter from Mr. Locker, which ran thus:

"Mrs. Easterfield told me. She wrote me a letter about it, and I think her purpose was to make me thoroughly understand that I was not in this matter at all. She did not say anything of the kind, but I think she thought it would be a dreadful thing, if by any act of mine, I should cause you to reconsider your arrangement with Professor Lancaster. I have written to the said professor, and have told him that it is not improbable that I shall soon marry. I don't know yet to what lady I shall be united, but I believe in the truth of the adage, 'that all things come to those who can not wait.' They are in such a hurry that they take what they can get.

"If you do not think that this is a good letter, please send it back and I will write another. What I am trying to say is, that I would sacrifice my future wife, no matter who she may be, to see you happy. And now believe me always

"Your most devoted acquaintance,

"CLAUDE LOCKER.

"P.S.—Wouldn't it be a glorious thing if you were to be married in church with all the rejected suitors as grooms-men and Lancaster as an old Roman conqueror with the captive princess tied behind!"

Now that all the turmoil of her life was over, and Olive at peace with herself, her thoughts dwelt with some persistency upon two of her rejected suitors. Until now she had had but little comprehension of the love a man may feel for a woman —perhaps because she herself never loved—but now she looked back upon that period of her life at Broadstone with a good deal of compunction. At that time it had seemed to her that it really made very little difference to her three lovers which one she accepted, or if she rejected them all. But now she asked herself if it could be possible that Du Brant and Hemphill had for her anything of the feeling she now had for Dick Lancaster. (Locker did not trouble her mind at all.) If so, she had treated them with a cruel and shameful carelessness. She had really intended to marry one of them, but not from any good and kind feeling; she was actuated solely by pique and self-interest; and she had, perhaps, sacrificed honest love to her selfishness; and, what was worse, had treated it with what certainly appeared like contempt, although she certainly had not intended that.

She felt truly sorry, and cast about in her mind for some means of reparation. She could think of but one way: to find for each of them a very nice girl—a great deal nicer than herself—and to marry them all with her blessing. But, unfortunately for this scheme, Olive had no girl friends. She had acquaintances "picked up here and there," as she said, but she knew very little about any of them, and not one of them had ever struck her as being at all angelic or superior in any way. Neither of the young men who were lying so heavily on her mind had written to any one, either at the toll-gate or at Broadstone, since the very public affair in which she had played a conspicuous part; and her consolation was that as each one had read that account he had said to himself: "I am thankful that girl did not accept me! What a fortunate escape!" But still she wished that she had behaved differently at Broadstone.

She said nothing to any one of these musings, but she ventured one day to ask Mr. Easterfield how Mr. Hemphill was faring. His reply was only half satisfactory. He reported the young man as doing very well, and being well; he was growing fat, and that did not improve his looks; and he was getting more

Frank R. Stockton

and more taciturn and self-absorbed. "Why was he taciturn?" Olive asked herself. "Was he brooding and melancholy?" She did not know anything about the fat, and what might be its primal cause; but her mind was not set at ease about him.

Things went on quietly and pleasantly at the toll-gate, and at Broadstone. Dick came down as often as he could and spent a day or two (usually including a Sunday) with Olive and her uncle. It was now October, and colleges were in full tide. It was also the hunting season, and that meant that Mr. Tom would be at Broadstone for a couple of weeks, and Mrs. Easterfield said she must have Olive at that time. And, in order to make the house lively, she invited Lieutenant Asher and his wife at the same time, as Olive and her young stepmother were now very good friends. Then the captain invited his old friend Captain Lancaster, Dick's father, to visit him at the toll-gate.

These were bright days for these old shipmates; and, strange to say, as they sat and puffed, they did not talk so much of things that had been, as they puffed and made plans of things which were to be. And these plans always concerned the niece of one, and the son of the other. Captain Asher was not at all satisfied with Dick's position in the college. He could not see how eminence awaited any young man who taught theories; he would like Dick's future to depend on facts.

"Two and two make four," said he; "there is no need of any theory about that, and that's the sort of thing that suits me."

Captain Lancaster smiled. He was a dry old salt, and listened more than he talked.

"Just now," he remarked, "I guess Dick will stick to his theories, and for a while he won't be apt to give his mind to mathematics very much, except to that kind of figuring which makes him understand that one and one makes one."

There was a thing the two old mates were agreed upon. No matter-what Dick's position might be in the college, his salary should be as large as that of any other professor. They could do it, and they would do it. They liked the idea, and they shook hands over it.

Olive was greatly pleased with Captain Lancaster. "There is the scent of the sea about him," she wrote to Dick, "as there is about Uncle John and father, but it is different. It is constant and fixed, like the smell of salt mackerel. He would never keep a toll-gate; nor would he marry a young wife. Not that I object to either of these things, for if the one had not happened I would never have known you; and if the other had not happened, I might not have become engaged to you."

The two captains dined at Broadstone while Olive was there, and Captain Lancaster highly approved of Mrs. Easterfield. All seafaring men did—as well as most other men.

"It is a shame she had to marry a landsman," said Captain Lancaster, when he and Captain John had gone home. "It seems to me she would have suited you."

"You might mention that the next time you go to her house," said Captain Asher. "I don't believe it has ever been properly considered."

It was at this time that Olive's mind was set at rest about one of her discarded lovers. Mr. Du Brant wrote her a letter.

"MY DEAR MISS ASHER—It is very long since I have had any communication with you, but this silence on my part has been the result of circumstances, and not owing, I assure you upon my honor, to any diminution of the great regard (to use a moderate term) which I feel for you. I had not the pleasure of seeing you when I left Broadstone, but our mutual friend, Mrs. Easterfield, told me you had sent to me a message. I firmly (but I trust politely) declined to receive it. And so, my dear Miss Asher, as the offer I made you then has never received any acknowledgment, I write now to renew it. I lay my heart at your feet, and entreat you to do me the honor of accepting my hand in marriage.

"And let me here frankly state that when first I read of your great deed—you are aware, of course, to what I refer—I felt I must banish all thought of you from my heart. Let me explain my position, I had just received news of the death of my uncle, Count Rosetra, and that I had inherited his title and estates. It is a noble name, and the estates are great. Could I confer these upon one who was being so publicly discussed—the actor in so terrible a drama? I owed more to society, and to my noble race, and to my country than I had done before becoming a noble. But ah, my torn heart! O Miss Asher, that heart was true to you through all, and has asserted itself in a vehement way. I recognized your deed as noble; I thought of your beauty and your intellect; of your attractive vivacity; of your manner and bearing, all so fine; and I realized how you would grace my title and my home; how you would help me to carry out the great ambitions I have.

"Will you, lady, deign to accept my homage and my love? A favorable answer will bring me to make my personal solicitations.

"Your most loving and faithful servant,

"CHRISTIAN DU BRANT.

"(Now Count Rosetra.)"

"What a bombastic mixture!" thought Olive, as she read this effusion. "I wonder if there is any real love in it! If there is, it is so smothered it is easily extinguished."

And she extinguished it; and thoughts of Count Rosetra troubled her no more.

She did not show Dick this letter, but she thought it due to Mrs. Easterfield to read it to her. "He has got it into his head that an American woman, such as you, will make his house attractive to people he wants there," commented that lady. "You have not considered me at all, you ungrateful girl! Only think how I could have exploited 'my friend, the countess'! And what a fine place for me to visit!"

It had been arranged by the two houses that Dick and Olive should be married in the early summer when the college closed; and Mrs. Easterfield had arranged in her own mind that the wedding should be in her city house. It would not be too late in the season for a stylish wedding—a thing Mrs. Easterfield had often wished she could arrange, and it was hopeless to think of waiting until her little ones could help her to this desire of her heart. She held this great secret in reserve, however, for a delightful surprise at the proper time.

But she and Olive both had a wedding surprise before Olive's visit was finished. It was, in fact, the day before Olive's return to the toll-gate that Mr. Easterfield walked in upon them as they were sitting at work in Mrs. Easterfield's room. He had been unexpectedly summoned to the city three days before, and had gone with no explanation to his wife. She did not think much about it, as he was accustomed to going and coming in a somewhat erratic manner.

"It seems to me," she said, looking at him critically after the first greetings, "that you have an important air."

"I am the bearer of important news," he said, puffing out his cheeks.

In answer to the battery of excited inquiries which opened upon him he finally said: "I was solemnly invited to town to attend a solemn function, and I solemnly went, and am now solemnly returned."

"Pshaw!" said Mrs. Easterfield. "I don't believe it's anything."

"A wedding is something. A very great something. It is a

Frank R. Stockton

solemn thing; and made more solemn by the loss of my secretary."

"What!" almost screamed his wife. "Mr. Hemphill?"

"The very man. And, O Miss Olive, if you could but have seen him in his wedding-clothes your heart would have broken to think that you had lost the opportunity of standing by them at the altar."

"But who was the bride?" asked Mrs. Easterfield impatiently.

"Miss Eliza Grogworthy."

"Now, Tom, I know you are joking! Why can't you be serious?"

"I am as serious as were that couple. I have known her for sometime, and she was very visible."

"Why, she is old enough to be his mother!"

"Not quite, my dear. In such a case as this, one must be particular about ages. She is a few years older than he is probably, but she is not bad looking, and a good woman with a nice big house and lots of money. He has walked out of my office into a fine position, and I unselfishly congratulated him with all my heart."

"Poor Mr. Hemphill!" sighed Olive. She was thinking of the very young man she had sighed for when a very young girl.

"He needs no pity," said Mr. Easterfield seriously. "I should not be surprised if he feels glad that he was not—well, we won't say what," he added, looking mischievously at Olive. "This is really a great deal better thing for him. He is not a favorite of my wife, but he is a thoroughly good fellow in his way, and I have always liked him. There were certain things necessary to him in this life, and he has got them. That can not be said about everybody by a long shot! No, he is to be congratulated."

Olive was silent. She was trying to make up her mind that he was really to be congratulated, and to get rid of a lingering doubt.

"Well, that is the end of him in our affairs!" exclaimed Mrs. Easterfield. "Why didn't you tell us what you were going to town for?"

"Because he asked me not to mention it to any one. And, besides, that is not all I went to town for."

"Oh," said his wife, "any more weddings?"

"No," said Mr. Easterfield, helping himself to an easy chair. "You know I have lately been so much with nautical people I have acquired a taste for the sea."

"I did not know it," said his wife; "but what of it?"

"Well, as Lieutenant Asher and his wife are here yet, and have no earthly reason for being anywhere in particular; and as Captain Asher seems to be tired of the toll-gate; and as Captain Lancaster doesn't care where he is; and as Miss Olive doesn't know what to do with herself until it is time for her to get married; and as you are always ready to go gadding; and as the children need bracing up; and as you can not get along without Miss Raleigh; and as Mrs. Blynn is a good house-keeper; and as I have an offer for renting our town house; I propose that we all go to sea together."

The two ladies had listened breathlessly to these words, and now Olive sprang up in great excitement, and Mrs. Easterfield clapped her hands in delight.

"How clever you are, Tom!" she exclaimed. "What a splendid

idea! How can we go?"

"I have leased a yacht, and we are going to the Mediterranean."

CHAPTER XXXVIII

"*IT HAS JUST BEGUN!*"

This wonderful scheme which Mr. Easterfield had planned and carried out met with general favor. Perhaps if they had all been consulted before he made the plan there would have been many alterations, and discussions, and doubts. But the thing was done, and there was nothing to say but "Yes" or "No." The time had come for the house party at Broadstone to break up, and the lieutenant and Mrs. Asher had arranged to spend the next few months in the city, but they gladly accepted Mr. Easterfield's generous invitation and would return to the toll-gate alter a few weeks preparatory to sailing, that the party might get together, for Captain Lancaster was to remain at the tollhouse. Mr. Easterfield also invited Claude Locker "to make things lively in rough weather," and that young man accepted with much alacrity.

Mrs. Easterfield was in such a state of delight that she nearly lost her self-possession. Sometimes, her husband told her, she scarcely spoke rationally. If she had been asked to wish anything that love or money could bring her, it would have been this very thing; but she would not have believed it possible. She was busy everywhere planning for everybody, and making out various lists. But, as she said, there is a little black spot in almost every joy. And her little black spot was Dick Lancaster.

"Poor Professor Lancaster!" she said to her husband. "We to

Frank R. Stockton

have such a great pleasure, and he shut up in close rooms! And Olive far away!"

"Are you sure about Olive?" asked Mr. Easterfield. "She has never said positively that she is going. I most earnestly hope that she will not back out because Lancaster can not go. If she stays her uncle will stay."

"And for that very reason she will go," said Mrs. Easterfield. "And I think Professor Lancaster will urge her to go. He is unselfish enough, I am sure, to wish her to have this great pleasure. And, talking of Olive, one thing is certain, Tom, we must be back early in the spring. There will be a great deal to do before the wedding. And, O Tom, I will tell you—but you must not tell any one, for I am keeping it for a surprise—I am going to give them a fine wedding. They will be married in church, of course, but the reception will be at our house. You will like that, I know."

"Will there be good eating?"

"Plenty of it."

"Then I shall like it."

All this was very well, but, nevertheless, this talk made the enthusiastic lady a little uneasy. It was true Olive had never said in words conclusively whether she would go or not. But she was extremely anxious that her father should go, and she implicitly followed Mrs. Easterfield's directions in making preparations for him, and was just as earnest in making her own; and her friend was certainly justified in thinking all this was a tacit consent.

As for the two captains, they were so delighted at this heavenly prospect that they gave up talking about Dick and Olive, and read guide-books to each other, and studied maps, and sea-charts until their brains were nearly addled. They were a source of great amusement to the young people when Dick came for his frequent short visits.

It was evident to all interested that Professor Lancaster approved of the expedition, for he entered heartily into all the talk about the various places to be visited, and all that was to be done on the vessel; and he did not bore them with any lamentations in regard to the coming separation between him and Olive. And, of course, every one respected his feelings, and said nothing to him about it.

The weeks went by; all the preparations were made; and at last the time came when the company were to assemble at the toll-gate and Broadstone before the final plunge into the unknown. Olive wished to have them all to dinner on the first day of this short visit.

"Our house is a little one," she said to Mrs. Easterfield, "but we can make it big enough. You know nautical people understand how to do that. What a jolly company we shall have! You know Dick will be there."

"Yes, poor Dick!" sighed Mrs. Easterfield, when Olive had left.

The Easterfields, with Lieutenant Asher and his wife, arrived very promptly at the toll-gate on that important day, and their drive through the bright, crisp air put them in a merry mood. They had hoped to bring Mr. Locker, but he had not arrived. They found two captains at the toll-gate in even merrier mood. Dick Lancaster was there, having arrived that morning, and they were none of them surprised that he looked serious. The ladies were not immediately asked to go up-stairs to remove their wraps, for Olive was not there to receive them. She soon, however, made her appearance in a lovely white dress that had been made for the trip under Mrs. Easterfield's supervision. Dick Lancaster immediately got up from his chair and joined her; and the Reverend Mr. Faulkner appeared from some mysterious place, and the astonished guests were treated to a very pretty marriage ceremony.

Frank R. Stockton

It was soon over, and the two jolly captains laughed heartily at the bewilderment of the Broadstone party. And then there was a wild time of hand-shaking and congratulations and embracing. By his wife's orders, Mr. Tom kissed Olive, which seemed perfectly proper to everybody except Mrs. Lieutenant Asher. She was also a young bride, with no similar experiences.

Later, when all were composed, Olive explained. "What has happened just now is all on account of Mr. Easterfield's invitation. I wrote immediately to Dick, and we settled it between us that he would ask for a vacation—they always give vacations when professors are married, and he knew of some one to take his place—and then we would be married, and ask Mr. and Mrs. Easterfield to invite us to take our wedding trip with them. Dick had to stay at the college until the last minute almost, and so we didn't say anything about the wedding—and we were both afraid of—well, we don't like a fuss—and so we planned this. And when Dick came he brought the license and Mr. Faulkner. And now I don't see how Mr. Easterfield can help inviting us."

Mr. Easterfield was standing by his wife, and as Olive finished her explanation he took his wife's hand and gave it a gentle squeeze of sympathy; and that heroic woman never flinched; nor did she ever say one word about that pretty wedding she had planned for the spring.

They had all nearly finished the fried chicken with white sauce, when Claude Locker arrived. He had missed the regular train and had come on a freight; had got a horse when he reached Broadstone.

"I am more tired than if I had walked," he grumbled. "I am always in bad luck! I am an unlucky dog! But you are so good you will excuse me, Miss Asher."

"That is not my name," said Olive gravely.

And with both eyes of the same size, Mr. Locker looked

around, wondering why everybody was laughing.

"Let me introduce Mrs. Lancaster," said Dick with a bow.

"Do you mean," cried Locker, starting up, "that this thing is really done?"

"No," said Olive. "It has just begun."

Choose from Thousands of 1stWorldLibrary Classics By

A. M. Barnard	Booth Tarkington	Edward Everett Hale
Ada Leverson	Boyd Cable	Edward J. O'Biren
Adolphus William Ward	Bram Stoker	Edward S. Ellis
Aesop	C. Collodi	Edwin L. Arnold
Agatha Christie	C. E. Orr	Eleanor Atkins
Alexander Aaronsohn	C. M. Ingleby	Eleanor Hallowell Abbott
Alexander Kielland	Carolyn Wells	Eliot Gregory
Alexandre Dumas	Catherine Parr Traill	Elizabeth Gaskell
Alfred Gatty	Charles A. Eastman	Elizabeth McCracken
Alfred Ollivant	Charles Amory Beach	Elizabeth Von Arnim
Alice Duer Miller	Charles Dickens	Ellem Key
Alice Turner Curtis	Charles Dudley Warner	Emerson Hough
Alice Dunbar	Charles Farrar Browne	Emilie F. Carlen
Allen Chapman	Charles Ives	Emily Bronte
Alleyne Ireland	Charles Kingsley	Emily Dickinson
Ambrose Bierce	Charles Klein	Enid Bagnold
Amelia E. Barr	Charles Hanson Towne	Enilor Macartney Lane
Amory H. Bradford	Charles Lathrop Pack	Erasmus W. Jones
Andrew Lang	Charles Romyn Dake	Ernie Howard Pie
Andrew McFarland Davis	Charles Whibley	Ethel May Dell
Andy Adams	Charles Willing Beale	Ethel Turner
Angela Brazil	Charlotte M. Braeme	Ethel Watts Mumford
Anna Alice Chapin	Charlotte M. Yonge	Eugene Sue
Anna Sewell	Charlotte Perkins Stetson	Eugenie Foa
Annie Besant	Clair W. Hayes	Eugene Wood
Annie Hamilton Donnell	Clarence Day Jr.	Eustace Hale Ball
Annie Payson Call	Clarence E. Mulford	Evelyn Everett-green
Annie Roe Carr	Clemence Housman	Everard Cotes
Annonaymous	Confucius	F. H. Cheley
Anton Chekhov	Coningsby Dawson	F. J. Cross
Archibald Lee Fletcher	Cornelis DeWitt Wilcox	F. Marion Crawford
Arnold Bennett	Cyril Burleigh	Fannie E. Newberry
Arthur C. Benson	D. H. Lawrence	Federick Austin Ogg
Arthur Conan Doyle	Daniel Defoe	Ferdinand Ossendowski
Arthur M. Winfield	David Garnett	Fergus Hume
Arthur Ransome	Dinah Craik	Florence A. Kilpatrick
Arthur Schnitzler	Don Carlos Janes	Fremont B. Deering
Arthur Train	Donald Keyhoe	Francis Bacon
Atticus	Dorothy Kilner	Francis Darwin
B.H. Baden-Powell	Dougan Clark	Frances Hodgson Burnett
B. M. Bower	Douglas Fairbanks	Frances Parkinson Keyes
B. C. Chatterjee	E. Nesbit	Frank Gee Patchin
Baroness Emmuska Orczy	E. P. Roe	Frank Harris
Baroness Orczy	E. Phillips Oppenheim	Frank Jewett Mather
Basil King	E. S. Brooks	Frank L. Packard
Bayard Taylor	Earl Barnes	Frank V. Webster
Ben Macomber	Edgar Rice Burroughs	Frederic Stewart Isham
Bertha Muzzy Bower	Edith Van Dyne	Frederick Trevor Hill
Bjornstjerne Bjornson	Edith Wharton	Frederick Winslow Taylor

Friedrich Kerst
Friedrich Nietzsche
Fyodor Dostoyevsky
G.A. Henty
G.K. Chesterton
Gabrielle E. Jackson
Garrett P. Serviss
Gaston Leroux
George A. Warren
George Ade
Geroge Bernard Shaw
George Cary Eggleston
George Durston
George Ebers
George Eliot
George Gissing
George MacDonald
George Meredith
George Orwell
George Sylvester Viereck
George Tucker
George W. Cable
George Wharton James
Gertrude Atherton
Gordon Casserly
Grace E. King
Grace Gallatin
Grace Greenwood
Grant Allen
Guillermo A. Sherwell
Gulielma Zollinger
Gustav Flaubert
H. A. Cody
H. B. Irving
H.C. Bailey
H. G. Wells
H. H. Munro
H. Irving Hancock
H. R. Naylor
H. Rider Haggard
H. W. C. Davis
Haldeman Julius
Hall Caine
Hamilton Wright Mabie
Hans Christian Andersen
Harold Avery
Harold McGrath
Harriet Beecher Stowe
Harry Castlemon
Harry Coghill
Harry Houidini

Hayden Carruth
Helent Hunt Jackson
Helen Nicolay
Hendrik Conscience
Hendy David Thoreau
Henri Barbusse
Henrik Ibsen
Henry Adams
Henry Ford
Henry Frost
Henry James
Henry Jones Ford
Henry Seton Merriman
Henry W Longfellow
Herbert A. Giles
Herbert Carter
Herbert N. Casson
Herman Hesse
Hildegard G. Frey
Homer
Honore De Balzac
Horace B. Day
Horace Walpole
Horatio Alger Jr.
Howard Pyle
Howard R. Garis
Hugh Lofting
Hugh Walpole
Humphry Ward
Ian Maclaren
Inez Haynes Gillmore
Irving Bacheller
Isabel Cecilia Williams
Isabel Hornibrook
Israel Abrahams
Ivan Turgenev
J.G.Austin
J. Henri Fabre
J. M. Barrie
J. M. Walsh
J. Macdonald Oxley
J. R. Miller
J. S. Fletcher
J. S. Knowles
J. Storer Clouston
J. W. Duffield
Jack London
Jacob Abbott
James Allen
James Andrews
James Baldwin

James Branch Cabell
James DeMille
James Joyce
James Lane Allen
James Lane Allen
James Oliver Curwood
James Oppenheim
James Otis
James R. Driscoll
Jane Abbott
Jane Austen
Jane L. Stewart
Janet Aldridge
Jens Peter Jacobsen
Jerome K. Jerome
Jessie Graham Flower
John Buchan
John Burroughs
John Cournos
John F. Kennedy
John Gay
John Glasworthy
John Habberton
John Joy Bell
John Kendrick Bangs
John Milton
John Philip Sousa
John Taintor Foote
Jonas Lauritz Idemil Lie
Jonathan Swift
Joseph A. Altsheler
Joseph Carey
Joseph Conrad
Joseph E. Badger Jr
Joseph Hergesheimer
Joseph Jacobs
Jules Vernes
Julian Hawthrone
Julie A Lippmann
Justin Huntly McCarthy
Kakuzo Okakura
Karle Wilson Baker
Kate Chopin
Kenneth Grahame
Kenneth McGaffey
Kate Langley Bosher
Kate Langley Bosher
Katherine Cecil Thurston
Katherine Stokes
L. A. Abbot
L. T. Meade

L. Frank Baum
Latta Griswold
Laura Dent Crane
Laura Lee Hope
Laurence Housman
Lawrence Beasley
Leo Tolstoy
Leonid Andreyev
Lewis Carroll
Lewis Sperry Chafer
Lilian Bell
Lloyd Osbourne
Louis Hughes
Louis Joseph Vance
Louis Tracy
Louisa May Alcott
Lucy Fitch Perkins
Lucy Maud Montgomery
Luther Benson
Lydia Miller Middleton
Lyndon Orr
M. Corvus
M. H. Adams
Margaret E. Sangster
Margret Howth
Margaret Vandercook
Margaret W. Hungerford
Margret Penrose
Maria Edgeworth
Maria Thompson Daviess
Mariano Azuela
Marion Polk Angellotti
Mark Overton
Mark Twain
Mary Austin
Mary Catherine Crowley
Mary Cole
Mary Hastings Bradley
Mary Roberts Rinehart
Mary Rowlandson
M. Wollstonecraft Shelley
Maud Lindsay
Max Beerbohm
Myra Kelly
Nathaniel Hawthrone
Nicolo Machiavelli
O. F. Walton
Oscar Wilde

Owen Johnson
P.G. Wodehouse
Paul and Mabel Thorne
Paul G. Tomlinson
Paul Severing
Percy Brebner
Percy Keese Fitzhugh
Peter B. Kyne
Plato
Quincy Allen
R. Derby Holmes
R. L. Stevenson
R. S. Ball
Rabindranath Tagore
Rahul Alvares
Ralph Bonehill
Ralph Henry Barbour
Ralph Victor
Ralph Waldo Emmerson
Rene Descartes
Ray Cummings
Rex Beach
Rex E. Beach
Richard Harding Davis
Richard Jefferies
Richard Le Gallienne
Robert Barr
Robert Frost
Robert Gordon Anderson
Robert L. Drake
Robert Lansing
Robert Lynd
Robert Michael Ballantyne
Robert W. Chambers
Rosa Nouchette Carey
Rudyard Kipling
Saint Augustine
Samuel B. Allison
Samuel Hopkins Adams
Sarah Bernhardt
Sarah C. Hallowell
Selma Lagerlof
Sherwood Anderson
Sigmund Freud
Standish O'Grady
Stanley Weyman
Stella Benson
Stella M. Francis

Stephen Crane
Stewart Edward White
Stijn Streuvels
Swami Abhedananda
Swami Parmananda
T. S. Ackland
T. S. Arthur
The Princess Der Ling
Thomas A. Janvier
Thomas A Kempis
Thomas Anderton
Thomas Bailey Aldrich
Thomas Bulfinch
Thomas De Quincey
Thomas Dixon
Thomas H. Huxley
Thomas Hardy
Thomas More
Thornton W. Burgess
U. S. Grant
Upton Sinclair
Valentine Williams
Various Authors
Vaughan Kester
Victor Appleton
Victor G. Durham
Victoria Cross
Virginia Woolf
Wadsworth Camp
Walter Camp
Walter Scott
Washington Irving
Wilbur Lawton
Wilkie Collins
Willa Cather
Willard F. Baker
William Dean Howells
William le Queux
W. Makepeace Thackeray
William W. Walter
William Shakespeare
Winston Churchill
Yei Theodora Ozaki
Yogi Ramacharaka
Young E. Allison
Zane Grey

www.ingramcontent.com/pod-product-compliance
Lightning Source LLC
Chambersburg PA
CBHW031059260626
47172CB00001B/139